Advance Praise for
They Call Me Ishmael

"Many visit Bougainville and—like John Kuhns—become enchanted by its physical beauty and its people. Not so many can use the experience as a setting for a wonderfully readable story. Kuhns frames the vicissitudes of his foreign protagonist within the intense pressures generated by the island's ethnic distinctiveness and fabulous natural wealth, as well as the geo-political competition that swirls around it. But the core of the novel is the legendary Ishmael. He is the novel's hero—and with Kuhns's story calling Conrad to mind, the reader will earnestly hope that in the sequel Ishmael's apotheosis is not redolent of Nostromo's."

—**Michael Thawley**, former Australian Ambassador to the
United States of America, Secretary of the Department of the
Prime Minister and Cabinet, and once frequent visitor
with fond memories of Papua New Guinea and its people

"A thrilling story of leadership, commitment, and friendship amidst the challenges of building a Pacific Island nation in the swirl of China's pervasive influence."

—**George W. Casey, Jr.**, General, U.S. Army (Retired)

"*They Call Me Ishmael* is a must read for world leaders from remote locations who are forced to teach themselves how to be great statesman in the face of overwhelming adversity."

—**Jason Osborne**, Senior advisor on more than ten successful
U.S. and international presidential campaigns and
the Pacific's preeminent campaign strategist

"*They Call Me Ishmael*, John Kuhns's sweeping novel about Bougainville, brilliantly portrays the epic story of Ishmael, a courageous and visionary leader who rises to power against all odds to overcome a tide of colonial overreach, gold mania, and civil war in a lush and mineral-rich South Pacific paradise."

—**Deborah Goodrich Royce**, author of *Finding Mrs. Ford* and *Ruby Falls*

"Readers will be captivated by this deeply moving tale about Ishmael, the people of Bougainville, and their heartfelt quest for liberty and freedom, especially in the face of an ever-expanding People's Republic of China, which covets their Pacific Island gem."

—**Jim Fanell**, Captain U.S. Navy (Retired), former director of intelligence and information operations for the U.S. Pacific Fleet, and currently a government fellow at the Geneva Centre for Security Policy in Switzerland

"Not only all Bougainvilleans, but all Australians as well as the Australian government, should be eternally grateful for people like Ishmael and John Kuhns, who together managed to create an honest, independent government in the South Pacific beyond the reach of Chinese control."

—**Paul Jordan**, Special Air Service Regiment (Retired), author of *The Easy Day Was Yesterday*

Also By John D. Kuhns

China Fortunes

Ballad of a Tin Man

South of the Clouds

THEY CALL ME
Ishmael

Bougainville is an island, an island of sorrow
Bougainville is an island, an island of pain
Bougainville is an island, an island of hope
Bougainville is an island, an island I love
Bougainville is an island, an island I love

Island of Sorrow, Bougainville Folk Song

THEY CALL ME
Ishmael

JOHN D. KUHNS

Post Hill
PRESS

A POST HILL PRESS BOOK

They Call Me Ishmael
© 2022 by John D. Kuhns
All Rights Reserved

ISBN: 978-1-63758-149-0
ISBN (eBook): 978-1-63758-150-6

Interior design and composition by Greg Johnson, Textbook Perfect

Post Hill Press
New York • Nashville
posthillpress.com

Published in the United States of America
1 2 3 4 5 6 7 8 9 10

For my parents Eileen and E.D.—
I think about you every day.

Contents

PART FOUR: ISHMAEL AND JACK

PART FIVE: ISLAND OF HOPE

THEY CALL ME
Ishmael

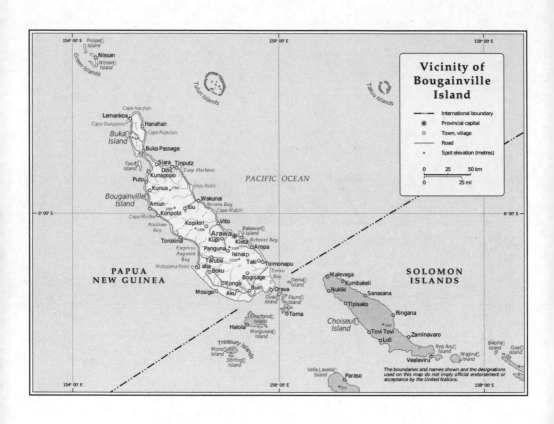

PART ONE

ISLAND OF SORROW

Island of Sorrow

The way some Bougainvilleans told me the story, Álvaro de Mendaña was the first white man to lie about Bougainville. He wouldn't be the last. The lies have always been about gold.

It is widely known that Mendaña, a Spanish navigator, was the first European to visit the Solomon Islands, landing—according to foreign academics deprived of the truth—on Santa Isabel Island in 1568. Also generally acknowledged is Mendaña's belief that the archipelago contained untold riches, causing him to name it the Solomon Islands. Supposedly, Mendaña believed that hidden in the islands' jungles lay the biblical city of Ophir, from which King Solomon received tribute of gold, silver, pearls, sandalwood, ivory, apes, and peacocks.

Regarding Mendaña's itinerary in the region, Bougainvilleans know better. Mendaña was correct; the Solomon Islands do contain vast riches. They're just not on Santa Isabel Island. The gold and copper and silver, as every Bougainvillean will tell you, are on Bougainville Island, where Mendaña's mendacity began. Bougainvilleans are certain that he first discovered Bougainville Island, not Santa Isabel Island. The men Mendaña sent ashore reported what anyone who visits central Bougainville can confirm today:the streams are full of gold.

Mendaña decided not to tell his Spanish patrons the truth, the story goes, and kept the knowledge of Bougainville—and its potential riches— for himself. He neglected to map Bougainville on his charts, behaving as deceitfully as the legions of white men who would follow him. His illicit behavior met with a justly deserved end. In 1595 Mendaña died of disease on Santa Cruz, one of the Solomon Islands nearby. For a time, the knowledge of Bougainville and its resources died with him.

It was left to Louis Antoine de Bougainville, a French navigator and later a naval hero in the American Revolutionary War (and also the namesake of the flowering vine Bougainvillea), to bump into Bougainville, the hitherto-uncharted member of the Solomon Islands—although its largest—200 years later, in 1768. Of course, Bougainville named the island for himself.

The European explorers were presumptuous to say they discovered Bougainville. It had been inhabited for approximately 30,000 years. Originally its people either migrated from islands further north in Papua New Guinea, aboriginal Australia, or East Africa. One prominent academic described a unique anthropological aspect of Bougainvilleans:

> "[A] trait shared by the present-day descendants of both northerners and southerners is their skin-colour, which is very black.... The presence of Bougainville as a 'black spot' in an island world of brownskins (later called redskins) raises a question that cannot now be answered. Were the genes producing that darker pigmentation carried by the first Bougainvilleans when they arrived? Or did they evolve by natural or 'social' selection, during the millennia in which the descendants of those pioneers remained isolated, reproductively, from neighbouring islanders? Nothing now known about Bougainville's physical environment can support an argument for the natural selection of its peoples' distinctively black pigmentation; therefore a case might be made for social selection, namely an aesthetic (and hence reproductive) preference for black skin."

However it evolved, their exotic ebony skin color is a badge of honor for Bougainvilleans; the blacker, the better.

Bougainville lies within Melanesia, a geographically and culturally distinct group of islands running in rough parallel to the northeastern coast of Australia, from New Guinea Island in the northwest along the Solomon Islands to New Caledonia in the southeast. Bougainville is itself an archipelago, including Bougainville Island (the largest), Buka Island (a lesser island directly across a narrow, river-like sea channel locals call the "Passage" from Bougainville Island), the Carterets, Mortlock, Nissan, and many other smaller islands and atolls.

A few hundred miles south of the equator, Bougainville's climate is tropical—very hot and humid—with substantial rainfall. It is located in the doldrums—there is little breeze. Bougainville is mountainous, and the inner portion of the island's terrain is challenging, beset by sharp peaks thrusting up from jungle-covered hills. Parts of Bougainville Island are rarely visited by humans. The Emperor Range, including its highest peaks, Mt. Balbi and Mt. Bagana, both active volcanoes, bisects the northern half of Bougainville Island, and in the south, the Crown Prince Range, including Mt. Loloru, an inactive volcano, does the same.

Geographically, Bougainville may be part of the Solomon Islands, but politically it has always been held separate—because of the gold, Bougainvilleans will remind listeners. In the days when colonial lines were drawn heedlessly on maps in European capitals, the political powers who most coveted the gold ended up with the island.

Bougainville is currently part of the Independent State of Papua New Guinea, known locally as PNG, but it exists culturally apart from them as well. Again, it's because of the gold, Bougainvilleans emphasize, and recent history confirms that. While both Bougainville and PNG are part of Melanesia, their people are distinctly different. PNG's mountainous mainland contains hundreds of linguistic groups across a testy, fractious land, whereas Bougainville is much less fragmented, and socially more benign. Unlike PNG, most of Bougainville's clans and lineages are matrilineal: when a man marries, he lives at his wife's home in her village. Bougainvilleans value family and land above all else. Authority for governance, regarding both social and civil matters, is customary: It runs with the land. Most important decisions in Bougainville are made by the chiefs—men and women—of the landowning families, clans, and tribes who have set social codes and civil rules for centuries.

Although well-endowed with natural resources, since Bougainville's discovery by Europeans, it has been cursed as a geographical and political stepchild. Due to the gold, it has always been picked over by, and belonged to, someone else: first the ill-fated Mendaña; then the half-hearted French; then more-determined Germans, who agreed with the English to divide the Solomon Islands between them, and then annexed Bougainville into German New Guinea (once again, to control the gold, Bougainvilleans say). After World War I, the Australians took control under a mandate from the League of Nations; the Japanese troops intervened during World War II's violent interlude, until the Allies ran them off in what many described as the most brutal battle conditions experienced during the Pacific conflagration; and then the Australians returned, having decided that Bougainville should be part of their Territory of New Guinea.

As the nineteenth century became the twentieth, at the same time the Germans established Bougainville's first coconut plantations, they reputedly began doing what attracted them to Bougainville in the first place—mining gold. While there are traces of equipment left over from various mining ventures, the secretive Germans left no evidence as to their mines' productivity.

The first fully documented mines, operated by Australians, were established at Kupe in the mountains of central Bougainville in the 1930s. Limited mechanical gold and copper mining expanded to the promising nearby areas of Atamo, Karato, Kopani, and Mainoki by the 1950s.

In 1967, in a backroom deal originally cut in Canberra, Conzinc Rio Tinto of Australia, Limited, later to be renamed the Rio Tinto Group, became the beneficiary of Australian and PNG legislation giving them exploration rights in and around Panguna, a mountain village in central Bougainville. In exchange, Australia received 20 percent of Bougainville

Copper Limited, the subsidiary Rio Tinto formed to own and operate its interests on Bougainville Island. Pursuant to Australian law, resources underneath the surface of the land were owned by the government. At the time, no one thought to discuss this with Bougainville's customary landowners, who, as Melanesians, considered their land and all its bounty—above and below the earth—theirs since time immemorial.

Mechanized exploration commenced, and word soon leaked out: the Panguna deposit was a bonanza. When Australian contractors showed up at Panguna on bulldozers waiving copies of the legislation granting exclusive rights to explore and expropriate land for mining, the Bougainvilleans had little understanding of what it meant or the grim changes portended. As the Panguna Mine was constructed, Bougainvilleans attempted to air their grievances peacefully. Certainly they protested the inadequate sharing of financial benefits derived from the resources taken from their land. But more fundamentally, as had happened from the date of the foreigners' first arrival, the Bougainvilleans petitioned politely for them to simply leave. The land didn't belong to them, and they had no right to be there.

The mining company saw fit to ignore them, as the Panguna Mine became the largest and most profitable copper and gold mine in the world. The cruelty of the deal for the Bougainvilleans was lost on their foreign visitors, who had convinced themselves they were merely following the law, and doing nothing wrong.

The final indignity took place in 1975, as PNG—including Bougainville—ceased being a territory of Australia and became the Independent State of Papua New Guinea. To provide the new country with economic substance, Australia transferred its interest in Bougainville Copper Limited to PNG, and the deal's new bedfellows also agreed to a generous revision of the company's taxation. Between dividends and taxes, lucky Papua New Guinea, eight hundred miles away, unburdened by the pressures of actual mining, and possessing a government most Bougainvilleans regarded dubiously, was to receive over 60 percent of the financial benefits of the Panguna Mine. This obscene amount was almost twice as much as that to be distributed to Bougainville Copper Limited and *its shareholders—who paid for the mine—and more than ten times the benefits flowing to Bougainville. Curdling estrangement into animosity, an inexpensive solution was ignored when PNG selfishly rebuffed Bougainville's petition for a more equitable financial arrangement.*

To some Bougainvilleans, taking up arms against PNG seemed inevitable, and the price—however horrific—of freedom. For many others, the languorous life in what was then PNG's most prosperous province outweighed the deprivations caused by rude foreigners and troublesome environmental damage. Few envisioned the actual consequences of what they would come to call the Crisis: a brutal conflagration reminiscent of ancient times, which would leave Bougainville broken, and in desperate need of a messiah.

Most Bougainvilleans have always considered themselves a group apart from the balance of Papua New Guinea's unruly population and corrupt government. If asked, a majority of this moral, ethical people would say that they have had no desire to join governmentally with Spain, France, Germany, Japan, or Australia, and they feel the same way about PNG. Don't even mention China. But over the years, no one bothered to inquire. They were too blinded by the gold.

PART TWO

ISHMAEL

2

Left for Dead

The incoming grenade meant certain death. An ocean swell rolled underneath Ishmael's longboat, and he stepped back toward the stern just as the high explosive device finished its descent from the sky. It hit amidships, disintegrating the vessel and sending a shard of the port gunwale streaking at Ishmael like an arrow. The fiberglass severed his left arm below the bicep; his four shipmates were killed instantly.

As Ishmael flailed in the sea, his first instinct was to scold himself. He had half-realized the splashes in the water around his longboat could be ordnance from onshore grenade launchers, but the growl of the boat's outboard engine had prevented him from hearing their telltale whine as they fell through the air. He pushed flotsam out of the water in front of him, trying to locate the Papua New Guinea Defence Force encampment they had been attacking onshore and get a glimpse of his antagonists. He peered north up the reef line toward Arawa in search of the Bougainville Revolutionary Army's other longboat; hopefully, they had seen his craft blown out of the water. He thought he heard the whimper of the other boat's engine as he bobbed in the seawater, dogpaddling to keep his head above the surface, but could see nothing in the flat light. It was only then that he realized his left arm was missing. He reached over for it. It hung by a strand of ligament from his elbow. He held his forearm with his good hand, lay on his back, and kicked his legs in the water, trying to float away from the wreckage.

Dawn had turned into day on the June morning in 1996, and the glassy Bougainvillean lagoon lay still under a cloudy sky. A mechanized vessel lurked, its engines grumbling, behind a strip of fog resting between the sea and the sky and obscuring the Pacific horizon. Ishmael knew it was a Defence Force patrol boat. He kicked his legs frog-like, floating with the current of the incoming tide toward the Kieta shore, listening in vain for his other BRA longboat.

"There's the motherfucker!" a voice cried out from the fog. The Pacific-class patrol boat's big engines snarled, and an angry gray prow nosed through the mist.

Four brown-skinned men in camouflage uniforms representing the First Royal Pacific Islands Regiment's Marine Element stood alongside the starboard deck as the boat pulled up, hove to, and lined its stern parallel to Ishmael flopping in the water. Two of the men dangled a pole with a fishing net attached to its far end over Ishmael, hooking his head in the trap line. Tightening the net around him, they hauled their catch toward the patrol boat.

It took all four crewmen to pull Ishmael's coal-black, muscle-bound body up onto the deck. As he lay there tangled in the net, one of the men came over and whacked him on the head with a gaff, as if he were a fish they planned to fillet for dinner.

"Get that net off him and stand him up for the captain," the man in boatswain mate's stripes said.

The three remaining crew members shucked and slid around Ishmael, their boots slipping on the steel deck made slick by blood and seawater.

"Rouse him quick," the boatswain's mate said. "Now. There's another armed longboat out there somewhere."

They stood Ishmael up and removed the net from his upper body. As he straightened, the man with the gaff whacked him over the head again for good measure, and Ishmael collapsed to the deck in a heap.

"Keep him alive!" an officer shouted from the bridge. The man emerged from the pilot house, nervously checked the horizon for the other longboat, eyed his expiring captive, and started climbing down a ladder to the deck. As he approached Ishmael, he adjusted the visor of his captain's hat and opened a writing pad. His national government was fighting a civil war against Bougainville's BRA renegades, and his orders were to find and capture their leader, who was rumored to be marauding in nearby waters. "Stand up, prisoner."

Ishmael did his best to stand.

"Firing detail, make yourselves ready," the captain barked.

Two of the crew stepped inside the boat's superstructure and returned with M-16s. They stepped forward side by side, clicked their heels, stomped the butts of their rifles on the deck, and stood at attention, ready to enjoy themselves.

Barefoot, Ishmael raised himself to his full height, prepared to meet his maker.

"Your name?" the brown-skinned captain said to Ishmael, a pencil in one hand and his pad in the other.

Ishmael stared wordlessly back at the captain.

"You are a member of the Bougainville Revolutionary Army. By the authority vested in me by the Royal Papua New Guinea Constabulary, I have the right to execute you for bearing arms against your government, and other treasonous offenses." The captain continued reading the prisoner a list of his transgressions, the officer's expression indicating he had something more important to do.

Ishmael kept his eyes on the captain's.

The captain snapped his writing pad shut. "Where is Ishmael?" he demanded, looking his captive in the eye as he made an attempt to smile, exposing rotted teeth.

Ishmael said nothing.

"Answer me, mate, or I assure you, I'll show no mercy."

Ishmael heard an outboard engine somewhere off in the fog bank. He needed to buy time. "What do you want with Ishmael?" he asked.

The boatswain's mate heard the longboat's engine too. "Begging your pardon, sir, but that's the other longboat!" he yelled to the captain.

The captain appeared exasperated. "Order arms," he called to the firing detail.

The two men raised their rifles.

"Where is your BRA leader?"

Ishmael heard the scream of the second BRA longboat's engine accelerating across the lagoon at the same time as he heard the report of his men's rifles. He looked off to starboard and saw the vessel closing fast out of the fog on a suicide mission, the rebel crew standing and firing, squaring off against superior odds in order to rescue their leader. Across from Ishmael, one of the Defence Force riflemen dropped his weapon, a hole the size of a dime below his eye starting to spurt blood.

As the rifleman collapsed to the deck, chaos ensued.

Ishmael stepped to the port gunwale, clambered over it, and tumbled into the sea. Holding his left arm with his right, he headed down and away from the patrol boat. Pumping his legs to move forward, he reached a depth of a few yards beneath the surface and leveled off. He willed himself to stay under, knowing that his thin chance of survival depended on not surfacing. Using his legs methodically, he tried to conserve strength while peering ahead through the Pacific seawater toward the coral reef. Fish swam by. His lungs on fire, he lied, telling himself he could swim underwater forever.

At the same time he heard the patrol boat's engines rev up, he could stay submerged no longer. He surfaced. Three hundred yards off, all he could see of the patrol boat was its receding stern, half-subsumed by foam, its engines churning franticly as it chased the other BRA longboat making for the safety zone inside the northern reef.

Ishmael bobbed in the sea alone, gazing toward the Kieta shore. He couldn't head straight in—that's where the Defence Force camp was. He'd have to swim south around Pok Pok Island, fend off the current, cut through the gap in the coral reefs, and head toward Toniva. He felt dizzy and weak. The beach was at least a couple of miles away. He'd never make it. He rolled on his back, said a prayer and, still holding one arm with the other, started pumping his legs.

3

License to Kill

The boy was chasing a coconut he had thrown into a wave and had run up over a hump on the sandy beach when he came upon Ishmael's body lying in the surf. The man's legs were covered by swirling foam and sand. He had done something funny with one of his arms. Somehow, one of them was holding the other out in front of his body, extending up the beach toward the shore, as if to keep it away from the wavelets lapping at his feet.

The boy tiptoed closer, stopped, and stared at the body, looking for any sign of movement. Flies buzzed around the back of the man's head where blood oozed out. The boy turned and ran up the beach toward town where his mother was selling vegetables at the Toniva market. He slowed down as he approached her so as not to attract attention. An only child, he behaved older than his ten years and had learned to be discreet. Catching his breath, he walked closer to her, grabbed her arm, and pulled. "Mummy, come quick."

Kneeling down behind her vegetables alongside another woman offering fish for sale, Beverly resisted her son's plea. "Not now, Jonah. Can't you see I'm talking to Amanda?"

Jonah tugged on her arm again. When she tugged back, the boy changed tactics, moving closer and whispering in her ear, "There's a dead man on the beach."

Her eyes growing wide and white against her smooth black face, Beverly turned away from her brown-skinned friend and pulled her son close to her. She said in a low tone, "Keep your voice down, and tell me where he is."

After Jonah explained, they got up and retraced his steps, Amanda watching them as they hurried down the shore.

When they got to Ishmael, Jonah said, "See Mummy? There he is. He hasn't moved; he's dead."

"Hush, child." Beverly looked up and down the beach for observers. The market was a long way off; she didn't think anyone that far away could see them. She dropped to her knees next to the body lying half-covered with sand. As the waves lapped over Ishmael's legs and trunk, she examined the rest of him carefully, staring at his dismembered arm. She moved next to his head lying face down in the sand. Shooing away the flies, she waited until a wave rolled up. Cupping clear water in her hand, she poured handfuls over the top of his head, washing the blood and sand from his hair and off the sides of his face. As she did so, she lifted the man's head back and tilted his face toward her.

"Saints preserve us!"

"What Mummy?" Jonah said. "What?"

"It's Ishmael," she said, barely breathing, she was so afraid.

"Uncle Ishmael?"

Beverly didn't answer. She glanced around once more for strangers on the beach. Then she scooped more water and poured it over the man's face, just to make sure it was really Ishmael. She thought she saw an eye flutter; it did again. Both of his eyes opened. Beverly caught her breath in her throat. "Oh my! He's alive." She ran over to the small thicket between the beach and the road, Jonah wordlessly scampering after her. After clearing a grassy area under the trees, she hurried back to Ishmael.

"Mummy, what are you doing?"

"Come over here and help me. He's going to die. We've got to get him into the shade. Take one arm. Please."

Jonah grabbed Ishmael's good arm, and Beverly took the other one by the shoulder. She signaled, and they pulled. At first, nothing happened. "Come on, Jonah. One, two, three…" This time they moved Ishmael's body a yard out of the surf.

Ishmael's face was being dragged through the sand. He coughed once, spitting out sand and seawater.

"Oh, sorry; sorry." Beverly stopped and knelt down beside Ishmael, brushing the sand out of his mouth. "Here, help me turn him over," she said to her son, and they rolled him over on his back. Beverly stood up, mopped the sweat off her brow, and grabbed Ishmael's shoulder again. "Once more. One, two, three…"

When Jonah couldn't pull anymore, Beverly stood behind Ishmael's broad shoulders, reaching her arms under his armpits and clasping her hands together behind his neck. Stumbling, she dragged him up the beach. She hauled backward, lurched a few steps, fell down on her seat, and then got up and pulled him again, and then again. Broken shells, sharp sticks, and flattened soda cans nicked her bare feet. Finally, she reached the thicket, dragged Ishmael's body under the bushes, and collapsed backward onto a patch of grass.

Jonah crept in and snuggled alongside her. "Mummy, what was Ishmael doing?"

"Not now." Out of breath, she rested, but only for a minute. Then she rolled over and examined Ishmael once more, fussing over his face, brushing the sand out of his eyes, nose, and mouth. "He's a very brave man. We've got to get him help, or he'll die."

"Can someone put his arm back?"

"I don't think so."

"Who can fix him?"

"Amalani can." Beverly leaned over and brushed the last sand off Ishmael's forehead. She lifted his good arm and laid it across his torso, and then very carefully took his severed forearm, still attached by a thin thread of tissue and sinew to his bicep, and laid it on his chest. "Come on, son. We've got to get home and wait for your father."

"Who's Amalani?" Jonah asked, trotting along behind Beverly as she walked rapidly back up the beach.

"Amalani Tarurava. A lady up in Roreinang," Beverly said, reaching out her hand and taking Jonah's, forcing him to trot alongside her. "She uses special medicine from the jungle."

Thirty minutes after they arrived at their house in Toniva, Beverly heard the front door open. Her husband, Leo, a big man, walked into the hallway, home from work at the Panguna Mine. He hung up his jacket and sat down on the chair in the hallway to remove his work boots.

Beverly looked out the window to make sure Jonah was nearby and saw him playing in the yard with Olivia, Amanda's daughter. "Leave your boots on," she said to Leo. "We must use your truck to run an errand."

He stood up silently.

"We need to go now," Beverly said, and started to walk past Leo in the hallway.

Leo grabbed her arm and turned her toward him. He studied her face. "What is it? I hate it when you get like this."

"It's your cousin. Come on; if we don't hurry, he'll die." She pulled her arm free and walked down the hallway to the front door.

"Ishmael?" Leo called out, striding after her.

She turned at the doorway and stepped in front of Leo. "Shush! The redskins will hear you." She looked over her shoulder for her son. "Jonah! Come here right now." The boy ran to her, and she told him to eat the dinner on the kitchen table that she'd prepared for him and then get to bed; she and his father would be back later that evening. "Don't you dare say a word about what happened today to anyone."

Beverly and Leo got in the truck and drove down their driveway. As they passed the house next door, Amanda, their redskin neighbor, watched them drive off through the village. She kept watching the pickup as it rolled out of Toniva, past the market and toward the beach beyond. The truck slowed a thousand yards down the road, its brake lights ablaze as it pulled up next to the thicket by the shore. It was the same place where she had watched Beverly and Jonah crawling around in the sand earlier that day.

Four hours later, Beverly and Leo's mission was complete. They had taken Ishmael from the bushes, loaded him into the bed of Leo's pickup, covered him with a tarpaulin, and drove two hours up into the hills to the village of Roreinang. Even though Defence Force soldiers patrolled the highway, Leo drove slowly and no one stopped them. It was well past dark when they arrived at Amalani's house. The three of them carried Ishmael from the truck into a room in the back of her house. Beverly glanced around inside; shelves holding bottles and potions lined the walls. After they laid Ishmael out on a bed, Amalani leaned over his chest, listened to his heart, looked up at Beverly and Leo and smiled. He was still alive. After thanking her, Beverly and Leo got into their truck and returned to Toniva.

When they got back to their village, it was pitch black. Beverly could hear the rustle of the palm fronds as the trees swayed over the house, but couldn't see them. There was no moon. She noticed the generator humming, and the lights still on, at Amanda's house. Beverly got along with her neighbor, but she knew that Amanda was jealous because she had neither a vehicle nor a man. In years past, such sentiments had been of no consequence, but the Crisis had changed everything. "I don't feel safe here anymore," she whispered to Leo.

Leo pulled the truck past Amanda's and stopped in front of their home. They didn't have a generator, and the house was dark. "We've lived here all our lives," Leo said.

"That doesn't mean it will ever be like it was before." Beverly checked to make sure Jonah was in his bed, closed up the house, and fell into a deep sleep.

The next morning, she was awakened by the sound of a chopper. The whump, whump, whump of the Iroquois helicopter's dual rotor blades was far off, but moving toward Toniva. Beverly felt her heart pound. Nothing good could come from the choppers. They carried members of the Royal Papua New Guinea Constabulary's riot squads. The thug-like policemen had been sent over from Port Moresby to keep order in Bougainville in the aftermath of the rape and killing of a pregnant Bougainvillean nurse by a group of redskin squatters on nearby Aropa Plantation, and counterattacks by Bougainvilleans. As far as Beverly was concerned, the possibility of order where riot squad men were concerned was laughable. They were the same low class of life as the squatters who had committed the crime in Aropa. Not ordinary redskins, they were highlanders from the mainland's remote mountain regions, where cannibalism was rumored to have been a fact of life up until the 1960s. Three square meals a day, a uniform, and a gun—a license to kill—was a dream come true for many PNG highlanders.

The chopper flew closer. Beverly expected it to fly over Toniva and keep going, but it didn't. She grew more afraid. Soon, it sounded as if it was tethered directly above their house. Still in her pajamas, Beverly left Leo in bed and called for Jonah, but in the racket from the chopper she couldn't hear her own words. She searched inside their house for her son, but couldn't find him. She looked out back by the pigsty; the boy was nowhere to be seen. She hurried back through the house one more time, looking in every corner for her son with no success, and then pushed through the front door and walked down the stairs.

The chopper had landed away from the trees, in the schoolyard a hundred yards down the road. Its big blades still, the helicopter's engine remained loud as it idled. A dozen uniformed men stood around the open bay of the chopper. They all looked in Beverly's direction. A jackbooted man wearing a tan riot squad uniform with stripes on his upper sleeves walked up the driveway through the trees toward her.

Beverly looked around for Jonah, but still didn't see him.

The riot squad officer approached and made an attempt to draw himself up in front of her. Dignity would be impossible; he was a stumpy, ugly man. His redskin face was already sweating, even though it was still early morning, and his eyes were black and bottomless. He wore a beret and carried a wooden night stick. He said, "I'm Sergeant Greyson Trull, Beverly. We have some questions for you." He looked her up and down, standing there in her pajamas.

She felt a chill come over her. "How do you know my name?"

"You know why we're here. Nothing will happen to you if you cooperate."

The front door slammed, and Leo walked up behind Beverly. He stood next to her and took her hand. "What's this about?" Leo said, looking down at Sergeant Trull. "We've done nothing wrong."

Down their driveway and farther off throughout the village, neighbors were starting to come to their front doors and look out. A few walked out into the road and tried to peer past the idling helicopter toward Beverly's front yard, but it was difficult to see through the trees. Partially hidden, Amanda sat on her front porch, watching expectantly.

Sergeant Trull said to Beverly, "We know that the BRA uses women to gather intelligence. We know they are using you. If you'll admit to your mistake, we'll go easy on you. We're all Melanesians here."

"You're wrong," Leo said.

Beverly said nothing.

"Well, Beverly? What did you and your son do on the beach yesterday?" Sergeant Trull asked.

Leo said, "Leave my wife and son out of this."

The sergeant stared at Leo. "Where's your cousin, Leo? Where is Ishmael?"

Beverly blurted out, "My husband wasn't involved."

The sergeant turned his attention back to Beverly. "I'm glad you've decided to take my point of view, Beverly." He looked her up and down slowly. "What are you wearing underneath those pajamas?"

Leo jumped on the runty sergeant, knocking him down and smashing him in the face with his fists before two of his armed men could run up and separate the two.

Sergeant Trull stood up and faltered backward for a moment, rubbing his bruised jaw. He picked up his beret from the road and brushed it off. Recovered, he stepped forward, thrust his shiny bald head directly underneath Leo's, and shouted, "Firing detail report!"

The two policemen picked up their M-16s from the driveway and came to attention, resting the butts of their rifles on the ground.

"Neutralize this man."

Both men swung the stocks of their rifles and whacked Leo over the head. As Beverly screamed, Leo crumpled to the ground, his scalp spurting blood. When Beverly tried to kneel down over Leo, the sergeant wailed the side of her head with his night stick, and then grabbed her by her hair and jerked her away.

Sprawled in the driveway, Leo lifted his head slowly, rubbed his scalp, and studied the blood covering his hand. He turned his face to look up at Sergeant Trull. "Go home, redskin. You're going to die here."

"We'll see who's going to die," the sergeant snapped. Holding Beverly by her hair, he pulled her until she was standing over her husband's body lying in the road. "You want to see what happens to people who don't cooperate?" the sergeant yelled at Beverly. He spat at Leo's head. "Finish him," he ordered.

The larger one of the two men with rifles handed his gun to the other. Taking a step back, he leaped in the air over Leo and came down with his knee on the back of Leo's neck, snapping it. Leo's body went limp, and his head rolled sideways.

"No!" Beverly yelled. "Noooo!" She fell down over Leo and hugged his body.

Sergeant Trull whacked Beverly in the head again with his nightstick, and gobs of her blood flew into the air.

"Where's Ishmael?" the sergeant yelled at Beverly. "What did you do with him?"

Struggling to remain conscious, Beverly didn't answer.

Sergeant Trull yanked her by the hair until she was on her feet, and then began pushing her toward her house. She tried to stop, and he hit her again hard with his night stick. As she stumbled up the front steps, blood covering her face, Jonah ran out of the bushes lining the front of the house, crying.

"Mummy! Mummy,"he sobbed. "It was me. It was all my fault," he said, his face streaming with tears. "I told Olivia about Ishmael, and then Amanda made me tell her. I didn't know this would happen, Mummy. I'm sorry," he screamed.

"Run, Jonah!" Beverly cried. "Run!"

Jonah stood there next to his mother, crying as he tried to hug her, not willing to move.

Sergeant Trull called to the men in his detail. "Grab him, bring him inside, and make him watch." He dragged Beverly the rest of the way up the front steps, and then pushed her through the front door into the living room. He stood her against the back of the couch and bent her over the cushions, pulling her pajama bottoms down to her ankles. He pulled down his pants and raped her.

When he was finished, he went to the kitchen and cleaned himself and his uniform. Zipping up his pants, he walked back through the living room. The two riflemen stood at attention behind Beverly, waiting their turns. "When you're done, cut her up and throw her to the pigs," the sergeant said.

As he walked out the front door, he saw Jonah standing wide-eyed in the corner.

"Bring the boy with you when you come," he called back to the men in the house.

Twenty minutes later, the Iroquois helicopter rose over the coconut trees, heading up the shoreline to the military base in Arawa. The crew was in a good mood, laughing and joking. When the chopper was several hundred yards above the sea, the sergeant left his seat in the cockpit and came back into the hold where Jonah was sitting numbly, his eyes blank and listless as he stared out over the jungle of Bougainville Island.

"The Good Lord told me He would forgive me if I did this for you," the sergeant said to Jonah. "You wouldn't have a life." He studied the catatonic boy's face, and then looked down at the sea. "Higher," he yelled to the pilot in the cockpit.

The chopper lifted, like a bird on the wind. At a thousand feet, they threw Jonah into the Anewa Bay.

4

Amalani

Amalani Tarurava spent the night tending to Ishmael in the space in the rear of her house she called her operating room. She sedated him with a pasty lozenge made from passionflower, which would leave him knocked out for the better part of a day. Outside the house, her husband, Elijah, threw logs in a pit and built a fire. When the flames were high, he heated water in several vessels, bringing inside the first kettle that boiled. Using the scalding water and clean rags, Amalani swabbed Ishmael's upper torso and his face and beard, removing sand, salt, and grime—anything that could cause infection, the immediate and most serious enemy.

When Amalani had cleaned Ishmael's body, Elijah helped her turn him on his stomach, and she cleaned his back and washed his scalp. Then the two of them dried him off, turned him over on his back once more, and began working on his severed arm. Elijah brought in a fresh pot of boiling water, and Amalani sopped it over the stump protruding from Ishmael's shoulder, swabbing and dabbing, removing loose bits of skin and tissue and dried blood, all the while softening up the surfaces of his wound, preparing them to be receptive for medicine. She did the same with the strand of ligament and tissue that connected Ishmael's forearm to his bicep.

She treated Ishmael's severed limb all night, keeping it moist, not letting it dry out. When he cried out and moved, she restored him to the middle of his bed and gave him more sedative.

When dawn came, Amalani sent Elijah out to gather the long stringy leaves of the sirivi plant. Once he had returned with a bushel of the leaves, she began crushing them with a mortar and pestle. Grinding the leaves into an oily paste, she added droplets of water into the mortar bowl until she produced a dark green gruel. Amalani put her head over the mortar bowl and breathed in the pungent smell of the sirivi oil. When she could sense the vapor entering her nasal cavity and affecting her, she stopped grinding, set that batch of sirivi aside, and ground more leaves. She ground sirivi leaves for several hours.

At noon, she told Elijah it was time for the bamboo procedure. He went outside and selected a long tapering bamboo stalk, not too thick in diameter, from the grove next to the house and cut it into meter-long lengths. Selecting a length of medium thickness, he checked to make sure it wasn't cracked, and sighted inside its barrel. Then he went into his tool shed and returned with a thin metal shaft. Using the shaft, from each end of the bamboo rod Elijah poked inside the barrel, puncturing the inner membrane walls and making a transit hole. He then scraped clean the barrel walls at one end of the bamboo rod until they were flush and unobstructed, and checked to make sure he could look inside that end and see all the way through to the pinhole at the other end.

When Elijah had finished preparing three bamboo rods, he put fresh wood on the fire and stoked the coals. After the firewood had finished its initial combustion, the flames died down, and the wood formed a robust bed of glowing coals. He fetched a metal framework from his tool shed and installed it over the glowing fire pit. Elijah laid the three bamboo rods horizontally across the length of the metal framework. Where they rested, the rods were inches above the smoldering coals, too far removed for the bamboo to combust, but close enough so that inside the bamboo the temperature would be exceedingly hot, above the boiling point, and convert the watery sirivi paste into a gas.

Amalani came out and collected him, and the two of them lifted Ishmael into a lounging position and stuffed pillows under his torso to prop him up. She demonstrated to Elijah how she was going to hold the pieces of Ishmael's damaged left arm together and where to blow the sirivi vapor. When they were finished, Elijah went outside to the fire and returned to the kitchen with a bamboo rod. Amalani took a piece of wax paper, fashioned a crude funnel, and stuck the furled point into the open end of the rod. Then she took a mortar bowl of liquid sirivi paste and poured it through the funnel into the hollow rod. As she poured more and more of the sirivi into the rod, Elijah leveled it until it was flat and full of sirivi. Amalani released the rod to her husband, who carried it out to the fire and laid it on the metal framework. In five minutes, the sirivi in the bamboo rod was bubbling. Elijah put on a pair of welding gloves and transported the hot, incandescent rod into the operating room. While Amalani gathered Ishmael's stringy ligament and held it between his forearm and his bicep and positioned the whole arm together in place, Elijah aimed the rod at the juncture and blew the sirivi vapor into Ishmael's wound until all the gas in the rod was spent.

They lay Ishmael down, filled the next two rods with sirivi, and repeated the procedure for two hours. When they had used all of the sirivi, they stopped, lay Ishmael's head back on a pillow, and covered his eyes with a moist cloth compress. It had been eighteen hours since Ishmael had arrived. Amalani and Elijah went into their bedroom, drew sheets as blinds across the windows to shield the sunlight, and went to sleep.

A few hours later, Amalani awoke when she heard Ishmael cry out where he lay in the operating room. As Elijah lay sleeping, she got out of bed and hurried around to the rear of the house. Ishmael was resting quietly, but the sun was high in a cloudless sky, and the room was too bright. She went to the clothesline, removed the sheets and the blankets she had been drying, and hung them over the windows of the operating room to block the sun. She felt Ishmael's forehead and exchanged the compress covering his brow with a new, cooler one.

When she went to leave the operating room, Ishmael's father was standing outside her doorway.

"Amos," she said, "you frightened me."

"I'd like to see my son," he said in a low tone.

Amalani led the way back into the operating room, closing the door behind her. She tied off one of the sheets covering a window, letting in enough light so that Amos could see Ishmael's face.

Amos bent over his son, and then moved closer to examine his arm, not touching him. He straightened up. "I don't want him to get infected."

"The seawater was helpful," Amalani said. "There is no fever yet."

"Can you fix his arm?"

"Curing the flesh is possible," she said. "But the bone? Parts of it are crushed. If he wants to keep it, he will need a bone surgeon. A western doctor."

"In Port Moresby?"

"No; PNG is too dangerous. Go back to the same hospital—the one in the Solomon Islands—where you took him after his gunshot injury. I hear they have a bone specialist—a Swiss man."

Ishmael stirred, groaned, and rolled over on his side. Amalani and Amos straightened him out and lay him back down in the center of the bed. When they were finished, his father stood next to the bed, staring at his son's arm.

"He must rest," Amalani said. "I will give him more sirivi in another hour."

"I will leave you," Amos said. "Thank you."

"Tell no one he is here. The Defence Force is handing out money for information."

Amos left, and Amalani rehung the sheet over the window. In the darkness, she leaned over Ishmael to check on him one more time.

His eyes were open, and he was looking straight at her. "How is my arm?"

Shocked that he had awakened, Amalani shushed Ishmael. She checked to see the door was closed, and then felt his forehead for fever. "Don't speak; you need the strength. No one must hear you."

"How is my arm?"

"Your father was just here," she said.

"I know. How is my arm?"

"If the Good Lord wishes, you will live." She adjusted the compress on his forehead.

"Tell my father to keep praying for me. He prays every morning at seven; I can feel it when he does. I need his strength."

"Your fighting days are over."

He stared at her as he considered her words. "Amalani, look at me."

She looked into Ishmael's eyes.

"Don't let them take my arm."

5

Born to Lead

After learning all he needed to know, Ishmael closed his eyes and slept the sleep of the dead. Safe in a hiding place in his village with Amalani, who had cared for him since he was a boy, he was alive—and he still had his arm.

Eight years earlier, in 1988, a twenty-year-old Ishmael hadn't wanted any part of hiding. It was a heady time for young Bougainvilleans to be out and about. A man named Francis Olu had galvanized a restive populace, calling its citizens to action. Olu had worked for Bougainville Copper Limited as a surveyor at its Panguna Mine, but he and a group of like-minded firebrands were fed up with BCL and the mine, PNG's corrupt national government, and the few greedy Panguna landowners who enriched themselves with mining royalties—what the Bougainvilleans called "fish compensation"—at the expense of the majority. Men were joining his new rebel militia, the Bougainville Revolutionary Army, and mustering out in Guava, Olu's village hidden high in the hills. Ishmael heard the news, took his father's shotgun, and headed up the mountain.

Ishmael probably wouldn't have wanted to be a soldier if his parents hadn't encouraged him to read. Ever since he was a young boy, Ishmael had devoured stories from *Commando Comics*. The covers were bright and colorful, the pages black-and-white cartoon artwork on newsprint, and the stories about fighting men in World War II. Most of the soldiers were brave, although to keep things real, a few cowards were portrayed. All were patriots, willing to die for their country, capable of noble actions one minute and joking with their mates around a campfire the next. The battle scenes took place around the world, including many in the Pacific. The combatants weren't typically black, but rather white members of the Allied Armed Forces—Brits, Aussies, Kiwis, even Yanks—but the men's skin color mattered little to Ishmael. They were heroes on Arthurian quests. He wanted to be like them, experience what they had done, and forge a character of his own.

Ishmael didn't learn only by reading. Many Bougainvilleans spent all of their lives on their island, but not him. When he was six, his mother Alice and his father Amos, teachers and missionaries with the United Church of Christ, moved the family to the PNG highlands. He remembered the airplane—the old type where passengers had to walk downhill to get to their seats—how its big engines rumbled and the plane bounced going through the storm clouds before landing in Mt. Hagen. Living in PNG in the midst of people Bougainvilleans called redskins, he realized for the first time how brown-skinned they were and how black he was, and what it was like to be different.

"Father, they're not the same as us," he said one day after coming home from school. "We're black, and they're brown."

"We're the color of the night," his father said proudly, his teeth pearly white when he smiled.

Ishmael liked his color better.

When it was decided that in 1975 Papua New Guinea would gain its independence from Australia, the Mt. Hagen mission closed and everyone had to leave. Ishmael and his family returned to Bougainville. Flying out of Mt. Hagan, he remembered their plane being full of white people going back to Australia. The men were somber and the women sobbing, crying about leaving their homes, escaping before PNG was overwhelmed by a sinister force Ishmael couldn't comprehend, embodied by a strange, new word: chaos. Chaos was coming to Papua New Guinea.

They moved back to Roreinang, where Ishmael had been born, a village clustered around a United Church mission on a ridge above Aropa. Ishmael was a middle child in a family that grew to six siblings, including three brothers and three sisters. Being born to teachers who were also naturalists, Ishmael thrived in the wild, learning many things from his father, including all about the spectacular tropical plant life that grew in the mist-covered hills of his homeland.

"Look, father," he said as he returned from a weekend of exploring in the jungle surrounding the village, proudly displaying a clutch of orchids that he had obtained by climbing cliffs and shinnying up tree trunks.

"Here, we must care for them," Amos said, taking the plants from Ishmael. "Watch me," his father instructed him. He searched the ground among the grove of palm trees behind their house and fetched several decaying coconut husks. With Ishmael looking over his shoulder, Amos packed the innards of the husks with leafy compost. "This is all the food the orchids will need," he told his son. Amos placed the plants root-first inside the curved shells, bound up each assemblage with a length of vine, and sprinkled water on the plants in their new homes. "Don't make the mistake others do with orchids," he advised Ishmael. "They don't need much water." He set the flowers in the shade by the side of the potting shed. "They'll recover and grow. They deserve to live long lives, just like you."

"I thought we could sell them in the Arawa town market," Ishmael said. He was somewhat disappointed; he had thought that proceeds from selling the orchids could pay for a new edition of *Commando Comics*.

"If you want to sell special flowers, perhaps one day you could sell these," Amos said, drawing Ishmael around to the opposite side of the potting shed where he kept his fenced-in flower garden. He led Ishmael down the rows of brightly colored adenium, lilies, and orchids, and stopped in front of a green, cactus-like plant with a round, white flower hanging from a stem. "Do you know what this is?"

"You told us once," said Ishmael. "You said it was the most valuable flower in the world, but I don't remember its name."

"That's the Queen of the Night," said Amos. "A botanist in Mt. Hagen got one in Sri Lanka, an island country like ours near India, and gave me some of its seeds. The flowers make magnificent perfume."

"Why are the flowers so valuable?"

Amos said, "Because as soon as you pick the flower, it dies. The only way for us to make the perfume would be to make it here—where the flower grows. That would cost a great deal of money, more than Bougainville has now. If we could do that one day, it might help propel our people to greatness; maybe you can make it happen."

Ishmael looked up into his father's kind eyes. "I will, father."

He was a good schoolboy too. His academic scores were high enough to qualify him to board at Hutjena Secondary School on Buka Island, the best high school in the Bougainville province. He performed well at Hutjena, and became friends with George Washburn, an upperclassman two years ahead of him. It seemed important to George to be selected by the headmaster as the head of his class, while Ishmael couldn't abide the politics necessary for such things. His passion remained anything involving the military: heroes, battles, guns, and warfare strategy. He wanted to go away to military school, but that was not possible for his family financially.

When he was sixteen, Ishmael's mother drowned in a freak accident. Her death staggered him. He loved her unconditionally and felt inconsolable guilt; he was away at school when she died and hadn't been nearby to help her. It was his first experience with the loss of a person close to him. Inside, he would grieve perpetually for her, but Ishmael's budding manhood caused him to remain stoic, rather than expose to others his susceptibility to sorrow.

After his mother's death, school didn't seem important anymore. Ishmael left Hutjena, and went to the Defence Force barracks in Arawa, determined to sign up and pursue what he was sure was his mission in life. He was rejected; at five feet, five inches, he was deemed too short. Disheartened, like everyone else at the time he applied to work for BCL at the Panguna Mine. While the people there were nice enough, they didn't hire him, leaving him even more adrift. He went to work for a logging company instead and belatedly grew six inches, while still hoping for a military career. Little did he know it would unfold in the Crisis right over the mountaintop, against two seemingly benign parties he had just encountered who would become the opposition: the Defence Force and BCL.

When Ishmael showed up with his father's shotgun at Francis Olu's BRA hideout in Guava, the last thing he'd expected was to be the only member of the BRA with a conventional firearm. Almost everyone else was armed with primitive weapons, including bush knives, spears, bows and arrows, and even slingshots used for killing birds. A few men packed homemade zip guns.

The BRA's initial adversary was a nasty one: PNG's riot squads. After the BRA grew to become a meaningful irritant, the Royal Papua New Guinea Constabulary, the national government's police force, stationed a riot squadron at the Panguna Mine, a few miles from Guava. In the beginning, the skirmishes between Bougainvilleans and the riot squads had little to do with what later burgeoned into a civil war, but instead stemmed from simpler rivalries involving skin colors, tribes and clans. The intensity and frequency of the incidents escalated, and neared the level of atrocity. Bougainvillean women were afraid to go out at night. Olu's band of BRA recruits, shoeless and unequipped, were outnumbered, but determined to account for themselves. The BRA leader welcomed Ishmael and turned him over to Glen Tovir, an experienced military man in charge of whipping the BRA into fighting shape.

Ishmael was excited to begin maneuvers, but, after a few days of training, was less than impressed. The BRA's activities weren't remotely akin to the type of action depicted in *Commando Comics*. Under Olu, the BRA's creed was not to expend men, ammunition, or energy in military attacks, but rather to spy on the enemy, filch provisions and supplies when possible, and then hide.

Ishmael regarded the BRA's strategy as one espoused by common thieves, and devoid of military impact. "I thought we were supposed to teach the riot squads some manners," Ishmael said carefully in a joking tone to Francis Olu when a group of BRA men sat around a campfire one night, but the great leader didn't even respond to the young newcomer.

Ishmael was pleased when finally dispatched on an assignment which might involve action: a stakeout on a well-travelled trail from Guava to Panguna. Where the path crossed a stream, its water flattened out and ran quickly through rock-lined banks. The villagers used the site to draw water, and Glen said it was a gathering place for riot squad troops up to no good.

A patrol led by Glen, accompanied by Ishmael, Wendell Bittyman, a middle-aged man, and Sebastian, his oldest son, waited in Guava until nightfall, and then slipped down a side trail through a jungle-draped ravine. Glen carried a zip gun made from a pipe, Ishmael his shotgun, and Sebastian a bush knife. Wendell had painted his face and wielded a bow and arrow.

As the men stumbled along the trail, the silence echoed danger to Ishmael. From years climbing in the hills above his village at all hours of the night, Ishmael knew that when the only sound was raindrops dripping off the tree leaves, the birds and wildlife were holding their breath and laughing at the clumsy intruders. While the BRA men lurched along in the dark, Glen warned Wendell to shut up twice, and Ishmael smelled home brew on Sebastian's breath.

Up ahead in the bush, a group of riot squad men was making as much noise as a pair of mating rhinoceroses. Behind a line of trees, the BRA guerillas nestled down in the moist earth, still warm from the heat of the day, and observed their foes ten yards across the stream in a clearing. Two of the soldiers were washing dishes, while a third filled canteens, and another did the same with kitchen water drums.

Listening to the riot squad policemen gripe about the food they'd just eaten for dinner, Ishmael held his breath, listened to his empty stomach complain, and admired their camouflaged khaki uniforms and high-topped leather boots.

After a few uneventful minutes, one of the riot squad men said in a loud, oblivious voice, "Someone's coming." The men ceased their chores and lumbered around, pulling their dishes and canteens out of the stream and backing away beneath the low bush a few paces off the clearing.

Ishmael could hear girls' laughter as they came closer to the stream. Carefully, he unlocked the safety of his shotgun.

As three girls, unaware of danger, entered the clearing, one of the soldiers spoke out of the darkness. "*Welkam,*" he said in pidgin.

"Oh!" one of the girls exclaimed. The three stood stock-still as the riot squad policemen emerged from the shadows.

"*Wanem nem blo yu?*" the talkative one asked.

Ishmael figured something would happen when the guy asked the girl her name, but he was unprepared for what transpired. He heard a zipping sound behind him, and then the bush crashing as Wendell, war paint glistening, stampeded into the clearing, knife drawn.

"What the hell?" one of the riot squad men managed to gurgle as the shaft of Wendell's arrow disappeared into his sternum.

The girls screamed.

Two of the riot squad men dropped their implements, turned, and ran, while a third, as he drew his Colt pistol, took a .50 caliber slug from Glen's zip gun in the middle of his face and was blown back into the jungle.

Ishmael straightened up from where he had been crouched in the bush, feeling like an idiot; he hadn't fired his gun.

"You could have got us killed!" Glen yelled at Wendell, who, ignoring him, was standing over the riot squad guy he had just skewered, the arrow sticking up out of the man's chest as he moaned and twisted, trying to wrest the three-foot projectile from his torso.

Wendell leaned over him. "*Skius*," he said politely, and stepping on the man's ribcage, ripped the arrow out of the guy, who cried out again. Wendell wiped the blood and flesh off the arrow's tip, spat on the ground next to the riot squad guy's head, and then bulled into the bush, heading up the trail back to Guava. Without a word, Sebastian crashed into the jungle behind him.

"We've got to get out of here," Glen said. "I'm sure someone heard us." He yelled after the girls to run back to their village, while Ishmael glanced around the clearing. Glen grabbed the dead man's Colt off the ground, and Ishmael gathered the canteens. Stepping around Wendell's victim, neither of them bothered with the headless body in the bush as they left the clearing.

Wordlessly, they scrambled up the steep trail toward Guava. Five minutes later, they caught up to Sebastian and Wendell.

"Your father's crazy," Glen said to Sebastian.

Sebastian ignored him and kept humping up the trail, following his father, with Glen and Ishmael bringing up the rear. At a switchback in the trail, Sebastian growled, "One of those girls was my sister," and resumed hiking up the mountain.

Ishmael had been looking right into the riot squad man's eyes when Glen blew his head off, and felt queasy for a few days. It took one more incident involving a Bougainvillean woman, riot squad thugs, and the mindless complicity of the mining company, to cauterize Ishmael for war, and transfix all of Bougainville as well.

The Aropa Plantation near Kieta was one of Bougainville's largest. When Bougainville had been part of German New Guinea, missionaries and planters had settled the flatlands from Arawa in the north past Kieta twenty miles south to Aropa and made Kieta the center of the colony. The area was cleared and planted with thousands of coconut palms by the 1920s. A microcosm of Bougainvillean colonial civilization, the Aropa Plantation included acres of coconut palms running from the hills down to the sea, a reef-protected lagoon lined by wharfs and docks, and a dignified plantation house surrounded by a mini-village including a blacksmith shop and stable, a small collection of stores, a laundry, and even a medical station.

When BCL blasted the Panguna Mine into a mountaintop overlooking the plantations on the coast, it didn't realize it was bringing with it urbanization problems unique to Papua New Guinea. BCL couldn't fill all of the Panguna Mine's personnel requirements with Bougainvilleans and recruited skilled management from Australia and workers from PNG, forcing on Bougainvilleans an unwelcome tide of foreigners—arrogant Australians and rambunctious redskins—as well as a host of environmental depredations.

For its workforce, BCL provided dormitories and living quarters in the Panguna Mine's two towns: Panguna Town, up on the mountain next to the mine, and Arawa, down at the harbor. There was limited accommodation for others, but that didn't stop anyone. The sylvan acreage of the Aropa Plantation in particular became a magnet for squatters, who, thanks to PNG's special, so-called "freedom of movement" land-use laws, were allowed to stay anywhere they could scratch out a camping spot. Perhaps if Aropa's benign plantation owners and missionaries had spoken up in the beginning, they could have staunched the problem. By the time hundreds of immigrants had washed up on Kieta's shore, including a large group of mountain tribespeople from Sepik, a remote PNG area alongside the Indonesian border, it was too late.

When a serial rapist—the Arawa Phantom, rumored to be a redskin—attacked a number of Bougainvillean women, emotions were stretched to the limit. It was probably the worst time for a group of Sepik redskins to go on a rampage and rape and kill the Aropa Plantation's nurse, a well-liked Kongara woman who was with child. Bougainvilleans were outraged. In Bougainville's matrilineal society, women are considered by many the most important members of the community. In a frenzy of retaliation, the BRA, including a young rebel named Washburn, swept down from the hills into the Aropa Plantation, killed several redskin squatters, and chased the remainder from the land.

The situation escalated. Truckloads of new riot squad troops arrived and retaliated by burning villages, raping women, and killing young Washburn, one of the first BRA casualties of the conflict. Reactionary behavior had been expected from the riot squads, but not mild-mannered Bougainvilleans. An angry crowd gathered on the tarmac at the Aropa Airport and burned an airplane and nearby government buildings. It was the first time something like that had happened in beautiful Bougainville, but it wouldn't be the last.

Perhaps if Francis Olu had chosen another time to light a match and spark the Crisis, Bougainvilleans might have been composed enough to observe all they were poised to destroy, and think twice. After all, hundreds of them enjoyed salaried employment at the Panguna Mine or other businesses sponsored by BCL. But for too many Bougainvilleans, what had itched under their skin for a generation had festered into a rash that demanded to be scratched until it bled. No longer would they mindlessly "belong" to Papua New Guinea, or allow their land to be mined, without a fair deal. The sooner they finished their divorce with the mainland, the better.

One afternoon in late 1988, pursuant to an armed holdup, Francis Olu stole a supply of Cordtex explosives from a BCL storeroom. The next day he went on the radio and warned that judgement day was coming. A week later, his men used a spool of detonation cord to blow up a transmission line pylon along the road that ran from Arawa to the Panguna Mine. The explosion cut off power to the town and shut down the largest and most profitable copper and gold mine on earth. The event made the evening news around the world. The Crisis was underway. Olu took to the airwaves again, but now he spoke of secession. BCL had no choice but to begin winding down mining operations. The company's engineers converted the Panguna Tailings, a wide gravel wash downriver from the Panguna Mine where they dumped stony residue after crushing rock to extract copper and gold ore, into a temporary airstrip. De Havilland Twin Otters, stubby bush planes that could take off and land on short runways, began flitting in and out of the western side of Panguna, removing valuable equipment, supplies, and personnel.

In March of 1989, the national government sent reinforcements to central Bougainville in the form of the army—three companies of Defence Force soldiers—and gave Francis Olu an ultimatum: he had twenty-one days to surrender. Olu had barely begun; his BRA was expanding rapidly, and his response indicated as much. He demanded that the national government and BCL pay reparations of ten billion PNG kina, approximately ten billion US dollars at the time, to compensate aggrieved Bougainvilleans. The twenty-one-day surrender period expired with no sign of Olu. The national government declared a state of emergency and turned the Defence Force loose to root Olu out of his mountain stronghold in Guava. In the first armed engagement between the Defence Force and the BRA, while searching through a village called Orami, two Defence Force soldiers were shot and killed by BRA rebels. It was the Defence Force's first casualties since World War II. In a sign of things to come, they promptly slaughtered seven villagers.

Ishmael graduated quickly from BRA trainee to squad leader. Like someone with years of experience, he knew what he wanted in a fighter.

"I'm going with you this time," said one of the young men who had joined the BRA recently, the darkness partially obscuring the multi-colored war paint he had applied to his face, as Ishmael organized men for a raiding party.

"That won't be possible," Ishmael said, as kindly as he knew how. "There's other work here in camp where you can contribute while you learn."

"You're not any older than I am," the young man protested. "You can't tell me what to do."

"I watched you turn and run when faced with the enemy last time, and if the going gets tough tonight, you'll do the same. Stay put," Ishmael said. He dropped a shell into the barrel of his shotgun, snapped it shut, and turning his back on the neophyte, walked out of camp.

Ishmael took extreme care when recruiting guerillas. The best ones were typically villagers from the cacao plantations down the road from Roreinang like Solomon and Sevy, quiet and dependable deputies who were fearless and could be trusted to cover his back. Perched in the hills around Guava, Ishmael and his chosen BRA patrolmen continued to conduct scavenger missions as they watched the national government's Iroquois helicopters begin to ferry in real soldiers from the Defence Force to supplement the riot squad police.

Like the birds of prey he had observed in the skies at home, Ishmael monitored everything moving on the land below, from Panguna Town all the way down to the Tailings, learning the habits of his enemy. He had been studying the careless riot squad men for weeks when the Defence Force soldiers began to arrive. Ishmael realized that the time for the BRA to take advantage of the riot squads' shoddy routines was fleeting. Their discipline was second-rate, but their equipment wasn't: their standard-issue weapon was the M-16 assault rifle, the same basic weapon as the one deployed by the US Armed Forces. Ishmael had studied the attributes of the M-16 in a Vietnam War-era firearms manual he had found. He wanted one.

He memorized the riot squads' actions and their hours, noticing how casually they treated their weapons and their lax behavior when off-duty. They displayed little caution, parading back and forth in their troop-carrying vehicles—TCVs—as if they were back home on Papua New Guinea's mainland. When the goons weren't on duty, they tossed their rifles aside, and no matter what time of day, they always seemed to have enough access to home brew to get plastered.

If Ishmael had an assault rifle—especially an M-16—he would sleep with it, and he never took a drink, nor did he allow his men to. He formulated a plan. Since the riot squad policemen didn't respect their weapons, Ishmael would relieve them of the responsibility. That would be the BRA's future source of weapons—not home-made zip guns made from pipes, but real armaments. Ishmael decided to organize a team of BRA fighters to hit the riot squads when they were most relaxed, after dinner when they were drunk. Every night, the riot squads ate at the mess hall in Panguna Town an hour after sundown. Later, their TCVs ferried them back down the road to their tents by the Tailings. The BRA guerillas would jump them *en route*. It would be a challenging mission, one which Ishmael was committed to lead, but some backup wouldn't hurt.

"Come with us," Ishmael said, trying to recruit some men carrying homemade zip guns who had recently swaggered into the BRA's camp, older guys he had respected as civilians in the days before the Crisis.

"So we can get our heads blown off?" they scoffed. "You've got a death wish."

Ishmael didn't blame the men for being afraid, but their attitudes weren't compatible with military objectives, no matter how ragtag the BRA might be. The BRA needed to take the fight to the enemy. Their success depended on it; it had to happen. Otherwise, what were they fighting for?

On a moonless evening, Ishmael, together with only his wingmen Solomon and Sevy, hiked down a mountain trail from Guava to a high bank overlooking Panguna Town and the road to the Tailings. In front of them, the road hung a ninety-degree turn to cross a bridge before heading down the steep hill toward the Tailings. Any TCV would have to slow to a virtual stop to make the sharp turn and cross the narrow bridge. Under the bridge, the Jaba River spilled out of the Panguna Mine's pit on its way to the Solomon Sea. In the blackness, Ishmael and his men slid to the bottom of the gravelly bank, hunkered under the downstream end of the bridge, and waited for a TCV to come along the road.

Everyone knew the plan: carrying shortened, point-sharpened bush knives, Solomon would take the right-hand, driver's-side door, and Ishmael would go after the guy most likely to be carrying a gun, the front passenger on the left; Sevy would cover them with Ishmael's shotgun. They had to pray that the riot squad guys sitting in the front seats of the vehicle didn't lock their doors, and that any passengers in the back seats would be too surprised to become engaged. Under the bridge, the dark water of the Jaba River was their escape hatch.

They heard the engine of the TCV before they saw any headlights. Ishmael craned his neck above the floor of the bridge and gazed up the road in the darkness. "Nogat, nogat," he called to the men, and they all shrunk back under the cover of the bridgeworks. A minute later, three TCVs slowed down to make the turn, then thundered over the bridge and continued down the hill toward the Tailings.

They waited ten minutes more before they heard the growl of another TCV engine. Ishmael straightened up from where he was hiding and peered up the road. "This one," he hissed to his men. "It's alone."

The driver downshifted as the TCV crawled up to the bridge and started to rumble across. When the vehicle approached the end of the span and began to pick up speed, Ishmael and his men sprang up from underneath the bridge and ran barefoot alongside the truck. Sprinting, Ishmael got even with the cab of the TCV, reached to grab the door handle, and swung up onto the vehicle's running board. He found himself looking through an open window into the shocked eyes of a riot squad policeman. They were head-to-head, and only a foot apart. Picking up the strong stench of jungle juice on the man's breath, Ishmael jerked open the door. He thrust his bush knife into the guy's ribcage and grabbed the man's M-16 where it lay across his lap.

"Hey!" the man cried, his nostrils flaring, eyes wild.

Ishmael jerked the M-16 out of the guy's hands and jumped backward away from the TCV. While he was in the air, he heard the

TCV's driver scream, saw the vehicle's trajectory jog off-course, and hoped Solomon had been able to similarly eject himself from the moving vehicle. Landing hard on his feet, Ishmael rolled backward, head-over-heels, still clutching the M-16 with both hands, and ended up in a ditch on his back. He bounded to his feet. He had taken a pounding, and the back of his head was bleeding, but he had his prize. It never occurred to him that the mission would be anything but a success.

The taillights of the TCV veered toward the riverbank as the vehicle picked up speed, bouncing down the hill. Dazed, Ishmael was checking the status of the M-16 when he heard shuffling and glanced up. In the darkness, Sevy was standing next to him, holding Ishmael's shotgun. "I didn't hear anything," Ishmael said to him. "Did you fire a round?"

Sevy said, "There was no need. Take a look."

They both glanced across the road just in time to see the TCV's taillights disappear down into the Jaba River canyon.

"Is Solomon with you?" Ishmael asked. When Sevy said no, Ishmael panicked. "Solomon?" he yelled. He bolted across the road to where the land fell away to the Jaba River. "Solomon?" he called again, his voice echoing down into the empty chasm. He would never forgive himself if something had happened to his friend from home.

"Mi orait," they heard. A moment later, Solomon hoisted himself up from the steep riverbank onto the road. He was covered with the driver's blood, but otherwise seemed fine, although disgusted; he hadn't been able to filch a weapon.

"I got my gun; where's yours?" Ishmael said, watching his friend's surprised face transform from a scowl to a smile as he got the joke. Everyone laughed; they were alive, and that was all that mattered.

The next day, Ishmael talked Solomon and Sevy into walking with him in broad daylight up the Panguna road, carrying his captured M-16 into the maw of the mine pit, in plain view of any observer. He hoped that riot squad policemen would see them, lose their cool, and chase after them; then, maybe, they could cadge a few more weapons. It wouldn't hurt if his own BRA comrades learned about the successful escapade as well, Ishmael concluded; they needed to know how much a dash of courage could accomplish. The young guerilla was bringing a new attitude to the BRA rebels.

From their perch in the Guava heights above the Panguna Mine, Francis Olu and Glen Tovir kept tabs on the BRA's military progress. Their most recent topic of conversation was George Washburn. Even though he was Bougainvillean, George had been a high-ranking Lieutenant in the Defence Force. When his younger brother was killed in the fighting with the BRA at the Aropa Plantation, George had taken leave to come home to Bougainville to bury him. Olu used the event to convince George to remain in Bougainville and change sides, offering him the title of commander of the BRA. George agreed, but indicated he had no plans to spend his time in the bush wielding a weapon on behalf of the BRA. He saw his future career to be one involving diplomacy and politics.

"Who was responsible for holding up that TCV and grabbing the M-16?" Olu asked Glen. "That's the kind of man we need in the bush."

"Ishmael," Glen replied. "You should have ten more like him. He's fearless, and his men will follow him anywhere. That M-16 was the first of many. Ishmael always has a plan. We should make him head of all military operations."

Over time, Ishmael assumed leadership of the BRA's military cadres, and their success in the field reflected it. From behind rocks and trees, they ambushed the national government's forces, helping themselves to assault rifles, self-loading rifles—SLRs—and two of Ishmael's favorite, M-249 tripod-outfitted machine guns. Ishmael didn't confine his weapons appropriation plan to PNG's armed forces. He and his men raided the Kuveria Prison for shotguns, retrieved high powered, twenty-two caliber rifles with telescope sights from the Arawa Shooting Club, and even dug up US and Japanese guns and ordnance at their mothballed, WWII military bases in Torokina.

While the BRA under Ishmael became a larger and better-equipped fighting force, the Defence Force proved ineffective. They had no answer for what they encountered in Bougainville's rugged terrain. Their maneuvers—standard insertion and extraction exercises—were worthless in a jungle war. They had no idea where the enemy was, where they were going, or how to get there. Even if the Defence Force had owned expensive artillery pieces—and they didn't—they would have been useless: the terrain was too difficult and the BRA rebels too elusive. An air campaign might have worked, but other than transport helicopters, the Defence Force had no aircraft, let alone any with installed armaments or electronic detection equipment.

During 1988 and into 1989, PNG's military leaders knew that Francis Olu was holed up in Guava but were powerless to capture him. The day after a foreigner with the organization that managed the Twin Otter planes was killed by a shotgun blast—the first white expat to die in the Crisis—BCL announced that it would close the Panguna Mine by April 1989. The mood of the ordinary PNG citizen became increasingly depressed—the mine was responsible for half of the country's economy. In a war in which PNG's riot squad policemen, not the Defence Force, remained in charge, morale in the army's ranks worsened. The Crisis had become Papua New Guinea's version of Vietnam.

The climax of the first phase of the Crisis took place on the road from Arawa to the Panguna Mine, in a village called Sideronsi. Because it was situated next to the road, BRA men used Sideronsi as a staging area for raids on BCL and PNG vehicles. After an attack on a Defence Force convoy, the BRA rebels involved didn't disappear into the jungle as usual, but instead holed up in the village. As a platoon of Defence Force soldiers gave chase through the collection of flimsy, thatched-wall houses, the small group of BRA men with antiquated weapons began firing at the soldiers out of windows and doors. After each exchange of bullets, the men jumped from house to house, reloaded, and then fired again. They were accurate and picked off many of their enemy. Outfoxed by the ragtag BRA fighters, the Defence Force troops took their anger out on the village. Soldiers sprayed anything in their path with hundreds of rounds from machine guns, SLRs, assault rifles, and even pistols, shredding houses and chopping people to bits. When they discovered that the BRA men had somehow managed to escape, the Defence Force's frustrated platoon commander ordered that the village be torched. Within an hour, the homes of hundreds of Bougainvilleans were reduced to ashes.

The international press learned what happened at Sideronsi, and sentiment directed at PNG's politicians was harsh. A survey indicated that across Bougainville, at least 1600 homes had been destroyed. The national government fell. Fingers were pointed in all directions, and as members of PNG's parliament stumbled selecting a new prime minister, a military coup was barely averted. In March of 1990, the national government and the BRA signed a cease-fire agreement, and the two sides declared a truce. When the chastened PNG political leaders told the Defence Force to come home, the riot squads evacuated overnight, fearing for their lives. BCL cleared out the next month and the Panguna Mine was closed, never to reopen. Bougainville was left to its own devices.

Basking in military and political victory, Francis Olu was convinced he could do nothing wrong. His aggressive, unpredictable actions had not been altogether Bougainvillean, but they had worked nonetheless. His grateful people, relieved that the fighting had abated, assumed that some type of future improvement would accrue to their lives, although most doubted that the final chapter of the Crisis had been written. A tentative Bougainville tried to return to its peacetime ways.

The BRA guerillas were happy to take a break; many of them had been fighting in the bush, away from their families, for over two years. While Ishmael looked forward to returning to his village to see his family, there was another he longed for: Roreinang's most beautiful young lady. While the name she was given at birth was Elizabeth, her friends teased her by calling her "Queennie," so she preferred "Betty." Her vision had been entwined in Ishmael's thoughts from the day he had left for war.

"Did you miss me?" he finally worked up the courage to ask her, as the two of them sat alone on a grassy bank along a mountain stream.

A wistful smile touched the corners of Betty's lips, but she didn't answer, seeming to be focused instead on the waters of the brook flowing past them.

"It's been almost two years," he lamented, their languorous conversation not the reception he had longed for from the girl of his dreams.

"Has it been that long?"

Ishmael turned away, his spirit crushed. He had thought she cared…and then his heart leapt as he felt her behind him wrapping her arms around his shoulders, her lips caressing his ear.

"I thought of nothing but you."

They were married soon afterward, and in a year Betty delivered their first child, a baby boy. Meanwhile, Roreinang, together with all of Bougainville, did what was normal behavior in South Pacific islands: while the world swirled around them, they took their time. Days turned into weeks, and weeks into months, as the cloud of the Crisis floated above the land, still dark and loaded but not in discharge mode. While no one was quite sure what the next day would bring, the interlude was peaceful. Ishmael had always wanted to be a cacao farmer, and began clearing and planting an orchard, happily working from dawn to nightfall. War had been an unpleasant experience for Bougainville; everyone hoped it would just go away.

No one realized it at the time, but the hiatus represented the high-water mark for both Francis Olu as well as the BRA in terms of widespread Bougainvillean support. Even though theirs had been Papua New Guinea's most prosperous province before the Crisis began, on the heels of the victory, no one could blame Bougainvilleans for expecting that even better days would soon follow. Until they didn't.

6

No Place to Hide

Francis Olu's biggest problem was that he had no plan to govern. Adept at pointing a finger at purported villains, he lacked solutions as well as the skills to implement them. In the aftermath of the cease-fire and the truce, Olu was supposed to lead a Bougainvillean task force to disarm, and subsequently negotiate, the terms of peace with the national government. Instead, in May 1990, before any discussion had commenced and after little consultation with his own people, he made a surprise announcement: Bougainville's sole objective was complete independence.

Olu's proclamation guaranteed that the Crisis would continue. The national government leaders felt duped, and debated reprisals. The BRA's supreme commander called Ishmael back from Roreinang and tasked him with making sure PNG's armed forces remained banned from Bougainville once and for all.

Ishmael was stunned by the turn of events. Even though he was only in his twenties, he recognized the difference between launching raiding parties and fighting a civil war for independence. No one in the BRA had signed up for such a major undertaking. But at that point, he remained loyal to his leader Olu and didn't question him.

Ishmael kissed Betty and his baby son goodbye, strapped on his M-16, and reported to BRA headquarters in Guava.

"Whose idea was independence?" some of the men grumbled as Ishmael arrived in the BRA's mountain camp. "We can't survive by ourselves."

"Focus on your tasks and stop complaining," Ishmael advised them, intent on maintaining military order, even as he wrestled with his own doubts. Independence was a noble concept, but he had joined the BRA for a simpler, more pragmatic reason: to rid Bougainville of oppression. Even though his men's fears were misstated—he had lived on his own in the jungle for weeks at a time, and his BRA guerillas could learn to do the same—he worried that for the entire population to go into survival mode over a prolonged period of time would weigh heavily on Bougainville's soul.

Olu's lack of diplomatic savvy weakened Bougainville, militarily and politically. Sentiment in PNG regarding Olu's position shifted from resigned cooperation to outright hostility. At home in Bougainville, disquiet brewed. Unanimity had always struggled to find a secure place in the people's mindsets, while jealousy and envy were much more prevalent. When the national government's pullout removed Bougainville's military adversaries, it left a vacuum in which local antagonists could settle old scores. For the first time, the protagonists were armed and less inclined to rely on traditional dispute-resolution methods. Bougainvilleans fought, sometimes violently, over everything: land, houses, vehicles, and even each other's wives and husbands. It was an ugly time for Bougainville.

Among Bougainvilleans most disenchanted by Francis Olu's performance, the citizens of Buka Island stood out. Although only separated from the larger Bougainville Island by the narrow waters of the Passage, Buka Island was bereft of precious minerals. With mining issues of no concern to them, many Bukans, as they were known, had rejected Olu's destructive agenda from the beginning. When, in a tribal argument, rogue antagonists posing as members of the BRA burned down Buka's iconic Hutjena Secondary School, Ishmael's old high school, Buka Island's citizens called it quits with Olu and his BRA. Organizing not just one, but two anti-BRA militias—the Bougainville Resistance Force and the Buka Liberation Front—the Bukans persuaded the national government to return the Defence Force to their island, and also to fund the local, anti-BRA insurgents. Soon afterward, the BRA lost control of Buka Island for the remainder of the Crisis.

Similar resistance militias sprouted up across the southern end of Bougainville Island, where, again, due to lack of mineral resource concerns and geography, the BRA was less of a factor. Fighting flared in the outlying regions. This time, however, a majority of the hostilities pitted Bougainvillean against Bougainvillean. Sensing an opportunity to recast themselves as the voice of reason and restore their standing in the Bougainville community, the national government's politicians clamored for their armed forces to resume beachheads at both ends of Bougainville Island.

Olu was adamant that the PNG armed forces be repulsed. Preventing their return—especially to Buka Island, where the most potent seeds of anti-BRA feeling had been sown—was critical to remaining in power as the leader of a unified Bougainville.

"I want you to meet Albert Musku," Olu said to Ishmael one day toward the end of 1991. "His family is from Guava, but he's now living in Buka. He has intelligence concerning PNG's military intentions, he's recruited men in Buka, and he can help us keep the PNG armed forces out of our northern territory."

"I know the Musku family," Ishmael said as he greeted the man. Ishmael didn't say anything else, but took a seat and studied their guest. He had always found that in important situations like the one he was in—evaluating a potential military ally—it was best to say as little as possible, let the other person talk, and concentrate on their words and expressions. As far as the Musku family, Ishmael felt it was immaterial to mention what everyone in Bougainville knew—that they had been accused of hoarding the Panguna Mine fish money that BCL paid landowners in the Guava area. Since the Musku family was from Guava, Olu had obviously chosen to ignore the issue, but Ishmael couldn't help thinking that being involved with them might represent an error in judgement. Still, he wasn't going to fall into the jealousy trap that plagued some Bougainvilleans; he would strive to weigh the newcomer on the merits.

Not that Ishmael accepted what people told him at surface value. The war had taken care of that, and had replaced his boyhood innocence with a healthy level of cynicism. From Albert Musku's outward appearance, Ishmael's reticence seemed well-placed. Wearing high, lace-up, leather paratrooper boots and a black leather jacket, the man appeared far too well-dressed to Ishmael, who, as usual, was barefoot in jeans and a T-shirt. Ishmael studied the man's weapon, a fancy Australian Parabellum F1 submachine gun with a distinctive, top-mounted magazine. He had heard that up north, the PNG armed forces paid big money to Bougainvilleans who agreed to help them— the kind of money it took to buy an F1.

"Where have you been fighting, Al?" Ishmael asked.

"I prefer to be called Albert," the man said.

Ishmael hesitated, not sure how to respond. "Sorry about that. I think I'll just call you Musku," Ishmael said. He was tempted to say, "I'll bet that's what your mother called you," in jest, but held his tongue, glancing at Olu to see his leader's reaction to Albert's pouty statement.

Apparently, the conversation wasn't that important; Olu wasn't paying any attention.

"I haven't been lucky enough to see any action yet," Musku rattled on, his excuse being that although Bougainvillean, he had been a member of the Defence Force, and was deployed overseas when the Crisis broke out.

Olu nodded his head supportively as Musku told his story, while Ishmael continued to listen.

"I was on assignment in Australia for paratrooper training," Musku continued. "It was impossible to get a flight home to join the BRA until now."

Ishmael had seen and heard enough. The man sitting across from him wasn't hard-bitten enough to be a guerilla, and if he was so desperate to join the BRA, he could have taken a boat home. "I'm certainly convinced that we must keep PNG's armed forces out of the northern end of the island," Ishmael said. "Unfortunately, I don't see how you can help us."

"He's got a plan. Listen to him," Olu urged Ishmael.

"I have," Ishmael said to Olu. He turned to Musku. "It's nothing personal."

Ishmael knew that in Melanesia, conversations about important topics didn't end quickly, so he wasn't surprised to see Musku waiting for him at the mess table early the next morning. The two men greeted each other and took their coffee in the mess hall, an outdoor grouping of rough-hewn log tables on the western edge of the Guava village. The sun rose over an unusually clear morning in the mountains of central Bougainville, which normally were shrouded in clouds. As they sat under a cobalt blue sky, they could see all the way to the Solomon Sea. Down the hills off to the southwest nestled the farming community of Bana; the Jaba River ran west to the Empress Augusta Bay; and to the north, white volcanic mist curled out of Mt. Bagana's cruel mouth.

"Here's why you would be smart to accept my help," Musku said, waving in front of Ishmael a stack of photographs, describing them as pictures he had taken of a new installation the Defence Force was building on the northern end of Bougainville Island. He pulled a photo off the top of the pile and pressed it flat on the wooden tabletop. "I used a Kodak camera out in the Passage on a friend's banana boat."

As he drank his coffee, Ishmael studied the photograph. He handed it back to Musku, who handed him another, and then another. As Ishmael viewed the snapshots, he was both surprised and concerned, but his face remained impassive. The photos showed dozens of men digging what looked like a fortress. The compound surrounded by Defence Force breastworks along the water's edge was unfinished, but already extensive; PNG's armed forces obviously planned to stay a while. Ishmael had not been up to the northern end of the island for some time and had no idea that the PNG armed forces had returned in such numbers. Past the compound, he recognized the outskirts of Tsiroge, a village on the northwestern tip of Bougainville Island. A small hamlet, its western edge was flanked by the sea, and was otherwise surrounded by coconut plantations. Strategically located, Tsiroge—especially the spot where the Defence Force was digging in—not only controlled the western entrance to the Passage, but the sea lanes running up and down the west side of Bougainville Island. There was no road on the west side of the island—the water was the highway. Ishmael sighed. "It looks like they're serious," he allowed.

Musku said, "I tried to tell you; we've got to get up there."

"Yes, yes," Ishmael said, standing up to signal the morning's unexpected conversation was coming to an end. He stacked the photos and handed them back to Musku, forming the same mental question regarding Musku's expensive Kodak camera that he had about the man's F1 machine gun: where'd he get the money? Surely, Musku was working for the other side; his greed was nauseating. Ishmael could never trust him, but he was convinced that the military threat at the northern end of Bougainville Island was real, and worth a fight. He sensed that if he wanted to act, he had little time.

"I can help you if you'll let me," Musku pressed, not willing to drop the subject.

"Thank you," Ishmael said, his eyes lingering on the last photo on the top of the stack, which showed men working in the compound but no sign of armed guards for security. "They don't seem to be worried about the BRA," he said, grinning at Musku as he spoke.

"You've got to hit them now," Musku urged. "They don't expect it. When they're done, the place will be impossible to defeat."

Ishmael was deliberately casual. "Nothing we couldn't handle—when and if we choose." When Musku's eyes questioned him, he offered no further comment. But he had made up his mind. It was critical that he squelch the PNG rebuilding effort as soon as possible.

"My guess is you've got a month; after that, they'll be dug in," Musku warned. He stood up at the table and gazed west down the Jaba River to its estuary at Marau, where spongy wetlands jutted out into the Empress Augusta Bay. "Tsiroge's three hours up the coast by boat," he said. "You wouldn't try to attack the north end of the island from here, would you?"

"Yes, it's a long way," Ishmael agreed. He looked up the western side of Bougainville Island, where clouds were already beginning to gather around the peaks of the Emperor Range. "We can't wage a northern ground war from here, but we can launch strikes anytime," Ishmael said. He looked at Musku, who nodded as if they were on the same page, and then Ishmael added, "When and if we want to."

Musku pushed ahead. "It's too long a ride for a northern attack on the same day. How many boats do you have?"

Ishmael said nothing.

Musku kept talking staccato-like, as if he were nervous. "The time is now. We'd be better off if you got there the day before. I could meet you nearby with my men from Buka, and we could stage the attack the next day."

"Could be," Ishmael said, tossing the dregs of his coffee into the bush.

"This location could be helpful." Musku slapped a Kodak photo down on the table as if it was his last card in a game of blackjack.

Ishmael glanced down at the snapshot. "Where's this?" he asked as he examined the photo that showed a wooden dock extending twenty yards out over calm seawater from a beach. There was no sign of human habitation. Towering coconut palms ran in long rows away from the beach toward higher ground.

"Madehas Island," Musku answered. "I'm sure you know it. It's used for coconut farming, and just a ten-minute boat ride from Tsiroge. There's only one family living there, on the east side facing the mainland."

Ishmael nodded. "I know the place. What were you thinking?"

Musku said, "The beach and the dock are on the west side of the island facing the Passage. For an attack on Tsiroge, we could make that area our staging ground. With the island blocking the view, the Defence Force in Tsiroge would never see us. Take a day to get to Madehas from Marau, and land in the afternoon. I'll bring over my men toward evening. We'll get organized and hit the Defence Force hard the next morning."

"Maybe someone told you that we've got a lot of men," Ishmael said, "but fighters are in short supply around here, and Tsiroge's a long way. If we pursued it, I would only send a small raiding party, not a major force."

"Of course," Musku said. "How many men?"

"Not many."

Musku got up to leave the table. "See you in Tsiroge?" he said to Ishmael, flashing a phony smile.

"We'll see." Ishmael was relieved to be rid of the man; he tried not to dwell on the notion that Olu had introduced them. He waited until he was sure Musku was gone from Guava, then went to find Solomon. "Get everyone together for a meeting. One hour." Unlike many Bougainvilleans, Ishmael was a stickler about promptness.

An hour later, Ishmael stood in front of fifty men. He had done the same thing twenty times in the past several years, but he still got a jumpy feeling in his stomach every time he sent young men out to die. Although he had no use for Musku and smelled a trap, Ishmael was resolute about raiding Tsiroge, and destroying the base the PNG armed forces were building. The action wouldn't be a raiding party; this would be a real military mission.

Ishmael's men gathered in the grass next to the mess hall. Most of them were lean and barefoot and wore tattered T-shirts and shorts or cut-off jeans. No one had shoes. A few had paint on their faces or beads in their hair, but only their firearms gave any hint as to their occupation. They could have been a farm crew out picking coconuts. As Ishmael had taught them, the BRA guerillas lived off the land, their diet mainly coconuts, fruit, and garden produce, except on infrequent days when Ishmael took them to the sea for fresh fish or someone would scavenge dried meat or chicken from a local market. Half of their guns had been plundered from PNG armed forces, while the rest were WWII vintage weapons from the arms dumps in Torokina, with a few zip guns thrown in. Everyone was armed; the days of bows and arrows were over. But ammunition was in short supply. Ishmael discouraged wasted ordnance—one bullet per target was enough— and everyone tried to finish a mission with a positive ammo count; otherwise, they might be short for the next sortie. The oldest recruit was forty, and there were many in their teens. Even though BRA guerrillas died in combat all the time, not a single fighter wanted to do anything else.

Ishmael's remarks were short. "The national government has dispatched a company of Defence Force soldiers to occupy northern Bougainville Island, and they're also funding local resistance groups. We've got to counter that hard and keep the PNG armed forces out of Bougainville. This will be an important operation. Get your weapons and supplies ready and make sure to find plenty to eat. I'll hand out orders three hours before we leave—it could be tomorrow, or it might be a week from now."

That was as much as Ishmael ever told them. He had found that if he said more, by the time he got to where they were going, the target was waiting for them.

Some of the men were angry about the anti-BRA militias, and one of them spoke up. "I've heard about these resistance groups from my family," he said. "My clan lives near Tsiroge, and they're loyal to the BRA. There are men up there who say they're with the BRA, but they're not. Those are the troublemakers. We've got to root them out and shut them up."

Ishmael said, "We don't want to get a reputation of accusing northern people of bad faith. We're going to strike quickly, against PNG military forces only, and then move out. It's not our mission to bother other Bougainvilleans."

Ishmael dismissed the men. For the next several days, he occupied himself solving his two biggest problems: ammunition and fuel. He dispatched a crew of men in a longboat carrying raw alluvial gold panned from the nearby Panguna Mine to the Solomon Islands. They needed to elude the blockade and get through to Choiseul, the nearest of the larger Solomon Islands—a one-hundred-mile trip that took all day—exchange their gold for cash with Chinese traders, and then return with bullets and fuel. He also made sure to get a message delivered to Musku, confirming that his force would arrive at the Madehas Island staging area the following Tuesday afternoon, and they would together hit the Defence Force installation in Tsiroge on Wednesday morning.

Ishmael's plans for Tsiroge were verification that the BRA was no longer engaged in a series of firefights, but pursuing a civil war. He was never concerned about his personal safety in armed combat—which came naturally to him—but fretted about his family and when he would see them again. Most of all, he wondered when—and how—Bougainville would be able to climb out of the hole it was sliding into. In his prayers, he thanked God that managing the government was Olu's responsibility, and not his.

As soon as his men returned from the Solomon Islands, Ishmael issued orders to move out. Fifty of the BRA's troops broke camp at zero five hundred hours and filed off the mountaintop in the darkness. When they arrived at the Panguna road an hour later, Ishmael split up the force. Led by Sevy and Steven Toppis, a fighter from Kongara, forty of the men climbed into four waiting Toyota trucks and headed up over Panguna Mountain and north on the coast road. When they were five miles south of Kokopau at the top of Bougainville Island, they would cut across the coconut plantations that dotted the land and attack the Defence Force position at Tsiroge from behind. If everything went as planned, they would commence firing at Tsiroge around noon on Tuesday afternoon—almost a full day ahead of when Musku expected them.

Ishmael directed the remaining team of ten men to pile into the open-back farm truck that waited for them at the side of the road and told Solomon at the wheel to make his way down to the port at Marau.

"I forgot to eat this morning; can we stop so I can grab a papaya?" Richard, a young trooper who was also Ishmael's nephew, called out ten minutes later from the rear of the truck, his words directed to Ishmael where he sat in the shotgun seat.

"Hold up," Ishmael instructed Solomon.

Solomon hit the brakes, and the truck lurched to a stop.

Ishmael got out and walked around to the back of the vehicle. "Richard, was that you?"

"I'm fine. I didn't mean it," said a muffled voice from somewhere in the crowd of men crammed in the truck bed.

"Get down here." Ishmael didn't yell, but spoke in a normal voice. "Now."

The men in the truck shuffled around, and a wiry kid pushed forward. He climbed down to face Ishmael standing in the road.

"Your weapon," Ishmael said, extending his hand.

Richard frowned and handed over his rifle.

"Your instructions were to fill your belly before we left on our mission. While you're walking back to camp, feel free to climb up a tree and eat as many papayas as you want. Maybe the fruit will fortify you and help you learn why, on a military mission, it's imperative that we obey orders. When you get back, report for kitchen duty."

No one said a word as Ishmael walked back to the front of the truck and climbed into his seat; Solomon kicked the vehicle in gear, and they continued rolling down the road.

At zero seven hundred hours, they boarded two longboats for the ride up the Solomon Sea along the west coast of Bougainville Island. Ishmael checked his watch. They were on track to arrive early, before noon on Madehas Island, as if he was indeed following Musku's plan of making the island a staging area and had simply arrived early. But Ishmael had no plans to remain on Madehas. He was convinced Musku was on the Defence Force's payroll and was helping them set up an ambush. Ishmael would arrive early and spoil the fun. Hopefully, Musku had accepted Ishmael's statement that he was only dispatching a small raiding party. If his plan worked, the Defence Force over at Tsiroge would be required to dilute some of their firepower to intercept him and his men at Madehas Island just as the main force of BRA rebels opened fire from the woods. With the Defence Force required to wage battle on two fronts against a large, well-armed foe, Ishmael expected to deal a crippling setback to PNG's new military plans in northern Bougainville. He hoped it would be enough; if the bolstered Defence Force regained beachheads on Bougainville Island, the BRA could be overwhelmed. Once more, he found himself questioning Francis Olu's judgement: befriending people like Musku, and assuming that the BRA could wage a successful civil war against the national government, were not good decisions taken by a wise leader.

When Ishmael and his men arrived at Marau, the sky was cloudless; they would be blessed with a dry, sunny trip. Solomon took the helm of one of the two waiting longboats, Ishmael captained the other, and they set out down the mangrove-lined estuary.

As his longboat glided downriver, Ishmael's thoughts continued to stray. It was less than a year earlier when he had navigated a similar longboat down another river, transporting his first load of cacao beans to the wholesaler in Buka. He had been so sure of himself then, certain that good things were on the horizon for him and his family, and for Bougainville. Now, his loved ones were hiding for their lives once again, and the BRA was embroiled in a civil war with no end in sight. He forced the irritating doubt from his mind; going into battle demanded optimism.

An hour later, they were in the open sea. The twenty-five-foot vessels skimmed north across a glassy Empress Augusta Bay until the Torokina headlands rose on their right. Beyond Torokina, like a green monster Mt. Bagana spewed white, wispy smoke from its mouth into the sky. Schools of flying fish chirped in and out of the depths, zipping along in parallel with the boats. After the second hour, they passed Mt. Balbi off to the right; Bougainville's highest point, it was half-covered by clouds. As the sun ascended and the temperature increased, the heat of the land rose skyward and wind began to blow, ruffling the water's surface. Speeding ahead at twenty knots, the longboats slammed up and down, throwing saltwater spray into the men's eyes.

An hour later, White Island rose up in the distance like a mirage over the salt flats that lined its shore. Shortly after eleven, they neared the Passage, on schedule. Ishmael called over to Solomon to throttle back his engine to reduce the noise of their approach. Solomon swung his prow in behind Ishmael's wake, and the two longboats chugged toward Madehas Island, a mile straight ahead. Along their line of approach, aquamarine-colored water covered low, tidal flats that ran into mangroves along the southern edge of Tsiroge. Toward Madehas Island, the sea remained deep and blue-green. As they motored toward the midsection of the island's eastern shore, Ishmael pointed his longboat at the family compound. Within a stone's throw of land, Ishmael and his men readied their weapons. They cruised closer, examining the small groupings of one-story houses, but saw no human activity. Ishmael called over to Solomon and instructed him to circle around the island's north side, warning that he might come face-to-face with the enemy; he would do the same thing around the island's southern end, and they would meet at the dock on the other side.

Weapons drawn as their longboat cruised around the end of Madehas Island, Ishmael and his men scrutinized every tree and bush. They saw no one; the island appeared to be deserted. As they approached the western shorefront, the wooden dock came into view, but no one was there. Although the land under the coconut palms along the beachfront was empty, the men did not relax. Up ahead, Solomon's longboat had completed its circuit and was moving down the western shore to join them.

The boats slowed as they approached the dock. The crews made their lines ready, and as the two longboats slid alongside the wooden planking, the men lashed them to crude piers formed from old coconut trees. Nine nervous BRA fighters climbed onto the dock, weapons held at the ready, peering into the coconut palms on the shore. Nothing stirred. After a few minutes, some of the men began to relax and stretch their legs. Ishmael strapped his M-16 over his shoulder and began walking up the dock to inspect the beach, a few of his men following behind. A lone hornbill, its silver-haired head glistening in the sun and wings outswept, carved a long arc over the island, the bird's shadow crossing the ground in front of Ishmael as he approached the sand.

Thirty yards past the beach, a slight Bougainvillean man emerged from behind a row of coconut palms and started walking slowly down a path toward them. Barefoot and naked except for a loincloth, he was old and frail.

"*Hai*," Ishmael called up the dock when he saw the man drifting wraithlike out of the trees.

The BRA men froze, their eyes fixed on the man as he walked toward them. A zephyr caused palm fronds to sway and clack together, and songbirds lowed and clucked as they flitted from tree to tree. Although the sea had little in the way of a swell, its wavelets seemed to crash as they lapped onto the sand on the beach.

The man called back, "*Wanem nem blo yu?*"

"We're friends, father," Ishmael said. "Who are you?" As he spoke he heard a low, mechanical-sounding rumble across the bay.

"Are you Ishmael?" the man asked.

Ishmael didn't answer immediately, in the quiet trying to discern what was making the rumbling noise. "*Yesa*, father." The sound was growing louder. "*Disla wanem*, father?"

"They're coming for you. I'm sorry. I wanted to get word to you, but I didn't know how."

The noise became unmistakable—it was a chopper. Not far off, it was closing fast.

"You must run," croaked the old man, standing still as the BRA men swirled into action.

Men ran back along the dock and started to untie the boat lines at the same time Ishmael glimpsed the aircraft. The Iroquois UH-1 helicopter was a mile or two away and headed straight for them, from where it had taken off a minute earlier at the old military parade ground on Sohana Island across the Passage. The rumor had been that during the truce, the national government had received munitions from Australia and outfitted their transport helicopters into gunships. Ishmael was about to find out. "Leave the boats!" he yelled to his men. "Get into the trees."

Moments later, machine gun ordnance laced the water and closed in on the men, rows of bullets converging as they tore the length of the dock. Two men were hit before they could reach shore. Frozen where he stood on the beach, the old man never had a chance. Cut in half by bullets, a thick, red stripe of lacerated flesh was the only thing connecting his left side to the right as he crumpled to the sand.

There was nowhere to hide except the coconut palms, their trunks providing meager cover. Making it there as the chopper swept overhead, Ishmael saw that the ship was not outfitted with fixed machine gun installations. The fire was coming from Defence Force soldiers laying prone in the open bay and firing assault rifles.

Some of the BRA men fired at the rear of the chopper as it passed over the treetops.

"Hold your fire until they turn around," Ishmael yelled. He looked back at the beach. He saw that the old man was dead, and watched his two wounded men crawling along the boards of the dock. "Make your way to the boats," he called to them. "We'll get you out of here."

The whump-whump-whump of the chopper diminished for a moment, then grew louder as it circled back. This time, it came in close over the treetops, the Defence Force sharpshooters firing down into the coconut palms. The BRA men made difficult targets, moving around the bases of the trees and unleashing flurries of bullets that pinged and clanked off the Huey as it passed overhead. "My rounds hit the ship," Solomon called over to Ishmael. "I saw them smack metal."

"They can't see us," one of the men exulted, others whooping as well.

"Forget the ship; try to disable the blades," Ishmael called out.

The chopper swung north out over the Passage, did a U-turn, and swooped back toward the island. On its third pass, the same thing happened: the Defence Force gunners blitzed the men where they hid in the trees. This time Ishmael and his men took cover in the lee of the tree trunks, then fired bursts at the Huey's blades as it flew by. A few found their mark.

The chopper didn't return immediately, but instead hovered over the other side of the island. Ishmael and his men could hear it, but the noise became far-off and different. When they next saw the Huey, it wasn't swooping back at them over the trees, but had risen up above the island and floated high over them, well out of the range of the BRA's small arms fire.

A minute later, grenades began exploding among the trees.

"No place to hide!" Ishmael yelled to his men. "Make for the boats."

Another barrage of grenades exploded in trees ten yards away from the men, shredding tree trunks and blowing holes in the ground. The men ran from their cover toward the dock. The first to reach the longboats loosened the lines while Ishmael and Solomon jumped into the stern of their boats and pulled on the starter cords. Two BRA guerillas each lifted a wounded man off the dock and lowered him into the longboats. Then they were off, in seconds moving out into the sea while getting ready to try to elude the chopper.

As they sped away from the island beach, they heard the noise of heavy gunfire across the bay. Ishmael looked at his wristwatch: it was noon. Sevy and Steven had commenced the battle at Tsiroge, and just in time. Ishmael looked up in the sky, expecting to be shark bait for the chopper, but instead watched the Huey hurry east, abandoning the prospect of a few guys in boats to help the land war brewing across the bay.

"Follow the chopper!" Ishmael called to Solomon.

It only took five minutes to traverse the bay. Ishmael followed a channel that wound through a mangrove swamp to where it ended alongside a plantation road that connected to the southern end of Tsiroge. In the distance, the volume of gunfire escalated. Instructing a BRA guy to guard the longboats and the two wounded men, Ishmael emptied his ammo bag, taking four thirty-round magazines for his M-16. He set his weapon to fire three-round bursts, and he and Solomon and the remaining men jogged up the farm road.

In ten minutes, they came upon the rear of the BRA war party.

"What's happening?" Ishmael said to Sevy, who emerged from where he had taken cover behind the trunk of a palm tree.

"We were shredding them until the chopper showed up," Sevy replied, not turning around as he held his rifle level, his eyes surveying the field for targets. "As long as that bird is overhead, we're in for a stalemate."

Between where Ishmael stood and the Defence Force's position was an open field. Sevy was correct; the BRA's attack had definitely surprised the Defence Force soldiers. A dozen lay dead in their shiny new uniforms along the breastworks lining the water to the west. Beyond them, more wounded soldiers lay where they had fallen or managed to crawl. The remaining men were hunkered down in the northwest corner of the battlefield, arrayed behind their breastworks under some trees, now facing the BRA forces inland rather than seaward. The chopper, hovering above the trees, had saved the Defence Force troops and changed the character of the battle. Controlling the entire battle scene, the Huey had made the field a no-go zone. With both forces pinned down, the two sides could be mired in a standoff for hours.

"We don't have enough bullets for a prolonged battle," Ishmael said as he pushed past a group of BRA men to get a better look at the battlefield. Steven Toppis and his men were dug into a line of foxholes at the front, firing sporadically. As Ishmael assessed the situation, new armed fighters filtered in at the rear of the BRA's trench line, men he didn't recognize, their eyes shifty. Ishmael hated fighting with men he didn't know. He grew alarmed. If they were Musku's men, armed and present in close quarters, they represented an ominous threat.

"Ishmael," he heard someone call out through the continued din of weapons firing. It was Musku, appearing fresh in clean clothes, as if he hadn't fired a shot, surrounded by the new guys. How could Olu possibly have concluded that this amateur could help him militarily, let alone as a truthful ally?

Ishmael's internal alarm bell was clanging on overload. Things had to change, fast. Ignoring Musku, he yelled to Sevy over the racket, "What's over there?" He pointed at the thicket east of where the Defence Force line ended.

"Coconut palms and bush," Sevy yelled back.

Ishmael pulled off the three-round burst lever of his M-16. He called instructions over to Sevy, where he stood firing behind the tree. "You and Solomon and Steven stay here, occupy the chopper, and hold down this position. In two minutes, launch a barrage at the main

Defence Force position and keep them pinned down. I'm going to take some men through those trees, outflank them, and break through their rear position. The guys in the chopper can't target us if we're in the trees."

"We'll go with you," Musku said.

Ishmael didn't respond to Musku. He turned and signaled to three of his men to join him. "Ready?" Without another word, he took off at a dead run. Circling back into the plantation trees, his M-16 held out in front of him, Ishmael made an end-run around the edge of the field and then entered the coconut plantation. He found a wagon road between two rows of coconut palms and followed it until it turned east, the wrong way. He jogged across more rows of trees until he found another wagon road heading west between two lines of palms, and then kept running. He could hear his men running behind him, but he was out in front of everyone by several lengths.

Behind a palm tree up ahead, a swatch of camouflage uniform appeared and then disappeared. Ishmael wasn't surprised; signs of the enemy meant he was closing in on his objective. Still at a dead run, he raised the muzzle of his rifle and, when the soldier next showed himself, drilled him. Ishmael sped by, looking down only enough to ascertain the man was out of commission. "Lord, forgive me," he automatically thought to himself, the same sentiment he felt every time he found a human being at the end of his gun barrel. It never occurred to him that a member of the enemy could be in the same position, and shoot him. He kept running, not hearing anything but his own breathing. He was almost to the other side of the field. Two Defence Force soldiers stepped into the path, and Ishmael fired twice. His shots—each finding its mark—were the last he fired at Tsiroge.

As he ran past the two wounded men on the ground, he heard something off to his right and glanced quickly over his shoulder. One of the men who had been with Musku had come out of nowhere and was now running parallel and slightly behind Ishmael on the wagon road. Carrying a shotgun, the man was running hard, as if the two of them were in some kind of a race. Ishmael glanced at the guy again to check him out—as Ishmael made eye contact and realized he knew him, the man flashed a devilish grin—and then, as Ishmael turned to see if anyone was on his left, he sensed something about to go very wrong. The turn saved Ishmael's life, since his head was off-center as the gunman stopped, aimed, and fired. A wall of lead from the shotgun blast whacked Ishmael from behind, spraying the right side of his head behind his ear and lodging along the full length of his trapezius muscle. Ishmael took two more long paces, a few shorter ones as his body told him it wasn't working, and then stumbled and went to his knees. A moment later, dazed and in shock, he stood up, struggled to find his balance, and instinctively strapped his M-16 over his good shoulder. He held his hands over the massive wound in his neck to staunch the bleeding and started to wander away from the fighting. His last memory was the would-be assassin smiling as he'd prepared to frag him. Treachery was something Ishmael would never comprehend.

7

Roreinang Coup

"He's going to die if he doesn't get blood soon," Solomon called to Sevy at the wheel of the ten-seater from where he lay in the back cradling Ishmael.

"We'll be in Wakunai in three minutes," Sevy said as they roared down the coast road, his eyes straining to see through the mud-spattered windshield into the Bougainville night. At eight o'clock in the evening, there was little traffic.

Splayed across the rear compartment, Solomon lay along Ishmael's right side, clutching tightly the rags they had bound around his upper torso, hoping to staunch the blood that was pouring out of the cavernous wound stretching the length of his neck and shoulders.

"Is he breathing?" Sevy cried out.

Solomon said, "I can't tell." He was afraid to look into Ishmael's eyes.

They barreled down a hill into a long, twisting turn. Sevy downshifted and then gunned the Toyota over the steel causeway that crossed the Wakunai River. "We're here," he announced. "The clinic's a block away." The Toyota rumbled along the cobbled road through the village and skidded to a stop in a driveway next to a low, one-story building.

The clinic was dark, but across the way house lights were on and a diesel generator hummed. "I'll go find the nurse," Sevy called as he jumped out of the Toyota.

Solomon crawled around Ishmael where he lay bleeding on the floor, climbed out of the ten-seater, and pulled open both rear doors. Behind him, he heard a woman open her door and answer Sevy, followed by sounds of a frantic conversation and hurried steps. "We'll need hot water," the nurse called out to someone, and then a flashlight beam bounced across the driveway next to the darkened clinic. Sevy and the woman arrived, followed by a wide-eyed boy dutifully carrying a lantern.

She unlocked the clinic and swung open the door, and the boy scooted inside with the lantern, lighting the interior space. "Hurry, bring him in," she said to the men. Sevy and Solomon lifted Ishmael out of the back of the ten-seater and carried him into the clinic. "In here." The nurse directed the men into a linoleum-floored room with two hospital beds arrayed on opposite sides and a curtain hanging from the ceiling to divide the space. "Willie, leave that lantern and go help your father with the hot water," she said to the boy, who put the lantern on the floor and ran out of the room. She yanked one of the beds away from the wall. "Put him here," she said.

Solomon and Sevy laid Ishmael on the bed.

The nurse took the lantern off the floor and placed it on a table between the two beds, for the first time illuminating Ishmael and the two men, all three awash in Ishmael's blood. Her eyes focused on her patient; she took hold of Ishmael's head with one hand while still holding her flashlight with the other. His eyes were closed, but when the flashlight beam shined in his face, he flinched and turned. "He's alive," she said.

She laid Ishmael's head down gently, straightened out his limbs, and then shined her flashlight into the wound running down his neck. Her lips pressed tightly together. "We have very little time," she said, walking to a sink in the corner, turning on a faucet, and scrubbing her hands. From a coatrack on the wall the nurse removed a medical gown, tied it on, and took down a stethoscope and hung it around her neck. She returned to Ishmael's bed, rolled a stool alongside, sat down, and took Ishmael's pulse. She held her hand across his forehead. "No fever," she said, sounding surprised. She placed the stethoscope over his chest and listened, then moved it up over his shoulder and listened some more. "Does anyone know his blood type?" she said as she got up, went in the other room, and returned with a blood-test kit. She pried a package of sampling strips from the kit, then looked at the two men.

They glanced at each other. "No," Solomon said.

The nurse tore off the wrapping of a sampling strip and placed it gently along the bloody edge of Ishmael's wound. After a moment, she examined the strip. "Good," she said, putting down the colored strip and looking back at Solomon. "You know yours?"

"No," he said again.

"Let's hope you're type A." She fished in the kit for another sampling strip. "Please go over to the sink and wash your hands good."

He did so, then returned.

"Hold out your forefinger." The nurse pricked his finger, squeezed out a drop of blood, then daubed it on the paper strip.

Solomon leaned closer, trying to determine what the nurse was doing with his blood and the strip of paper.

"Nope. No good." She looked up forgivingly at Solomon. "There's nothing wrong; you're just not type A." She turned to Sevy. "You're next. Go wash your hands."

Sevy scrubbed his hands in the sink and returned.

The nurse repeated the procedure. "Okay," the nurse exhaled a moment later, mopping her brow and pushing her hair out of her eyes. "Yours is good. The same as your friend here," she explained. "We've got to hurry. We're going to do a blood transfusion; you must give him some of yours. Sit up on that windowsill so it can run downhill."

While Sevy hoisted himself up on the windowsill, she left them for a moment and then returned with soap and water and a batch of medical devices wrapped in plastic packages. She cleaned Ishmael's left arm, opened one of the packages, removed a syringe, and injected penicillin into his shoulder. Then she took Ishmael's forearm, bent it, and straightened it, looking for a good vein. Finding one, she injected a transfusion needle into Ishmael's forearm, and when she was finished, scrubbed Sevy's forearm and did the same to him. Then she connected the two men via a clear plastic tube. "This might make you dizzy," the nurse said to Sevy. "Try to lean back against the wall." A few moments later, the transfusion line ran red.

"Here's hot water," Willie announced as he entered the front door, lugging a steaming bucket of water.

"Bring it here," his mother said. When he put the bucket down next to the bed, she said, "Run back and tell your father we'll need more." As the boy ran off, she went over to the sink to wash her hands again. "Come over here and wash up," she ordered Solomon. "You're going to have to help me."

"First his T-shirt," she said to Solomon when they were both scrubbed and standing over Ishmael's bed. "Lift him up a little," she said, and as Solomon raised Ishmael into a reclining position, she leaned over him and used a pair of surgical shears to snip the front of his T-shirt from his belt-buckle to his throat. "Now over on his left side," she told Solomon, who pulled him that way. Ishmael groaned. "That's a good sign," the nurse muttered as she pulled away the back half of his T-shirt.

She extracted the sections of the bloody shirt from Ishmael's bed, dropped them by the sink, then scrubbed her hands again. Returning with a canister of powder and washcloths and bandages, she started in on Ishmael's wounds, cleaning around their periphery, swabbing with hot water, and then sprinkling the open flesh with raw sulpha powder. Once Ishmael was cleaned and washed and sterilized, the nurse and

Solomon wrapped bandages and tape around his torso, neck, and head until he was unrecognizable.

"That's enough for now," she said to Sevy, and disconnected the transfusion tube. Only then, after two hours had gone by, did she take a breather, sitting on her stool and rolling it backwards so she could lean against the wall.

"Thank you," she said to the men. "I'm Cathy."

The men looked down at their feet, mumbling their thanks and their names.

"It's a miracle he's alive, you know. Another inch, and that shot would have destroyed his carotid artery," she exhaled. "When did this happen?"

The guys glanced at each other. "We're not sure," Solomon said. "Maybe two o'clock?"

"Two o'clock?" she exclaimed, her face incredulous. "Why'd it take so long for you to get here?"

Sevy hung his head. "We couldn't find him. There was a gun battle in the woods. We didn't know where he was."

"It took us hours," Solomon said. "He was lying in the road; it was dark when we got there."

She said, "So you weren't with him when he was shot?"

"No."

"That explains it, I guess," she said. "Part of it, anyway."

"Explains what?" Solomon asked.

"You realize he was shot from behind," she said, examining their faces.

Their blank expressions confirmed nothing.

When it was clear they were not going to comment further, Cathy moved on. "He can't be moved for a while, but his wound needs expert attention. It's bound to get infected. I'm going to try to remove the fragments of lead shot and stitch him up tomorrow, but he needs to go to a hospital. A doctor must look after him. It would be a punishing trip, but he should go to the Solomon Islands. Their hospital has good doctors, and whoever is trying to kill him won't be able to bother him over there."

Ishmael spent several days in Wakunai recovering. After a week, he told Cathy he felt strong enough to travel. The day before they left, Sevy drove up into the hills to Roreinang and returned with Ishmael's father Amos. With the two bodyguards, Ishmael and his father left Wakunai harbor in a longboat at dawn and pushed against headwinds down the Slot the entire day. They spent the night on Choiseul Island, and early the next morning got back on the water and powered another hundred miles to Gizo. Cathy had given Amos a syringe and several doses of sedatives, and Ishmael made good use of all of them. They arrived at Nasatupe Airport in Gizo in time to make the afternoon plane connection, and landed in Honiara, the capital of the Solomon Islands, late that night. Under a false name, they checked Ishmael into the National Referral Hospital. Even though his wound could have been only caused by a gunshot, no one questioned him.

The sun was streaming into his hospital room window the following afternoon when Ishmael finally stirred.

Amos was sitting in a chair next to his bed, studying his son's face. "How are you?" Amos asked.

Ishmael nodded his handsome head. He had never shaved, and a beard was starting to take shape.

"We haven't been able to talk since you went back up to Guava," Amos said.

"No."

"Do you know who shot you?"

"I know him, but I won't retaliate. He was just following orders."

Father and son studied each other.

Ishmael said after a moment, "What's more important is that I know who was responsible."

"Is there a lesson involved?" his father asked.

Ishmael thought about the question, taking time to organize his thoughts, knowing his father would scrutinize his response. "Yes," he said. "It's good to be a fighter. That's what I prefer to do. I'd rather leave the politics to others. The leaders, they call themselves. But I've learned that I cannot."

"Why?"

"There are lives involved. Men die when leaders make the wrong choices. I don't know that I can make better ones, but I can no longer accept someone making bad decisions that put my men at risk. Even if it's the supreme commander."

* * *

After his neck injury during the attack on Tsiroge, Ishmael recovered slowly and remained out of action for two years. No one stepped up to take his place. George Washburn, the BRA's commander, didn't come up to the bush and rarely wielded a weapon in a firefight. Not every fighting organization's battle performance varies directly with its leadership, but the BRA's did—they were lost without Ishmael. From when he had joined the BRA in 1988—even though he was only twenty at the time—until his injury took him off the field in late 1991, the BRA fought high above its weight class. When he was sidelined, things regressed.

Ishmael's absence not only led to lackluster military action by the BRA, but also created a power vacuum that the Bougainvillean politicos abused.

From its first days as a colony, the roots of power in Bougainville had been consistent: the chiefs provided the people with a strong sociocultural base for the day-to-day; the priests and nuns and pastors dispensed religious guidance for the afterlife; and law and order involving true crime—a rarity in Bougainville—was meted out by the office of the local Australian kiap, an all-powerful sheriff, judge, and jury system that existed from colonial times until Papua New Guinea was granted independence. Australia, Oz-like, stood behind the green curtain in case something truly supernatural was required. Nothing else was necessary.

There was no day-to-day role for what currently would be called government. In colonial times, Bougainville wasn't governed; rather, in the true sense of the word, it was administered. Occasionally, white men in pith helmets or bush hats would show up from either Canberra or Port Moresby, but it was understood that their presence was a formality. They were not corrupt, but they did little and possessed no day-to-day power; after issuing proclamations, they left.

Confusion set in when the colonial era ended. Yes, the chiefs and the religious orders would remain, and there would be some type of police force, but what to do about the white administrators? No one thought to ask the important questions: Were they really needed? What did they do? In the absence of clearer thought, everyone assumed these positions needed to be filled. Now that the Australians were leaving, they would be replaced by Bougainvilleans. The few Bougainvilleans lucky enough to become well-educated, the group Bougainvilleans called the elites—spelled the same way we spell it but ironically pronounced *elights*—realized that the vestiges of this useless political apparatus could be theirs for the taking. They wanted to wear the pith helmets. All that was needed was a little hot air. Bougainville politics was born.

Francis Olu was among the first Bougainvilleans to figure this out. Neither a chief nor a priest or a policeman, Olu's role was nonetheless clear—at least in his mind. From his Guava stronghold, he announced to the world that his organization, labelled by him as the Bougainville Interim Government, would fight to the death in order to achieve independence. Someone else would do the fighting, to be sure, but Olu, the supreme commander, was in charge. It's easy to see why he concluded that Bougainvilleans must have been in agreement, for they said nothing. The national government had certainly reacted with displeasure, and began to ferry armed forces back to Bougainville, but that didn't bother Francis Olu. He—or rather his forces—had vanquished those foes easily, and could do so again.

This time around, the national government also utilized a naval blockade of Bougainville and enforced an embargo of critical supplies like medicine, fuel, and foodstuffs. Olu didn't give it a second thought. He had planted an extensive garden in Guava; as long as it was tended, he'd have plenty to eat. For too long, that's what Olu did. Later, he heard grumblings, and after months turned to years, complaints surfaced. People were hungry, and those who needed critical medical attention were dying. Everyone was tired of fighting, and a few were beginning to openly question why they had revolted in the first place.

After the wounded Ishmael was carried off the Tsiroge battlefield, his scarred body needed years to recover. Only as 1994 ended was he able to leave his village, visit more populated areas, and speak with the people. It became clear that Bougainville's morale was flagging. Diplomacy may not have been Ishmael's chosen métier, but someone needed to convince Francis Olu to take charge. "You've got to come down from Guava and meet with your public," Ishmael urged Olu one day as they spoke in his garden on the edge of a mountainside.

"Take a look at that beauty," the supreme commander said to him, holding up a plump onion. He dropped it in his burlap bag, overloaded with fruits and vegetables. "My people know what I stand for; they don't need to see me."

"Your men do," Ishmael said, trying to keep the sharp edge out of his voice.

"My men? That's your job."

"I can lead them into battle, but you must give them hope."

"They have hope."

"How can they, when they think their leader is hiding?"

Ishmael's words hit their mark. Reluctantly, Olu agreed to come to a special meeting near the Arawa town market, where people could see and hear him, and he would pass on a few encouraging words to his loyal subjects.

Two weeks later, after Ishmael made all the arrangements, Olu didn't show.

"It's too dangerous down there," he sniffed when he saw Ishmael the following month. "Tell the people to come to Guava. They should move up here anyway; life's too decadent in the flatlands."

Slowly, the thin air of his mountain aerie got to Olu, who finally conceded that his fellow Bougainvilleans needed some inspiration. He devised an excellent solution: their land would receive a grander name. And so it was done: Bougainville would now be the Republic of Me'ekamui (in local dialect, the "Holy Land"). Blissfully uninformed in his garden in Guava, Olu also reached the conclusion that neither the Republic's name nor its leadership required any debate or election process: Olu would be not only the BRA's supreme commander, but president of the Republic of Me'ekamui as well.

One day, Olu was surprised by a visitor. Jasper Kaboose was a Bougainvillean politician who had, prior to the Crisis, been the premier of Bougainville. This meant that he presided over an insignificant, powerless entity, a governmental unit with even less substance than its parent, PNG's national government. At least PNG could levy, and try to collect, taxes. Kaboose, and the other Bougainvillean politicians like him—Liuman Mogol, for example, the regional member who represented Bougainville in the national government's parliament—had seen the Crisis render their positions useless and were grasping for any remaining claim to authority, let alone financial reward.

Kaboose, a genial and intelligent man, convinced the supreme commander of what every Bougainvillean who did not live in Guava knew firsthand: Olu's reign wasn't working. It had been six years since he had ignited the Crisis. Rather than improve people's lives, the insurrection had done the opposite. Bougainville was withering, and unless Olu made significant adjustments, circumstances would get worse.

Olu had no interest in coming down off his mountain, and he had things to do. He gave Kaboose five minutes to describe what changes were necessary.

Doing his best to display careful, respectful reflection, Kaboose replied that the BRA men—indeed, all the people—would be happier if the government were more inclusive, if Kaboose had a role, for example. Say, vice president.

Olu could scarcely believe his good fortune. The saccharine aspirant sitting across from him was merely a job seeker. He was no threat; rather, he was willing to politic on Olu's behalf with the BRA men and the people at large—the very thing Olu abhorred. After another hour of discussion, he sent Kaboose down off the mountaintop with a shiny new title: vice president of the Republic of Me'ekamui. Later on, after Kaboose learned how to push Olu's buttons and convinced the Guava hermit that people would rise up unless further steps were taken, Olu tossed in an additional concession and agreed to make Kaboose co-president. Since the BRA needed Ishmael to focus on battle, Kaboose took George Washburn under his wing to maintain some cosmetic support from the more militant members of the BRA.

While the three politicians were up on the mountaintop telling each other lies, the Crisis dragged on, not standing still for either side. The blockade was lethal and had turned Bougainville Island into a cocoon. Inside, there was no oxygen, and everything was dying. Meanwhile in PNG, yet another new national government with a sharpened Bougainville policy had taken over; they wanted an end to the war. They reinforced, re-equipped, and emboldened the Defence Force and the riot squads. Arawa was retaken, and they began an offensive to recapture the Panguna Mine. Advancing easily at first, PNG's armed forces smelled victory and began to tighten the noose on the BRA. Surely, the dissipating rebel forces were exhausted—they had been battling for years. But at the last minute, a change took place within the BRA ranks, and they stiffened. The Panguna Mine remained in rebel hands.

Disappointed, the Defence Force sent spies to learn what had gone wrong with their offensive. The information they gathered was surprising. Adjustments had been made within the BRA; the rebel force was no longer shrinking, but growing again, and now numbered over two thousand fully-armed men. The guerillas' camp was no longer in Guava, but in Roreinang, the home of their leader, the young fighter named Ishmael. He had fully recovered from a serious injury and was once again leading the BRA; as long as he remained in charge, the BRA was a potent force.

Thanks to long periods of time hibernating in his mountain lair, Olu had grown almost as uninformed about what was going on in Bougainville as the Defence Force. He hadn't seen his field marshal Ishmael in a year, since the aborted town meeting in Arawa. After Ishmael repulsed the Defence Force's bid to retake the Panguna Mine, it dawned on Olu that a disheartened military leader represented a potential threat. He invited Ishmael to come to Guava for a powwow.

As in the old days, Ishmael respectfully accepted, and made the long trek up to the mountain retreat to meet with the supreme commander. They sat down at a table in Olu's house; a boy brought them coffee. Olu had grown a long beard, and looked older.

"I don't know why you wanted to move our base of operations down to Roreinang. I suppose every man's most comfortable in his own village," Olu said, looking into Ishmael's eyes as if he understood him.

In the old days, Ishmael would have nodded and accepted the leader's statement whatever his inner feelings, but no longer. "My personal desires had nothing to do with the decision," Ishmael said. "We moved to Roreinang because it's closer to PNG's base camp at the Aropa Airport. It's much easier to send raiding parties to grab their weapons and supplies."

"It's working?"

"Yes, yes; most of the time." Ishmael managed a thin smile. Walking up the mountain to Guava, he had considered asking Olu to explain unanswered questions—about his relationship with the traitor Musku, or the aborted town meeting in Arawa—but decided it was a personal conceit, which had no place in a meeting about important matters like the future of Bougainville.

"I'm glad we're pressing the opponent," Olu said, slapping his hand on the table. "Push them into the sea." He stood up and gazed out the window across the mountaintops. "I have spoken to my friend Noah Ponsa about harvesting Bougainville gold," he said. "I want to get him here to talk to you about that."

"My men don't care about money. They want to know your plan for them," Ishmael said.

"Why, I just told you," Olu said, fervent. "We're fighting for independence."

Ishmael tried a conversational tack. "Have you ever considered that perhaps, at this point in time, independence is too much to ask—of not only PNG, but Bougainvilleans as well?"

"Out of the question."

Ishmael did his best to remain calm. "Many of your people would be relieved—and pleased with your leadership—if we pursued a more graduated freedom."

"Nonsense," Olu said, taking a drink of his coffee. "We'll fight till the last man."

"That is no plan."

The passion drained out of Olu's face as he stared across the table at his young military leader.

Ishmael said, "The men need to know why they're fighting."

Olu's enthusiasm turned to irritation. He raised his voice, saying, "They're fighting for the Republic of Me'ekamui!"

"You can't say that to fighters whose families are starving, whose old ones and babies are dying."

"We must fight to the death."

Ishmael stood up. "Your men need to hear much more than that from you."

"Tell them to come hear me in Guava."

"You should come listen to them in Roreinang." Ishmael walked out, his mood hardened in the chilly mountain air.

The breaking point occurred after Bougainville's rumor mill brought the people a glimmer of hope. PNG's new prime minister, Nathaniel Chan, seeking a peaceful solution to the Crisis, had proposed a temporary ceasefire in order to negotiate a peace agreement with Francis Olu in the Solomon Islands. Bougainvilleans held their breath, hoping for an end to their misery. Two weeks later, a mind-numbing update spread like wildfire: Francis Olu had pulled another no-show; he hadn't even seen fit to attend Chan's meeting. Ishmael spoke to Kaboose the next day. "I have a message to deliver. Meet me at Olu's."

Ishmael was out of time; the BRA, indeed all of Bougainville, needed clear direction toward a solution. He trudged up the trail to Guava. When he arrived, his M-16 strapped over his shoulder, Olu and Kaboose were standing in front of Olu's house.

"Please come inside," Olu said.

Ishmael stood his ground, his body ramrod straight. "Your nonsense must stop now."

Olu, rarely at a loss for words, could do nothing but stare at Ishmael; Kaboose's sweaty face dripped in fear.

"The future of the BRA, and the men's vision for Bougainville, will be determined at a meeting to be held in Roreinang next Tuesday. Be there." Ishmael turned on his heel and walked back down the mountain.

The ethereal atmosphere of Roreinang was enhanced by the quiet stream whispering though the village as well as the melodic tones of the United Church's choir echoing off the hills. Olu and Kaboose arrived together and were escorted to a dwelling that Ishmael was building for his family on a bluff overlooking the village rooftops. The event was held outdoors in one of Amos's gardens. Olu and Kaboose were given honorary seats at a table set up on a stage-like platform. Surrounding the garden were hundreds of tents, lean-tos, and smoking campfires, accommodations for a war camp of more than two thousand men. Beyond the mist, the hills of Kongara and the peaks of the Crown

Prince Range encircled them in a setting fit for a story about the Knights of the Round Table.

Shortly after the guests sat down, the sound of men marching rumbled over the land. Many men. Coming up the road from the village, two thousand BRA rebels marched three abreast, brandishing their weapons. On and on they came; Bougainville had never seen so many fighters in one place before. They thronged around the stage and filled the garden.

Sitting at one end of the table, Ishmael kept his seat. Glancing over at Francis Olu, he said, "These men want to hear your plan."

Olu looked at Ishmael, defiance in his eyes. He stood up and looked out over the BRA guerilla army. "I am your supreme commander," he said, and began to speak.

"Tell us why we are fighting," yelled someone in the crowd.

"We are fighting for our homeland," Olu said, and hearing a murmur of approval, was spurred on foolishly to add, "and we will fight to the death!"

"No!" men in the crowd yelled. Someone fired his weapon into the air, a dozen followed, and then every member of the BRA stood and fired bullets into the sky, the noise as deafening as the din of a pitched battle. Ishmael glanced over at Kaboose, whose blubbery face was shaking, as if he were going to cry. Beyond him, Francis Olu had remained standing, but wore a wild expression, as if he expected to be grabbed and torn to pieces.

Ishmael stood. He signaled for the men to be quiet, and waited several minutes until they calmed down and found seats in the grass. Then he looked down the table at Francis Olu. "These men need a plan," he said. "Fighting to the death is not a plan. We have been willing to die so that Bougainville could be free. That has always been our goal, but it is not a plan for today. Independence will happen in the long run, but for now, we must negotiate with the national government and put an end to the fighting. We will gain our freedom at the point that God wishes." He looked over at Kaboose, who was trying to regain his composure.

"I agree," Kaboose said as he struggled to his feet.

The men in the crowd cheered.

Olu blustered, "We will never negotiate!"

Catcalls erupted from the crowd. They rose to their feet as one, and some of them started firing their weapons again.

Ishmael calmed the men. He said, "Whoever is with me and Kaboose and prefers to negotiate, stay here in Roreinang. Those who want to fight to the death, go with your supreme commander back to Guava."

In the ensuing minutes, Olu and a small band of supporters filed out. That day, although nothing was ever announced, Francis Olu's control of the BRA—and his significance in Bougainville history— began to wane.

Ishmael's men told him he should become supreme commander, but he disagreed. He had always felt the title was grandiose. He needed a label implying a stature beyond military, one that reflected his new diplomatic resolve. Effectively, he had already been the BRA's military leader for years and would continue to do so, but in the future, he would never again leave things up to the politicians. He selected a title which reflected military and diplomatic functions, as well as island culture: chief of defence.

Ishmael and Kaboose made a pact. Even as the sides continued fighting, Kaboose would approach the national government and propose discussions toward peace. The BRA would deliver battlefield success, and Kaboose would use that as leverage to attain Bougainville's best terms at the negotiating table.

The Defence Force did its part to steel Bougainville's resolve. Following a preliminary round of negotiations in Cairns that Nathaniel Chan arranged with Kaboose, members of the Defence Force breached the temporary ceasefire by shooting at Kaboose and a group of unarmed BRA rebels. It was part of the Defence

Force's new, no-nonsense belligerence, designed to culminate with a victorious, D-Day-like invasion of Bougainville that would end the war: Operation High Speed.

Building up for the offensive, the Defence Force pitched camp alongside the harbor in Kieta and began stockpiling men and supplies. Watching them from the hills, Ishmael's appetite was whetted. He had never seen such a rich target: guns, ammunition, and supplies. He knew what the Defence Force was thinking: Other than the exception of a couple of months, Kieta had been in the hands of the Defence Force and the riot squads since the beginning of the Crisis. Surely not even Ishmael would be crazy enough to launch a raid on such a secure location.

Ishmael hatched a plan: he would strike them from the water. He ordered two of his longboats from Marau to circle the island at night, then meet him and his men in the Arawa harbor. The Defence Force would never know what hit them.

8

Adam's Rib

From the BRA's early days, Ishmael had been its guerilla leader, but as its chief of defence, he wouldn't remain unscathed for long. His arm wound occurred only a year after the Roreinang coup. After the mutilation of his neck and back, the laceration of Ishmael's arm made him, once again, a serious battlefield casualty. This time, he had an idea what to expect. There was one difference. When he had been shot, after he awoke he realized he was alive; that was enough for him to know he would be all right. This time, the same thought hit him like a hammer every morning from the first day he gained consciousness: could they save his arm?

Lying in the operating room behind Amalani's house, Ishmael forced himself to be patient. He knew from before what a slow process healing was. He watched Amalani and Elijah as they moved around the room doing their chores, especially when they blew the sirivi vapor into his wound. The heat from the gas alone gave him a recuperative feeling. After several days, he was, for the first time since gaining consciousness in Amalani's house, able to shift his body over on one side so he could look down at the juncture of his arm while they worked on it. He was profoundly disappointed. "I can't see anything happening," he said to Amalani.

"Don't talk," she said. "The sirivi works on the flesh from the inside; you won't be able to see much difference for weeks." Whenever Ishmael was conscious enough to speak, Amalani knew he needed more sedative. She didn't like sedating him, but knew that if she didn't, the pain would be excruciating.

Ishmael began to eat solid food, but still lost ten pounds. His energy returned, although his head ached. He wanted to talk, but he knew better than to do so; he needed his body to heal first. Most of all, his arm hurt. It throbbed all day.

Slowly, the flesh from the upper and lower parts of Ishmael's left arm began to stitch together. He would flex his arm, and was happy when it took a while for the strands of the mending tissue to be stretched apart.

Amalani watched Ishmael's eyes as he willed himself to heal. She leaned over and pressed her cheek alongside Ishmael's forehead. "You haven't shed your fever," she said.

"I'll be all right."

She pursed her lips. "Your arm's telling you that we can heal the flesh, but we can't fix the bone."

"I'll be all right."

Betty came to see him every day, and so did Amos. At first he and his father talked about little things, like the flowers Amos had planted in the yard, or the new saplings in the cacao orchard.

One day Ishmael asked, "Do you think I'm going to heal?"

Amos never misrepresented anything to his son. "We can't answer that here," he said. "The bones in your arm were crushed. We can't fix them—only a western doctor can do that. We can get you fit to travel, and then we must go back to the hospital in the Solomon Islands. This time we need a specialist. Amalani says they have a Swiss orthopedic expert."

The day came when Ishmael told his family he was fit enough to undergo his operation in the Solomon Islands. The trip would involve the same travel itinerary they had employed years earlier. His wife, Betty, had not gone with him the first time. Their son had been a baby, security was tight, and the trip would be arduous. For the past few years, Betty had been patient and careful—Defence Force soldiers constantly followed her when she went to the market in town—and had accepted that she would see her husband infrequently during the fighting.

This time was different. Ishmael would be gone much longer—Amalani advised them that recovery could take months—and there was a chance he wouldn't live through the procedure. Betty would not be denied: no matter how tortuous the journey, she wasn't leaving her husband's side. She and Amos, together with Sevy and Solomon as bodyguards, busied themselves making preparations.

"You must get the Swiss orthopedist," Amalani insisted. "No one else will do."

The conditions of their journey were similar to those experienced years earlier—grueling. Two days pounding through the waves across the Pacific in a twenty-five-foot longboat, everyone seasick, and then a plane ride in a Cessna that bumped and whumped in similar fashion through the clouds down to Honiara.

Ishmael awoke the next afternoon in his hospital room to the sound of Solomon having a calm but firm conversation with a hospital orderly. The orderly was telling Solomon that no visitors other than immediate family members were allowed in the room except during visiting hours. Solomon was, in a pleasant way, telling the orderly that he and Sevy were the patient's bodyguards, and those rules applied to regular people, but not to this patient. Solomon won.

Ishmael awoke again later, in time to hear a more serious conversation, this one between his father and Betty and a Solomon Islander in a white coat who looked like a doctor. Amos and Betty had tight expressions on their faces.

The man seemed inappropriately casual as he discussed Ishmael's condition. "I've never heard of a patient whose arm has been severed having enough remaining stability in the bone material for the arm to be properly reattached. Some things just aren't possible for the human body."

Amos and Betty said nothing, but glanced over at Ishmael.

Seeing that Ishmael was awake, the doctor prattled on, but made his comments at him directly. "There's nothing wrong with a man your age undergoing an amputation," he said, putting on his most genial bedside manner. "The success rate is high. Once the procedure is done, you will still have a chance to learn how to be a productive member of society."

"Who are you?" Ishmael asked.

The doctor walked toward Ishmael's bed. "I'm Dr. Taboa," he said. "I'm your physician here at National Referral."

Ishmael said, "We asked for the Swiss orthopedic expert."

"I'm afraid it doesn't work that way here," Dr. Taboa said. "At National Referral, you are assigned doctors on a first-come-first-served basis, especially if you don't have a regular physician here in the Solomon Islands. Besides, Dr. Oberlicht is very busy; he wouldn't be able to see you."

"I'm not comfortable with him," Betty said as the doctor departed, not even waiting until the man had closed the door.

Despite the serious situation, Ishmael had to smile. His wife was usually the picture of grace and decorum, except where any threat to her family was involved. He gathered his group together. "Betty's right. You heard the man. The Swiss doctor's name is Oberlicht. We've got to find him."

It took until that evening for Amos to track down Dr. Hermann Oberlicht, who was indeed a Swiss orthopedic specialist at National Referral Hospital. His office was in another wing of the building. Once Amos found the location on a hospital map, he went there and verified Dr. Oberlicht's name on his office door. Amos sat on the floor and camped out the rest of the night until the doctor arrived for work at seven in the morning.

A half hour later, Amos and the doctor entered Ishmael's room. As Sevy and Solomon rubbed the sleep out of their eyes and left, Dr. Oberlicht gazed after them with a quizzical expression. Betty, sitting next to Ishmael, greeted the doctor. "Thank you for coming," she murmured.

"Of course," the doctor replied, getting Ishmael in his sights. "What seems to be the trouble, Mr....? Your father is a very insistent man."

"My name is Ishmael," Ishmael said, and then began describing his condition. The doctor was only half-listening. He inserted a thermometer into Ishmael's mouth, pulled back the bandages around his arm, and peered at the wound. Then he went to the sink, scrubbed his hands, put on his stethoscope, and examined Ishmael. He leaned closer over Ishmael's wound and used a wooden tongue depressor to poke the flesh. He poked it harder, and Ishmael winced. "That hurts, doesn't it?" the doctor said, while Ishmael didn't respond.

He stood up straight, removed the thermometer from Ishmael's mouth, and read it. His eyes widened slightly, and he held his hand over Ishmael's forehead. "How did this happen?"

Everyone listened as Ishmael answered the doctor.

"Are those two men with you soldiers?"

"Yes."

"They look young." His lips pressed tightly together, Dr. Oberlicht turned his attention back to Ishmael's arm. "Who cared for you up to this point?"

"Amalani," both Amos and Betty answered at once. "A nurse in our village," Betty explained.

"You're very lucky," the doctor said to Betty. "Amalani knows what she's doing, and your husband has healthy, resilient flesh." He sighed. "The bone is another question. The only way to get answers is to operate."

"Let's make it happen," Ishmael said.

Doctor Oberlicht tried to smile. "I wish it was that simple. I won't know until I open you up whether I can repair the bones in your arm or not. For your arm to be saved, I'll have to take bone from another part of your body. If the bones in your arm are not useful, I'll have to amputate."

"You can't amputate."

The doctor shook his head. "I can't make you any promises. I won't know until I operate."

Ishmael considered what he had just heard. "Where would you get the new bone?"

"Just like Adam in the Bible. One of your ribs."

"When can we do this?"

"It must be soon. There is substantial infection where the bones have crumbled and are rubbing together. You must have surgery in a day or two, or the infection will spread."

This time, Betty waited until the doctor had left the room. "He's the one," she said.

The next day, as they wheeled Ishmael on a gurney to the operating room, he smiled up at Dr. Oberlicht walking alongside him. "Doctor Oberlicht?"

"Yes?"

"Don't make it necessary for me to come looking for you."

As Ishmael awoke after surgery, his consciousness was dreamlike, as if he was floating over the sea. He tried to tick through the events of his life. He couldn't get past the last day, in the longboat attacking the beach. Then he did the same thing he did in the water that morning—reached over for his arm—and it was still there.

9

Money Changers in the Temple

Over the months as Ishmael's arm knitted together in Honiara, he and Betty and his father kept track of family news, and also rumors of political and military events from Bougainville. To their surprise—and contrary to the normal pace of things in their homeland—much changed in a short time.

Ishmael had suffered his wound in the latter stages of the Defence Forces's Operation High Speed, the military offensive that the national government had hoped would turn the tide of the war. Instead of a crowning victory for PNG, the campaign was a disaster. The opening stumble had been the battle at Koromira, where for the first time Ishmael and his BRA forces had captured a Defence Force forward base camp and recovered enough munitions and supplies to last years. Another battle initiative, the Defence Force's invasion of the entrenched BRA militia at Aropa Airport, had also been a fiasco.

The incident at Kangu Beach came next. Members of a local resistance group—purportedly allies with the Defence Force, but secretly angry with the soldiers for hitting on their women—staged what was supposed to be a friendly volleyball game at a place near Buin called Kangu Beach. After getting the Defence Force men drunk, the locals turned on them and killed twelve. It was the Defence Force's worst day of the Crisis. When the Defence Force retaliated by assassinating Theodore Miriung, a Bougainville lawyer and politician who had functioned over the years as a mediator, Prime Minister Chan had seen enough. As discipline and morale within his government's military plummeted, he withdrew his men from Bougainville.

"They'll be back," Ishmael said to his father, thinking it would be a good time for Kaboose to ramp up the peace negotiations.

"No," his father said. "The rumor is the national government is going to hire Sandline, a group of British and African mercenaries."

Ishmael thought about it. The British? Imagine fighting them. All he could think of were the stories in *Commando Comics*. And Africans? He heard they were all seven feet tall.

Hoping he would recover enough to fight trained mercenaries, Ishmael returned home to Bougainville in 1997 at the same time Chan signed a contract with Sandline. Ishmael never retook the field. Sandline didn't mark a new phase of the Crisis, but the beginning of its end. Once the news was leaked to the press, international condemnation followed. The so-called Sandline Affair soured an already demoralized Defence Force, who mutinied and temporarily took over the national government until Chan was forced to resign. Bill Skate was elected as the new prime minister with a clear mission: end the Crisis.

In December 1997, Ishmael, Kaboose, Washburn, and others cleared the decks, sponsoring the Burnham Agreement, which negotiated away all internal arguments so that Bougainville could present a unified front to the outside world. In 1998, Skate invited a team led by Ishmael, Kaboose, and Washburn to meet and negotiate in Christchurch, New Zealand. The group produced the Lincoln Agreement, a mutual cease-fire and disarmament arrangement. Ishmael and Kaboose signed the agreement and went home, while George Washburn surprised his colleagues: abandoning the BRA, he accepted an overture from the New Zealand government to remain in-country as a student.

The cease-fire held over the next three years, and in 2001, Ishmael and the other Bougainvillean leaders, together with a cast of international diplomats, entered into the Bougainville Peace Agreement. The Crisis was over. Twenty thousand people had perished, approximately 10 percent of Bougainville's population; most had been casualties of the blockade.

Ishmael was exultant. He had wanted his life to amount to something, and so far it had: he had played a role in significant events, but, more importantly, he and his fellow Bougainvilleans had taken meaningful steps toward becoming citizens of the world.

Unfortunately, in the aftermath of the Crisis, Bougainville was saddled with two problems that would plague it for decades: bad police, and worse politicians. In the beginning, Ishmael didn't consider either his responsibility, but that changed. Still, he could only deal with one at a time.

It was as if the authors of the Bougainville Peace Agreement assumed there would be no crime in Bougainville, for they left no tools with which it could be addressed. Both sides had agreed that Bougainvilleans would not bear arms: the only guns the police controlled would remain locked inside the station house. Before the Crisis, Bougainville had possessed an excellent police force, whose roots were grounded in the Australian kiap system. The BPA replaced it with the Bougainville Police Service, which reported to the Royal Papua New Guinea Constabulary. The arrangement turned out to be a very bad idea. While only a few riot squad thugs managed to infiltrate the ranks of the Bougainville Police Service, those who did wasted little time in educating their colleagues on how to infect their work with corruption.

As the BPA became the law of the land, Ishmael moved back to his home in Roreinang, intent on being a cacao farmer. When he had grown up, crime in Bougainville was virtually nonexistent. The Crisis changed things. Bougainville's poverty was pervasive, and debilitating. No one had any money, but they had expectations—it had been the wealthiest province in PNG only ten years earlier. For the ten years the Crisis raged, there was no police force to speak of, but plenty of rivalries and conflicts, whose passions sometimes spilled over into crimes against property, and worse. Bougainville's larger towns— Arawa and Buka—remained more diverse, and people didn't know each other well. Post-Crisis, a certain level of crime became a fact of life, but Ishmael couldn't accept it. He and his men had not risked dying for an island community where people needed to be afraid; that was what they thought they were eliminating.

Ishmael started getting calls from his former BRA men, now known as ex-combatants, asking him to mediate disputes across the island, in the Arawa and Buka neighborhoods as well as the villages. In the beginning, the calls were sporadic, and most were about civil disputes. A few, however, involved more urgent matters. The people all told Ishmael the same story: The Bougainville Police Service wouldn't lift a finger to solve violent crime. The only thing they wanted to do was negotiate arguments the "Melanesian way," where they could reduce the offense to financial dimensions, and extract a cut for themselves.

In the first years after the BPA was signed, there was still no government and less supervision, and Ishmael began getting dozens of calls. He had decided that helping Bougainville solve its crime problem was as much his responsibility as leading the BRA in battle: He was the best person for the job, so it fell to him to do it. He couldn't handle everything and, where possible, urged families to solve their own problems, but if a matter was significant, he didn't turn it down.

As people learned of Ishmael's availability, the calls increased. When someone had a serious problem, the advice became universal: "Call Ishmael." As a consequence, on the weekends he was usually in his truck all day Saturday; Sunday morning during church hours, he might get some rest. He started recruiting BRA ex-combatants like Solomon and Sevy to help out; that wasn't enough, so after a while he recruited more men. Ishmael didn't want Arawa to spiral out of control, so he got a house in town and moved his family, which now included a baby girl, there on the weekends.

One Friday evening, Joe Sipo, a guy who had made zip-guns for Ishmael's BRA guerillas, called Ishmael in Arawa. This was the third time Joe had called, and Ishmael knew his problem. The guy next door had been hitting on Joe's daughter, who lived downstairs in Joe's house with her husband. The neighbor was starting to get physical. He wouldn't take no for an answer, and had taken to grabbing the girl's ass when he was drunk. The husband was too afraid of the neighbor to do anything, but Joe had had enough.

The pervert was at it again and had trapped Joe's daughter in his garage. "He's blasted on jungle juice—I'm going to kill the motherfucker!" Joe yelled over the phone.

Ishmael hung up, walked down the hallway, and grabbed his .410 bore, pump-action shotgun off the rack. It was the lightest weapon he owned. He removed its quarter-ounce slug shells and chambered medium-grade pellet shells instead. If he had to shoot someone, he wasn't planning on killing them.

"I heard that guy on the phone," Betty said, standing in the kitchen, wiping her hands with a dishrag. "Are you sure that tiny shotgun is going to be enough?"

Ishmael kissed his wife, told her he loved her and would be home by dinner time, and headed out the door to his pickup truck. It took two minutes to drive around the block to where Joe lived in Section 17 and pull into his driveway. Ishmael switched on his brights and left the truck running as he jumped out, shotgun in hand.

The wack-job from next door was standing out in his driveway in front of his garage, one arm tightly wrapped around the neck of a young woman who had to be Joe's daughter, his other holding a bush knife to her throat. The girl had been roughed up with bruises on her face, and her nose was streaming blood. Joe, bobbing and weaving off to one side, was yelling at the guy while holding one of his zip-guns in the pretense of aiming, except he knew there was no percentage in aiming a zip-gun. The bullet could go anywhere, which had to be the only reason Joe hadn't fired. A timid-looking guy who was undoubtedly the husband and a woman in a bathrobe who Ishmael recognized as Joe's wife were standing in front of Joe's house screaming.

"All right, all right—shut up!" Ishmael yelled.

Everyone kept screaming.

Ishmael pumped the .410 and unloaded a shell into the side of the wack-job's garage, disintegrating the windows and spraying glass everywhere.

The explosion shut up the screamers—except for the girl, who kept wailing.

"Let her go," Ishmael called over to the wack-job.

"Fuck you," the guy said, tightening up on the girl and making her scream louder.

Ishmael pumped the .410 again. "At three, you're losing a leg," he said to the wack-job. "One...two..."

"Fuck you."

Ishmael aimed low and away from the girl and fired, filling the outside of the guy's upper thigh and hip with lead and rolling him halfway up his driveway.

The girl ran over to her parents.

Ishmael called over to the husband. "Get him to the hospital as soon as you can, before he loses too much blood. His family is going to blame you if he dies." He walked over to his truck, climbed in, backed out of the driveway, and headed home for dinner.

* * *

It wasn't just violent crimes; property issues came up too.

Arawa had four banks before the Crisis, including a local branch of Bank South Pacific. During the Crisis, all the banks in Arawa where the fighting was concentrated were burned to the ground. They stayed that way, their foundations covered with weeds, long after the hostilities ended.

Since no banks remained in Arawa, there was no source of cash in town. BSP still had a branch in Buka, which became the only source of cash in all of Bougainville. For any Bougainvillean to withdraw or deposit cash in the bank required three days: one day to make the drive or boat ride to Buka, one day to wait in line with hundreds of other Bougainvilleans trying to do the same, and the last day to return home—assuming things went smoothly.

The Savants were a prominent Arawa family. Mathias Savant had been a bank manager before the Crisis, and was usually the first person Jasper Kaboose had consulted on financial matters. His wife Anita was one of Arawa's largest landlords. They were both big supporters of Arawa town government. Given Matty's banking background, the town leaders asked him to speak to BSP about replacing its bank branch, so Arawa would once again have an in-town source of cash.

"BSP's not going to do it," Matty and his wife commiserated with Ishmael one day when they ran into each other at the market. "I talked to their president at a UN conference," Matty said. "He said we'd just burn it down again."

Ishmael shook his head in resignation. It was one more thing to add to the pile of reasons why Francis Olu's warmongering had been a bad idea—except for the overarching fact that Bougainvilleans were a little closer to having their own country.

"I had an idea," Anita said to Ishmael. A former schoolteacher, she was one of the smartest people in Arawa. "You could tell BSP you wouldn't let anyone burn down the bank." She smiled at Ishmael, as if he was a favorite student.

"Thanks, but what would that do?" Ishmael asked.

"Why, you know exactly what it would do," Anita said. "It's just like when you signed the Bougainville Peace Agreement as the chief of defence. Everyone saw your signature there, and for them it was like a guarantee that it's going to happen—you know, all those conditions, disarmament, and the independence referendum and all."

Ishmael knew that much was true. That was how he'd lived his life every day since the Crisis had ended. He had stopped shooting on the battlefield, but that didn't mean the fight was over. He hadn't realized it when he had hiked up the mountain to join up with Francis Olu, but for him this was all part of a greater struggle. Winning the shooting war meant nothing unless it led to a better life for Bougainvilleans over the long run.

"How about it?" Matty said. "Would you sign a written statement, giving BSP your personal guarantee that no one would burn down their new bank building?"

It didn't take Ishmael long to make up his mind. Central Bougainville needed a bank again, and Arawa was full of BRA ex-combatants who would help him make sure nothing bad happened to the new bank building. "Yes."

Ishmael delivered his written guarantee to BSP the following week, and the bank built a new branch office in Arawa within the calendar year.

Ironically, the Bougainville Police Service had the same problem. The Arawa police station had also been burned down in the Crisis. Not only did the Royal PNG Constabulary not have any money, but, even though the Crisis was over, they still made a tempting target for angry Bougainvilleans with scores to settle. Ishmael guaranteed their building too, and they quickly erected a new facility. After Ishmael did the same for them, so did PNG Power, the Kieta Port Authority, and the Aropa Airport.

Ishmael's other challenge was Bougainville's politicians. Until the late 1960s, there had been no such thing. Feeling their way, amateurs stepped into the shoes of retreating Australian administrators, hardly an ideal circumstance in which to learn the ropes. Bougainvilleans were thrust into situations where they couldn't simply administrate, but actually had to govern. Doing so while avoiding the infection that accompanies money and power was something many found impossible.

The most questionable character in Bougainville's short-lived political history was one with a familiar face, a man who reappeared on the scene as soon as the Lincoln disarmament agreement was signed. Although not Bougainvillean—he was half from PNG stock, with the other half Chinese—Liuman Mogol had become a local politician before the Crisis: he was the regional representative of the province of the North Solomons (as Bougainville was known at the time) in colonial Papua New Guinea's first representative assembly. When the bullets started flying, he fled to Port Moresby. Now that the coast was clear, he was back, trying to make an end run around the BRA ex-combatants. Mogol whispered to his supporters in PNG's national government that he—not Kaboose or another BRA candidate— was a better choice to initiate a political rapprochement between Bougainville and PNG. He proposed that Bougainville form a new provincial government within PNG, with him serving as the first governor. Mogol's proposition encountered irate opposition from the BRA ex-combatants. Despite his oily assurances that he was working for the good of all Bougainvilleans, the Mogol plan was scuttled.

Mogol's ingratitude toward Bougainvilleans who had given their lives so that he could live might have been explained away as typical politics were it not for the fact that he had once been a priest. Notwithstanding, Christian values like piety or truthfulness appeared to count for little with him. Mogol kept trying to convince the people that even though he was not Bougainvillean and had abandoned them during the Crisis, he was the one who should wear the pith helmet. Without doing their homework, Bougainvilleans listened— in the minds of many, Mogol remained a priest—and voted for him, and in the end got what their ignorance deserved. Mogol, who was not even in Bougainville during the Crisis, insisted on being a prominent signatory to the Bougainville Peace Agreement, which said all one needed to know about the man. His political success was—unfortunately—a searing indictment of Bougainvilleans as well.

Before and after the completion of the BPA, Mogol and Kaboose were the two most significant contestants for Bougainville's head political office, jousting while several interim government organizations were tried on, and then discarded. Finally the BPA was signed, which led to the formation of the Autonomous Region of Bougainville: a special autonomous zone of PNG's national government with its own constitution, democratically-elected president, and legislature, but no control of most police or taxation functions. The first elections were held in 2005, with Jasper Kaboose, Liuman Mogol, and George Washburn vying for president. Kaboose won. Francis Olu, who only a year earlier had proclaimed himself "King of Me'ekamui," died a month later of unknown causes.

Although Mogol had always been a spurious character, his loss to Kaboose in the presidential election helped guide the man to a pact with the devil. Once again, Mogol quit Bougainville. He talked PNG's national government into sending him to Beijing as ambassador to the People's Republic of China from 2007-2010, where he collaborated with the Chinese on plans for a shared future that would come back to haunt Bougainvilleans.

Kaboose's representation of Bougainville was, if anything, even worse than Mogol's. His reputation was saved only by his premature death via a heart attack while in his third year in office. Kaboose's presidency got off to a lurching start as Joe Wobely, his choice for vice president, had to be removed from office for public drunkenness. Meanwhile, Kaboose had bigger problems. He had been involved in Bougainvillean politics long enough to know that Bougainville was penniless, and that the national government—despite the fact that the BPA required it to fork over millions annually to Bougainville—would welch on its obligations. A desperate man, he made a juicy target for carpetbaggers.

One day in Kaboose's first year in office, Ishmael was contacted by George Washburn. Given that there was strength in numbers, was he available to accompany George to Port Moresby on a critical mission for the president? Ishmael could hardly say no, although he wanted to when George told him more about the specifics of their assignment. Money men who George portrayed as Bougainville's saviors waited for them, and it was urgent that they fly back to Bougainville with a deal. Ishmael couldn't help but wonder: what did he or George know about sophisticated financial matters?

As the four men ordered drinks at the bar of Port Moresby's Ela Beach Hotel, an unpleasant sense of familiarity hung over the three Melanesians in the group. Sergeant Greyson Trull, formerly of the Defence Force, had been the batman for Lieutenant George Washburn when he had been a Defence Force officer. Although Ishmael had never met Trull, he knew him by his malodorous reputation, especially as solidified by an infamous Toniva incident in which three Bougainvillean family members—distant relatives— were killed. Now a civilian, Trull was accompanied by his Australian squire, a tall, slightly humpbacked man from Queensland named Lucien Sump, to whom George seemed overly deferential. When for Ishmael's sake Sump spent a minute putting the faces in context and made the mistake of describing Greyson as his driver, the former Defence Force thug practically had to be restrained before calming down and ordering another beer on Lucien's tab.

Early on in the conversation, Ishmael resolved to say as little as possible.

Lucien Sump started things off by launching a lead balloon. "Guys, thanks for coming. Sorry to disappoint you, but I can't get distracted at the moment. If I don't come up with five million kina for my PNG timber deal, the whole thing is going under."

"Forget the timber deal," Greyson said. "That's about millions. George is talking billions."

"It's all arranged," George said, trying to sound authoritative. "As President Kaboose's financial advisor, I'm here to cut a deal for twenty million kina to bail out Bougainville." He stole a glance at Greyson, who nodded at him for reassurance, and ignored Ishmael staring at him.

Ishmael absorbed with difficulty what he was hearing while trying to remain calm. He knew nothing about George being Kaboose's financial advisor, and he had no idea what Bougainville was giving away for twenty million kina.

Lucien stared off across the Port Moresby harbor into the sun setting over the western mountains. "They always promise billions with these banana republic deals, and it always turns out that there's nothing there."

George said, "Tell him, Greyson."

"Haven't you been listening?" Greyson asked Lucien, his face screwed into a scowl. "I told you. The Panguna Mine is worth billions, and it's not a fantasy; the hole's already in the ground."

It seemed to Ishmael like Lucien had had a lot to drink before he and George had arrived, and it was clear from Lucien's blurred expression that Greyson's impatience was well deserved. Nonetheless, now the Australian began to concentrate. "Wait, you meant Rio Tinto's mine?"

"Yes, goddamnit. I told you all about this," Greyson barked.

"But what about the mining company? Rio Tinto?"

"They're gone," Greyson said, exasperated. "Besides," he said, pointing at George, "his client's the goddamned president, bird-brain."

Lucien looked at George with newfound interest. "All right, all right," he said, folding his long arms on the table and leaning forward. "Now I'm listening. What's the deal?"

George said, "There's a fortune in the ground in Bougainville. It's already proven; you don't have to go find it. Just tell us what your investors need for the twenty million kina; we don't have a lot of time."

"Can you first limp along enough to get the mine reopened and show some results?" Lucien asked.

"No, no," George said. "The government doesn't have enough money to pay its employees—including the president." With a serious expression on his face, he added, "Besides, the man needs expert medical attention. He's got a heart condition."

Lucien tried to buy time. "The first thing I've got to do, mate," he said to George, "is find five million for this timber deal, or it's going under."

Greyson said, "Forget your timber deal. It's another five million kina down the rathole. Do the twenty million with George in Bougainville, and you'll practically own the place. Just tell the man what you want in return," he coaxed.

Lucien leaned back and looked around the table. He didn't try to hide the exasperated expression on his face, which advertised that he was a long way from home, about to lose his ass on a timber deal, and now his knuckle-headed driver—of all people—had introduced him to a guy who said he was a commander of the army in Bougainville, a place everyone knew was shot to hell.

What Lucien said next seemed predictable to Ishmael; when backed into a corner, men tended to take matters out on the audience. Sump was probably thinking that if they expected him to be a hero, he would reciprocate by squeezing Bougainville dry.

Sump said, "My investors and I would need to receive seventy-five percent of all of Bougainville's resources." He eyeballed the men for emphasis.

George couldn't return his stare.

Ishmael was stunned. He couldn't believe what he was hearing. They had fought the Crisis for this? Kaboose would be crazy to consider such a deal, but if he was stupid enough to do it, he'd be drawn and quartered in the Buka Town square.

"Now we're getting somewhere," intoned Greyson, pulling a pencil and a piece of paper out of one of the purse-like reed bags the PNG men carried around. "Twenty million kina gets you seventy-five percent of Bougainville's mineral resources."

"No, no; that's not what I said," Lucien replied.

"I just wrote it down," Greyson said, holding out his scribbled notation to Lucien as if it was obvious, like the results of a pregnancy test.

Lucien said, "I said seventy-five percent of *all* resources, not just mineral resources."

Greyson's expression turned blank.

"Bougainville's got a lot more besides copper and gold," Lucien explained, trying to reassert himself as the senior member of the deal team, as compared to his driver. "There's oil and gas, timber..." his voice trailed off as he looked at Greyson, who was grinning at him like a Cheshire cat. "What?"

"Don't you think you're getting a little greedy?" Greyson said, leering at Lucien.

George looked like a lost dog.

It appeared to Ishmael that Lucien was hooked. Being greedy seemed to comport with his constitution, and the way his face ticked made it clear he wanted to close the deal. There were billions in copper and gold, and probably oil and gas too—and it was only going to cost him twenty million smackers. Fortune favored the brave. Lucien said, "All right then, I'll drop it to seventy percent. By the way, a flimsy memorandum of understanding won't suffice—my agreement's got to be memorialized with actual legislation."

Greyson waved at the waiter. "Check."

Ishmael got up from his seat, made an excuse about his abrupt departure to Sump and Trull, and leaned over George's shoulder. "You can't do this, and neither can Kaboose. If you try, I'll oppose it."

As Ishmael left the room, he heard George's voice as if he had just woken up. "Are we leaving?"

"Didn't you hear him? We've got a deal," Greyson said. "Give Jasper a call and tell him we'll be on tomorrow morning's plane to Buka."

"What about my timber deal?" Lucien said.

Greyson said, "When am I going to be able to stop spoon-feeding you? Screw the timber deal. We're going to Bougainville."

South Pacific Goliath

The sordid transaction involving Jasper Kaboose, George Washburn, Lucien Sump, and the twenty million kina reached prime time two years later. Kaboose and Washburn had ignored Ishmael's advice, as well as the words of many others who learned about the ridiculous deal. On behalf of the government of the Autonomous Region of Bougainville, they had accepted twenty million kina, approximately the same amount of US dollars, from Impregnable Resources, Lucien's company, and sold Bougainville down the river. They also gave Lucien the documentation he requested: the agreement between the parties was not merely a contract, but actual legislation. What saved Bougainville was that Kaboose was naïve enough to believe he could execute binding law with no approval by his legislature, and Lucien was stupid enough to accept that and allow the check to be cashed. As the rumors leaked out, Bougainville went into a slow burn. When people learned the news was true, they called for Kaboose's head. Australian journalists swooped into Buka to do an exposé, but Kaboose inconvenienced everyone by suffering a heart attack and dying.

After Lucien steered his company into a series of worthless investments in Bougainville, it went under, and he was left to develop the plot for his next act while Bougainville turned to another amateur. James Tonic, who had replaced Joe Wobely as vice president under Kaboose, was elected to serve the unfinished portion of Kaboose's term. Tonic managed to remain in office with no incident, but was removed later from a subsequent government post for gross misconduct.

After those embarrassing candidates, in the presidential election of 2010, it must have come as a relief for many Bougainvilleans to be able to vote for Liuman Mogol, a former priest. The rumor was that, not leaving anything to chance, Mogol's Chinese collaborators fixed a majority of the ballot boxes while the unwitting press chalked up his landslide victory to the public's adoration. To pay them back—and demonstrate business prowess to his voter flock—Mogol's first presidential act was to sign six memoranda of understanding with Chinese state-owned enterprises, after which he declared Bougainville's economic challenge solved. Most of the Chinese companies never graced Bougainville's shores, and those that did left soon afterward. For the remainder of his ten-year reign, Mogol did nothing to help Bougainville's economy, which remained in ruins.

The poor performances turned in by Bougainville's early presidents pushed Ishmael toward a career change. He had steered Bougainville through the Crisis and reduced crime, but its biggest remaining challenge was to fix the government. In 2015, he decided to run for Bougainville's highest office.

Ishmael sounded out the competition. Not surprisingly, George Washburn was seen to be his strongest challenger—if he was running. Ishmael and George would both receive stout support from ex-combatants. If they both ran, they would split the vote and probably ruin each other's chances; if only one man ran, he could count on a major block of support. George had run in 2010 and had fared poorly. Surely he would agree that it was Ishmael's time.

George and Ishmael had a respectful relationship during their days with the BRA, mainly because they had not gotten in each other's way. In the aftermath of the Crisis, they had taken different paths.

George's biggest problem was overrating his capabilities. Deeming himself Kaboose's financial advisor was absurd: Bagman was a better job description. It was as if the headmaster back at the Hutjena School had told George he was special, and he decided to simply believe him, rather than looking in the mirror from time to time.

Ishmael tracked down George and spelled out his thinking about the upcoming election. He should have been more suspicious when George readily agreed, telling Ishmael he wouldn't run and wishing him the best. But when the writs were filed, Ishmael discovered that George had indeed thrown his hat into the ring. Predictably, the ex-combatant vote was split, allowing Mogol to win. Ishmael came in second, while George finished back in the pack.

Afterward, Ishmael noticed that George was avoiding him, similar to the behavior he'd exhibited after the disastrous Port Moresby meeting with Lucien Sump. Not wanting George's behavior to complicate his life, he confronted him.

"I don't hold your decision to run for president against you, you know," Ishmael said to George after seeking him out at a political rally. "I'm sure you felt really bad about it. That's enough of a cross to bear."

Coming in second in the presidential race wasn't a total loss. Ishmael learned a lot. Running for office was more complicated than he had thought. He had made mistakes: he assembled no financial support or organization; worse, he had taken people at their word. He was mulling over the issues when the topic surfaced again in an unexpected way.

Ishmael received a call from Leki, a woman who worked at the Gold Dealer in Arawa. Her boss had a problem—his mining partner had stolen their excavator—and they needed Ishmael's help. The guy's name was Jack Davis. He was a white foreigner, an American, who had first come to Bougainville a couple years earlier and gotten involved in the gold-buying business. Everyone around town had originally thought Davis was partners with Lucien Sump, the other white guy in town, but over time it became clear he was on his own.

Ishmael met Jack Davis at his office at the Gold Dealer and helped him solve his problem with his landowner partner. Afterward, the American asked Ishmael an odd question: "Would you ever consider running for political office?" Ishmael told Davis he had run once, and it had been a disappointing experience. Davis said, "I think you should reconsider. If you did, my American friends and I would be first in line to support you." Ishmael was grateful to Davis for saying as much and told him so, but he had no idea whether he could believe the guy or not. Most of the white foreigners who came to Bougainville flew in, scouted around trying to make a quick buck, and took off. Davis had seemed like a reasonable guy to Ishmael, especially when he heard from his friend Bishop Unabali over at the Diocese of Bougainville that Davis was taking the bishop and a group of Bougainvillean chiefs to introduce them to industry and government officials in the United States. But if the man was legitimate, what was he doing in Bougainville?

One day in August 2019, Ishmael saw George Washburn's number on his mobile phone. George never contacted him unless he had a reason. Ishmael texted him back, and they agreed to speak while attending an ex-combatant gathering the following week.

"I'm inviting you to an important meeting," George said when they got together, as if he was doing Ishmael a favor.

Ishmael said, "I hope it's not to have a drink with Lucien Sump and Greyson Trull in Port Moresby."

At first it didn't seem like George got the joke, but then his lips flattened into a tight smile. "No, this is a real deal. A big one."

"What's it about?" Ishmael asked.

George said, "It's an investment conference. There will be some important people there, and they're helping me bring good news to Bougainville. These guys are talking about investing billions."

"What do you need me for?" Ishmael said. All he could think about was the disastrous session at the bar of the Ela Beach Hotel, and how he never wanted to do anything remotely similar again. He also had learned not to place any faith in George's judgement regarding people or financial deals.

"Come on, my brother," George said, playing the Melanesian card. "This is about Bougainville. You're an important guy. These guys want to meet you, and I told them I'd get you to come."

Uncomfortable with flattery, Ishmael changed the subject. "Where's the meeting?"

"Vanuatu, in Port Vila, the capital. Have you been there?"

"No."

"You'll love the place. We're staying at the Iririki Island Resort, a fancy hotel on the beach."

Ishmael winced. "That's not my style. I don't think I can afford it."

"Oh, don't worry about that," George said. "It's free. These guys are paying for everything."

"Are you serious? Why?"

George said, "I told you. They want to meet you."

Something smelled. Ishmael had heard that George had been hanging around with Chinese guys—supposedly he had actually travelled to China—and it might be better if he was along for the ride, if only to keep tabs on George. After all, the last time he'd practically given Bougainville away. "Are these guys Chinese?" he asked.

George was caught by surprise, and his face looked like he didn't know whether to smile and agree or backpedal. "Maybe some of them."

That meant yes—even more reason to go.

"Who else will be there?"

"You're the guy they want to see. They may invite some others; I'm not sure." George was getting impatient. "What do you say?"

"When is this happening?"

"Whenever you can go."

This was no investment conference. "I could probably get there for a day or two."

"Great," George said, a smile of relief crossing his face.

The following Monday they met at the Buka airport. Resplendent in a sports jacket and slacks, George handed Ishmael his tickets and an itinerary. "The hotel where we're staying has a casino, if you want to stay a couple of extra days."

"Thanks, but I'm probably going to need to get back," Ishmael said. He carried his bag with him on the plane; he had packed for one night. Rather than his standard Bougainville outfit of jeans, a T-shirt, and bare feet, Ishmael made a concession to foreign travel: he wore a collared Lacoste shirt and tennis shoes.

Flying business class all the way, they travelled from Buka to Port Moresby and, after staying overnight in a hotel near the airport, caught a morning flight to Vanuatu the next day. Their plane touched down in Port Vila at two o'clock local time.

As George and Ishmael walked down the plane's airstair, a youthful Chinese woman in a blue uniform waited on the tarmac, holding a sign saying, "Ishmael and Washburn." As they stepped off the airstair, she waved at Ishmael. "Over here, General Ishmael. Welcome to Vanuatu!"

Ishmael didn't know what to think. No one ever called him General, even during the Crisis.

The young woman looked over Ishmael's shoulder. "Hello again, Commander Washburn," she said, her overly made-up face frozen in a big smile as if she were welcoming home family members. "Pleassse," she said, sweeping her arm to the side and guiding the two men away from the airplane toward a black Mercedes limousine purring on the tarmac. "Follow me, gentlemen."

The car's driver was also Chinese, uniformed, and wearing a peaked driver's hat. Ishmael stepped into the back of the limousine. "Hello, General Ishmael," a Chinese man said, sticking his hand out at Ishmael from where he sat inside the limo. "Call me Rudy." As George pushed in behind Ishmael and sat down next to him, Rudy greeted George the same way the Chinese woman had, as if they had met before. The woman hopped into the shotgun seat up front, and the driver pulled away.

A sunny, hot day outside, it was cool and quiet inside the air-conditioned limo. Making note of the level of development in a country that was new to him, Ishmael intentionally didn't say anything as he gazed out the tinted windows at the landscape rolling by. He liked visiting new places and tried to familiarize himself with what he could see of Vanuatu. Rural countryside around the airport quickly gave way to residential and then commercial neighborhoods. Port Vila appeared on a par with Port Moresby, but cleaner.

"Have you ever been here before, General Ishmael?" Rudy asked. Ishmael shook his head.

"You're going to love it," Rudy assured him.

As they came into what looked like the center of town, they turned off the main highway into a long driveway flanked by luxuriant tropical foliage and colorful flowers, and cruised up toward the entrance of the Iririki Island Resort.

Ishmael sized up the hotel. He didn't consider himself an expert, but during the Crisis he had attended his share of international dispute resolution conferences overseas in nice hotels and knew enough to form a basis of comparison. The Iririki wasn't as large as the Ela Beach Hotel, but, if anything, it seemed more expensive. He was glad he wasn't footing the bill. The reception building was small but elegantly designed and appointed, and surrounded by clusters of bungalows. Through palm trees and thick groves of birds of paradise, he could see past an expansive pool complex to the sea. The hotel was crowded, and there were people everywhere—all Chinese.

The limo circled the reception area of the hotel and stopped at the front door. "The Iririki Island Resort Welcomes General Ishmael and Commander Washburn from Bougainville," read the sign hanging over the entrance. "Welcome, gentlemen," Rudy said from his seat. The young woman got out of the shotgun seat and opened Ishmael's door. "Pleassse," she said, sweeping her arm toward the front door of the hotel. Ishmael got out of the car, his bag slung over his shoulder, and walked toward the glass double doors that formed the main entrance. When he got a few yards away, the door opened, and two young Chinese people bounded out, followed by a blast of air-conditioning.

"Hello, General Ishmael," they said in unison, the young woman dressed in the same blue garb as their airport escort and the young man wearing a dark suit and black-frame glasses. "Let us help you with your luggage," the guy said.

"That's okay," Ishmael said. As he got inside the reception area, an older Chinese woman came out from behind the reception desk and approached him with a hotel key folder. "Welcome to the Iririki, General Ishmael. Robert here will show you to your room," the woman said, handing a brown-skinned guy in a bellman's uniform Ishmael's key folder together with some hotel literature.

Robert nodded at Ishmael; he was the first person Ishmael had seen since they landed who wasn't Chinese. "*Welkam*," Robert said to Ishmael, who returned the greeting in pidgin. "Come on mate, follow me," the man said, taking Ishmael's elbow and steering him toward a narrow, garden-ensconced walkway with bungalows on either side.

"Meet back here for lunch in ten minutes," Rudy called after them.

Ishmael followed Robert down the walkway.

The man didn't utter a word until they turned a corner. "Here we are," Robert said, stopping and using a key to open the electronic door lock. They entered the suite, featuring a bedroom and a separate sitting area with a desk. Robert took a minute to turn on the air conditioning and show Ishmael how to use the television. He finished and peered at Ishmael. "How's Bougainville these days?"

Ishmael said, "We're doing all right. Have you been there?"

"I was a cook for the Defence Force."

Ishmael studied Robert's face, which was light and freckled; maybe he had come from one of PNG's outer islands.

"I know who you are," Robert said. "Your BRA guys embarrassed us."

What could Ishmael say? He just smiled.

Robert started to grin. "I'm telling you, man," Robert said. "You guys were good," and the two of them started laughing. Robert glanced at his watch. "I got to go; Ms. Wu will be all over my ass. Can I ask you something?"

"Sure," Ishmael said.

"What are you doing with the Chinese?"

Ishmael explained that he wasn't with them; he was there at George's invitation.

Robert's eyes flickered with hesitancy. "Oh, we all know Commander Washburn." He peered back at Ishmael. "I could tell you stories about what's happened in this country. Keep those guys off your island, if you know what's good for you," he said as he left the room.

Ishmael sat down on the edge of the bed. He told himself to simply tolerate whatever the day was going to bring him, get out of there as soon as possible, and never accept another invitation from George. He started to unpack his bag, but then changed his mind, left it unopened on his bed, and headed back to the lobby.

"There he is," Rudy said overenthusiastically when Ishmael returned to the lobby. George was there too. He seemed unwilling to make eye contact with Ishmael, as if he were embarrassed about something. "Everyone ready for lunch?" Rudy asked. "We're a little behind schedule." Not waiting for any response, he led the way down a hallway toward a Chinese lady who beckoned from a boardroom doorway.

As soon as Ishmael entered the boardroom, he realized why the Chinese had chosen to use a military title when addressing him. Almost all of the men in the room were in uniform—army green and navy blue—except for the young attendants, and one small man in a dark suit.

Everyone went through their *ni haos* and hellos, all smiles as they took turns greeting their friend Commander Washburn. Then Rudy took over. "General Ishmael, I'd like to introduce you to our hosts, Major General Wu of the People's Liberation Army Ground Force," he said, gesturing toward the guy in the green uniform, "and his naval counterpart, Captain Yu."

Both men squared their shoulders and saluted.

"Hello," Ishmael said, looking at George for guidance.

Rudy didn't wait for any response. "Let's take our places, shall we? General Ishmael, you're the guest of honor; please allow the hostess to escort you to the table." He took Ishmael by the wrist and handed him off to the young lady who had preceded them into the boardroom. She guided Ishmael to the rear of a large round table with a lazy Susan in the center. A starched white napkin curled in a tube and arranged like a phallic symbol sat erect on the tablecloth in front of him.

"This is the seat of honor, General Ishmael," she said, pulling out his chair.

Major General Wu took the seat to Ishmael's right, and Captain Yu the one to his left, with George one seat away.

As Rudy and the hostess herded the men to the table, the sole Chinese man not in uniform remained standing. He walked out into the middle of the room. "Good afternoon, General Ishmael; greetings again, Commander Washburn. I am Mr. Zeng; I am speaking on behalf of these men and the People's Liberation Army of China in welcoming you here to Vanuatu." He bared his yellowed teeth in a grimace intended as a smile. "We are honored by your presence. Thank you for coming from Bougainville." He made a short bow and glanced over at the hostess sitting off to one side, and she handed him an electronic control device. He clicked it, and a screen dropped from the ceiling midway across the room. *China Strengthening the South Pacific* exclaimed the first slide, with a graphic of two hands clasped together over an ocean background.

"I'm not sure how much you know about the extent of China's deep friendship with the South Pacific," Mr. Zeng said, "so we thought we'd show you this brief presentation." The wrinkled man proceeded to flip through slides illustrating China's close involvement with a dozen Pacific island jurisdictions, from Yap to Chuuk to Kiribati, ending up with Vanuatu. Each slide was covered with photographs of infrastructure projects—highways, bridges, dams, mines, and ports—and happy islander faces. "China has lent Vanuatu over three billion RMB," Mr. Zeng said, his stained teeth clipping together as he pronounced each word, looking toward Ishmael. "Almost two billion kina."

A door at the rear of the room opened silently, and waiters began ferrying in Chinese dishes and placing them around the center of the big table. No one began eating until Captain Yu urged Ishmael to eat something, and then everyone dug in.

Mr. Zeng flipped a slide, and an island map familiar to Ishmael popped up. "Now we're poised for one of our biggest investments yet in the South Pacific," he said, moving closer toward the table and gazing at Ishmael. "The Solomon Islands." As if on cue, everyone clapped. Ishmael glanced over at George, who was clapping along with the rest. "Next week, we will announce a three-billion-RMB program of investment there," the little man said. Another slide flipped down, showing a chart with Chinese investment figures overlaid on photos of a mine, a road, a hydroelectric project, and an island port. Using the electronic pointer in the control device, he touched the red laser dot on the island of Tulagi, and glanced over at Ishmael. "I imagine you've been to Tulagi?" Mr. Zeng asked. "A fine, deep-water port. Not as good as Arawa's, of course."

The man leered at Ishmael. "None of these places are as valuable to us as your homeland," he said, clicking the control to drop a slide of Mt. Bagana onto the screen, "and that's why Bougainville is so important to all of us in this room." He flashed his yellowed teeth again. "It would be the jewel in our South Pacific crown." Mr. Zeng nodded over at George, who stood and moved to the center of the room. "Now Commander Washburn will educate our Chinese friends here who are new to Bougainville about our plans for your wonderful islands."

George took the control device from the man. "Bougainville is my home," he said to the Chinese in the room, "and we need to do so much. Thanks to our friends in China, it can finally happen." He flipped through several additional slides, each using a backdrop of green Bougainville jungle superimposed with images of new bridges, highway-like roads, a huge airport, and ports teeming with cranes and fishing vessels. "Here is what truly sets Bougainville apart," George said, and introduced the last slide, an aerial view of the Panguna Mine. The illustration was not one of the tired old photos showing rusting trucks at the bottom of the pit, but an artist's sketch of a new, vibrant mine with dozens of vehicles and millworks with conveyor belts, all set forth behind a photoshopped, shiny pile of gold Doré bars. "The current value of the ore in the Panguna Mine is nearly seven hundred billion RMB," George intoned to a buzz of exclamations.

When George was done, he handed the control to Mr. Zeng and sat down. The others buzzed in animated Chinese. Mr. Zeng walked closer to the table and looked at Ishmael. "So now, General Ishmael, perhaps you understand why it was so important for China to meet you."

Ishmael just stared back at him.

"China knows that Bougainville is about to experience two threshold political events," the man intoned. "First, you will undergo a referendum, which we are told by everyone will result in Bougainville seeking its independence. Next, there will be an election in the spring to select the person who will lead the newest nation on earth—and then that person and Bougainville must wrestle with the impossible task of accessing the capital to pay for prosperity." The man smiled unctuously. "These are delicate events. Independence and elections can create chaos." He walked back out to the center of the floor, flicked the control once more, and George's smiling face appeared on the screen, rounded and moon-like, with *George Washburn, President of Bougainville 2020* emblazoned in gold letters across the bottom of the frame.

The Chinese people in the room clapped politely.

Ishmael's ears burned with a mixture of anger and humiliation.

"So you see, General Ishmael," Mr. Zeng said, "it's very important that the only man who could possibly make George Washburn's candidacy difficult agrees not to run against him." He clicked the control, and another photo with a backdrop of the Panguna Mine appeared, this one dated from the Crisis, showing a riotous crowd demonstrating on the ramp going down to the pit. "We also can't have this type of uncontrolled behavior ruin our joint opportunity for prosperity," he said. "So that the Panguna Mine can produce a golden dream for all concerned, Bougainville must elect the correct leader and enforce real law and order." The man stared at him. "It's very clear, General Ishmael, that the only person who can guarantee both of these things is you."

On Ishmael's right, Major General Wu could no longer contain himself. "I'm involved in the Southern Theater Command; that's Hong Kong and Macao. We can give your men in—I believe you call your army the BLA—the latest weapons and training for anti-riot control. It will be important for the people to fear the rule of the Washburn government." At this, Captain Yu broke in. "How many men are currently enlisted in your army, General Ishmael? We'd also need to train them for duty in the atolls as we transform them the way we did in the South China Sea."

Everyone in the room peered at Ishmael.

He said nothing.

Mr. Zeng started to chuckle. "Well played, General Ishmael. Your inscrutability approaches ours." He signaled to the hostess, who glided out of the room, the door swinging behind her. "Forgive us for getting ahead of ourselves," he said as the woman reentered the room with the young man from the reception area, each of them carrying two bulging sports equipment bags, setting them down on the floor next to the little man and leaving. Mr. Zeng looked over at Ishmael. "To show our appreciation, General Ishmael," he said. He kept staring at Ishmael, who didn't respond. "One million US dollars will take you many places in the world. Of course, we would require a written agreement before releasing the funds."

Ishmael looked around the table at the Chinese men staring back at him, waiting for his answer. George gazed out the window. Ishmael forced himself to stand and started to side-step around the table. He got as far as the bags, where Mr. Zeng waited for him, smiling like someone about to hook a fish. "I'm sorry," Ishmael said, looking down at the man's wrinkled face. "I need to use the men's room."

"Of course," the man said, doing a poor job at stifling his surprise.

Ishmael pushed through the door into the reception area. The Chinese manager saw him and came out from behind her reception desk. "Can I help you, General Ishmael?"

As Ishmael wondered what to say, Robert appeared.

"Can he please show me the way to the bathroom?" Ishmael said, pointing to Robert.

"Sure, mate, right this way," Robert said, and the two men walked out of the room and down the hotel walkway.

As they got to the door of the men's room, Ishmael grabbed Robert's elbow. "I've got to get out of here," he said. "How can I get to the airport?"

Robert didn't seem at all surprised—rather, almost pleased. "No problem, man. You can grab the eleven o'clock flight tonight to Fiji if you like," he said. "Where are your things?"

"My bag's still packed, sitting on the bed in my room."

Robert pointed through the bushes lining the walkway. "The highway's right out there, about three hundred yards or so. Wait inside here until I bring you your bag, then sneak through those bushes out to the road. You'll see a Tastee Chicken snack shack across the highway. I'll call my brother and get him to pick you up there in his cab in ten minutes. His name is Tommy; he looks like me; his car is red and has a taxi light on top."

"Thank you."

"Don't mention it. I know who you are, Ishmael. Everyone at the Defence Force still talks about you. You can pay me back with a vacation weekend at the beach in Arawa sometime."

As the plane took off for Fiji later that night, Ishmael made a mental note to contact Jack Davis, the American who owned the Gold Dealer in Arawa, as soon as he got home.

PART THREE

JACK

11

No Alibi

What happened in Bougainville wasn't something I planned in advance. That would be giving me too much credit. If, after what transpired, I was accused of making frivolous life decisions, I wouldn't be able to put up much of an argument.

It all started one day at my office in New York City with a telephone call from my movie friend Clyde. He and his partners produced films and dabbled in reality TV shows. Like all Hollywood promoter types, Clyde kept lines out on the water to reel a person in if they got hot. No way had he mistaken me for one of those. More likely, he just needed me to raise some capital. It didn't matter; I liked Clyde, in spite of the smarmy business he was in. He said he had a deal to discuss and asked if he could drop by with some friends the next morning.

"Jack, you know about Bougainville, right?" Clyde said as he strolled through the door of Davis Partners' reception area shortly after nine. He was carrying a cardboard tray of Starbucks coffees, two strangers in tow.

"Not a lot," I said. Witt Francois, our Haitian receptionist who I'd taken a chance on after he introduced himself to me aboard the

New Haven line train, took the tray from Clyde and showed the men into the boardroom. While Witt delivered their coffee together with a cream and sugar service, I waited for everyone to get situated.

After spending most of the previous ten years living and working in China—and making and losing a fortune in the process—I was back in town, wondering what I was going to do next to make some money. In the meantime, this was how I spent my day. Davis Partners was a boutique investment bank, a "deal shop." I had owned a majority interest in the place for twenty-five years, and had continued to operate the firm even when I was working overseas. Our offices were in the center of Manhattan on the eighth floor of the Graybar Building, next to Grand Central Terminal. Although we were small, the world came through our doors. We did quality deals and represented access to serious capital—large amounts of money. Usually, supplicants wanted Davis Partners, on behalf of their company, to raise money from financial institutions, our preferred set of investors. Sometimes our visitors got carried away and asked me to invest my own money in their deals. I never did that—before Bougainville.

Back in New York, the investment banking business had changed, and so had my personal life. My wife—the love of my life—had died. Our four sons had grown up and moved on, one by one shaking my hand and saying goodbye at the front door of the big brownstone on the Upper West Side where we raised them. I loved our family home, but now it was a lonely reminder of a life I had lost. My story thus far had been one most would envy, and being the boys' father topped it all; I would do anything for them. Surprisingly, fatherhood had turned out to be my highest calling. It had totally fulfilled me, but now it was over as an everyday occurrence. My days felt incomplete. I was older, but not ancient. Surely, some last chance to round out my existence remained. Nothing ordinary would do. Perhaps foolishly, I clung to the hope that momentous possibilities awaited, just out of sight. I accepted that, as usual, I would be required to do my bit to round the prospect into shape. Something was coming; surely, I would recognize it as circumstances unfolded.

I sold the brownstone, moved to our farm in Connecticut, and for the first time in my life became a commuter. Every morning I caught the train to Grand Central, taking the five a.m. express to make sure I got a seat and arriving at the office a few minutes after seven. At first, the new routine matched my rededicated enthusiasm for business. I looked forward to each new day and couldn't wait to get started. Whether coincidently or purposefully, the work was all-consuming; the notion of another woman was nonexistent. In any event, I had never determined what possible explanation I could offer the boys, although I think maybe it was just my realization that I could never find anyone like their mother. Then, over time, the investment industry slid downhill, mainly because of the new breed of people involved.

Clyde didn't feel compelled to introduce his two friends, and like many of the recent crowd crossing our transom, they didn't possess the good manners to introduce themselves either. The shorter one was sloppy and sweaty. Once seated in the boardroom, he became fixated on the task of emptying a half-dozen teaspoons of sugar into his coffee. Testing it, he slurped some. Coffee dribbled down his chin into his beard, a threadbare, scraggly affair, and I could see drops of the liquid glistening on his skin. It made it difficult to look at the guy. His outfit didn't help. Over a grubby white T-shirt, designer jeans, and hiking boots, he wore a down vest, even though it was August— definitely a Hollywood wannabe.

If I'd been told the other guy was Ichabod Crane's long-lost cousin, I would have believed it. Tall and gawky with a slight hump marring the contour of his upper back, he was older than me. To give him credit, his clothes were rumpled but well-made, and he had a handsome, intelligent face.

"I know Bougainville's an island in the South Pacific," I answered Clyde. "I think the Marines went there after Guadalcanal…and I believe something else happened there later, some type of conflict involving a big mine?"

"The Marines obliterated the Japs is what happened," interrupted the sloppy guy in a self-absorbed way.

I never threw anyone out of Davis Partners, no matter how rude.

Conversation ended for a moment while the rube tried to determine if we were all going to follow his lead and get sidetracked chattering about the US Marines annihilating the Japanese. When it became obvious that we were not, he reached over and extended his hand. "Rolly Maloney," he said.

"Jack Davis," I said, shaking his with little enthusiasm.

Rolly said, "I'm a student of history. Of you too; I looked you and Davis Partners up on the internet. Clyde brought us to the right place to finance our movie."

"I'm sorry—terribly impolite of me," the tall, skinny guy said in an Australian accent as he leaned across the boardroom table and extended his hand. "I'm Lucien Sump." He smiled, affecting a schoolboy expression that, despite his age, he got away with.

"It's not why we're here, but listen to their movie idea," Clyde said to me. "You're going to love it."

I wanted to tell Clyde there was no chance I would love anything Rolly had to say, but that wasn't my style.

"I'm an executive producer of *Yukon Gold*," Rolly said, glancing at me for affirmation.

I waited. One thing I learned as an investment banker was to size up a person by their ability to make a pitch. I never nodded my head; that just gave them a crutch, a false sense of security. I let them convince me—if they could.

Rolly forged ahead. "I met Lucien here in a bar in the airport in Seattle. He told me all about Bougainville? The crocodiles and all? The two of us cooked up the idea for a sequel to *Yukon Gold* over a couple of White Russians." He grinned again, continuing to be pleased with himself. If nothing else had done so, his choice of bar drink sealed his fate with me.

"Thus was hatched *Monster Gold*," Lucien said through tightened lips, as he read my unimpressed reaction.

"Don't you love it!" Clyde exclaimed, the way he did sometimes.

Rolly morphed into director mode. "Imagine footage of guys panning gold…when along comes a croc—and it's dinner time!" he exclaimed, chomping his arms and hands together, croc-wise, for emphasis.

"You're going to have to start by telling me what *Yukon Gold* is," I said. This meeting was going to be a total waste of time. I glanced intentionally at my watch.

Rolly and Clyde gave me funny looks.

"I guess *Yukon Gold* is a movie, but I haven't heard of it," I explained to Clyde. "You know financing movies is not our thing."

Rolly seemed stupefied by my comment. "*Yukon Gold* is one of the most profitable reality shows on TV," he said. "I'm an executive producer," he repeated, "and Clyde and his partners own the syndication rights. I've already sent some of the *Yukon Gold* regulars down to Bougainville to scope things out."

In the train wreck of a conversation, Lucien tried to reassemble the pieces. "Look here, we didn't come to your office to pitch a movie," he sputtered. "The true subject is billions in gold. Bougainville is Treasure Island. I'm the chiefs' man on the island, the government has finally passed its mining law, and I can deliver mining licenses."

"How many mining companies are operating in Bougainville now?" I asked.

Lucien forced a guileless expression onto his face. "You'd be the first new one." He affected a reassuring smile.

"But what about the big outfit that's already there?" I started to ask. Rolly interrupted once more, mouthing more nonsense about *Monster Gold*. I reached over and put my hand on his shoulder.

Smiling so he wouldn't take it too hard, I said, "Do me a favor and stop talking." I turned back to Lucien. "Tell me more about the gold."

Lucien said, "That's why Clyde suggested we come to New York. We need investors to join up with the Bougainville chiefs to mine gold. *Monster Gold* is a fig leaf, a way to get a few bucks into the hands of the local landowners so they'll allow us to mine gold from their streams."

Clyde added, "We're in. I've been to the island. The place is a shithole, but there's gold everywhere. We've cut a deal with Lucien and his chiefs, and we're prepared to invest—that is, if Davis Partners agrees to finance the rest of the deal. We're just doing the phase one part: no exploration, only alluvial mining—just mechanically extracting gold from the streams, like they do in *Yukon Gold*. Simple stuff, with a super-quick payback. We'll make a fortune."

"Who would manage the business?" I asked.

"That's me," Lucien said. "I've got a ton of experience, and I live there. Plus I have the backing of the chiefs, as well as George Washburn."

"Who's he?" I asked.

"The George Washington of Bougainville. He's the ex-commander of the BRA—the local militia."

Crossing my arms, I leaned back in my chair. "Like I tried to ask earlier—what about the people who control the big mine? Don't they have something to say about competition?"

Lucien answered, "You're talking about Rio Tinto and their local subsidiary, Bougainville Copper Limited. Their site—the Panguna Mine—was the cause of the civil war way back when and has been shut down for twenty-five years. We don't even know if they're coming back. We're not involved with their tenement. We've got our own sites, in partnership with George and the chiefs."

The absence of competition always appealed to me. Perhaps the meeting wouldn't be a waste of time after all. "I think I heard you use the term 'billions'?" I said.

"Most reports from qualified geologists estimate that the ore remaining in the Panguna Mine alone is worth over fifty billion dollars," Lucien replied. "The sixty-four-dollar question is: how many Panguna Mines are there on Bougainville Island?" He grinned.

I figured the answer would be scintillating. I didn't say anything, expecting Lucien to hit me with the number, but he waited me out. "Okay, okay, I give up. How many?"

"Probably four to five."

I'm sure my face reflected relief, let alone interest. I looked over at Clyde as he beamed back at me. I said, "I guess you're off the hook—for now." Shame on me if I wasn't interested in an island with billions in gold; a place like that might offer me a way to double down on my recent losses in China. "But I'd have to know a whole lot more about your deal before we'd consider raising money for it, and I can't imagine how I'm going to do that."

Lucien quickly interjected, "Be my guest in Bougainville."

"What about *Monster Gold*?" Rolly interrupted.

Everyone ignored him.

"How much would your group put into this deal?" I asked Clyde.

"Take Lucien up on his offer, and I'll pay for your trip," Clyde offered, giving me his Hollywood two-step.

I kept looking at him.

"Business class all the way," Clyde said.

Stupidly, I didn't totally dismiss the notion of going ahead. My next question confirmed me as an idiot. "How do you get there?"

12

Perfect Timing

Normally, someone from the investment world wouldn't dream of entangling themselves in a place like Bougainville. Back when I was one of them, I took a different point of view: such an attitude may not have been short-sighted, but it was definitely short of imagination.

I began my career as an investment banker, and then became an investor. There's a difference. When I graduated from business school, I was hired by Salomon Brothers, a big Wall Street investment banking firm. For five years, investment banking is what I did, both at Salomon Brothers and then at J.J. Laurel & Co., a smaller firm with a prestigious list of partners, including two men who ran for president of the United States. Investment banks, unlike regular banks, don't make loans or accept deposits. We raised money for corporations, governments, and projects, selling issuers' equity and debt securities to financial institutions and individuals. An investment bank is nothing more than an agent, a middleman. You're perpetually conflicted, and it's easy to turn into a financial whore.

I became an investor when the investment banking firms that employed me asked me to raise money for management teams that didn't know what they were doing. Trying to help as best I could, I would watch, dismayed, while the person at the controls caused the mission to fail. They say that all business entails a jockey—the head of the company—and a horse—the business its leader is trying to ride. Business problems were usually the jockey's fault. True, either could be flawed, but even if a horse was ill, a good jockey could often cure it.

Just like a good jockey, a skilled investor can make a horse their own. My first shot at being an investor involved an electric power company. Before I took the reins of my own enterprise, an experience while working at J.J. Laurel & Co. taught me what to avoid. There, I had signed up California Power & Light, a fledgling client trying to develop a fifty-megawatt project making electricity from the Central Valley's orchard cuttings. But the head guy, Franz El Paso, was better at running up bar tabs than he was at managing the company, and I watched a perfectly good project sink into the California desert. Soon afterward, together with Bobby McDermott, my partner at J.J. Laurel & Co. and Salomon Brothers before that, we took a shot at establishing our own power company, Catapult Energy, to try what Franz had failed to do. We succeeded, but not because we were any smarter than Franzie: we just stayed sober and went to work every day.

People who don't know me assume that someone who attended business school and went on to a Wall Street career must suffer from an odious desire for money. Not me. In my view, the sole purpose of earning money was to make life more convenient. Life was not about money; it was about opportunities. I was never interested in money for its own sake; the opportunities came first. I had to be careful telling investors that; some of them might hold it against me.

Over time, I learned that the truly good opportunities, like Catapult Energy, come along once in a blue moon. Building a business is like creating an artwork. You choose the right mediums—the plan, the people, and the product—and hope the timing is right. When it is, you've got to jump.

These days, practically the only people coming up with new business concepts are computer programmers, and it's very competitive out there, even for the techies. For an undergraduate art major like me, the optimum place to hatch a new business was more likely to be overseas, in those parts of the world that hadn't caught up with civilization as we know it. The more exotic, the better.

While investment banking stopped being my vocation in favor of investing, it remained a good way to pay the bills while I waited for lighting to strike. That was Davis Partners' role: to serve as a comfortable place to hang my hat and make a few bucks while I waited for a business opportunity to be born that I could mold and shape.

Over the period of time I was in the industry, investment banking had become a lousy business. Some rogues got greedy, and then the politicians killed the Street with legislation and regulations. At one point, my colleagues were known as captains of industry, but more recently, the mainstream media informed the public that everyone in the financial sector was a crook. Even though you went through twenty years of schooling, bootstrapped businesses that grew to employ hundreds of people, and paid your taxes, the prevailing narrative seemed to indicate that the world would be better off without you.

When I first entered the investment banking industry it was glorious, and there were hundreds of investment banks across the country. Now there are only about ten firms left, most concentrated in New York City. When we took Catapult Energy public, the investment bankers' offering expenses totaled a quarter million dollars: a reasonable sum. Years later, when we listed the shares of another company I created, Middle Kingdom Hydroelectric Corporation, the bill was close to three million. With the industry the way it is, it's virtually impossible for small but promising companies to raise money, flushing them into the maws of the venture capitalists—the biggest financial whores of all.

If you're paying for the cost of complying with today's investment banking regulations, there's not much left over with which to hire good people. When I left business school, becoming an investment banker at a prestigious Wall Street firm was enough to get me to kneel down by my bed and say my prayers every night, not just on Sunday at church. Except for those at the industry's top ten firms, many people in the business today are a lower form of life than even the politicians who regulate it. By 2015, most of the personnel I was forced to hire would have been just as comfortable out on the street dealing a hand of three-card monte.

I felt like something was missing in my life, didn't like the investment banking business anymore but needed to replenish my bank account, and was looking for one last investment opportunity as a jumping-off point. Along came Clyde, looking to finance a gold mine in a far-off place called Bougainville. The timing was perfect.

13

With the Philistines

I might as well describe what happened to me in China before I get too far into this story. It's the reason I found myself back in New York City, on the rebound.

I first traveled to China in the 1980s on behalf of my first power company, Catapult Energy. We specialized in developing hydroelectric projects. Allis-Chalmers, the sole remaining US manufacturer of hydroelectric turbine-generators, had filed for bankruptcy and left its customers in the lurch. We were desperate to find an alternative equipment manufacturer. Much to my surprise, a Chinese-American friend told me that salvation waited in his ancestral homeland, which was, in his words, "the hydroelectric capital of the world." It was the truth, but I'd had no idea. That just shows how insular Americans were back then.

I found myself involved in something that, up to that point, sounded like a non-sequitur: an American travelling to the People's Republic of China in order to bail out his business. I probably wasn't the first, but I definitely wouldn't be the last. If I had to queue up those who also drank Kool-Aid from the China trough, they'd form a line that would stretch around the block. Unlike me, they were people from well-known organizations like General Motors, Coca-Cola, John Deere, and Goldman-Sachs.

Back then, as long as one could deal with the lack of Western conveniences, China was like a fairyland.

The people—at all levels of life, from business leaders to the busboys at the hotels—treated foreigners like royalty. Foolishly, most of us convinced ourselves we deserved it. After all, we were Westerners. We possessed things that our deprived Chinese friends lacked, which we were certain they found important too: university degrees from Ivy League schools; nice cars; summer homes at the shore; and a certain amount of international *savoir faire*. We misled ourselves. What's worse, I suspect that my Chinese friends were aware of our self-congratulatory delusions—but played along.

The truth was, the cosmetic ornamentation of our lives mattered little to most Chinese. They simply needed foreigners for their money. Whether it was a Chinese company looking for capital, or a gold-digger at the bar in a hotel lounge seeking a wealthy husband, all but a few were after the same thing. As soon as the intractable Chairman Mao died in 1976, the more flexible leaders who followed him went to work on a well-conceived, nationwide plan. Everyone was in on it.

In China at the time, there were barely a few dollars of equity. Sure, they had large banks with millions in deposits, but no economy can go farther than its available equity will take it. Other than a handful of secretive, wealthy families holed up in Hong Kong, China had almost no sources of equity, but the country's leaders needed the economy to grow rapidly, and for that they needed investment capital. They plotted to lure Americans to the "Middle Kingdom" to spend—or better yet, invest permanently—equity dollars. The more well-intentioned the parties—read naïve—the better.

The suckers weren't limited to business types. University professors and administrators, journalists and media people, a clutch of US presidents out in front of a broad swath of American politicians, as well as leaders from other Western nations, climbed on the China bandwagon. Even some military leaders did so, although most remained rightfully dubious. In the end, stupidly, most of us believed the same thing: Not only did the Chinese like us, but they wanted to *be* like us too. While we foreigners spent most of our time coining profits, reserving little capacity to contemplate the long-term meaning of our activities, it was easy to assume that the Chinese would, after their country was fully developed, naturally take their place alongside the other heavenly bodies in the universe: our universe.

Who would have ever thought that it was all part of a well-conceived, subversive plan? I could see a few patterns emerging, but I didn't put it all together until it was too late.

My impression was that China would continue to be a big, profitable sandbox in which to play, and I was happy to do so. Back in 1984, as Catapult Energy's engineering team and I finalized the price of our first Chinese hydroelectric equipment purchase, we became giddy: the turbine gensets would cost a mere 30 percent of their American counterparts. (We only learned much later that our joy was more than surpassed by that of our counterpart, the Chinese turbine-genset manufacturer, which had been prepared to sell us equipment at 10 percent of US market, if necessary.)

Thanks in part to our inexpensive Chinese equipment, Catapult Energy's business plan met with financial success. After we sold the company, it was only logical that I would revisit China while organizing my second power company, the New Land Power Corporation. And after we sold New Land, when I needed to draw three of a kind in 2006, it made perfect sense to go back to China to establish the Middle Kingdom Hydroelectric Corporation.

Unlike my two earlier power companies, which were headquartered in the New York City area and developed projects primarily in the US, Middle Kingdom was a total China play. Headquartered in Beijing, the company developed and owned twenty-seven hydroelectric projects, all located in the PRC, and employed over a thousand employees; all but a handful were Chinese.

I created the business plan for Middle Kingdom, and with our management team I financed, owned, and operated our company's hydro projects. But our bet at Middle Kingdom depended entirely on one guy: Lin Boxu. Our princeling.

There are many types of relationships one can have in China, but there's only one that truly matters: if you want to get things done, you must be partners with a princeling. The United Kingdom has the royals, the United States had the Kennedys, and the People's Republic of China has the princelings. These lucky few—no more than a couple hundred, give or take—are the progeny of the Chinese Communist Party's founding fathers. If you are partners with a grandson of Chairman Mao, you're partners with a princeling; if you're partners with a granddaughter of Deng Xiaoping, you're partners with a princeling. If, on the other hand, you're partners with the governor of a major Chinese province—but the governor is not of princeling lineage—you're seated in general admission.

Lin Boxu's grandfather was a key elder statesman of the CCP. Close friends with Sun Yat-sen, he'd been one of Chairman Mao's most trusted advisors and his first finance minister. The man was revered in China, as was his grandson. Our princeling had little to do with the company's day-to-day business, but that didn't matter. Middle Kingdom became the largest foreign-owned power company in China, but we wouldn't have been allowed to exist without Lin.

Lin's corporate title was meaningless for Western purposes—he was chairman of Middle Kingdom's Beijing subsidiary—and he didn't take an active role in management. Other than on payday, he only came to the office on the days when I was in town. In China at that time, employees were not paid electronically, or even by check; rather, it was cash on the barrelhead. We kept a safe in the office, and every fortnight, Lin liked to stand at the door at closing time, handing out envelopes of one-hundred-RMB notes to the employees.

I considered Lin a good friend. Sure, the basis of our relationship was commercial, but we liked each other. We talked about art—me discussing twentieth-century contemporary work, and Lin describing his collection of Chinese antiquities, one of the highlights of his life. At Lin's invitation, I took my family to stay with his at his second home in Sydney, Australia, where we spent ten days touring the eastern seaboard of the country and snorkeling in the waters of the Great Barrier Reef. I trusted Lin completely.

Lin and I had first gotten to know each other when he sent Chinese emissaries to Wall Street to inquire about the possibility of raising equity investment for a portfolio of Chinese companies that he controlled. When his colleagues told me who they worked for in China, I knew that serving Lin's interest could lead to much greater opportunities. Davis Partners proceeded to raise millions in US institutional equity financing—the best kind—for several of Lin's companies, and a strong relationship was forged.

Later, when I learned that Lin's father had been the head of Beijing's Ministry of Electricity, I came up with an idea. I suggested moving beyond raising money from US investors for Chinese companies to establishing our own US-registered company to pursue hydroelectric power projects in China. Lin was equally enthused, but cautious. "Would your investors be interested in that?" he asked.

"Some of them have questioned why we haven't done it already," I answered.

"What else do we need to do?"

"The institutions won't give us a dime to establish our own company unless we have skin in the game," I said.

Lin did what all Chinese do when they're not sure of what's being said, and acted inscrutable.

I knew he probably didn't understand my idiom, and I didn't want him to be uncomfortable. "We must invest equity capital ourselves," I explained. "My management team and I will probably need to put up a million, but you only need to invest a fraction of that."

"How much?" The tone of Lin's voice indicated that my answer really mattered.

"Truthfully? My guess is they wouldn't do it unless you invested a hundred thousand."

"RMB?"

I shook my head. "Dollars."

Lin stared down at his shoes, and then raised his head and grinned. "I'm Chinese. I'm supposed to be getting money from Americans to do deals in China, not the other way around." I didn't say anything.

"You think this will work?"

"I'm sure it will."

Lin agreed, we assembled our grubstake, and Middle Kingdom was born. It thrived, and both of us made millions as the value of our investment skyrocketed. We took the company public and listed it on the New York Stock Exchange; soon, Middle Kingdom was recognized around the world. As most Chinese power companies spewed pollutants into the sky while arguing that they had no options, here was an outlier—a foreign-registered entity, of all things—demonstrating to anyone who cared that clean, renewable energy was a viable alternative in the PRC.

Ron Jones, my favorite US regulatory lawyer, used to counsel me about trying to be too aggressive in the face of governmental forces you can't control. When I urged him to push the Federal Energy Regulatory Commission for favorable rulings, he urged me to be cautious.

"What difference does it make?" I asked.

Ron took a while to answer me. "Well, the first ruling you win is fine, like a little shiny light you hang on a tree during the holidays. But if you get too ambitious and hang a slew of those lights in the branches, you never know. Those commissioners might take a step back and say to each other, 'That's not merely a tree with lights—that's a Christmas tree.'" He eyed me carefully. "The last thing you want to be with the FERC is an attention-getting Christmas tree."

Unfortunately, success turned Middle Kingdom Hydroelectric Corporation into a Christmas tree. Our audience wasn't the FERC, but the Chinese Communist Party. It turned out that they didn't just view us as an irritant; they wanted us gone. In the US, if we had found ourselves at cross purposes with the powers that be, we could have litigated and appealed. In China, there was no contest.

On October 1st, 2012, in Beijing, six years after we had founded Middle Kingdom, our receptionist Rachel buzzed me at my desk.

"There's someone on the phone from the PLA," she said. "They're asking for you."

"What?" I turned around and looked through the glass wall separating my office from Lin's. "Lin should take this; is he here today?"

"He was earlier. I don't know where he's gone; today's a holiday, after all. You'd better talk to them," she said.

"Go ahead and put the call through," I said. In a moment my phone buzzed again, and I picked up. "Jack Davis."

"*Ni hao, Daviszhong,*" someone said, and continued in language that was unintelligible—until they pronounced the last three words, "People's Liberation Army."

"I think this must be a mistake. I don't know who you are."

"No, *Daviszhong.* We talk you."

"Look, I need to get my partner Lin to speak with you. Do you know Lin Boxu?"

"No, *Daviszhong;* we talk you. We want buy your company."

"Sure you do." Thinking it was a crank call, I hung up.

An hour later, Rachel announced that I had a visitor. From her voice, I could tell she was nervous. I walked out to the lobby to find several uniformed officers of the People's Liberation Army milling around in front of the reception counter, together with a wizened Chinese man with greasy hair and an ill-fitting, dark suit.

"Ah, *Daviszhong,* is it?" the man said when I appeared. "*Ni hao, ni hao,*" he greeted me, never looking me in the eye. "My name is Mr. Zeng. Pleassse," he said the way a Chinese waitress does when she's directing you to your table. As if he had been in the company's office before, gesturing with a sweep of his arm, he invited me into my own boardroom. We sat down at the end of the table while the army stooges stood at attention along the wall.

I had been in China long enough to learn that anytime the PLA sends a uniformed delegation led by someone in a suit, it's trouble.

"Will you have tea, Mr. Zeng?"

The little man held up his right palm. "No, *Davizzhong*. No tea. We talk now. We want buy your company."

"I'm very sorry, but it's not for sale."

"We wish you say yes." As he said the words, he held his rust-colored teeth together and stretched his lips across them into what was supposed to be a smile, his eyes blinking slowly like a lizard's.

"I'm sorry."

They arrested me the next day via an exit ban at the Beijing airport.

It was Friday. I always flew back from Beijing's Terminal 3 to JFK on the Air China flight, leaving at one in the afternoon on the second and fourth Fridays of the month. When I handed my passport and travel documents to the immigration officer in the plexiglass booth at the airport, she glanced at me oddly before pushing a button on her desk. I remember thinking that I had gone through the process a hundred times and had never realized that immigration officials had buttons on their desks. A lone PLA officer in camouflage and a beret, wearing high, hobnailed boots and carrying a short-barreled machine gun slung over his shoulder, stomped across the marble floor behind the row of immigration booths until he got to the one where I stood. He slapped his heels together as he turned toward me, and then motioned for me to come his way. When I was a yard away from him, he held his two hands out toward me as if in prayer and nodded at me like I should imitate him. I didn't want to—I had a feeling what would happen next—but didn't think I had much choice. I put my hands together; he jerked a set of plastic, strap-like handcuffs out of his back pants pocket and cinched them around my wrists, cutting me, and, in front of hundreds of dumbfounded international travelers, led me away.

The PLA officer took me to an airport jail facility, just an ordinary office really, windowless, with iron bars lining the single door inside and out. There were two other miscreants in the room, both Chinese, and some ordinary police officers who didn't speak English. One of them was playing games on his mobile phone. I turned away from the policemen, pulled out my mobile phone, and was trying to send a text to Zhu Zhu, my assistant, when one of the policemen saw what I was doing and grabbed my phone, yelling at me in Mandarin.

I sat alone in the jail cell for three hours before a police officer who spoke English arrived. She blew into the room and made a fuss greeting me, hanging up her coat, arranging a chair at a desk across from where I sat, and unpacking and assembling her computer. I didn't speak. After several minutes adjusting her computer, the woman squared up in her seat and blurted out, "You know why you're here."

I told her the truth, which was that I had no idea.

Her mobile phone rang. She answered, and handed the phone to me. "Pleassse. Your lawyer."

It was Zhu Zhu on the phone with my lawyer. They explained what was going on. The People's Liberation Army had arranged to have me arrested and slapped with an exit ban, which meant I was prohibited from leaving China. After some negotiations, I was being released to the custody of my attorneys. My lawyer said the PLA was my antagonist; they were trying to intimidate me for some reason. Their pressure was unlikely to end anytime soon, and at a minimum, I would have to pay a significant amount of money to be able to get out of the country. I could probably leave China in a week or so, but this could happen again, and likely would continue until they got what they wanted. When she pushed me to explain things to her, asking what the PLA was after, I balked, telling her I didn't know and needed to speak to Lin.

Zhu Zhu and Mr. Xie, my driver, picked me up outside the departure terminal an hour later. "Have you spoken to Lin?" I asked Zhu Zhu.

"No. No one can find him."

"Christ almighty." I had no idea what was going on. "How much did it cost us to get me out?"

"Five hundred thousand dollars."

"Jesus Christ." I kept trying to call Lin, but couldn't get him. In an hour, we were back at the Poly Centre, our office building in downtown Beijing. It was the end of the workday and start of the weekend, and people were streaming out of the building. I rode up in an empty elevator with Zhu Zhu. As the door opened at our floor, I stepped out and came face-to-face with Lia Chen, our Beijing CFO, who was waiting with a group of people to take the elevator down.

"Oh, Jack, I'm sorry," she cried when she saw me, the blood draining from her face as she held her hands to the sides of her head, wailing as she moved to the rear of the car, as if she was trying to get away from me.

I stepped out into the hallway, disturbed, as the elevator doors slammed behind us. "What was that all about?" I said to Zhu Zhu. "Lia looked at me like I was dead."

Zhu Zhu was tough, but it was still difficult for her to say this to me. "It's your loss of face. Now, for her, you *are* dead."

After more legal wrangling and additional bribes, I flew home a week later. For days I tried to reach Lin with no luck, which had never happened before. Finally, I gave up trying to call him and sent him an email saying we needed to speak about the PLA's actions as soon as I returned to Beijing. I received no response to that either. Meanwhile, Zhu Zhu was right; as far as our demoralized organization was concerned, it was indeed as if I had died. I received no communication from anyone at Middle Kingdom.

I did get a curious email from my friend Miao Wang in Beijing. A financial analyst, Miao and I first met when he applied for a job at Middle Kingdom. Even after I explained that we were only hiring engineers at the time, Miao continued to press me every few months for a position, explaining that he really wanted to work for a company with both a Western pay scale and transparency. Over time, I came to know Miao well and found that I enjoyed him, even as he kept pressing me for employment. I never hired Miao, but that didn't prevent us from becoming good friends. I discovered that he was extremely well-connected to the upper levels of Beijing's political hierarchy, which didn't hurt.

Miao's email said he was looking forward to working with me in the future, "wherever that might be." I wondered where Miao thought I was going. His English wasn't perfect; I attributed his quirky message to mistaken syntax.

I was taking a risk by returning to China, but I had no choice. There was no way to resolve the problems remotely. A few days before my pending departure for Beijing, I received an email from Jing Cao, one of our Chinese shareholders. He asked if I could detour to Hong Kong on my way to Beijing; he and a group of fellow Middle Kingdom shareholders wanted to meet with me. It was a standard request. I agreed, and indicated that I would adjust my flights and stop by his offices when I came through Hong Kong the following Tuesday.

Ushered into Jing's boardroom the next week, I was surprised. At least fifteen people were seated around the table, all Chinese and looking serious. Other than Jing, I knew only one of them, Mr. Zeng, the wizened man sitting at the far end of the table. He was the same PLA operative who had visited my office in Beijing and offered to buy Middle Kingdom. This time, he was equally efficient, but took a different approach. "Mr. Davis, I'm confused," he said, not looking confused in the slightest. "Why are you, a *laowai*, the chairman and chief executive officer of Middle Kingdom Hydroelectric Corporation, a company doing business in China?"

A conversation that starts that way isn't a conversation.

At the end of our brief meeting, as he ushered me out of the boardroom, Jing handed me a thick document. It might as well have been a cold mackerel. I glanced at the cover; it looked like a proxy statement.

Outside in the reception area, I sat down and studied the paperwork. It was a proxy statement, all right—only a draft, but its message was clear. A group of Chinese investors, ignoring SEC protocols—which was illegal, but following the rules would have tipped us Americans off—had scoured the world's financial capitals to find Middle Kingdom stock for sale. They paid large premiums—mainly to Middle Kingdom's greedy American shareholders, organizations managed by people I thought were my friends—to acquire 60 percent of Middle Kingdom's shares. As soon as the papers were filed and the proxy was finalized, they—that is, the Chinese guys sitting in Jing's boardroom, representing the People's Liberation Army, whomever— would own a majority of Middle Kingdom's shares. They could call a special board meeting, throw out the old board and management, vote in replacements, and do whatever they wanted with Middle Kingdom. They could even make the company go away.

Depressed and feeling ill, I flipped through the pages of the draft proxy statement, gathering the pertinent facts. Past the boilerplate, I arrived at the shocking news in the back. The tops of my ears began to burn. The Chinese shareholders had already prepared a new slate of directors to govern Middle Kingdom, led by their new Chair- man—Lin Boxu. The saliva ducts inside my mouth began to secrete, what happens right before I puke. I had staked my financial future on Middle Kingdom. Losing control of the company could wipe me out and put me on the brink of ruin. I hurried out of the building and walked back to my hotel, the Mandarin Oriental, in a daze.

I went to the Captain's Bar, ordered a drink, downed it, and ordered another. Gathering myself, I pulled out my mobile phone and punched in Lin's number. When he answered, he sounded close by. I said, "Are you in Hong Kong?"

"No," is all he said.

He never sounded like he did that day on the phone. I knew it wasn't good, but I needed to push ahead anyway. "Do you know what's going on?" I asked lamely.

"No."

I cleared my throat. "Have you seen the proxy statement Jing's group is planning to send the company?"

"No."

Foolishly, I felt a pang of hope. "I've been trying to get ahold of you for weeks. I'm sure this is all related to my exit ban last month. I just met with Jing and a group of Chinese investors. They told me that they want to throw me out—as well as my American management and board members—replace us with Chinese people, and take over the company. They gave me a draft proxy statement summarizing their intentions. It says you're the chairman of the new group."

"I would never agree to such a thing," Lin said.

"Really?" Maybe I had a fighting chance. With a princeling on my side, anything was possible.

"I need to speak to some people," Lin said. "I'll call you back."

"Please do, Lin. Thank you. I'll wait in my room for your call."

He never called. I never saw Lin again.

That is, until Bougainville.

14

The Land of the Unexpected

On Labor Day weekend in 2015, I spent the last days of summer at my beach house in Watch Hill, a resort town on the rocky Rhode Island seacoast. As soon as the holiday was in the books, I planned to fly to Bougainville to check out Clyde's gold-mining venture. Davis Partners could use the fees, but I can't say I was looking forward to going.

Googling Bougainville, I read everything I could find. After doing so, I concluded that most readers would have crossed it off their travel lists. For me, its prospects appeared uncertain, yet hopeful, in a perverse sort of way. The place had gone through a brutal civil war—what the locals called "the Crisis"—and outward appearances indicated that even though the event had ended fifteen years earlier, Bougainville hadn't recovered. Lucien Sump hadn't overstated its resource potential—experts named the Panguna Mine one of the world's largest and most profitable, and Bougainville Island among the earth's most prospective sites for precious minerals—but despite latent riches, the place seemed like a rudderless ship with no one at the helm. To add to the intrigue, I learned that Bougainville, currently an autonomous region of Papua New Guinea with its own elected president and legislature, was scheduled to conduct an independence referendum within the next five years, and right after that, would hold new elections. Depending on the outcome of the referendum, the person who won the presidential election might well become the leader of the newest nation on earth. Maybe I was the only one dumb enough to form this conclusion, but it smelled like an opportunity.

Lucien had flown back to Bougainville, but he was still making his presence felt. He weighed in every couple of days, usually via email, and even telephoned from Bougainville a few times via scratchy, overseas telephone calls. He pressed to make sure I followed through on my pledge to visit what he termed "my island." In somber tones, he also warned that if I didn't get there soon, someone else might show up and apply for mining licenses at "our sites." I guess he didn't realize that every amateur employed the same type of lame threats.

Googling Lucien, I found his background more troubling than Bougainville's. Although early in Lucien's career he'd had a nice cup of coffee via a gold-mining deal on the West Coast, everything else he'd touched had gone bust. I ran into a lot of people like that: lucky bursting out of life's starting gate, they'd convinced themselves they were better than everyone else and didn't have to work as hard, but after that, nothing good happened. Apparently, after the Crisis, Lucien had come to Bougainville at the invitation of its first elected president, but the guy had died in office, and Lucien's prospects seemed to have evaporated. I couldn't tell if he had any management skills, but I doubted it. He was the deal's weak link.

My due diligence on Bougainville did confirm that Lucien was telling the truth as far as his buddy George Washburn was concerned. George's name was mentioned in most of the literature I read about the Crisis. There was even a film made about the war, titled *The Coconut Revolution*, but for some reason Washburn's name didn't come up.

After the meeting with Clyde and Lucien in our New York office, I ran the idea of financing an alluvial gold mine in the South Pacific past Elizabeth Krupp, my business partner of twenty years. She told me I was out of my mind. Armed with that appraisal, I figured I'd better call the guys who were my best sounding boards before I went down there, see if they thought Elizabeth was right.

Royce Morgan was a fund manager, and the savviest guy I knew in the investment business. Starting with Catapult Energy, I had been lucky enough to attract Royce's investment funds as an investor in most of the companies I started. Before I described any situation to him, I rehearsed. He didn't have a lot of time, and even less to suffer fools. He lived a couple blocks away from me in Watch Hill. When I got him on the phone, he said he was still in town but leaving shortly; if I met him at his hotel in the next hour, we could have a cup of coffee together before he left. Thirty minutes later on the veranda of the Ocean House, Royce listened politely. Squinting his slate blue eyes, he said the situation sounded somewhat "remote," compared to a normal Davis Partners' financing, but then ended the conversation the way he always did, saying he hoped I would be happy. He offered to participate as a small investor, as long as I put my own money into the deal as well.

Doctor Sid was my other go-to guy. He and I had been classmates at Harvard Business School. Among the smartest guys in my section, he had been a physician on the staff at Memorial Sloan Kettering before realizing he was bored and in the wrong line of work. He found his way to HBS. After graduating, he had worked in the family business and made a lot of money, but still didn't feel he'd found his true calling. One day in 1989, Doctor Sid told me about his hunch that when the Iron Curtain fell, there would be thousands of Russian contemporary paintings for sale—cheap. For anyone with a few bucks daring enough to fly over there, a bonanza was possible. I said it sounded good to me. A decade later, the National Gallery of Art in Washington, DC sponsored a major show featuring the best of a new collectors' category that had taken off like a rocket: early twentieth-century contemporary Russian painting. The show featured prominently several works from Sid's collection. Doctor Sid had invested in Davis Partners and Middle Kingdom, and I had always made him money, although never as fast as he would have liked. He thought the Bougainville situation was as ripe as Russia before the Iron Curtain fell, and advised me to forget the idea of financing the transaction for Clyde. He thought we should do the deal ourselves.

Feeling more sure of myself, I reached out to Clyde to get debriefed on everything he had learned while down in Bougainville.

"The place is a shithole," Clyde said.

"I recall you expressing that sentiment."

"Seriously, there's no place to stay except Lucien's house, which is a dump. There are no restaurants—none you'd want to eat in, anyway. And, oh—you'll owe me bigtime for this—it's critical you hit the duty-free in Hong Kong on your way there."

"Otherwise, it's jungle juice martinis?" I said.

"How'd you know about jungle juice?" Clyde asked.

"You'd be surprised at some of the places I've been."

"I shouldn't be telling you this, but my partners think you're crazy. Don't think you've got to do this for me."

Once Lucien learned that Clyde and I had formalized the details of the trip, he stopped hounding me. We agreed that I would shack up at his place in Bougainville, arriving on a Tuesday and departing a week later. I told Lucien I needed to meet the chiefs and see the mining sites. Most importantly, I wanted to meet with someone in the government in charge of issuing mining licenses.

I left for Bougainville the following Friday. Only three years earlier, before the Chinese expropriated my hydroelectric company, I had travelled to China every two weeks for ten years. I thought I had a good idea what to expect on my current trip, but I was wrong. The civilized Cathay Pacific people got me as far as Hong Kong, but then, heading south over the endless Pacific, I was stuck on Air Niugini the rest of the way. I kept track of the time as I hopscotched across the international date line and multiple time zones. By the time I finally landed in Buka, one of Bougainville's two tiny air strips, it would be over thirty hours in airplanes and airports since leaving New York City.

It's impossible to fly to Bougainville without going through Port Moresby, the capital of Papua New Guinea. My flight from Hong Kong arrived at Port Moresby's international terminal at six in the morning, and the plane to Buka didn't take off from the domestic terminal until ten. Lucien explained that the terminals were next to each other, but just in case, he would send a man to collect me off the plane. The guy would help me navigate customs and immigration, take me down to the domestic terminal, and buy me a cup of coffee.

My flight from Hong Kong to Port Moresby was full of Asians, as well as a large group of young Americans in Birkenstocks who made sure everyone knew they were anthropologists. Eight hours out, the captain announced we would be landing soon. I looked out the window to get my first glimpse of Papua New Guinea. As we coasted through the cloud layer, it was still dark to the west, but eastward, over a jagged mountain range, the first rays of dawn struggled to breach the horizon. Port Moresby floated in a basin at the foot of its outlying hills as if suspended on a cracked pie plate of brownish dirt. As the plane circled the airfield, I viewed a landscape that would be difficult for anyone to describe with affection. Barren hills ranged below us, pocked with a rash of scraggly, bush-like trees. Down in the folds of dust-covered ridges, tin-roofed farm dwellings lay assembled out of accumulated junk, incapable of shielding their denizens from either weather or predators. I saw little humanity, and no livestock. The plane cruised lower, enabling me to make out pathetic attempts at real estate development, PNG-style. Arrayed in grid-like neighborhoods amid piles of garbage, rows of houses made entirely of corrugated metal sat baking on iron stilts, devoid of the two staples most critical to suburban life: vehicles and shade.

We landed on schedule, just after six a.m. Exiting customs and immigration with Lucien's guy nowhere to be found, I located the front door of the international terminal. Still inside the air-conditioned space, I asked someone who looked like a hotel concierge to direct me to the domestic terminal.

She folded up her clipboard and regarded me oddly. "Why are you going there, sir? The hotel buses stop here."

I explained that I wasn't staying at a hotel in Port Moresby, but transiting to a domestic flight. She then eyed me with real concern. "If you'll give me a minute, I'll arrange security for you." She spoke into her walkie-talkie.

That seemed excessive to me. A New Yorker, I knew there were certain places in the city where a person couldn't go, but it seemed inconceivable the same circumstances could be present in an international airport. "My friend told me that the domestic terminal was right next to the international one," I said, craning my head to have a look around. Then, through the automatic sliding glass doors streaked with beads of condensation, I saw the group of security guards outside the international terminal. There were five of them, all holding chrome-barreled, pump-action shotguns.

"That's right, sir," the lady said, smiling efficiently. Having solved my problem for the time being, she waited for someone to come to my aid and, in the meantime, returned to her hotel paperwork.

I stepped out of the terminal to take a look around for myself. As the doors glided apart, the rough, humid air wrapped around me like a sooty blanket. The guards wore brown and yellow uniforms saying they worked for a security company named Guard Dog. While they stared at me, I cased the place. Up to the left, the terminal ended, but down to the right, a long, dark walkway extended about five hundred yards to another building. "Is that the domestic terminal?" I called over to the security guards. When they responded that it was, I voiced my thanks to both the men and the concierge inside and started walking.

I encountered no surprises at first. The scene was reminiscent of most developing world airports I had visited. Across the street in the gloom, families sat quietly along the curbstone like birds on a wire, waiting for relatives. But then I saw others, loners or small groups of men who appeared less benign. As I spotted them, they receded into the shadows of the parking lot, lurking behind cars. They were watching me. I heard something behind me and turned to see a couple of the shotgun-toting security guards trailing me to provide impromptu protection. The concierge had been right; my short walk was ill-conceived. Not something I would advise the Birkenstock crowd to do.

I arrived at the domestic terminal just in time for the incoming dawn. Inside, the place was already bustling. Unlike the international terminal, the domestic building was not air-conditioned, and the atmosphere was stifling. I walked past a dozen check-in agents beleaguered by overburdened baggage queues stretching fifty yards, congratulating myself because I had only brought carry-on luggage.

A few minutes later, my ticket in hand, I passed through the security checkpoint. The alarm was triggered—probably by my belt-buckle—but the security lady just smiled and waved me through. It was because I was a white guy, I realized. It wasn't right; why should I be treated any better than the locals?

Once in the departure lounge, I exchanged some currency, then visited the café in the corner. I forked over a ten-kina note for a cup of coffee and the local newspaper, and sat down to read Port Moresby's *Post-Courier*. On the front page above a garish color photograph, a headline guided the reader to the feature article inside: *"American Woman Raped, Loses 3 Fingers on the Kokoda Trail, Page 2."*

Before I could read what had happened to the woman, I heard someone calling my name. "Jack Davis," a voice boomed through the terminal. "Jack Davis," the man called again. Everyone in the terminal craned their necks.

I looked up to see a stumpy, brown-skinned man in a T-shirt and cargo shorts approaching, reminiscent of one of Snow White's dwarfs. The man stomped toward me, his bearded face etched with a frown, thighs and calves looking like they were stuffed with bowling balls, and unlaced Timberland boots coming halfway up his shins. He did his best to appear oblivious of the commotion he was stirring up.

Clomping past the security machinery and into the terminal, he paid the security guards no heed as he blustered through. "Jack Davis," the guy yelled again, although he didn't need to. He had spotted me, the only white guy in the terminal, and was headed straight in my direction.

"Jack Davis?" the guy said for the last time as he arrived where I stood to greet him, the top of his shiny bald head six inches below mine. When I nodded, he said loudly, "You're early," as if I should have told the Air Niugini pilot to hold my plane until the man arrived at the airport first. He eyed the lurid front page of the newspaper on my table. "Come on. We'll bring your paper, but leave the coffee. I've got orders to buy you breakfast," he said. With that, he swept up my newspaper, folded it under his arm, and began to hoof it back the way he had come, waving me the wrong way through the airport security apparatus as the guards there saluted him, grinning among themselves at his antics, as if he was some sort of local hero.

The stumpy man didn't offer to take either of my bags. I followed him outside to the parking lot, where a guy in ratty clothes waited next to a beat-up compact car with its engine running. It occurred to me that these guys might not have anything to do with Lucien Sump, but there wasn't much I could do about it at that point.

"Say hi to Eki," the stumpy guy said. "Sit in the back seat," he ordered as he jumped into the car's shotgun seat. "Stop at the Gateway so I can get some cash," he said to Eki.

With Eki at the wheel, we putted off, the interior of the car well over ninety degrees Fahrenheit. I tried to roll down my window, but it wouldn't budge. Straining to reach thirty miles per hour, Eki's car sounded like it was near death, its muffler about to fall off. The stumpy man sat oblivious in the front seat behind Eki's shattered windshield, reading my newspaper.

Around the corner, a sign alerted traffic to the front gate of the Gateway Hotel. We turned into the driveway. The hotel compound was surrounded by a ten-foot chain-link fence topped with concertina wire. Inside, a trio of guards with the same style of pump-action shotgun as the guys at the airport lined the front stairway leading up to the hotel's reception area. Eki pulled up, and the person I had started to think of as Stumpy hopped out.

I saw him inside the lobby using a cash machine. A minute later, he returned to the car and we were on our way. "Now take me and Mr. Davis to the weigh-in," I thought I heard him say to Eki.

Stumpy didn't seem inclined to ransom me, and I grew more comfortable—to a point—with the notion that he worked for Lucien. Sometimes, after a trial period as I learned their redeeming features, I ended up amused by characters like him, and other times they turned out to be jerks. With Stumpy, I leaned toward the latter. "I've got two questions," I said to him over the racket made by Eki's car.

He craned his bald head around and looked at me.

"What do I call you?" I said to him.

"Sergeant—I'm retired—Greyson Trull, ex-PNG Defence Force, at your service," he said.

"That's a mouthful," I said. "How about Grumpy?" It sounded better than Stumpy. I intended my remark as an icebreaker, and hoped he got the joke.

"You said you had two questions," said Grumpy, not amused.

Eki managed to coax his vehicle to the top of a hill, and once beyond, picked up speed. We buzzed by auto shops and industrial yards along one side of the highway, scrubby flats packed with corrugated tin shacks on the other.

"What were those three men with shotguns doing back at the Gateway Hotel?" I asked.

Grumpy's eyes blinked back at me as if I were stupid. "You saw me using the cash machine, right?"

"A cash machine is all it takes to merit a shotgun squad?"

Grumpy didn't say anything, but turned around and went back to reading my newspaper. "Did you see this story?" he asked me, not lifting his nose from the pages of the paper.

"I didn't get that far."

"The stupid rapists were walking around after the fact, each of them wearing one of the girl's fingers tied around their necks. No wonder they got caught. Dumb motherfuckers."

Eki started to slow down to make a left turn. Across the highway was a parking lot surrounded by the obligatory ten-foot chain-link fence and concertina wire. Next to the parking lot sat the Weigh Inn Restaurant, a scruffy, two-story structure. The gate to the lot was closed. Out front, two security men holding shotguns perused Eki's vehicle, recognized its front seat passengers, opened the gates, and waved us in.

"I'm sure I can guess your response, but I've got to ask anyway. What's this crew doing here?" I said.

Grumpy gave me his "you-must-be-stupid" expression again. "People pay cash for breakfast."

We went inside the Weigh Inn, and Grumpy ordered me a serviceable meal of scrambled eggs and bacon. When I was finished, I pushed my plate away. "What do you do for Lucien?"

Grumpy acted like I had said something offensive. "*What do you do for Lucien?*" he mimicked. "I don't work for Lucien. I'm the brains of the organization."

"What organization?"

Grumpy said, "The one you're flying over to Bougainville to meet with. BROL," he said, using a term I'd never heard before. He looked at his watch. "Let's get you back to the airport."

We were driving along the highway, the airport five minutes away, when Grumpy decided to speak without being prompted. "My job is to advise the leaders of Bougainville."

"Who's that?"

"The first one—Jasper Kaboose, Bougainville's first president—died in office. The guy who's president now, Liuman Mogol, is worthless; he's a former PNG-born priest and half-Chinese. The next president will be George Washburn. You'll meet him later today in Bougainville. I was his batman when he was a lieutenant in the Defence Force, before he left to become the commander of the Bougainville Revolutionary Army. You know about the Defence Force?" he asked, but didn't wait for my answer. "It's those guys right there," he said, gesturing out the window as we rolled by a campus-like military compound. "My boys."

"What about some guy named Ishmael?"

Grumpy twisted all the way around in his seat, so he could look me in the eye. "What the hell do you know about Ishmael?"

I was surprised by his reaction. "Very little," I confessed. "When I was on the internet learning about Bougainville, I watched *The Coconut Revolution*, a movie about the Crisis. I thought it would contain a lot of information about George Washburn, but he wasn't mentioned. The film's trailer said it starred Jasper Kaboose and Francis Olu, who I gather was the titular head of the BRA, but this guy named Ishmael stole the show. He came off as an absolute tiger. It's funny; I can't find much else about him on the internet, not even his last name. I just wondered if you knew what happened to him."

"You don't want anything to do with Ishmael."

The remainder of our return trip to the airport took place without incident. As Eki came to a stop at the terminal entrance, he reached over the seat to hand me his business card. I thanked him, got out of the car, grabbed my bags, and was getting ready to skedaddle when Grumpy rolled down his window.

"You're forgetting something," he said, not lifting his head from the newspaper. "I paid for breakfast, and Eki gets a hundred kina."

I tried to reach across inside the car to hand Eki a hundred-kina note, but Grumpy swiped it. Then he held up two fingers in my direction.

"A hundred kina for breakfast?" I exclaimed. "That's thirty dollars."

"Welcome to the land of the unexpected," he said, smiling for the first time through stained teeth as I forked over another hundred-kina note. Grumpy resumed reading as Eki pulled away. Thirty minutes later, mercifully, my plane left Port Moresby behind in the dust.

15

The End of the World

Jetting on a steep trajectory up into bumpy clouds, we passed over the Owen Stanley Range of Papua New Guinea's mainland. I looked down. Rather than Port Moresby's sad terrain, the land below had turned wild but majestic, emerald-green and mountainous. I saw no roads or buildings. It was hard to believe people actually lived down there, and easy to understand why it took so long to discover that Papua New Guinea's highlands teemed with humanity. Primitive when Margaret Mead first arrived in the early part of the twentieth century, things couldn't have changed much. We climbed to cruising altitude. Tall cumulous clouds cast blue shadows across a perpetual, silvery sea. After two days of travel, my destination at the end of the world was only an hour away.

Soon after the flight attendants served tea and soft drinks, the captain advised us to fasten our seatbelts for the landing in Buka. I looked down to see a coastline dotted by a score of green, tufted atolls ringed with white sand beaches and acres of aquamarine shallows. Offshore, reefs formed natural breakwaters protecting the mainland. We circled the airport to land into the wind, giving me a panoramic view of both Bougainville and Buka Islands, and the narrow waterway between them that the locals called the Passage. In Buka Town, no two structures were alike. All sat on stilts and were topped with brightly colored, corrugated metal roofs held in place with logs and loose stones. Tall stands of coconuts, lined up in orderly, colonial rows, swayed in the gauzy humidity. We landed and coasted up to a small, open-air terminal that looked like it had been around since World War II. A crowd of people gathered outside one end of the building. Most were very black, their faces handsome, eyes bright, and skin smooth.

I walked off the plane, passed through a couple of security guys checking people's luggage, and went out to the parking lot. I scanned the crowd for Lucien Sump but didn't see a white person anywhere. It was blazing hot. I set my bags down and removed my bush jacket. Realizing I should have changed into shorts and a T-shirt for this leg of my journey, I looked in vain for shade.

Two women holding umbrellas for protection from the sun approached me. "Good afternoon," they both said, their voices nervous, but almost musical. "Please," they said in English with a lilt to it, offering me their umbrellas, their striking faces showing shy smiles and perfect, white teeth.

"Oh no, I couldn't do that," I said, smiling back at them. "You're very kind."

"Please, please," they said, more confident, growing insistent. "We don't want anything to happen to a visitor, and this must be very hot weather for you," the taller one said, taking on a measure of local responsibility.

I said, "You're right about that." As they edged closer, people started to push behind me to get out of the terminal, and the three of us found ourselves jammed together under the shade provided by the two umbrellas. I said, "Here, we can share."

The women nodded at me. The taller one examined my face. "You're not Australian?" she said, frowning.

I guess my accent gave me away. "No. American."

"American," they repeated in unison, broad smiles of relief lighting up their faces. "We love Americans," the shorter one said.

Just then I heard a car horn honking, and saw Lucien waving at me from a Toyota Land Cruiser with a taxi sign painted across its doors. I turned to the women. "My ride is here. Thank you, ladies. You've made my day," I said, shaking their hands and giving them an appreciative smile.

"You are most welcome," the shorter one said. "We hope you enjoy our island."

I hoisted my bags and walked toward the Toyota, where Lucien and a large group of men, clad in T-shirts and shorts, waited.

"Welcome to Bougainville," Lucien called as I got closer. "Gentlemen, meet Jack Davis, my new investor from America," he said to the crowd of men gathered around him. He selected one in front and nudged him my way. "Jack, say hello to Chief David."

A slight man no more than five feet tall with bluish-gray cataracts clouding his eyes limped forward and offered me his hand. When I took it and said hello, he wouldn't let go. I studied the old man's face; he couldn't see.

"Chief David is our senior member," Lucien added, "while George here is our fearless leader." He moved Chief David to one side and parted the group of men so that a big guy in the rear could squeeze through. The man pushed forward and shook my outstretched hand. "Hello," he said. "I'm George Washburn." He was taller than most of the men around him, close to my six-foot height, with a handsome face, prominent forehead, and aquiline nose under a hairline that was starting to recede.

I knew about George Washburn, a leader of the Bougainville Revolutionary Army, from my internet search, and had heard more about him from both Lucien and Grumpy. "I'm Jack," I said. "Nice to meet you. I understand you were a military leader for Bougainville during the civil war."

"Yes," George said. "People here call that war the Crisis." His kept smiling, his expression vague, as if he was unsure what to say next.

"Things are looking up now, thanks to men like George," Lucien said, "and guys who fought beside him, like Steven Toppis here." As if he were a schoolteacher on a class trip, Lucien reached behind George into the group and pulled forward his next candidate for introduction.

The man was the blackest human being I had ever seen, so black he was almost blue. His lustrous skin smooth and shiny, he was the size of an NFL linebacker. He grabbed my hand, his paw as big as a baseball mitt. "Steven," he said, grinning. "Welcome to Bougainville." His mouth was blood-red, as if he were Count Dracula's cousin. It was my first introduction to betel nut, the nut from the Areca palm infused with a nicotine-like chemical, and the South Pacific's favorite addictive substance. "Excuse me," Steven said politely, as he turned and spit a stream of red slime ten feet behind him and wiped his mouth.

Lucien introduced me to several more men, all chiefs, he said—Richard, Jacob, Ben, Mark, Suston, Francis, and others whose names I didn't hear or remember—who had come to Buka to honor the special visitor from America. Lucien seemed as he'd described himself in New York: the chiefs' man in Bougainville. He announced that we were late for lunch, and everyone piled into the Land Cruiser like horses heading for the barn.

Lucien took the middle front seat and told me to ride shotgun. When everyone had piled into the rear compartment and Chief David had scrunched himself into the tiny space on the front seat behind the stick shift, the taxi driver put the vehicle in gear, and we headed toward town. As I would learn, they called this version of the Toyota Land Cruiser a "ten-seater" for a reason: that was how many people it seated. That is, if three sat across the front seat and seven more lined the bench that rings three sides of the rear space of the vehicle. We had more than ten, and with a group of men who had been out sweating in the hot sun and one guy who'd been in planes for thirty hours, it smelled that way.

"If it's all right with you, Jack, we're having lunch with the mining department," Lucien said. "We're not up at this end of the island much, so it's best if we take care of that now."

"Sounds good."

Buka Town, with a population of a few thousand spread north of the Passage, was the home of the Bougainville government. The town was small, so we didn't need to go far. In a few minutes, our driver pulled alongside the mining department's ramshackle compound. Lucien invited me to accompany him inside while the others waited in the car. Other than to be seen with an American investor guest, Lucien's mission inside was only to verify with the women at the reception desk that they had made a lunch reservation for the group. His Australian accent became more clipped and pronounced when he spoke to the women. The way he addressed them, one would have thought they worked for him, not the mining department. Confirming that they had indeed set things up at the restaurant down the street, but not thanking them, he instructed the staff to contact their bosses and inform them they were expected promptly; we would wait at the restaurant. Back in the ten-seater, the driver dropped us off on the town's main drag a few minutes later, and Lucien herded us across the street to Reasons, a hotel and restaurant complex located alongside the Passage.

Trailing behind the group as we walked from the road to the restaurant, hopscotching red betel nut spittle all the way, I saw that most of the men were barefoot. Those who wore shoes—universally flip-flops—shucked them when they entered the building, as if they were visiting someone's home. A table for twenty was set on a balcony with views of the Passage, the South Pacific's answer to the Gulf Stream. A mile wide, the seawater in the Passage ran fast like a river, clear and blue and deep. Longboats, their outboard engines whining, darted to and fro. As if in slow motion, a lone fisherman in an outrigger canoe paddled by.

Once we were seated, Lucien called the waitress over. "Good afternoon," he said to her, confusion in her eyes as she contemplated the task of serving twenty people. "I'll make this easy for you. For starters, bring out two loaves of bread," he said, and when she looked more confused, added, "They like to eat bread while they wait." He gestured over the heads of the Bougainvilleans. "These men," he said, "all of them," he emphasized, "will have your half-chicken and chips." Turning to me he said, "Take a menu and let me know what you want. The surf and turf is good."

"I'll take chicken and chips too."

"You sure?"

I nodded. "And some water."

"I'd like a steak," George said, sitting next to Lucien.

The waitress departed and returned with glasses and pitchers of tap water.

George asked her to bring him a Coke.

The bread came next, two big loaves in plastic bags, but it didn't last long. The men devoured it and asked Lucien if they could have some more. He ordered two more loaves; it came, they inhaled those too, and then the people from the mining department arrived.

Our side stood up, and introductions were made. We were in the presence of Ferdy Mimosa, the minister of the Department of Mineral and Energy Resources and an elected member of Bougainville's House of Representatives; Gideon Donglu, the executive director of the mining department; the head geologist, a registrar, and some minor officials. The one woman in the group, Lesley, the executive director's assistant, seemed like the smartest of the bunch as she passed out copies of the new mining law and her business cards, answering a few questions from some of the chiefs. After the introductions, the mining department people took seats at the other end of the table. The waitress came, and they all ordered steaks. Under the table I thought I felt Lucien flinch from sticker shock. Then, while the food was prepared, we got down to business.

Lucien said, "George, I'll get things started, and then why don't you say a few words." With that, he stood up and surveyed the government officials at the other end of the table. "I'd like to start by introducing Jack Davis, my new American investor, from Wall Street—where the money is," he grinned.

I raised my hand in greeting.

Lucien continued. "I want to thank the mining department for coming to this get-together. As you know, our group of chiefs represents most of the customary landowners in central Bougainville. They are here to make a statement. We're anxious to get our licenses, bring mining back to Bougainville…and stop being beggars on our own land." As he uttered the last phrase, Lucien's voice turned strident, almost adversarial. The mining department people didn't smile.

Lucien sat down, and everyone immediately started talking among themselves in Tok Pisin, the local pidgin language that most islanders in Melanesia use as their *lingua franca*. A few minutes after Lucien had spoken, George used his fork to clang his water glass until everyone stopped talking. Then he rose and started speaking slowly in a sonorous tone, as if his was a burdensome but necessary task. George also urged the department officials to move ahead with their licensing work, but unlike Lucien, didn't scold them. "Please welcome Jack Davis, BROL's new investor," he said inaccurately, using the name of the organization I'd heard Grumpy mention earlier that morning. "Lucien went all the way to New York City to find him and bring him back to Bougainville."

The food arrived. Since we were in Australia's sphere of influence, I should have known that chips meant French fries. Conversation ceased, the Bougainvilleans attacked their meals, and no one said another word except for me and Lucien.

"I'm not BROL's investor," I said to Lucien.

"No, of course not."

"What is BROL, anyway?"

"Us," Lucien said as he gestured over the heads of the men at our end of the table. "I'll fill you in later."

After the dishes were cleared, the next hour contained presentations by the mining department personnel. Most of what I heard corresponded with what I'd learned on the internet. After the Crisis, Bougainville, now officially named the Autonomous Region of Bougainville, had earned a measure of governmental separation from Papua New Guinea but had done virtually nothing with it. Ten years after the first Bougainvillean elections, the government had finally gotten their act together to pass Bougainville's mining act in 2015, pursuant to which the crew at the other end of the table would soon be taking applications for, and issuing, mining licenses. No mining had taken place since Bougainville Copper Limited, Rio Tinto's subsidiary responsible for its Bougainville operations, had departed the island when the Crisis erupted back in 1989. Beyond that, the department guys couldn't have been more obscure. The executive director did welcome me, saying, "We need foreign investors," but didn't seem enthused.

When it seemed apparent that no further information from the mining department would be forthcoming, I leaned over to warn Lucien. "I'm going to have to pry some specifics out of them about the licenses."

Lucien whispered, "Don't be a fool. We've submitted the applications, and they're evaluating our paperwork now. The last thing we want to do is give them a reason to hold up the process."

"Try telling that to an investor."

Lucien hissed, "You don't understand. These licenses are child's play; the only important issue is obtaining them. We've applied for them, and they'll be granted."

As Lucien argued his case, George, still eating, leaned his head our way to listen.

Lucien gestured toward George. "Do you really think they're going to deny the commander of the BRA?"

George raised his eyebrows at me as he kept chewing.

Speaking softly but loud enough for both men to hear, I said, "I'm sorry to be a bother, Lucien, but you're the one who doesn't understand. I'm here to perform due diligence for Clyde, and it's got to be done. Either I get the answers I need from these guys, or we'll never be able to finance this deal."

Lucien said, "For now, you're going to have to take George's word for things." He glanced toward the BRA's intrepid commander for support.

George kept chewing his steak.

Maybe it was just that I'd been on a plane for thirty hours and was tired, but the interlude with Lucien and the mining department was a real downer. If anything, the man seemed to have an adversarial, almost colonial relationship with the government officials, and his dismissal of the importance of the license information was amateurish. I had serious doubts as to whether Clyde and I could rely on him. "I guess we'll need to revisit the topic later," I said to avoid an open argument, half-thinking that maybe I ought to see if I could catch an earlier flight off the island.

I didn't get the chance. Lunch adjourned soon afterward. We said goodbye to the well-fed mining department crew and headed back out into the blazing sunshine alongside the Passage, picking our way through the crowd. Bougainvilleans chewing betel nut were in the majority, both men and women, young and old, reddish juice hiding their teeth when they spoke or smiled. Children flitted around like moths, contenting themselves with their soft drinks. When they were finished, they tossed their empty cans onto a huge, tide-washed pile that shimmered in the sun along the shore.

At a depot-like spot on the waterfront, a swarm of longboat water taxis jockeyed. For a fare of two kina, they ferried passengers across the Passage from Buka Town to the south side. Dozens of men, women, and children, barefoot or in flip-flops, squeezed under the cover afforded by a grove of leafy shade trees until it was time to go. The boatmen beckoned and cajoled, and the customers dithered, trying to determine which longboat would leave shore the soonest. Then, their craft selected, the travelers lugged bags of rice bound for their cooking fires, or burlap sacks full of cacao beans or copra for the processing mills, dumped their cargo over the gunwales, and clambered aboard.

The jaunt across the Passage, salty spray whipping across our faces, lasted barely a minute. Once on Bougainville Island, we squeezed into Lucien's ten-seater and shoved off for Arawa, the heart of central Bougainville Island's mining region, four hours away.

Our route, which I was told was the only improved thoroughfare, ran from one end of Bougainville Island to the other. For the entire distance, about one hundred miles, the road hugged the reef-lined, eastern edge of the island, the Pacific a stone's throw beyond. After ten minutes, the electric power distribution wires that had extended south from town ended, and a layer of civilization came to a halt.

Bougainville Island not only needed more electrification, but a better road. Its primary use was for foot traffic. Along the way at any time, Bougainvillean men, women, and children, using machetes to clear their way, popped in and out of narrow, tributary paths leading off into the thick, green bush. Our ten-seater billowed dust as it clattered down the rock-ribbed thoroughfare, the racket often so loud that it was impossible to talk. The ten-seater was one of only a handful of vehicles on the road. After an hour, I hadn't seen any brand other than Toyota; I now began to appreciate how it was that they were the largest car company in the world.

The majority of the people I saw were school-aged children. In matching-colored, uniform-like smocks and shirts, they walked single file along the road as they headed home from school, sometimes being forced to jump out of the way of vehicles careening down the road. None of the children wore shoes. Whatever troubles plagued

Bougainville, no one had told them; as our vehicle flew by, all the boys and girls smiled and waved, their bright faces cheerful and welcoming.

At irregular intervals, we came through village clusters, some featuring a store or two. An hour south of the Passage, the settlements thinned out and tended gardens expanded. Armies of stout banana trees lined the road, bunches of green fruit curling down from stalks at the top. Papaya trees sprouted alone like sentries, the tops of their trunks at the leaf-line heavy with clusters of green pods, the ripe yellow ones ready to drop. Flowers—a dozen varieties of lilies, purple and red adenium, and hordes of moonflowers—were everywhere, most growing wild, with some planted along the roadside. We pushed on, and the land took on an agribusiness aura, our Toyota whistling through forests of coconut palms standing in dignified rows. In some areas the terrain appeared wild, as if untouched by man, with native sugarcane and dense jungle bordering the edge of the road.

Every fifteen minutes or so, we passed roadside prayer grottos harboring crosses, indicating a church was somewhere down the path. From time to time, sparkling ocean vistas appeared through the trees as if captured in Winslow Homer watercolors. Off-shore, I could see bright white lines of waves foaming over the reefs, while closer in, lagoons lapped up onto sandy beaches. To the landward side, the rugged Mt. Tore and the taller, volcanic Mt. Balbi, a wispy white cloud spiraling out of its maw, strained their green shoulders toward the sky.

Lucien saw me looking at the mountains and pointed to one further south. "That's Numa Numa, an extinct volcano. Below it are the remains of the Numa Numa Trail, a road built by your Army Corps of Engineers in the big war." As he drove us around a bend in the road, we encountered a surprising sight. Even though Buka Town had been sun-drenched, straight ahead in the sky loomed a thick, black cloud, ready to dump its contents on us. It began to pour a minute later, the raindrops so dense and heavy on the roof of the Toyota it sounded like we were inside a drum. Lucien said loudly over

the din, "It's always raining somewhere in Bougainville. Wait 'til you go up to the mountains."

As quickly as the rain had started, it stopped. We slowed to ford a rushing stream and, once across, stopped at a sandy beach to stretch our legs. The sun reappeared, as quixotic as the island itself. At first glance, Bougainville was gorgeous, a South Pacific paradise. Off to the west beyond the Emperor Range, the sun was beginning to set, its golden rays gilding a plantation on the slopes of Numa Numa. At the mountain's base, orderly rows of coconut palms ran toward the road, as if someone had brushed a comb through the green vegetation. But when I turned the other way to watch the surf roll to the shore, a wave containing a kaleidoscope of multi-colored plastic bags, spent flip-flops, and crushed soda cans slopped its catch up onto the beach like so many dead fish, joining tons more flotsam lying in decaying heaps across the sand.

Two men from our group of chiefs, standing together in the tall grass talking to one another, approached me.

"I'm Richard," said the little man who had been sitting directly behind me in the ten-seater. "From Atamo," he smiled through betel nut-stained teeth. "English no good."

I told him his English was fine. To make conversation, I pointed off toward the plantation. "What are those dark green trees underneath the coconut palms?"

"That cocoa," Richard said. "Foreigners call it cacao. It make chocolate," he said. "Many cocoa trees in Atamo."

"I think Richard's village has the most cacao trees," the second man chimed in as he inched closer, taller than Richard and roundish. "I'm Suston. I don't have a plantation like Richard, so I must earn my living playing the piano," he said, splaying out his fingers and wiggling them, his eyes twinkling behind gold-framed glasses. He wasn't chewing betel nut, and smiled with big white teeth set in pink gums. Both men seemed extraordinarily gentle.

"He can play piano with his toes. I see him," Richard said, and both of the Bougainvilleans chuckled.

"Where do you play your piano?" I asked.

"Not here," Suston said, and we all laughed. "Italy," he said, his face growing more serious. "I must go six months each year. It's my living," he said, using the phrase again.

"Five more minutes and we're out of here," Lucien called out to everyone.

As I started to head back to the car, Suston put his hand on my forearm. "Can you please answer a question?" he said, as both men faced me.

"Sure."

"Will you go back to America, or can you stay here and help us?"

I didn't know how to respond. I said that perhaps I might return in the coming months, but I needed to learn more information first. Then, out of time, we all got back in the Toyota and kept driving toward Arawa. Richard continued to speak to me through the transom from the back of the ten-seater, doing his best to try to convince me that I should stay in Bougainville, that I would like it. In addition to cocoa, he said, there was lots of gold in the streams in Atamo. He would show me.

I had wanted to speak to George Washburn, who was sitting next to me in the front seat, but he slept the entire time.

When we had been on the road a little more than three hours, Lucien came to life. He peered through the twilight to our left. "If you look over there," he said to me, extending his arm to point across a grassy field, "you'll see my backup plan."

I gazed in the direction he indicated. "You mean the cows?"

"Those aren't just cows," he sniffed. "That's as fine a Brahmin herd as you'll see this side of Queensland."

"What will you do with them?"

"Sell beef, of course," Lucien answered, speaking with more confidence than necessary. "A beast a day."

I suppose I could have offered encouragement, but I thought Lucien would benefit from a little honesty. "To these people? I can't imagine they've got the money. How many pounds does one cow produce?"

Lucien couldn't have felt that strongly about his cattle herd; he dropped the subject. In another fifteen minutes, he spoke again. "We're coming through central Bougainville now," he said. "Mining country." Five minutes later, he gestured at a dirt track running off to the right. "That's the cutoff to Atamo, one of the sites Clyde signed up for. You know Chief Richard? The little guy you've been talking to? That's his village. We'll visit it tomorrow."

"Where's the next site?"

"Isina; George's village."

"Are they the places with the best alluvial gold?"

I could tell Lucien heard me, but he didn't answer.

I thought the issue was important enough to come at it from another direction. "Are all these guys chiefs?"

"That's why they're with us. BROL's chiefs."

"Who are the most important ones?"

"Why?"

"Didn't you tell me these would be the first mining licenses issued since the Crisis?" I asked. "I'm just wondering if Clyde's sites were chosen partly as a result of politics between the chiefs, not just for their gold."

Lucien sounded annoyed. "Don't be absurd."

"I guess we'll know the answer when we sample the streams."

"What do you mean?" Lucien asked.

I said, "In the end, that's the only way we'll be able to select our sites. In a place where there's gold everywhere, it's one of the advantages of alluvial mining, if you ask me. When there's not enough gold, we'll just move to another river."

Lucien smirked. "What else did you learn in your weekend mining tutorial?"

"You got me there. I barely know a trommel from a wash plant," I fibbed. I had actually spent time researching the topic of alluvial gold mining, but didn't want Lucien to know. Later, when I asked him questions, I wanted to be capable of evaluating how knowledgeable—and truthful—he was.

In the meantime, for the next fifteen minutes I played along, saying I was eager to learn from him. I let Lucien make like a geologist, lecturing me about Bougainville's tectonic plates. As we approached a bend in the road, Lucien said, "Now for a change of pace. This is a place called Manetai. Do you see that steel tower in the jungle off to the right? That's another one of BROL's projects."

In the jungle along the road, a rusted hulk loomed twenty feet above the tallest trees. "What is it?" I asked.

"It's a limestone crushing and lime calcination facility. It produces high quality lime, a commodity Bougainville can sell anywhere in the world. Thanks to George here, BROL owns it, and we'll be redeveloping it soon."

I knew a few things about developing infrastructure projects, enough to suspect it might be the first of Lucien's schemes that made any sense. "If the lime quality is decent, that sounds promising."

I saw that George had woken up and heard Lucien's lead-in, and I hoped he would add something, but he just looked at me, his eyes expressionless.

Ten minutes later, we arrived on the outskirts of Arawa. As we drove by a huge metal shed alongside a tank farm, Lucien said, "That's ours too. Bougainville's first bio-diesel project."

"You've been busy," I said. Looking closer, I saw that the facility was frayed at the edges, its equipment rusting. "It doesn't appear to be operating," I added a moment later, my comment directed at a guy who, in my mind, was turning out to be an unfocused charlatan.

Lucien kept driving, lips pressed tight.

We came around a sharp corner into what looked like the center of town. Arawa bore little resemblance to Buka Town. As opposed to a ramshackle jungle settlement, Arawa looked as if someone had plucked a '60s suburb out of Long Island and plopped it into the jungle. As Lucien described it, that's what had happened. Beginning in 1968, Bougainville Copper Limited, Rio Tinto's operating subsidiary on the island, was commissioned to spend billions building not only the Panguna Mine, but two employee towns: Arawa along the sea and Panguna Town on the mountain next to the mine.

Arawa's streets were arranged on a grid, with curbstones and sewers; downtown was a series of strip malls. Or what was left of them. Most of the buildings were charred and bombed out, the way Washington DC looked after the Martin Luther King riots. "There's our butcher shop going up," Lucien said as we passed a skeleton of steel girders over a bare cement slab.

"Do any of your projects actually operate?" I asked, chuckling intentionally, hoping Lucien would take my question as constructive rather than rude, but he didn't see fit to answer. I tried again. "Who do they belong to anyway?"

"BROL."

"What exactly is BROL?" I asked.

"Bougainville Resource Owners Limited."

"I didn't see any mention of BROL in the paperwork on Clyde's deal."

"It doesn't need to be mentioned. Things work on a handshake basis in Bougainville. Everything in your mining deal that goes to the chiefs finds its way to BROL first, including the fees you guys owe for the licenses."

"What fees?" I asked, surprised.

"BROL's fees for preparing the applications," Lucien snorted. "A lot's been done," he said, his manner indignant, as if I was taking his work for granted.

I said, "I'm sorry if I've offended you. Clyde never said a thing about fees."

"Clyde agreed to pay me a hundred thousand dollars when the three licenses are issued," Lucien snipped. "We shook on it. I'm sure it's in the agreement."

I dropped the topic, but made a mental note to look; I had an electronic version of the executed agreement on my computer. I had read it a couple of weeks earlier, but hadn't seen anything about fees payable to Lucien, let alone BROL.

After a pregnant pause, Lucien did a bad job feigning laughter. "We need to get paid for our assistance, but we've got no interest in your small-time alluvial deals; BROL's hunting bigger game." He glanced over at me and raised his eyebrows. "Exploration."

"If that's the case, why isn't BROL pursuing exploration now?" I asked.

Lucien said, "That's the way the mining department has decided to play things out. Alluvial applications come first."

We arrived at Lucien's house after dark. Thanks to BCL and the Panguna Mine, Arawa, unlike 90 percent of Bougainville, was connected to an electrical grid, and the houses were lighted. Lucien pulled the Toyota up the driveway to his house, a one-story bungalow.

"Why are all the houses in Bougainville on stilts?" I asked.

"Earthquakes," Lucien answered. "We get at least one a quarter; we're in the Ring of Fire."

We all clambered out, and other than Lucien, the men headed to what looked like utility rooms underneath the house on the ground floor.

"Follow me, Jack," Lucien said, opening a swinging gate to a set of stairs and beginning the climb up to the house's front door on the first floor.

Before I did so, I put my bags down and began saying my goodbyes to the men, but Lucien interrupted. "They're not going anywhere; they'll sleep here. You'll see them tomorrow. Come on, follow me," he repeated, and led me up the stairs. "Hustle up; the mosquitos out now are the ones with malaria."

"Where will the men sleep?" I asked Lucien as I followed him up the steps.

"Down there," he scoffed. "On the concrete driveway, in the shower stall, on a bench. They can sleep anywhere." He unlocked the front door and led me through the kitchen and down a hall to my room. The interior was dimly lit, but I could see enough to validate Clyde's assessment.

Lucien put a package of chicken parts for stew into a pot of water and switched on a gas range that looked like it had come with the house. Outside, I could hear the chiefs cooking something over a fire. Ten minutes later, Lucien and I sat down to eat, the two white men eating by themselves upstairs, the black men having dinner downstairs. I told myself that if I ever had my own place in Bougainville, that would never happen.

I was starved, and Lucien's meal was decent. For a nightcap he made the two of us Bougainville Cocktails, as he called them: Scotch and Sprite, in a highball glass with plenty of ice. Maybe it was the oppressive heat, but I found my drink surprisingly good. Then Lucien said good night, telling me he was going down below to look after the chiefs. I stood outside on the front porch and watched him as he moved through the men, making sure they had food, and noticed that he handed out two kina notes to each chief.

I went to my room, and out of habit checked my mobile phone— no bars. I turned in and slept until four the next morning, when the roosters started crowing under the house. I got up soon afterward, made myself some instant coffee, and we were off to inspect alluvial mining sites by eight.

That day, I learned three things about gold in Bougainville. First, it was as plentiful as advertised. There was gold everywhere; all you had to do was get to a stream and follow the panners. Second, as a cash crop, panning gold was propping up all of Bougainville; coconuts and cacao weren't even close. Third, there was an opportunity:

Bougainville's panners had no exit strategy, no straightforward means of getting paid cash for their gold.

Lucien drove a group of us north to Atamo first. We turned off the coast road after twenty miles, and Chief Richard guided us up a single-lane road paralleling a river through coconut plantations and cacao orchards. For several miles, I watched a stream of men, women, and children walking in single file along the road, jumping out of the way as we barreled by in Lucien's ten-seater.

We came into a clearing, where beneath some trees sat an open-air building. A man in a white clerical robe stood at the doorway watching us.

"Atamo church," Richard said.

"Are those people along the road all coming here?" I asked him.

"Yes," he said, smiling. "School for communion."

"How far must they walk?" I asked.

He frowned. "Three kilometers, maybe four?"

We kept driving. After a few miles, we took a right-hand fork in the road, continued for ten minutes, and then stopped in a clearing. I followed Richard and Suston into the rain-soaked jungle a hundred yards until we came to a wide stream. Beneath a canopy of tall, leafy trees was a panning camp, comprised of a thatched-roof lean-to and a smoldering campfire. Alongside the camp, a dozen men and women were working in the stream. We watched them for a while, then Richard brought me over to a group of six panners. Two men were pushing and shoving boulders out of the way, two more were shoveling gravel from the river bottom into a pile by the riverbank, and two women were panning material from the pile.

Richard spoke to one of the women, and they stopped what they were doing. One untied a small glass vial from around her neck and held it out to show me what was inside. The material looked like shiny sand. I asked Richard how much gold was in the vial. He spoke to the women, and they answered in pidgin.

"Five grams," he said. "A good day."

"That's about two hundred fifty dollars' worth of metal for six workers," I said aloud, standing next to Suston, who nodded his head in agreement. "How long have they been panning today?" I asked.

Richard spoke to the women, and then turned to me. "Four hours," he said, holding up four fingers.

I said, "What if they had the types of machines we're going to bring in here—mechanized digging equipment and sluices?"

"Really big money," Richard said, as both he and Suston grinned like little kids with ice cream cones.

"How about if these people were picking cacao beans instead?" I asked.

Richard looked at me, confused, and Suston explained my question to him in pidgin. A crease formed on Richard's forehead. "No big money with cocoa," he said, shaking his head. "Panning make money."

"When they are done, who do these people sell their gold to?" I asked.

Richard looked confused, and conferred again with Suston. "Oh, yes, yes," he nodded, now understanding the question. He smiled. "Maybe you?"

When we got home that night, Lucien was otherwise occupied, sitting out on the front porch, staring at the computer on his lap.

"Can I interrupt you?" I asked him.

He glanced up at me, seeming somewhat irritated, clearly in the middle of something.

"Sorry, but I was just wondering, if you're saying that the big upside here—exploration—comes along later, why go to all the trouble to license an alluvial gold mine, assemble machinery, and hire men? Couldn't someone just open a business here buying gold while they waited for the exploration activities to start?" I asked. "I've talked to some of these chiefs. It sounds like they've got no one to buy their gold, no one they trust, anyway. Where I come from, that sounds like an opportunity to make some dough."

Lucien sat up straight and looked me in the eye. "That's not the deal on the table. I'm not allowing that."

"Why not?" I stammered.

Lucien didn't respond, but made a point of ignoring me and refocusing on his computer. His refusal to continue the conversation told me all I needed to know. Buying gold was indeed a good business opportunity; for some reason—maybe having to do with fees—it just didn't fit into Lucien's plans.

I went to my room, swabbed myself with mosquito wipes, mixed a Bougainville Cocktail in the kitchen, and walked downstairs to what passed for Lucien's lawn. Some of the men were cooking over a fire, and I saw Suston's face illuminated by the flames.

"Just the man I was looking for," I said as I walked over to him.

He looked at me, his eyes widening with curiosity.

"Why did you ask me yesterday about whether or not I would stay?"

Suston looked around, then took a few steps backward to draw us away from listeners by the fire. "We have no one," he whispered. "Nothing has happened in Bougainville since President Kaboose died. Our government has failed us; President Mogol is only interested in himself. Lucien and George and BROL have done nothing—promises for fifteen years, but no results. Lucien is just a middleman. He says you belong to him, but we know that's not true. We need someone to believe in us who can truly help us. The independence referendum is coming, and we don't know what to do."

"Tell me what will happen when the referendum comes."

"Of course, we will vote for independence," he said.

"But what kind of government will you have? Where's the money going to come from?"

"This is what you must help us do," Suston said, his eyes pleading.

"I'm a foreigner," I said.

"You're an American. We've been waiting for you to return since World War II."

16

A Leap as Big as an Ocean

My first visit to Bougainville ended a few days later, after a long, bumpy ride from Arawa back to the Buka airport. As my flight to Port Moresby took off, I looked out my window over the treetops of Bougainville Island with ambivalence.

The prospect of financing Clyde's gold-mine deal appeared dim. What had happened during my meeting with the mining department officials was enough to send any investment banker a negative signal. Lucien Sump, the person Clyde and I had assumed we could count on to be the deal's local lynchpin, was no businessman. Relying on him to manage a mining enterprise would be a disaster. Even if he was honest—which I doubted—the man couldn't finish anything he started. The chiefs seemed taken with him, at least for the moment, but that might simply be an indictment of them. It sounded like he hadn't been able to deliver much in the way of results over the years, and had lured me there because the chiefs had told him to find money or else. Not that Lucien was a cretin. He was certainly civilized. A good conversationalist, he and I could talk about anything. He'd put me up in his house, squired me around the island, cooked dinner, and served those wonderful Bougainville Cocktails every night.

The problem wasn't just Lucien; it was Bougainville too. The place was raw, its fundamentals primitive. Things could change, but it would take a gargantuan effort.

On the other hand, in terms of the bigger picture, Bougainville held enormous appeal—if I was crazy enough to try to embrace it. The resources were as magnificent as advertised—all told, the place was probably sitting on hundreds of billions of mineral resources—and Bougainville's people were not only lovely, but welcoming; Richard and Suston had practically offered me the reins to the place. If there was any chance that I could ride such a horse, I would never forgive myself for not trying.

With a thirty-hour trip in front of me the following day, I had plenty of time to be honest with myself. I needed to be careful; I was a sucker for situations like this. But I couldn't shake my conclusion: While Bougainville's challenges were daunting, it had even better answers. It offered the biggest shot at upside I had experienced in my life.

A moral and ethical people who shared their umbrellas with strangers and walked three miles one way to go to church was a solid foundation on which to build any nation. That Bougainville possessed documented resources worth billions was both staggering and, additionally, compelling. Mix that together in a vacuum—a population desperate for freedom, but not practiced enough to take on independence by themselves and asking for help—and things definitely got interesting. With those elements, Bougainville could accomplish a lot, if it—or maybe *we*, should I choose to get involved—could find a strong, honest leader.

So far, the people I'd met who might fill that role were less than inspiring. I had expected much more out of George Washburn. There had to be a person of real character out there somewhere. As the sun's rays shimmered across the Pacific, I allowed myself to consider the possibilities. A strong relationship with the right person at the helm of a Bougainville under full sail could be huge, especially if I was around to help rig the masts. Relationships are one thing, but a relationship with someone captaining a new nation? Who on earth had *that*?

I landed in Port Moresby. My next flight didn't leave until the following morning, so I checked into the Airways Hotel. I had no idea what I would find: I made the reservation online because it appeared to be the closest hotel to the airport. Entering the lobby, I couldn't have been more surprised. The Airways was an elegant oasis—in Port Moresby, of all places. A marble-floored, teak-inlaid jewel box, the hotel's public spaces were beautifully designed—and delightfully air conditioned. Its rooms were simple but well-furnished, its staff meticulous; it even offered spa services. The best feature was its restaurant, the Vue. Several stories up by elevator on the top floor of the hotel and cantilevered out above a terraced, garden-covered slope, an open-air bar and dining area resided alongside a sanctuary-like pool. Patrons were treated to magnificent vistas of airplanes taking off, the sea dotted by harbor islands, and the Owen Stanley Range, all bathed by sunrises and sunsets.

The beautiful bartender, as splendid as the hotel, sealed the prospect of my return.

After spending most of the afternoon in my room on my computer, I went for a swim in the pool in the early evening, showered and changed, and found my way to the bar for a drink. Ceilings fans overhead whispered in the soft air. Off to the west, the sun was going down over the Indonesian hills. The dining area was crowded, but no one else was at the bar. I pulled out a stool at one end and took a seat. Down at the service end of the bar where waiters stood in line to pick up drinks, a lone bartender was mixing what looked like a martini. She was slim but well-endowed, and her hair was long and jet black. Wearing a leotard that left nothing to the imagination, the shirttails of her white cotton blouse were tied in a bow across her bare midriff.

"I'll be right there, sir," she called over to me.

"Take your time," I said. "Am I allowed to smoke in here?" I asked as I removed from my shirt pocket a Cuban Cohiba cigar I had purchased in the lobby sundry store.

"Of course, sir," she said. "This isn't Australia."

I recognized the woman's accent as Filipino. She glanced toward me again, and to the apparent exasperation of the attendant waiting for the martini, stopped mixing the drink. She reached underneath her bar, gathered some things, and glided toward me carrying a tray with a cigar-cutter, a box of matches, and an ashtray. The closer she got, the more beautiful she became.

"Many thanks," I said as she placed the things from the tray down in front of me and offered me a gorgeous smile.

"Always a pleasure," she responded, looking just as good heading the other way as she returned to finish mixing the martini.

I tore open the cigar's plastic wrapper and sliced off its tip with the cigar cutter. The bartender glanced my way one more time, and, again abandoning the attendants waiting for drinks, returned as I finished preparing my cigar. She took the matchbox, removed a match, and looked at me. "Ready?"

"Yes, I am."

She lit me up.

"Thank you."

"Always a pleasure," she said again, and repeated her wonderful smile. "Would you care for a drink menu?"

"Do I really look like someone who orders a drink off a menu?"

She laughed. "No sir, and from your accent, I guess you're not Australian either." She looked at me with what appeared to be mild affection. "I make an excellent martini."

"Maybe next time. I just need something light. I've got a long flight early tomorrow morning."

She said, "I've got what you want. Wait one moment while I take care of my drink orders."

"Sure," I shrugged. I studied her backside again as she went down to the other end of the bar, then took a long drag on the Cohiba as I watched the last rays of the sun burnish the top of the Owen Stanley Range.

She returned in a minute with a full glass of white wine. "That smells like a great cigar," she said.

"It's a Cohiba. A Cuban one," I said. "You can't get these in the US."

She set the glass on a coaster in front of me, crossed her arms, and watched me, her eyes discerning, waiting for my reaction to her selection.

I took a drink. The wine was delicious, dry and light, with a gravelly taste, something the rest of the world has not yet been able to duplicate. "*Magnifique*," I said.

She raised her eyebrows. "You are correct," she said, flashing her radiant smile as if I was a participant on a game show. "It's white Burgundy."

If I returned to Bougainville, I was definitely stopping overnight at the Airways.

The next morning, I hopped an Air Niugini flight via Honiara, the capital of the Solomon Islands, *en route* to Fiji. At the airport in Nadi, I boarded a Fiji Airways plane, and after ten hours and a decent night's sleep, coasted into Los Angeles. Any time I found myself passing through LAX, I headed for the lounge, got a drink, and called my friend Bobby McDermott, who lived in town off Wilshire Boulevard. I dialed him up and filled him in.

"Don't forget, I spend every day with these Hollywood yahoos," Bobby said. "I wouldn't raise a dollar for any of them."

"Yeah, but I'm not exactly flush with choices. I guess I'll have to wait until someone new comes into my office with a better proposition; maybe something on Mars."

"Wait a minute," Bobby said. "You're going to pursue the situation, right?"

"It doesn't sound like you would."

Bobby said, "Forget what I would do; it's what you should do. It's not like you to walk away from something like this—there's too much at stake. I just don't think you should waste your time financing a rinky-dink gold mine for some movie producer. Go back to New York, line up Royce Morgan and some of your other friends, and get back to Bougainville and make something big happen."

Bobby's parting words echoed the plan I had begun to formulate in my head. It might turn out to be a decent one, if I could organize the capital. Most importantly, I needed to figure out a means in Bougainville of making money quickly. If I couldn't do that, the effort would die stillborn.

Clyde was my first call when I got back to the East Coast. We agreed to meet Saturday morning at our normal rendezvous point near his home in Greenwich, the Glory Days diner on Putnam Avenue. I wasn't exactly sure how to play things. Somehow, I had to tell him his deal sucked, but I wanted to do it myself.

As we arrived together at the front door of the diner, Clyde said, "I just signed up the best vampire film director in LA, but he's going to cost me a million bucks." We slid into one of the diner's red leather booths, and a waitress pushed a pot of coffee, cups and saucers, and menus across the table at us.

Clyde's comment made it sound like he was trying to back out of Bougainville; I hadn't expected him to make things so easy for me. "Film the movie in Bougainville," I said. "You can save a bundle. With all those people chewing betel nut, you won't have to import extras."

"My director doesn't leave LA," Clyde said without smiling at my joke, working hard to stay serious. "These things happen," he said by way of an apology, spreading his hands apart as if defenseless.

"Speaking of movies, what's the word on *Monster Gold*?" I asked.

"Please," Clyde said, "Rolly was smoking something that day in your office. He was just along for the ride; I was going to take him to pitch media companies later. I had no idea he was going to behave the way he did. Sorry twice."

"So just for the record, I can tell the Bougainville chiefs that there's not going to be a movie with crocs eating gold panners any time soon?"

Clyde laughed. "Not one that I have anything to do with."

"Am I hearing you say you're not interested in your mining deal either? Are you totally out?" I asked as matter-of-factly as possible, studying the menu I had seen a hundred times.

"Maybe not completely?" Clyde shrugged. "If you still want to raise money for the deal, we could stay in for a piece if you need some friends. Say ten percent?"

"That might be helpful," I said, looking around for the waitress. "You paid for me to go all the way down there. You want a written report?"

"Naw."

The waitress came to our table, and we ordered. Clyde got what he always did, an omelet, and I ordered scrambled eggs and bacon.

"I might as well tell you: there's no way your mining deal can happen," I said.

Clyde poured himself another cup of coffee, waiting for my explanation.

I said, "It's not the kind of business you can manage remotely. Someone's got to be there every day. Lucien's not the guy."

"Why am I not surprised?" Clyde said as the waitress brought our breakfast and replaced our empty coffee pot with a refill. "Not that it's critical information for me at this point, but what's the matter with him?"

"It's a long story," I said. "I don't want to waste your time."

"Could he help at all?" Clyde asked, salting his omelet.

"He's probably more trouble than he's worth." After a week in Bougainville, American food tasted extraordinary.

Clyde buttered a piece of toast. "How does Lucien make any money down there?" he asked. Follow the money: that was always how Clyde approached things, why he was a good movie producer.

"I didn't get that far. It can't be a lot, that's for sure. There's not a lot of anything down there." I laughed. "I can just hear the mining analyst at Fidelity if I invited him down to do due diligence, their guy on our financing list who's always ready to jet off on an exotic boondoggle, but never invests. *Where do you stay?*" I mimicked.

"So you didn't like it either."

"I wouldn't go that far."

"What could you possibly like about the place? Did you go swimming?"

"No." I had to think for a minute about how to answer his first question. "I liked the people."

"They don't even wear shoes."

"True."

Clyde laughed. "You felt like a fish out of water, right?"

"Did you see *Hamilton*?" I asked.

"Of course."

"I felt more like him, if you want to know the truth."

Clyde looked at me funny. "What are you trying to tell me? You're walking away from Bougainville, right?"

"Not exactly."

"You really are crazy."

From the look on his face, I guess I must have shocked Clyde as I told him I thought Bougainville had potential, and I was thinking of forming a company to invest there over the long-term. I was careful to thread the needle, not oversell things. The rights to Clyde's mining deal might come in handy—three licensed alluvial mining sites, the first in Bougainville since the Crisis, could be worth something—but I needed him to back out too. If he didn't, I had a problem. Clyde had introduced me to Bougainville. He was a client, which meant I had fiduciary obligations. If he said that he still wanted to do his deal and would take it to another firm, that would have been the end of me and Bougainville.

Sometimes, I wish that's what happened.

But I knew Clyde pretty well. Bougainville was a distraction. All he wanted to do was make movies. "Yeah, maybe I should lead the charge on this, really get involved," he joked when I asked. "Not."

"One last thing," I said. "Lucien tried to tell me you guys had an understanding that when his organization delivered the three mining licenses, you'd owe him a hundred thousand dollars. I double-checked your agreement; there's nothing in there about that."

"The man's a pig."

"I take it that means no."

"Do I look that stupid to you?"

I saved the part for last where I asked Clyde to invest. As we got up to leave, I told him that I needed to raise capital for my mission, and I'd like to take him up on his offer of a 10 percent investment. It wasn't so much his money: the last thing I needed was for Clyde to circle back some day and say I had duped him. I was relieved when he agreed to everything. He even picked up the breakfast bill.

Now, Bougainville's problems would no longer be Clyde's, but mine.

When I got home, I lined up Elizabeth, Royce, and Doctor Sid for a conference call, and later that day I gave them my thoughts about putting together a new company to invest in Bougainville. I admitted that I knew nothing about the mining business, and also confessed I had not yet learned enough about Bougainville to put together a viable business plan. I proposed we start with the alluvial mining deal Clyde had already teed up, but I held out no assurances we'd see it through to a closing. Maybe we could indeed make some reasonable cash mining alluvial gold, but if we played our cards right, we could help create a country too—and there had to be a huge upside in that.

My colleagues didn't exactly fall all over themselves to say it was a brilliant idea, but no one told me I was crazy either. I contacted several additional investors I had worked with on similar ventures in the past, including Richard Abderman, my rabbi from Drexel Burnham; Dixon Perth, an Australian solar developer Elizabeth and I had been in business with for twenty years; Peter Aristotle, a Greek shipping tycoon who had been an investor in Middle Kingdom; and Clark Howard from American Express. In the end Clyde punted, which is what always happened with the Hollywood crowd. By the end of 2015, we had formed a new company, Mt. Bagana Resources Limited, named after the volcano, and capitalized it with a seed money equity round of a total of one million dollars from eight of us.

These people were my best investors, and among my closest friends. Bougainville was going to have to pay off. If it didn't, I would have to remain on the far side of the ocean.

17

Sump's Lost Mines

In early January 2016, around the same time Clyde finalized the paperwork transferring ownership of his mining deal to my new company, I was barraged with emails and phone calls from Lucien Sump. He tried to bring up his pending compensation for the mining licenses once more, but I shucked off the topic, preferring to give him the word in person.

Lucien shifted to housekeeping business. He had just heard from the officials in Bougainville's mining department. We had only two months to get a sampling crew into the field, gather some data, and submit the information required for our mining license. He recommended Arly Beane, one of the Alaskan guys from the cast of *Yukon Gold* who Rolly Maloney had mentioned when we had all met in my office in New York. Arly lived north of Anchorage and was available to take my call. Lucien also said that Andy Kristos, his "highly credentialed British geologist"—to use his words—would be available.

At first, I had no intention of using Arly Beane; I was dubious about anyone recommended by Rolly Maloney. It was only when I consulted the mining want ads and telephoned a few alluvial miners that I realized I would be forced to reconsider. A half-dozen people, men and women, hung up on me when I told them I was calling about an alluvial mining opportunity in Bougainville. The only guy who'd speak to me told me that he'd require half the action to consider alluvial mining on an island in the South Pacific.

Arly was going to have to do. I held my nose and called him. The connection was scratchy, and soon I understood why. Arly was speaking to me via his mobile phone from a snowcat he was driving, grooming the slopes at a two-bit ski resort in Alaska. I couldn't understand much of anything he said. It might have been partially the phone line, but my sense was the problem was mostly Arly. In a series of tedious phone calls, Elizabeth and I negotiated a compensation agreement with Arly and his crew—his son Bryce and his nephew Gary—and a travel schedule.

I left for Bougainville on a Monday morning in mid-January. When I arrived at Lucien's house in Arawa on Wednesday afternoon, he introduced me to Andy, his geologist who had arrived a day earlier from Jakarta. Lucien had said Andy was British, and perhaps he was— he had a very light complexion—but one of his parents had to be Asian, most likely Thai. His English was atrocious, and he was an impossible person to read. During dinner that night, I asked him a lot of questions but learned nothing. Either he didn't view me as his client, or he just plain didn't know the answers. I made a mental note to hire my own geologist when the work got serious.

The Alaskans were due to arrive in Bougainville the next day. I had booked rooms for them at the Arawa Women's Centre, a training school funded by international charitable foundations for Bougainvillean women seeking employment in the hotel industry overseas. It had hot showers, was reasonably priced, and was only two blocks down the street from Lucien's. The specter of the Alaskans' costly roundtrip tab to Bougainville helped me focus on my mission at hand: find some good alluvial sites; map and sample them so we could file the information with our license applications; and learn as much as I could about alluvial gold mining in the process. I wasn't really counting on Lucien to deliver the alluvial mining sites he had specified to Clyde, but it would put me ahead of the curve if they actually proved out.

The Alaskans planned to adjust to the time zone changes on Thursday and show up at Lucien's ready to go to work first thing Friday morning. I had been up since seven when Arly knocked on Lucien's screen door at ten a.m. He was alone, his face pale and flaccid, cheeks flopping over his jawbone every time he talked. Under a wispy mustache, sweat covered his upper lip. He removed a hexagon-shaped hat with flaps over the ears, the kind old people wear so they don't exacerbate their sun poisoning.

I looked at my watch. "Where's your crew?" I said as I stood up to meet Arly.

"You must be Jack," the walrus look-alike said as he stretched out his paw at me, yawning. "Where's the coffee pot? I need a jolt."

Only after Lucien turned on the range to boil some water did Arly answer my question.

"My kids? They're still too tired," he said with a stupid grin, continuing to stand in everybody's way in the middle of the kitchen.

Lucien organized Arly a cup of instant coffee, and we waited for him to take a few gulps. "All right, men," Lucien said three minutes later. "Finish up, and let's roll. I'm taking you to two of my favorite mining sites." He peered at me and Arly and grinned. "The best news of all is that they're both close to the road."

"We're going to need to rent an excavator," Arly announced to me, as if he was commenting about the weather.

"That's a big machine. How much will one cost?" I asked Lucien.

Lucien blinked; it appeared he had no idea. "What do you figure, Arly?"

"Oh hell, I ain't got a clue," Arly said.

Their oblivious response made my stomach knot up, what happens when you're paying the bills. "Is there an equipment rental yard in town?" I asked Lucien. "I'd like to check out our options."

Arly took a last gulp of coffee, and then we got into Lucien's Toyota and drove a couple of blocks to an equipment yard. The compound sported a half-dozen junked vehicles and was surrounded by a chain-link fence and a wide gate blocking the entrance. A couple of mongrelized German shepherds lounging in the dirt raised their heads, sniffed, and went back to sleep. A young man opened the gates and let us in. Lucien spoke to him, and then we filed into a darkened shed to examine a fleet of beat-up construction machinery.

"That'll do just fine," Arly drawled, pointing out the biggest excavator.

Just then, an older Bougainvillean man walked into the shed. He was taller, his bearing dignified, and he wore a collared shirt, pants, and shoes. He stopped a ways off and called to the young man, who scurried over to him. They spoke. The older guy glanced at our group, scowled, and reeled off some loud words in pidgin to the kid. Then, leaving the four of us standing there, he walked out of the shed and disappeared into a house next door.

"What was that all about?" I asked the young man, Lucien standing next to me, appearing oblivious. "Was he the owner?"

"Yes, owner," the young man said. "He say *no gat.*"

I looked at Lucien, who just shrugged.

"What's *no gat* mean?" I asked the kid. Before he could answer, I heard a door slam and saw the older man walking back toward us, the scowl still on his face.

He got a few paces away from me and stopped. "Who are you?" he said to me in English. "Are you the one paying for this?"

"Yeah…" I said, not sure what he wanted.

"I need to talk to you," the man said, gesturing for me to follow him.

We walked over to a cluster of frangipani bushes twenty feet away. I could smell the fragrant blossoms; bees buzzed around, circling in the air above our heads. I edged under the wispy shade offered by the bushes; the sun was blazing, and it had to be ninety-five degrees.

"You're with the wrong guy," the man said. "Lucien Sump's cheated me for the last time. I won't rent to him."

"Okay," I said, trying to recover. "Sure." I started to turn around and walk away, but then thought better of it. "Thanks for letting me know."

"It's not you. You're with the wrong guy," the man repeated, shaking his head, and walked back into his house.

Lucien never opened his mouth. My guess is he knew what might happen when we went to the man's yard and just rolled the dice. He backed his ten-seater out of the equipment yard and drove us out past the edge of town, along the road to Buka, and stopped at what looked like a service station.

"Dead end," Arly declared as he peered through the windshield. "No excavators."

Lucien started to put the ten-seater into reverse.

"Hold it. Turn off the truck for a minute," I said, staring out across the equipment yard. "I see a backhoe." I got out of the truck and started searching for the owner.

An hour later, the smaller backhoe rented for a reasonable price, we headed back to Lucien's, picked up Chief Richard, and stopped at the Women's Centre for Arly's crew. The two younger guys, dressed in long-sleeved shirts, long pants, and heavy work boots, shuffled out and, without a word, climbed into the rear of the vehicle. Their heavy clothes were already stained with sweat, and their faces were burned as red as boiled lobsters.

As we headed up the road to Atamo, everyone was silent. I waited five minutes before turning around to look at Bryce and Gary in the rear compartment. "Let me guess," I said. "You feel asleep on the beach yesterday."

They nodded, in too much pain to talk.

When Lucien reached the turnoff for Atamo, a three-man crew driving the rented backhoe waited for us on the side of the road; as we headed into the Atamo bush, they followed along. Lucien took

Atamo's main road through coconut and cacao plantations, the same single-lane dirt road I had traveled during the fall when I was there for the first time. He said to his geologist, "Andy, take us to the first spot I showed you on the map, up the Queen River in the southern bush." In the back seat of the ten-seater, Andy shuffled some of his maps, leaned over, and compared notes with Richard. Meanwhile, the two baked Alaskans took Lucien's spoken word as their cue to begin talking. For the next half hour—and every minute I was in their company until they left—the only thing I heard them speak about was gear: any kind of vehicle, whether cars, trucks, motorcycles, excavators, or backhoes; or guns, including Bushmasters, pistols, shotguns, and bazookas.

Five minutes later, we came to a junction and took the left fork. When I had come to Atamo with Richard the first time, we had taken the road to the right.

We continued for only a short way when Lucien slowed to round a corner and rolled up to a ford-like crossing. A rain squall had just stopped, and the trees were drenched, their long, blade-like leaves dripping like showerheads. A heron, disturbed while standing in the stream, launched itself effortlessly and flapped upriver.

Andy tugged at Lucien's sleeve. "Queen River," he said.

"Right," Lucien said. "First site, men," he announced, guiding the ten-seater into a shady spot under a grove of banyan trees and switching off the ignition. Everyone climbed out, Arly and the kids so sweat-drenched they looked like they had gotten caught in the river.

"You guys must be roasting," I said, standing there in my T-shirt and shorts.

Arly sneered, "At least we're not going to get malaria."

I was no expert on tropical diseases, so I didn't bother to tell Arly that, as far as I had observed so far, if one took precautions like generous amounts of repellant outdoors and ceiling fans indoors, the mosquitoes were manageable. I wasn't a mining expert either, but the site felt as wrong as Arly's clothes. They say that gold in a stream likes to roll downhill, but if that's true, it wasn't going to do so there. Only about five miles off the coast road, the land was as flat as a beach. The river was wide and deep, filled with boulders and running high and fast; its water was far too energetic for panners. Obviously, the place wasn't conducive to alluvial mining; if it had been, we would have seen panners everywhere. To double-check, I walked upstream along the riverbank for a couple hundred yards, and then reversed and did the same downstream. There wasn't another soul in either direction.

When I returned to the crossing, the kids were floating in the river in their clothes, the water cooling their sunburned faces. Arly was digging a hole in the overburden along the riverbank. Using the backhoe's bucket to hoist shovelfuls of earth and gravel, he swiveled around and deposited the material in a pile by the crossing. The kids got busy panning the pile. Over the next couple of hours, Arly shoveled a hole in the riverbank the size of an automobile, and the kids panned and panned. Whenever they reduced the residue in the bottom of their pans to liquid slurry, they poured the mixture into a quart-size glass jar.

"How much material do you think we sampled this morning?" I asked.

Sitting in the river like a couple of rubber ducks in a tub, Bryce and Gary looked at other. "Maybe a couple yards?" Bryce said.

Gary nodded. "Yeah, two ton or more."

"And if you had to guess, how much gold has that yielded?" I asked.

They both looked at me and shrugged.

I walked down to the stream next to them, picked up the glass jar, and peered into the muck in its bottom. "I'll make you guys a bet," I said. "The first time I was here, Richard took me to a place upstream. The six panners I saw working that day, using hand tools, found five grams in four hours. With this big machine sucking fuel from the time we got here two hours ago, I'm laying odds that's more gold than you're going to find in the bottom of this jar, and I don't care if you work all day."

"Don't worry, Jack, you're going to find plenty of gold," Arly called over to me, taking a break as he shut off the backhoe. "It's all around us."

"I know it's all around us," I said. "Like I said, I watched those villagers before. That's all the more reason why I can't understand why we're digging in a place where there isn't any."

Lucien didn't say a word, but instead occupied himself extracting lunch from a cooler: Spam sandwiches and water. As soon as we finished eating, we headed south on the coast road for George Washburn's site in Isina.

Or rather, his wife, Francine's, site, as Lucien had made sure to tell me the night before. He had explained what I had learned on the internet, that Bougainville was part of Melanesia, where land was owned customarily, as opposed to via written deed filed at the county courthouse. Over the ages, according to custom, the land—from rock to tree to river—had been owned by clans, tribes, and families, and remained so perpetually. In Bougainville, most customary land was owned via matrilineal lineage. When a man and woman married, the land remained owned by the woman, and the man would live in the woman's house, in her village. We were paying a visit to a site on Francine's family's land, not George's. As Lucien had explained this, I had found myself wondering why neither George nor Francine was going to accompany us.

Lucien turned off the main road onto a dirt track a few miles south of Kieta. At the turnoff, two local men who were friends of the Washburns signaled us to pick them up. We stopped, and they squeezed inside the rear compartment of the Toyota. Then, directing Richard in pidgin, they guided us up the dirt road for a while, then off on a grassy path running through pleasant hills planted with cacao trees. Ripe cacao beans, orange, pod-like growths coming right off the wooden branches, hung everywhere.

After a mile, Richard directed Lucien to turn right, and he followed a fork in the path curling around a grassy rise and down into a shaded streambed. Ahead, a small brook trickled through a rocky, gravelly dell, flattened out below, then disappeared into the cacao orchard. Richard told Lucien to stop; we had arrived at the Isina site.

The bright sun, no longer overhead but off to the west, was blocked by tall coconut trees and jungle. Even so, it was extremely hot. In the orchard thick with cacao trees, there was no breeze. Arly and the Alaskans got their panning gear out of the rear of the ten-seater and, along with the local guys, hustled into the shade and began work. I headed for shade myself, along with Chief Richard. Lucien went underneath a grove of palm trees and lay down to take a nap, Andy following him.

Arly and the crew had been panning for an hour when I saw a man walking up the orchard path carrying a machete. "Chief Richard, there's a man coming," I said, trying not to sound too concerned. I had learned that everyone in Bougainville, even young children, carried machetes to clear the jungle paths where they walked. Still, seeing someone walking toward me with a large, razor-sharp bush knife was disconcerting. "Arly," I called over to the crew. "Better hold up for a minute. We've got a visitor."

Richard greeted the man in pidgin. George's two locals walked over, but said nothing.

The man's expression betrayed little. He spoke in pidgin to Richard. The two locals, who I had assumed were sent by George to help us navigate this sort of thing—local land issues—just stood there. Arly and the guys walked slowly up out of the shaded glen. Over by the palms, Andy stood still as a statue; Lucien was still asleep.

The man and Richard kept talking in a conversational tone, as if they were friends and the only people there. Finally, Richard turned to me, that little betel nut smile across his face. "You must talk now," he said.

"I'm not sure what to say," I stammered, before the man stepped closer.

"Is okay, I speak English," he said.

"Thank goodness," I said, almost laughing with relief. "I'm sorry. Chief Richard has probably told you that we're friends with George Washburn?"

"Yes," he replied.

"I'm sorry," I said. "I meant to say Francine Washburn."

The man looked at me carefully, squinting in the sunlight. "Did they tell you this Francine's land?"

"Well, yes," I said. "Is that wrong?" I asked, straining to look over the man's shoulder at Andy. "Andy, please do me a favor and wake up Lucien," I called. "He needs to get over here."

The man smiled thinly, showing no teeth as his lips pressed together, as if he wanted to be civil to me but would have behaved differently if he had been speaking to a Washburn. "Francine always say that. Not true," he said, shaking his head. "This not their land."

"In that case," I said, "please forgive our being here. Would you like us to leave?"

"Yes," the man said.

Arly and the crew packed up their gear quickly while the man waited in the clearing for us to leave. Lucien woke up, dusted himself off, and wheeled the car around.

I had waited while everyone else climbed aboard when the man stopped me before I could shut the door of the Toyota. "Are you in business with Lucien?" he asked, not seeming to care whether Lucien heard him or not.

I wished I would have been able to say no. "Yes," I replied.

The man with the machete gave me the same expression I had received from the guy at the equipment yard, and walked off.

We drove slowly out of the plantation and down the hill. I waited to speak until after we had dropped off George Washburn's two locals at the main road. As Lucien headed back to Arawa, I turned around to face Arly in the rear compartment. "Was there any gold on that hillside?" I asked.

"Hell no," he replied.

I said to Lucien, making sure my voice was loud enough so everyone inside the ten-seater could hear over the engine, "Will you please tell me why we were at either of those sites today?"

I couldn't believe Lucien's response. "Those are as fine a couple of sites as you'll see in Bougainville," he replied. "We just didn't find any gold today."

My mother always taught me that when you don't have anything nice to say, say nothing. That night, I went to sleep feeling extremely depressed.

The next morning, the roosters under Lucien's house woke me on schedule; the dawn was still an hour and a half away. My feet hanging off the end of the twin bed, I killed some time thinking about what to do next. Lucien and the team he had assembled were morons; there was no way I could rely on any of them to pursue an alluvial mining business. My fallback plan was sounding better by the minute. I didn't need to mine alluvial gold: I could just set up a business to buy it from panners until I found some miners who knew what they were doing, or the government authorized exploration, or both. Buying gold seemed much simpler than mining it. I might even make more money that way. I got out my computer and ran some numbers. According to my calculations, buying gold and mining alluvial gold were both money-makers, but the investment in equipment and time was much higher for mining than setting up a buying operation.

An hour later, I headed for the bathroom to take a shower. As I soaped myself down, I tried to keep the water inside the shower stall; Lucien's shower curtain was long gone. Finished washing, I remained in the shower and shaved. I looked down and noticed plant life—a fern—growing out of the drain. I studied the drain some more, assuming that at some point I would need to be ready to engage silverfish, if not small animals, emerging from it. When I finished my shower, I placed my razor and my bar of soap back on the spot along the top of the shower stall where I had stored them, being careful not to nick myself on the half-dozen rusted razor blades lying alongside.

I toweled myself off and returned to my room. When I dressed and went into the kitchen, Greyson Trull was sitting at the table.

"Grumpy; for a moment I thought I was having a bad dream. To what do I owe the pleasure?"

"Good morning, Captain America. You owe BROL one hundred thousand dollars. I'm here to collect."

As Grumpy spoke, Lucien strolled in and sat down at the table, as if we were all one big, happy family.

Without responding to Grumpy, I stepped to the counter to make myself a cup of coffee. I brushed a swarm of ants off the countertop, grabbed a coffee cup, rubbed its cruddy inside surface clean with a paper towel, and heated up some rainwater in a pot on the range.

"I've been trying to tell you," Lucien said, his words puncturing the silence. "Clyde and I had an understanding. He agreed that when BROL filed his mining license applications, he would pay us a fee. The last part of the deliverable was a tour of the sites; that happened yesterday."

"Those were hardly mining sites," I said, grabbing the instant coffee and milk and sugar out of the refrigerator. "Like you said, they were just places close to the road." I made my coffee, walked over by the back door, and craned my neck to look outside as a tepid sunrise exposed dishwater-gray clouds gathering over Panguna. "Do you think it's going to rain today?"

As Lucien started to answer, Grumpy interrupted him, repeating, "You owe me one hundred thousand dollars."

I took one gulp of my coffee and poured the rest down the sink. "I don't owe you anything, Grumpy; take it out of what you overcharged me for breakfast in Port Moresby last time. Lucien, I'm not sure what arrangements you have with this guy, but I don't want anything to do with him," I said. "If you want to get these mines financed, tell Grumpy to take a hike. It's him or me. As far as your BROL organization, I don't owe it a dime."

"No fees, no mines," Lucien threatened, helping to make my future business decision an easy one.

I walked out the front door and down the street to the Women's Centre, using the walk to help me calm down and sort things out. When I got to the hotel, I introduced myself to the woman at the reception desk. She was unusually tall and elegant, and had a gorgeous smile.

"How much for breakfast?" I asked.

"Twenty kina. That includes eggs and breakfast meat, four pieces of toast, fruit, and coffee or tea."

"What's your name?"

"Leki," she said.

"Okay, Leki, I'd like breakfast, please. I only need two pieces of toast." It was a cheerful, clean dining room. I wasn't alone. A Bougainvillean couple sat speaking in low tones; as I took a seat nearby, they smiled at me. My Alaskan miners were nowhere to be seen; they'd probably roll out of bed around noon. A group of Bougainvillean women occupied a round table, talking in pidgin. Two white women sat across the room. From their sour expressions, I figured they were NGOs. I could hear a few of their words: Australian. From the NGOs I had met, I got the feeling that all of them disapproved of people like me: We were capitalist pigs. God help me if I admitted to being a budding gold miner.

Leki poured me some more coffee. I watched her glide around the room serving the customers, and finalized my plan.

"Are you finished?" she asked a few minutes later.

"May I take a look at a room?" I asked.

When the breakfast crowd cleared out, Leki led the way up a stairway from the dining room to a covered, open-air walkway that ran perpendicular from the road. The walkway overlooked a large, cultivated flower garden, bordered by fragrant groves of frangipani. Off down a path sat an alfresco cottage with a thatched roof, sheltering a seating area with benches around its perimeter. Beyond the cottage, under a grove of banyan trees, I could hear a river flowing over stones. Leki led me along the walkway past several closed doors. We stopped, and she opened one. The small room had a double bed, was clean, and, much to my surprise, was air-conditioned.

"How much is this one a night?" I asked.

"One hundred kina," she said.

"Do you have any vacancies?"

"Yes. This one," she said, pressing her lips tightly together.

"How about a lower rate per night if I wanted to stay a long time?"

She said, "I will ask the management."

"All right, please do. In the meantime, I'll take this one for now," I said. We went back downstairs. I paid my breakfast tab together with a gratuity, gave Leki one hundred kina for the room for the night, and told her I'd be back soon.

When I returned to Lucien's, Grumpy was downstairs with the chiefs. Lucien was on the porch and waved me up. "I'm terribly sorry about Greyson," he said, leading me into his office. "I think you know how these highlanders can get, but I really need that money. Some of it's to pay him, you see," he said, raising his eyebrows, as if I should appreciate the position he was in. He sat down and sprawled back in his chair. Strewn with papers, his desk was as big as an aircraft carrier and took up half the room. "Please, take a seat," he said, gesturing across the table, but other than his, there were no chairs in the room.

I went on the front porch, grabbed a plastic garden chair, and carried it into Lucien's office.

"I'll make it easy for you," Lucien said. "Make it fifty thousand, but I really need the cash today. I've got to pay him." Lucien stood back up and started pacing.

"I've reviewed the agreement you signed with Clyde; I've got it on my computer if you want to see it," I said. "There's nothing about fees. Try again." I watched Lucien stomp up and down the room for a while. "I'm just curious: how do these Bougainvillean chiefs like a Defence Force thug in their midst?"

"They don't care."

"Have you ever asked them?"

Lucien stopped pacing, and looked at me, exasperated. "Look, none of us will like it if Greyson gets desperate."

"Grumpy's not my problem."

"I wouldn't be too sure about that."

I said, "Why don't we start over; show me the license applications."

"There they are, finished and filed," Lucien said, sweeping his hand over a six-inch stack of eight-by-eleven manila envelopes.

"There must be fifty documents in that pile. Show me mine."

Lucien smiled his schoolboy smile. "Take a look if you want. You don't trust me?"

I looked at the stack of envelopes. "I'm not going to root through all that."

Lucien looked at me, a resigned expression on his face. "I'll be happy to resolve the topic later today, but first Greyson and I must go up to the cattle ranch to tend to some business."

"You go ahead. I've got to do some work on my computer."

Lucien got as far as the front door before he turned around to look at me, as if not sure what to do next, before stomping out. I knew what he was thinking: what was I going to do in his office while he was gone? *You don't trust me?* I felt like saying.

I listened until I heard Lucien and Grumpy drive off, then returned to Lucien's office and surveyed the entire room. Except for the big desk covered with papers, it was devoid of furniture—no filing cabinets or bookshelves. I sorted through the stack of manila envelopes Lucien had urged me to examine and found the ones labelled Atamo, Isina, and Kopani.

I opened the envelope marked "Atamo" and pulled out the paperwork. It contained Lucien's notes and copies of letters from him to various investors, including Clyde. I sorted through the sheaf of documents. Lucien had solicited money from at least four different investor groups regarding Atamo, "one of Bougainville's most prominent alluvial mining opportunities." I realized that I could spend millions on Lucien's designated mine in Atamo, and other investors could show up one day and claim they were the rightful owner. There was no evidence of an Atamo license application to the mining department ever being filed—not a shred of paper, nor a receipt. I opened the Isina envelope. Its contents were similar; so was Kopani's.

I stacked the envelopes on Lucien's desk the way I found them and continued to inspect the piles of papers on his desktop. I saw a dish full of business cards, and was about to turn to the next pile when I recognized Lesley Gage's card on top. I remembered her from the lunch at Reasons, the one who had struck me as the only competent person in the mining department group. I sat down and dialed the office number on her card from my mobile phone.

She picked up. "Hello?"

"Ms. Gage, you probably don't remember me, but I'm Jack Davis. I met you last fall at Reasons when…"

She interrupted me. "Mr. Davis; of course I remember you. Lucien Sump's investor from New York City. Are you calling from New York? I know it's cold there. I attended Cornell."

"Cornell? Good for you, but you must have felt like an icicle."

"I got used to it. What can I do for you?"

"Well, I'm trying to get a copy of the license applications that Lucien filed for those alluvial mines. You know, the three he wanted my firm to finance? I haven't been able to obtain copies of either the applications or the actual licenses. I just need to verify their existence, for my due diligence files, of course."

"Of course." She remained silent for a few moments. "Mr. Davis, I don't want to get anyone in trouble."

"No, no."

"We haven't taken any applications for alluvial licenses. We can't; we just ratified our mining legislation last year, right before we met you. Also, in Bougainville there's a moratorium against mining that can only be lifted when the local landowners request it; that hasn't happened anywhere yet. To be honest, my bosses were confused. They didn't understand why Mr. Sump and Mr. Washburn invited us to lunch; they assumed it was so Mr. Sump could demonstrate he knew people like you from Wall Street. I don't think we'll have rules and regulations about mining for quite a while. We need lawyers to help us with that."

"How long will that take?"

"Maybe a year? That's just a guess, of course." She laughed. "It's Bougainville, Mr. Davis."

I thanked her and hung up, went to my room and collected my bags, and walked the two blocks down the street to the Women's Centre. It was a sober stroll. Lesley Gage had verified two things for me: not only was Lucien, my host and original introduction to Bougainville, a fraud, but getting anything meaningful accomplished there was going to take much more time than any Westerner would consider normal. For what would prove to be an early iteration of many interludes to follow, I asked myself if I should just fly home and refund everyone's money. Reminding myself that the few times I had quit something, I had regretted it profoundly, I walked on.

When I got to the hotel, Leki gave me a key to my room and asked me if I wanted dinner. I said I would like to eat around seven, dropped off my bags in my room, and walked back up to Lucien's to wait for him in his office.

He arrived about three, circled his desk, and slouched in his chair. "Is it too early for a drink?" he said.

"If I were you, I'd have one."

"Why's that?"

I said, "I talked to Lesley Gage while you were gone."

Lucien appeared genuinely puzzled. "Who's that?"

"She's with the mining department. The woman we met at Reasons?" I said. "I'm just curious. What's it take to get you embarrassed?"

"What the hell does that mean?"

"These Bougainvilleans need people like you and me to have solutions for them. Don't you realize that? That's not altogether the optimal approach, but that's the way it is for now, until we can change things. In the meantime, people like us have got to deliver here. Has that ever occurred to you?"

"You're clueless. You haven't got the first idea what these people think of you," Lucien said.

"Fine; please enlighten me."

His face twisted in a sneer. "They're using you. They're the coffee, and you're the dregs."

"Did they teach you that in Australia?"

"We're not as naive as Americans," Lucien said, looking like he wanted to spit at me.

"Your mines are a fraud, Lucien. There are no mining licenses. It's impossible to even file applications. There's a moratorium in Bougainville against mining, and the mining department won't have written rules and regulations for another year. Don't think these Bougainvilleans don't know you're full of shit. I've already had a couple of them tell me I shouldn't have anything to do with you."

Lucien's face darkened as he set his jaw. "I've got news for you. You're going to pay me—and like it—or you'll never be able to apply for a mining license in Bougainville."

"I hate to disappoint you, Lucien, but I don't want a mining license. I'm setting up a gold-buying business instead."

"You can't do that," Lucien hissed. "You're only here with my permission," he said, his eyes bugging out. "I need you to leave."

"I'm on my way—out of your house, anyway," I said. "But I'm not leaving Bougainville. See you around town. No hard feelings."

I didn't slam Lucien's door when I left; no sense getting emotional. At first, I tried to convince myself I was just turning one page in a longer story. But the more I thought about it, the more I realized that wasn't accurate. I wasn't even starting a new chapter; it was a whole new book. Jettisoning Lucien meant I had no one to rely on in all of Bougainville. If I truly wanted to pursue my plan, the work couldn't be done remotely. I would have to do everything myself; I would need to make Bougainville my home. I know I was supposed to be smarter, but it never occurred to me not to plow ahead.

18

Thank Goodness for Friday

I couldn't sleep that that night. The more I thought about it, the more I realized that my Bougainville decision confronted me with a stark reality. My apprehension wasn't so much about the challenges arrayed in front of me, but rather what I was giving up.

I would be required to say goodbye to significant aspects of my life, things I had thought would be a part of me forever. It was a life that had been comfortable, full of success and sunny days. Yes, of course, I had realized that my boys were in their own orbits now, with their own moon and stars, and I was no longer the sun. It was one thing to accept that, and another to say farewell to the magical family life we had enjoyed together: the birthdays, the holidays, the camping trips, and swimming and sailing and playing golf in Watch Hill. Most of that would now be shelved for an undetermined period of time. As far as Davis Partners, there would be no place to hang my hat when I returned home. I had often considered how painful closing the firm would be, but this was more like tossing the company off a cliff. While I would relish severing ties with the intolerable regulators and greedy landlords, saying goodbye to my partners and employees, let alone the legacy of the firm, would be crushing. I fought to remind myself: a payoff in Bougainville could represent my promised land, much the same way as the vague, misty worlds rumored to exist on the far side of the flat earth appealed to the ancient explorers. For reasons I didn't fully comprehend, as ephemeral as the objective may have been, it only made me want to attain it more.

Thank goodness for sunny island mornings. I awoke with the energy that accompanies new hope, took my laptop, and went downstairs to the Women's Centre dining room and ordered breakfast. The first thing I needed for my Bougainville gold-buying business was a name. I wanted something that sounded official, a name that would give Bougainville's panners trust and confidence in a new entity that aspired to buy their alluvial gold at a fair, transparent price. By the time I finished my second cup of coffee, I had decided on the Gold Dealer; it would be a wholly-owned subsidiary of our parent company, Mt. Bagana Resources Limited. Next, I did what anyone who needed to make money would do: opened my computer and started producing a cash flow projection. At that point, the prospects for the business appeared robust. I didn't know then that Bougainville numbers lied.

All that day, whenever Bougainville's internet would let me online—which was not often—I devoured information on panning alluvial gold, and tried to learn how to deal it, assay it, and melt it. I searched for specific information about alluvial gold in Bougainville, but there was nothing available. Instead, I made do with studying alluvial gold businesses around the South Pacific, across the Solomon Sea in Papua New Guinea, in Fiji, and all the way down to New Zealand and Australia. I learned that worldwide, the practice of gold dealers was to buy alluvial gold at a discount to the world market price of bullion and try to make money on the spread in what appeared to be a business based on volume.

It didn't take much time to figure out that, like most enterprises, gold buying was not simple. I would be in way over my head. I would need equipment: scales, a furnace for melting alluvial gold at high

temperatures, Doré bar molds, crucibles and other miscellaneous tools, and a secure vault to store my gold and cash. The single most important items were XRF spectrometers, the first a stationary device to be utilized in the melting facility, and the second a portable one for buying gold in the bush. When their lenses scanned alluvial material, these machines analyzed the purity of the alluvial gold and distinguished it from other less valuable precious minerals like silver and copper, as well as impurities. Consulting price lists, I was shocked: a single XRF gun cost as much as a medium-priced automobile.

I kept seeing website information for a California company which described itself as a worldwide manufacturer and distributor of small-scale alluvial mining equipment. I checked to see if they had a location in Papua New Guinea; they did, in Lae, the industrial center of PNG. I noted their address and telephone number, called them, got a salesman on the line, and obtained the store's hours and location. On the spur of the moment, I asked him if he could recommend any experts in the alluvial gold business; he took my email address and told me he'd ask around and get back to me.

In terms of personnel, I learned from the literature that I would need gold buyers, melters, and cashiers. I quizzed Leki about people in Arawa with knowledge of alluvial gold mining or gold buying who could help me. She told me that she knew plenty of panners, but there were no assaying or melting experts in Arawa. She explained that most of the panners sold their raw alluvial gold up in the bush to middlemen who came down from Buka representing Chinese or Indian money guys from PNG. The middlemen had no sophisticated assay equipment and low amounts of cash. Leki said that the panners didn't like it, with transactions often ending in disputes, but they had little choice. I was encouraged—it sounded like my competition was disadvantaged—but that didn't solve my immediate problem. I needed to find a lieutenant who was not only an all-round alluvial gold expert, but also someone trustworthy who wouldn't loot the till.

I emailed Elizabeth to discuss the topic with her, and even reached out to my sons for their thoughts. All of them gravitated to the obvious solution—look for someone in Alaska, the alluvial gold-mining capital of the world—until I reminded them about Arly and the baked Alaskans, as well the difficulty I had found sourcing an interested miner in Alaska pre-Arly. After trolling through some mining employment websites and a few impossible telephone interviews, it seemed like finding a good person would take a miracle.

I spent my first day as a gold dealer on the internet, and didn't leave the Women's Centre. After a few days, I felt I knew enough to venture out into Arawa to search for an appropriate physical location: something centrally located and secure. Leki advised me that Arawa had been ravaged by the Crisis, and there were few habitable commercial spaces available.

I learned that Lucien Sump's former company, Impregnable Resources, had also established an ill-fated gold dealing and assaying operation in Arawa, right around the corner from Lucien's equally star-crossed butcher shop. People told me that Lucien, using his company's shareholder money of course, had spent real dough establishing Impregnable's melting and dealer business, but had never bought a single gram of gold. It sounded like Lucien's formula: decent idea, lousy execution, and a potentially cheap entry point for the next guy. I went to investigate.

The sun was high in the sky, and heavy clouds, the color of a Glock pistol and already bulging with moisture, were threatening to erupt over Panguna as I walked from the Women's Centre to Arawa's business district. It was my first time to set foot downtown. The cityscape was depressing. The former commercial hub for thousands of Bougainvilleans, redskins, and expats, where BCL had spared no expense, had been destroyed and dispirited. Arawa resembled what it had been reduced to in the Crisis—an urban combat zone—even though the fighting had ended twenty years earlier.

Other than the palm trees, I could have been standing in Sarajevo in the aftermath of the Balkan conflict. Faded signs advertised a Lloyd's Bank and a Shell service station as well as squash courts and a beauty salon, the businesses all long gone, their mournful buildings boarded up with chain-link fencing and iron bars. Most of Arawa's city blocks had been vandalized, set afire, and destroyed, combustion outlines still marking what little survived of crumbling concrete-block walls and burned-out roofs open to the sky. Men and women lazed on the streets and sidewalks like the moss and ferns growing in pavement cracks, having nothing to do and nowhere to go. Other than a few pathetic shops selling trivial goods like stationery and mobile phone top-ups, Arawa was less a town now than simply a roadway junction that hosted the region's large open-air market and served as a depot for vehicles dropping off and picking up coconuts, cacao beans, and people.

I hunted down Impregnable's former address. It was a one-story industrial building with its entrance off Arawa's main street via an inner courtyard designed for both foot and vehicular traffic. I knocked on doors up and down the street until I retrieved the name and phone number of Anita Savant, the landlady. When I called her, she said she would be happy to show me the property. An hour later she arrived, fished a large key ring out of her woven reed pocketbook, and let me in.

The building had not been used in years. Thick, ten-foot cobwebs hung from iron girders bridging the corrugated tin ceilings, bats clustered upside down in the eaves, and rat droppings were everywhere. Plant life grew out of cracks in the concrete floor. Divided into two large rooms, one side of the building functioned as a product showroom, with the other side a workspace. A doorway in a corner of the workspace side led to a fenced-in, exterior yard for operating the melting furnace. It was my lucky day; in opposite corners of the workspace were two, one-of-a-kind rooms: a wood-paneled cashier's office, with a window that housed an air-conditioner sleeve, and a huge, walk-in vault. There were also facilities that I learned were rarities for rental space in Bougainville: an interior kitchen and a separate bathroom with shower, both with running water.

A week later, the building belonged to Mt. Bagana Resources, pursuant to a long-term rental lease. The Gold Dealer, a gold buyer located in the center of Arawa, the epicenter of central Bougainville's gold-mining district, would be open for business as soon as I could clean it up and obtain employees, machines—and customers.

"How do I get around here without a car?" I asked Leki that night in the dining room.

"PMV," she said. "Public motor vehicle." For dinner, she served me a single lamb chop with the thickness and toughness of shoe leather, and a pile of sweet potatoes. It was a meal that I learned was typical for Bougainville: light on protein and heavy on starch. A few minutes later, Leki returned to my table with a bottle of drinking water and a piece of paper. She placed the bottle down in front of me and handed me the paper; she had written three local phone numbers on it. "These are PMV drivers," she said. "Where do you want to go?"

"I need some basic supplies," I said, and showed her my list.

"Call this driver for short trips in town," she said, pointing to the top number on the paper. "There's a general store called STI down the street from Impregnable's building."

"Wait a minute. How did you know I was taking that building?"

She flashed her incandescent smile. "Everyone in town knows."

The next day, I walked down to the general store. Inside, I accumulated mops and brooms, detergent, and hand tools, and piled them up at the checkout counter.

The distinguished man at the cash register introduced himself as Stanley, the owner. As I pulled out a wad of kina to pay him, he rang up items while yelling in pidgin out the front door. A young man in dreadlocks shuffled inside and stood at attention. Stanley handed me my change and gave the youngster some instructions, and he emerged from a storeroom a minute later with two empty cardboard boxes.

Stanley looked over at me. "You're moving into the Impregnable building?"

"Yes."

"Where's your crew?"

"I don't have a crew."

Stanley looked at me like I was crazy, and then a thin smile crossed his face, and he nodded toward the young guy. "This is Charlie. He'll give you a hand with your supplies. Take him with you; he can help. He's three kina an hour."

"You sure?" I asked. "I don't want to steal your help."

"He's not my help," Stanley said. "Take a look outside. Charlie's just standing around out there like everyone else in this town, praying someone like you comes along. You can trust him; he's from my village. If you need anything else, just let me know; we'll try to help."

Charlie—Charlie Tuku was his full name—picked up one of the cartons and followed me across the street. We started by bagging trash and scrubbing down every interior surface in the building. The following day, Charlie brought in a cat, and the rats disappeared. He borrowed a ladder from Stanley and used it to climb up into the corners of the roof with a bamboo pole; from there, he flushed out all the bats. He introduced me to Philip Tibola, an electrician who I hired to rewire and reequip the interior and exterior light fixtures and install fans for the customers and an air conditioner for the cashier's office. We brought in Joe Sipo, a carpenter, to build walls to separate the assay area up front from the melting area in the rear. At the front entrance, Joe erected walls and doors with a Plexiglas window for a reception area and assay room. Vandals had tried to open the vault and had damaged it in the process. I emailed Elizabeth, who was able to locate a safecracker in Sydney; he flew up and repaired the lock.

After a couple of months cleaning, wiring, and woodworking, I was close to completing the renovation of the building and opening the business. I had grown impatient; I couldn't wait to start making money. It had taken much more time than I had expected, but I was learning that everything in Bougainville took longer. I deluded myself into thinking that equipping and organizing the Gold Dealer would be the hard part; buying gold would be easy. I emailed my sons, predicting that I was going to make mountains of cash.

That weekend I needed a break and decided to explore Arawa's beachfront. On Saturday morning, in shorts and a T-shirt, I walked to the end of my street, took a right onto the coast road, and kept going south. The road skirted some shacks and stores, and then, through a scattering of palms, I caught sight of the sea. I veered off into the bush, high-stepping through underbrush. Skirting mountains of flotsam that had probably taken twenty years to accumulate, I arrived at the shore. The sand wasn't white but a dark muck, a mixture of volcanic, magnetite-suffused runoff, and mud. I took my shoes off and sampled the water. It didn't feel like the sea, more like a warm bath. The sand was almost black, the trash everywhere. I moved south, hoping to find a better stretch. That's when I noticed the sand flies. At first there were only a few, and I brushed them away. They kept coming, and then there were more, tiny ones, and they began to swarm. At first, I didn't think they were biting me, but then I realized the flies' bite involved some kind of a delayed-reaction system. I hadn't felt anything at first, but now I could feel the flies biting me for sure. Dozens of red marks appeared on my arms and legs. I stumbled off the beach, back onto the coast road, and home. I examined myself and counted hundreds of bites.

All of them itched; a few of them stung. I took a shower, made myself a couple of stiff drinks, and went to bed. I was miserable all night. I usually toughed it out with minor maladies, but in the morning the bites were swelling. I emailed my sons, and they were unanimous: I needed to have someone look at me. When I went across the street to the Arawa Hospital Clinic early the next morning, the doctor confirmed my concern.

"You people must taste very good to these sand flies," he said. "I can go out on that beach a hundred times and never get bit." I didn't take his words as insulting, but just matter-of-fact. "I don't want to alarm you, but there is a strain of sand fly here in Bougainville—and I have no idea which type of fly has bitten you—that lays its eggs inside those bites. Then more will grow inside of you. It's your choice; you can wait around to see what kind of sand fly it is, or you can go to the Pacific International Hospital in Port Moresby, and they'll take care of it. They're the hospital in Moresby for expats like you. They've got a treatment that gets rid of the eggs." He looked at me as I was leaving. "Didn't anyone tell you not to walk on the mud beaches here?"

I felt really stupid staring back at him, but I couldn't think of a word to say.

"Stick to the white sand beaches. There's no critters there."

I flew to Port Moresby at noon. When I arrived at the airport, I fished Eki's business card out of my backpack and called him. Surprised to hear from me, he was happy to take me to the hospital. I registered as a patient with the administrative staff, and then a nurse spent the balance of the day sticking the needle of a syringe full of something in each of several hundred bites up and down my legs and arms. So much for playing tourist on the beach in Arawa.

I was trying to decide when to go to Lae to check out equipment when two news flashes accelerated my schedule. First, the Bougainville government announced that within the next twelve months, its mining department would begin taking applications for alluvial gold-mining licenses in a limited number of locations. That was good news for me and Mt. Bagana Resources; I wondered if Lucien would be competition. But it was the last straw for Rio Tinto, the big international conglomerate that controlled BCL, who perhaps had deluded themselves into thinking they might still manage to finagle their way back into Bougainville's good graces. They announced they were calling it quits, cutting BCL loose, and giving their shares in the subsidiary to the Bougainville and PNG governments. Now I had two reasons to go to Lae, and the sooner the better. I needed equipment for my gold-dealing business, and I needed to find someone who could not only help me run that, but get me ready to pursue alluvial gold mining as well.

Thankfully, at that juncture, the guy from the equipment store in Lae emailed me back: The man I needed to speak to was a cousin, a geologist named Michael Candi. He was available anytime to meet me at the store in Lae, and his email and telephone number were provided. I called Candi, telling him I was looking for someone with experience in alluvial gold to work in my gold-buying business, and to potentially prepare some mining license applications. With no hesitation, he responded that he was my guy—a trained geologist who had received his degree from the University of Papua New Guinea. I debated telling him that I wasn't seeking a trained geologist, but after the debacle with the Alaskans, I figured any locally trained expert would be an improvement. I asked if he was available to meet me at the store in Lae at the end of the following week, and he agreed to do so. I booked a round-trip air ticket.

I was going to need more money. I emailed Elizabeth. I described my progress with the Gold Dealer, and suggested that maybe her plans to produce and distribute a film trailer about Bougainville could come in handy. When she got my message, she called me to discuss the subject further.

"How's it going?" she asked when she got me on what she said was her third try. The line was very scratchy.

"I'm fine, I guess," I said. It had been weeks since Elizabeth and I had talked, probably the longest gap in our conversations since we had met years earlier. I did my best to sound upbeat, but I doubt I was persuasive. I had been in Bougainville for three months straight—after working all over the world, it was the longest time I had ever been away—and even though I tried not to think about it, talking to someone from home dredged up empty feelings.

"What exactly were you thinking for my sizzle-reel?" she asked. "I was designing it more for investors than locals."

I said, "If you could modify it so we could show it to both audiences, that would be helpful. We need a device to get to know the Bougainville chiefs and their panners better. Lucien has been our only contact with them until now."

"We can't believe a word he told us."

"Agreed," I said. "All the more reason for us to open direct lines of communication and make new friends."

She said she would get a production crew hired for the sizzle-reel and book her trip that day.

At dinner the following Thursday night, I told Leki I would be gone for a while.

She looked truly alarmed. "You're going home already?"

I laughed, but made a mental note not to joke about that subject, at least not with Leki. "You're not getting rid of me that easy. I've found a workspace and a good helper in Charlie; now I need tools," I said. "I'm just hopping over to Lae for two days. When I come back, it'll be time to get some customers."

Friday morning, I flew to Lae. Other than transiting the Port Moresby airport, it would be my first experience on the PNG mainland. The flight from Kieta took an hour. As we circled over the central stretch of the Owen Stanley Range, I could see Nadzab, the Lae airfield that had once been a WWII military base, lying at the seaward end of a long green valley. It was sunny, and the view was gorgeous; fields of sugar cane waved in the wind.

We landed, and my vision of the verdant Papua New Guinea terrain was squelched the moment I entered the airport. Dark and ominous, I doubted there was a more depressing airport terminal anywhere on earth. Uniformed men from Guard Dog, the security company whose employees I had seen in Port Moresby, operated the hotel transit system. Guard Dog vans, sporting the company's yellow-and-brown German shepherd logo and displaying various hotel destinations, idled along the curb, the vehicles wrapped with chain-link armor, their vacationing passengers no doubt horrified.

I hailed a taxi from the line, gave the driver the address of the equipment store in Lae, and we headed down a potholed road to town. The highway between the terminal and town—PNG's largest industrial city—seemed a clear indictment of the government: a corrupt, inept entity that couldn't even get its act together to gift wrap what had to be one of its best, most well-traveled vistas, a gorgeous landscape of lush fields and cultivated plantations. The potholed roadway lasted a half hour, and then emptied its traffic into a new, four-lane, divided highway, complete with electric lighting and traffic fixtures. The conga line of vehicles sped up, and the taxi driver hit the gas.

"Chinese build," the man said, peering at me via his rearview mirror.

"Why?"

"They want our gold," he said, a look of distaste crossing his face.

We arrived in downtown Lae ten minutes later. The streets were hot and dusty. From the literature describing it as PNG's industrial center, I had expected Lae to be a major urban area, but it was smallish and hilly, its prewar perimeter fighting a losing battle against squatter-fed urban sprawl. The taxi driver dropped me off at a strip mall in front of a storefront whose signage advertised mining equipment.

A PNG guy in khakis and expensive Timberland work boots who had to be Michael Candi was standing outside with a shorter, stubbier guy in shorts wearing a leather, Australian-type bush hat. I said hello, and Michael introduced himself and his colleague, Tete. Tete offered me a friendly but muted hello, blurred by a slight stutter. Other than Grumpy and the travelers and staff I had encountered coming in and out of the Port Moresby airport, Michael and Tete were the first locals I had met from PNG. Michael's skin was definitely lighter—he never would have passed for a Bougainvillean—but Tete's coloration was darker; he might have passed for either.

The three of us went inside the store, where Michael's cousin, the salesmen, waited. The place wasn't at all like what I had envisioned a mining equipment store to be: a dusty, industrial space crawling with prospectors and geologists. The air conditioning was nice, but it felt like we were in a place where someone shopped for stereo equipment.

"I understand you're a gold miner," the salesman said with an oily smile after we had all exchanged introductions.

"Not yet," I replied. "For now, I'm just trying to learn the gold-dealing business. It would certainly help if I knew a little more about how all this stuff works."

Tete screwed up his courage. "Y-y-you want to know your customers-s-s-s," he said, trying to cut off the last of his stutter.

"Exactly," I said, a little louder than necessary, happy that he had gained enough confidence to talk; it was also a smart thing to say.

"Just stick with me, partner," Michael said, trying to reassert himself into the lead position in the conversation. "Your problems are over."

I let Michael and his cousin lead us down an aisle until we came to the melting equipment. I examined the boxes on the shelves. The equipment was indeed melting machinery, but it was electric, not gas-fired. The smallish furnaces looked hobby-sized. It was all they had.

"Take the biggest one," Michael said as his cousin took a box containing the largest electric furnace off the shelf and set it on the counter in front of me. "It'll be worth it."

I saw Tete watching me, but he didn't say anything. I examined the labelling on the box, but I couldn't read it: the equipment was made in China. "Someone's going to have to tell me how much volume this unit will handle; it doesn't look adequate." I looked at Michael and his cousin. "Do either of you know?"

"A lot," Michael said.

Tete couldn't contain himself. "No, no," he said, shaking his head, picking the box up off the counter and handing it back to Michael's cousin. "This is an electric furnace. In Bougainville, the current in the grid won't be strong enough. These furnaces won't melt your gold."

"Hey, Tete," Michael said, "He said he likes it."

I said, "No, I didn't. Go on, Tete; what are you saying?"

Tete looked perturbed. He started to speak, stuttered, and stopped. Then he signaled me to follow him outside. Michael and his cousin chose to wait inside in the air conditioning. Outside, the sky was cloudless but hazy, and the sun beat down on the asphalt parking lot. Lounging next to a beat-up jalopy, a group of guys stood watching us.

Tete saw me looking at them. "They're not going to do anything," he said.

"If you say so."

"They're *raskols*, but don't worry; I know them," he said.

"What's a rascal?"

"It's a different word here," Tete explained. "*Raskols* are PNG mafia." He changed gears. "Sorry, but this is the wrong place for you. Michael and his cousin are trying to take your money because they think you're a rich white guy and you don't know any better."

"That's been known to happen. What are they telling me that's wrong?"

"Everything," Tete said. "This store is for amateurs, wealthy foreigners on vacation from Australia who come to PNG to pan gold. There's nothing inside that you can use. You're going to need to go to Australia if you want new equipment. You can buy stuff here in Lae, but it will be secondhand." He didn't stutter once.

"Where can I buy secondhand equipment?"

Tete said, "Lae has many places for that; it just takes time. There are many melters in the hills, and when they go out of business, they sell their machinery here. If you give me a list, I can look around down by the docks and find it for you. It would take me a week or so. I know what you need: a furnace, Doré molds, some crucibles."

"Would Michael let you?"

Tete looked surprised. "I don't work for Michael. I know him from my job. He's a geologist; he doesn't know anything about this stuff. Michael's a friend. He asked me to help him. So here I am." He shrugged.

I said, "Well, how do you know so much about this stuff? Who *do* you work for?"

"The MRA."

"What's the MRA?"

"The Mineral Resource Authority; PNG's mining department."

I started to feel better. "What do you do for them?"

"I'm a manager of their small-scale alluvial mining program."

I felt even better. "I guess that's a pretty good job?" I said, hoping it wasn't.

"It's okay." Tete grinned. "I like the gold business."

"I just want to make sure I heard you right. I think you said that if I gave you a list of everything I needed, you could find it in a couple of weeks."

"Yes. A week, I think. Maybe a little more," Tete said.

"How much would it cost?" I asked.

"Give me a minute." Tete went inside and came back out with paper and pencil. He asked me to specify the equipment I thought I needed and scratched down words and numbers on the paper. He told me he was adding some tools and supplies and recorded those amounts too. When he had asked me twice if there was anything else, he added up the columns and sighed. "All right," he said, scratching his head. "Yes; too bad. For everything, sorry, it's expensive."

"How much?"

Looking pained, Tete said, "About two hundred thousand, before shipping. The most expensive things are the XRF guns; they'll be fifty thousand apiece, used."

"Dollars?"

"No, no; kina."

Maybe I shouldn't have, but I couldn't help grinning. "You're saying I can get all that stuff for only seventy thousand dollars?"

Tete looked relieved at my reaction. "Yes. But before shipping."

"Well, how much is shipping?"

"A small container is six thousand kina."

"So what? That's still only seventy-two thousand dollars," I said out loud. I looked back at him. "Do they sell used vehicles in Lae?"

Tete said, "Yes; this is the best place to buy vehicles in PNG. I know the dealers, and I can test-drive them for you."

"Could you find a secondhand Toyota five-door while you're locating the used equipment?"

"Yes. That will only take a day."

"How much would a good, used Toyota five-door cost?"

Tete stuttered, "N-n-ninety thousand kina; m-m-maybe ninety-five."

"Can you fit a Toyota five-door in a container?"

"No. They ship vehicles separately. That costs about twelve thousand kina."

"How long does it take the ship to go to Bougainville?"

Tete said, "I'll have to check; I know they leave every two weeks."

I looked at Tete. The sun was very hot, and his face and beard dripped with perspiration. "It's hot out here. I'm sorry to keep you."

He shrugged, wiping his face. "It's always hot here."

"How much would you charge me to do all this?"

Tete reverted to his earlier, timid persona. "I don't know. Whatever you say is okay."

I studied him for a moment. "I've got a better idea. What if, after you put the stuff on the boat, you flew over to Bougainville? That way, you could help me set it up and check the place out."

Tete surprised me. "Y-Y-You mean you might offer me a job?"

I laughed. "I don't know if I should tell you this, but it's like you fell out of the sky. Yeah, the thought crossed my mind."

"I would like that," he said. "My friend Gideon Donglu tells me he really likes Bougainville."

"Who?"

"H-H-He's the executive director of the Bougainville mining department," Tete said. "Another friend from the MRA."

Some days are just better than others. "That's good to know. Now that you mention it, I think I met the guy." I looked Tete in the eye. "Well, what do you think?"

"I'd have to tell my family. W-W-What's my name? I mean, my title?"

"I'll explain later, but where I come from, someone who rescues a helpless foreign castaway is called 'Friday.'"

19

Elephant Country

I had been back from Lae a week when I saw the Australian road crew outside the house they occupied across the street from the Women's Centre packing up their pickup trucks like they were leaving.

I admired the house. At first glance, it was a typical, pre-Crisis BCL manager's house. A single-story ranch structure, it sat up on iron stilts one floor above ground level over a two-bay, concrete-floor carport, with the ground floor containing utility rooms. The more I passed by the house on my way in and out of the Women's Centre, the more I realized that—for Arawa, anyway—it was a good one. It had a large, wrap-around porch providing, because it was on a corner and one could see in several directions, excellent views. It had always impressed me as being secure, with a ten-foot chain-link fence topped with barbed wire enclosing the yard and gardens, and phosphorescent lights in the carport that switched on automatically after dark. My cooking repertoire barely rose above boiling water, but the Women's Centre, with its dining room open for breakfast and dinner, was across the street. For natural foodstuffs, there was a street-corner produce market two blocks away. Across the other street was the Arawa Hospital Clinic. Not exactly Memorial Sloan Kettering, but at least it was close. The street ran from the sea straight up to the Arawa hills, was paved smooth with asphalt, and had no potholes. That doesn't sound like a big deal, but I'd gotten waylaid on Arawa streets with potholes as big as the Grand Canyon, and wanted to avoid them.

I hustled across the road and through the driveway gates to where the men were loading their trucks. "Are you guys leaving?" I asked someone covered with tattoos.

"That we are, mate," he said.

"Has someone already leased the house in your place?"

"The devil, I expect," a bald guy with a full beard said, grinning when he saw my confusion. "I don't know, mate; I don't think so. Just ask Stanley."

"Who's Stanley?" I asked.

"The landlord?" the tattooed guy yelled. "The guy who owns the general store."

I signed a lease with my friend Stanley that afternoon and spent the weekend cleaning the house, picking up the trash in the gardens, and buying sheets and towels, supplies, and groceries. For personnel at the Gold Dealer, I added to Charlie by hiring Leki and Shirley, another lady from the Women's Centre, to be cashiers; Joe and Clepson, two experienced gold melters; and Ates and Steven, gold buyers with connections. All I needed was someone to handle security, and I would be ready for business as soon as Tete arrived.

"Have you heard about the man they call Ishmael?" I asked Leki on Monday when we were in the office.

Her eyes widened in a questioning glance. "Yes."

"I was thinking of asking him to provide us with security," I explained.

She was silent for a moment. "You're a foreigner. I don't know if he'll do it, but tonight I'll ask him."

"How do you know Ishmael?" I asked.

"Everyone knows Ishmael."

When I got to the Gold Dealer the next morning, Leki told me Ishmael had agreed to meet me and would stop by at ten. Later that morning, Joe, one of my recently hired melters, stuck his head in the door of the cashier's office where I was going over some recordkeeping with Leki. "Ishmael is here to see you." The way Joe announced the man's arrival made it sound like he was proud that Ishmael was visiting his new place of business.

Ishmael stood in the reception area waiting for me. I checked my watch—ten o'clock. It was my first experience with punctuality in Bougainville. He stared back at me through dark, intelligent eyes. Barefoot in a pair of jeans, he looked as if sculpted from rippled wire; there wasn't an ounce of fat on him. His bearded face was coal black, chiseled, and handsome in a brutal way. Ishmael's beard tried unsuccessfully to cover up a massive scar that started behind his right ear and ran down his neck all the way to his triceps. His upper torso was barrel-like, pecs and biceps stretching his T-shirt to its limit, but there was something amiss with his left arm; it was noticeably shorter than his right one. If you had told me the man was thirty, I wouldn't have questioned it, but he was probably fifty.

"Hi, I'm Jack Davis," I said, offering my hand. "Sorry, but I don't know your last name."

"Call me Ishmael," he said, shaking mine. His fingers felt crooked; apparently, his neck and arm weren't his only war injuries.

"Welcome to the Gold Dealer," I said.

"Yes. Maybe for you the place will operate," he said, studying my face to see my reaction.

We both laughed.

"Would you like to sit down? I have an air-conditioned office. Some water?"

"No thank you." He looked at me expectantly.

I said, "I'm planning to buy gold here, so there will be cash and gold on the premises. I can lock up everything in the vault overnight, but when I'm open, I'll need security."

Ishmael craned his neck, taking in the reception area and the doorways. "I'll just look around?"

"Sure." I gave him a five-minute tour of the premises.

"Why are you doing this?" he asked when we had finished.

I can't say I was surprised by his question; it was a legitimate one. "Well, it looks like there are lots of people panning gold, but they're getting ripped off. I'm betting I can help them, and make money too."

"You're trying to build a business and make money; you're not one of those NGOs," he ascertained, seeming satisfied with the conclusion.

"Hardly."

Ishmael said, "It's not as easy as it looks. Many foreigners have tried, but most give up quick. The guy here before you never even opened for business."

"I will."

Ishmael didn't say anything for a moment, like he was thinking it over. "You are American?"

"Yes."

"What type of security do you think you need?" he asked.

"You tell me. Is Arawa anything like Port Moresby?"

Ishmael's eyes amused, he looked at me as if regarding an idiot. "No, no."

"Sorry; I just don't know. Do you think I need one guard or two?" I knew my question sounded stupid, but it was all I knew to ask.

He said, "Let's take a ride in my truck."

I followed him outside and climbed into his pickup. It was a black Ford four-by-four, probably the only Ford pickup in all of Bougainville, the word "Independence" painted in white letters on each door. We pulled out into the main street. As we drove, Ishmael's eyes scanned the streets and sidewalks in front of him, surveying the town as if it was his. He said to me, "Roll down your window so people can see you."

I didn't know where we were going or what we were doing, but did what he said. We cruised around downtown Arawa, up and down streets and alleyways.

"Where do you live?" he asked me.

"Well, you're going to think I'm an idiot," I said, "but I don't know the name of my street."

I think he laughed to make me feel better. "Don't you live over by the bend down market?"

"Now I really feel stupid," I said. "There's a market at the end of my street, but I didn't know it had a name."

A minute later, Ishmael swung the Ford past the market at the foot of my street. "You're on this street, right? That's the *Bendaun* Market—pidgin for 'bend down.' There are no seats there, so the ladies must kneel down in front of their produce." We cruised my street and then drove across the Tupukas River Bridge. "This is the Town Market, where the town of Arawa pays for a marketplace building with seats and stalls," he said, gesturing to the large, roof-covered market I walked past every morning on my way to work. As he headed up a side street, he pointed straight ahead. "The Big Trees Market," he said as we drove underneath an arch formed by two, grove-sized banyan trees on either side of the road. "Many markets here, but not so many stores," Ishmael explained, like a city father.

Passersby waved to Ishmael. Several times, people signaled him to pull over. Short conversations took place in pidgin, and then we moved on. After an hour, when we had covered the entire downtown area of Arawa, he brought me back to the front door of the Gold Dealer.

Ishmael said, "I think that should be enough. People know you're with me now."

"Really? That's it? I'm going to have a lot of gold and cash in there. I don't mind paying."

"You don't need to."

Ishmael was the first Bougainvillean with something to sell me who hadn't asked for foreigner-scale compensation at the outset. It seemed too good to be true. "If I change my mind, can you provide a man or two to watch over the place?"

"Yes, yes."

"All right then, I guess for now that's good enough. I'm thinking the best thing would be some kind of periodic maintenance fee arrangement. I'll draw up a contract. How much do I pay you, and when?"

He shook his head. "No money."

"Come on. You should get paid."

"I do this for Bougainville. You live here, so you get it too."

Ten days later, Tete called from Lae. The equipment and Toyota five-door were on the interisland freighter, bound for the Kieta port, and Tete had a reservation on an Air Niugini flight in two weeks. The day he arrived, I arranged for a PMV to take me to the Kieta airport to pick him up. After I fetched him and his luggage and the PMV returned us to the house, I unlocked the front gate and started up the stairs to the front door, when out of the corner of my eye, I saw Tete behind me with his bags heading to the utility rooms downstairs.

"Where are you going?" I called down to him.

He looked at me as if the direction he was taking was the natural order of things. "I'll sleep down here."

"You're upstairs," I said, "in the room next to mine." I waited until he came up the stairs. "It's just me and you here so far," I said, unlocking the front door and holding open the screen door for him. "Would you like a beer, or water?"

He stopped in the doorway and grinned, seeming surprised. "A beer?"

"Yeah; they've been sitting in the back of the refrigerator, so they should be ice cold."

"Yes, please. A beer."

"Coming up. I'm not a very good cook, but I made fried chicken for dinner. You like chicken?"

Later that night, I was sitting outside on the front porch when I overheard Tete in his room speaking to someone on his mobile phone. "I told you. He's white. I'm sleeping in the room next to him, and my bed was made with clean sheets when I arrived. He gave me a cold beer and made me chicken dinner."

The following Monday, the first day of September 2016, the Gold Dealer opened for business. My plan was simple: buy as much gold as I could, as cheaply as possible. Naively, I thought Bougainvilleans would make it easy for me to do so.

I couldn't have been more wrong. My easygoing days in Bougainville had come to an end. I had first set foot on the island a year earlier, moved there six months ago, and made modest progress, notwithstanding a short detour to deal with Lucien. I had leased and equipped a functional gold dealer location, rented a serviceable house, obtained a used car, and opened a business. Working with things in Bougainville wasn't as straightforward as it was stateside, but it could be done. It was working with Bougainvilleans that made Bougainville challenging.

Most Bougainvilleans had difficulty with time; it didn't seem to matter to them. I could make an appointment to meet someone at ten, and they might show up at eleven, noon, or not at all. Since their time didn't matter, they assumed yours shouldn't either. Another annoyance was the feckless confusion over Bougainville versus PNG standard time. Bougainville, being eight hundred miles east of Papua New Guinea and geographically part of the Solomon Islands, was in a different time zone, one hour ahead of PNG. That didn't seem to register with Bougainvilleans. Despite their ambivalent feelings about PNG, most of them set their clocks and made their appointments using PNG time, but just as ambivalently: sometimes they did, and sometimes they didn't. When chaos ensued, they didn't understand why.

The chiefs were a conundrum. Bougainville's male chiefs wanted you to believe they ran the place. In some ways they did, but in most respects, the notion was preposterous. Since much of Bougainville was a matrilineal society, not all chiefs were men; some were women. I had no problem with the female chiefs. Bougainvillean women were strong: They not only raised the children, but also did most of the work earning the family's livelihood. Sometimes they gave me the feeling they didn't need men, but just tolerated them. My guess was that if the women were in charge, Bougainville would have fewer problems.

The male chiefs were another story. Most were dignified, astute men and could be chief-like, but some were lazy and gutless, and when given any opportunity to speak, utter windbags. At times when Bougainville needed leaders to stand up and step forward, my impression was that many of them would be checking out the exits.

I had been introduced to the chiefs through Lucien and had been happy to make friends, viewing them as cultural vignettes, snapshots of Bougainville. For an initial period, I harbored a quaint view of the chiefs as a sort of dignified royalty, akin to what Sitting Bull was to the Sioux. Now that my gold-dealing business required me to develop harder-edged, business understandings with the chiefs, I presumed I could rely on them. How foolish of me.

I had assumed that the chiefs, being chiefs, had something to do with what happened to the gold being panned in their village. When I discussed the subject with them, they had not discouraged me. My business plan for the Gold Dealer involved a win-win arrangement: the village panners would pan the gold, the chiefs would direct the panners to sell their gold to the Gold Dealer, and we would allocate a percentage of the transaction's proceeds to the village coffers to pay for things like medicine and schoolbooks. My miscalculation was to expect the chiefs to do work and be responsible.

To close the deal and launch the Gold Dealer, Elizabeth and I decided to throw a get-to-know-you event for the chiefs at the Women's Centre. The party would feature a screening of Elizabeth's film and get the chiefs enthused about the Gold Dealer. We sent the word out and made sure everyone knew the food was free. Charlie even took a couple of guides and hiked up into the bush to invite chiefs in the remote villages.

In retrospect, the only thing that produced the overflow crowd was the free food. To start things off, Elizabeth previewed her film, entitled *The World is Watching*, and everyone liked it. Next, I began a short presentation about the Gold Dealer and our business plan for the chiefs' participation. Unfortunately, the staff mistakenly put the food out on the buffet tables just as I began my remarks, and at that point, no one in the audience was interested in anything except jockeying for position in the feed line and heaping as much food on their plate as possible. People were going back for seconds before I finished.

The food didn't prevent the chiefs from getting our message, and when it came their time to speak, everyone wanted to get into the act. One by one, the chiefs got up and bloviated, telling their colleagues how committed they were to convincing the panners in their villages to sell their gold to the Gold Dealer, and that we were all in this wonderful effort together.

Elizabeth was scheduled to leave the following day. "Do you think it worked?" she asked me about the previous evening, standing downstairs next to our five-door as Tete prepared to drive her to the airport.

"I'm optimistic," I said; I really was.

I never saw most of those chiefs again. They had broken bread with us, and then stood up in front of dozens of witnesses and pledged mutual support; things that in my world back home meant a lot. But, as it turned out, it meant little to the Bougainville chiefs.

Charlie explained it to me. "Living up in the bush, when you're walking by the chief's house on your way home from working in the gardens, especially if you have a heavy load, you might leave a pineapple at his door. Otherwise, since he's not out working himself—he's the chief, after all—he might not have enough to eat. That's all most chiefs do: sit out front of their house and talk to the other men in the village, while the women do all the work. You'll never see a chief panning; that's hard work in the hot sun. As far as what the chiefs promised you about the panners in their village? They lied. No chief's going to tell a panner who to sell his gold to; that would be too much work. The panners would never listen to the chiefs anyway."

I discovered that the pattern exhibited by the chiefs at the Women's Centre was typical of many Bougainvilleans: you can offer them something, and, if it's valuable, they may take it, but that doesn't mean you're going to get what you expected in return.

Back when I was in a mood to be more understanding, I chalked up the failed results of my marketing debacles to basic culture clash. Take the topic of entrusting a chief with money. Initially, I had assumed that any chief in a position of authority and deserving of respect would behave accordingly. Not necessarily. One day, Steven Toppis, the guy Lucien had introduced me to who I thought would make a good NFL linebacker, came into the Gold Dealer to see me. He explained that he had a friend, another BRA ex-combatant named Damien, who had a big panning operation in the mountains down by Buin. We didn't buy much gold from the Buin area because most of the panners that far south ran their gold via longboats over to the Solomon Islands and sold it to the Chinese in Honiara. I had always assumed that those panners were getting hosed by the Chinese dealers and would make a good marketing target for us. Steven told me that if I gave him ten thousand kina—a sizeable grubstake, almost three thousand bucks—he would go down and start a relationship with his friend Damien, buy his gold, and bring it back to the Gold Dealer; we would split the profits. Steven was a major chief in the island's hierarchy, and a significant ex-combatant with the BRA. I gave him the money.

Steven disappeared for over a month. One Saturday I was walking to the general store through a skid-row section of Arawa full of dive bars and brothels. As I walked down an alley, Steven stepped out of a doorway. He recognized me and flashed his big Dracula-like grin, red betel nut spittle dripping off his lips. He was plastered. I tried to ask him what happened to my ten thousand kina, but realized conversation was useless. Steven kept trying to say something to me. As I tried to walk off, he wouldn't let me, laughing but grabbing me.

"Give me money," he finally managed to say, his breath like kerosene.

I gave him fifty kina and kept walking. Steven never said another word to me about the ten thousand kina.

When I told Leki what happened, expecting sympathy, I got the opposite. "You gave him ten thousand kina?" she asked, stunned that a white man could be so stupid.

Blaming the chiefs didn't solve my business problem. If I wanted to deal in gold, I was going to have to go out and buy it myself. Every day, I took Steven and Ates, our gold buyers, bales of cash, and the portable XRF gun, and went up into the jungle.

It took one of those early trips into the bush—to a boomtown-like man camp, a bivouac for dozens of transitory miners on the side of Mt. Bagana—and the words of Lawrence Queen, a well-known geologist, to knock some sense into me about the key to Bougainville's kingdom.

The trip was to Karato, a gold-rich region on the west side of Bougainville Island. Francis Makira, the Karato chief who was our contact, said panners had struck a bonanza there, a big vein of ore close to the surface in rocky ground. A gold rush ensued. Hundreds of panners from all over the island scrambled to the site, high up on the slopes of Mt. Bagana. A hive of thatched huts sprang up overnight, and there was plenty of gold for sale. All we had to do was get there and bring cash.

We packed a million kina, as well as food and sleeping gear. Roundtrip, the journey took a couple of days. Travel on the west side required boats; there were no roads, and walking across the broad, steep mountains was too difficult. Together with Chief Francis and Ates and a couple of local bearers to carry our supplies, we left Arawa in our crew truck at six in the morning in order to hit high tide correctly for the seagoing portion of the voyage.

Ten miles north of town on the way to Panguna, we pulled up to the Me'ekamui toll gate. Roosters were still crowing when I signaled a greeting to the guard. He recognized me, raised the bar, and we passed through. The Me'ekamui area was home to the insular group of Bougainvilleans originally led by Francis Olu. After Olu declared himself king of the Me'ekamui and some Bougainvilleans objected, Olu and the Me'ekamui installed the toll gate to discourage skeptics, and retreated into the clouds. They had made people's lives difficult at one point, but that was twenty years earlier, during the Crisis.

With the locals, the running joke was that the Me'ekamui gate was the *de rigeur*, first stop in Bougainville for any wannabe white journalist or NGO. Trying to be cool in front of the camera, sporting three-day beards, and wearing out-of-place clothing and hastily procured leather wristbands for a touch of authenticity, these pretenders whispered into their microphones that they were entering the land of the Me'ekamui, Bougainville's deepest, darkest jungle haunt, where foreigners were *verboten*. Everyone knew the Me'ekamui had been largely benign for years and currently used the gate only to generate cash. The only people who paid them were the white journalists and NGOs.

The dawn was breaking over the Pacific as we crested the ridge east of Panguna, passing through tufts of mist sticking to the mountainside like cotton candy. It was a clear morning, unusual for Panguna, and against a burnished ivory horizon we could see southeast all the way across the Slot to Choiseul Island, the nearest large member of the Solomon Islands. Along the road, acres of pink and red impatiens blanketed the hillsides, giving way to ferns in the deep folds of the jungle. Rivulets gurgled and trickled down sheer rock walls, while streams crashed down creases in the mountainside where the road switched back and forth. Topping the ridge at two thousand feet above sea level, we coasted west toward a still-dark Solomon Sea fifteen miles away, down the steep mountain road until we came into the main intersection of what had once been Panguna Town.

There were hundreds of panners in the Panguna area, and we bought a majority of our alluvial gold from the region. I had often been up to Panguna Town, replete with bombed-out buildings, rusting factories, and mangled vehicles. I felt the same way every time I drove through the place: A lost village of the damned, it had to be one of the most disheartening, discouraging places on earth. It was impossible to view Panguna Town's families—like persistent weeds sprouting from nuclear waste, making do in rotting, roofless structures, mothers stringing wash in the rain between walls green with fungus—without feeling an enormous sadness. Yes, the Crisis resulted in Bougainville taking important steps toward freedom. But it also caused the total destruction of a well-intentioned town built to house and employ thousands, including a vast number of Bougainvilleans. It was easy to conclude that Bougainville might have been better off trying to settle their differences with PNG in a more peaceful fashion. But two peoples, villagers and foreigners, had fashioned an understanding that teetered on an unstable foundation. One side didn't know they needed to speak up loudly to be heard, while the other side wasn't listening and foolishly thought they could rely on written agreements and lawyers, which, in Bougainville, counted for nothing. When Papua New Guinea's political leaders, a fattened, corrupt third party, stuck their greedy snouts into the mix, all was sure to come crashing down.

Our road left Panguna Town's wreckage behind and dropped down off the mountain along the Jaba River, into the so-called Panguna Tailings, where gravity and the strong rains that came daily to Panguna had washed the crushed sediment from the big mine toward the sea.

This was where the white journalists came to produce their stories, and the NGOs came to wring their hands. When someone who didn't know better saw the Panguna Tailings for the first time, a vast, gravel-strewn wash, it was easy to conclude that mining must have abused the land, that the moonscape that lay before them couldn't be natural. The truth was in between, but journalists trying to become news anchors needed simplistic conclusions, and NGOs needed afflictions, even if both had to invent them. Their drivers in their shiny new vehicles made sure they got through the Me'ekamui gate by eight in the morning and up to the Panguna Tailings by ten, and then, when the thunderheads formed and began to shake, informed their charges that they must leave no later than noon. They didn't stick around in Panguna to ride out an afternoon storm, to live through the Niagara-like squalls of rain that drenched the landscape daily. Every day, the Jaba River washed boulders the size of tables and chairs down its fall line, as well as millions of tons of gravel, sand, trees, and houses annually, leavened with a few dead bodies; unfortunates caught trying to ford a maelstrom and get home to their village before nightfall.

We left the riverbed behind and pointed across the island toward Marau, a dark, swamp-like port village on the edge of Empress Augusta Bay. Steven, our other gold buyer and a skilled waterman, collected us there in our longboat at eight. We set out across the sea, up the west side of the island, in bright sun and windless conditions. An hour later, right on time for high tide, Steven headed the longboat toward the salt flats lining Karato's jungle-covered shore. With surf breaking around us, it looked as if Steven was going to catch a wave in the longboat before it lumbered through the chop toward the flats fronting the mouth of the Karato River. On the west side, there was no coral reef, but the land itself was porous limestone. As we slipped across a lagoon separating the sea from the river, I looked down to see forests of seaweed growing out of white stone formations below us in water as clear as gin, schools of fish darting in and out of the boat's shadow.

Steven hung a sharp right turn, and we left the saltwater shallows of the lagoon and entered the Karato River's muddy, freshwater estuary. As we moved upriver, for the first hour we saw nothing but mangroves. The bushy plants grabbed and clawed at the riverbed, their thick wooden roots the size of small trees, leafy branches speckled white with egrets. Hammocks sprung up, small green hillocks where over centuries mangroves had composted into islands of earth, sprouting other flora from seeds deposited by the water and the wind.

The hammocks began to knit together, producing riverbanks and higher ground. In ten more minutes, we entered the kingdom of the sago palm. The tall, bushy trees lined the banks, sometimes blocking out the sun. Francis explained that the sago palm was the basic foodstuff of his village. The tree was like a banana plant, easy to propagate and requiring no maintenance. The locals waited until the flowers appeared at the top, when the tree was anywhere from seven to fifteen years old. Then they cut down the tree and split it, extracted the starch from the length of the trunk, and also harvested the leaves for housing materials. The sago starch was Karato's staff of life; it was used to make pancakes, bread, and biscuits, as well as noodles and puddings.

As Steven maneuvered the longboat around dead tree trunks lining the shore, the river switched back and forth every quarter mile or so, getting narrower, the banks and palms crowding closer. We needed to travel eastward to get to Karato, but the river did not run that way directly. It snaked back and forth every quarter mile or so, requiring as much as ten miles of river travel to advance one mile toward our landward destination.

Francis sat up front, erect, squinting in the sun as he stared upriver. "Watch for crocs on the logs."

We all focused intently on the sun-dappled logs lying across the river, but saw nothing.

"There's one," Francis said as we came around a bend, but when the rest of us spotted the log, all we could see was a muddy swirl in the water next to it.

"Pull up to the bank there," Francis said as we swept around another bend in the river.

Steven nosed the longboat to the shore where Francis pointed, and the chief hopped off the bow like a deer and scrambled up the bank and into the jungle, Ates following behind him. They were only gone a minute and then reemerged, beckoning for me to come. While Steven watched the boat, I climbed up the riverbank, crept ten yards into the bush, and knelt as I got closer to the edge of the river where it curved around the bend ahead of us. Francis put his finger to his lips and pointed through the trees. On a logjam of palm trunks lying straight in front of us, a half-dozen crocodiles ranging from six to ten feet long lay as if dead, their mouths wide open as they slept. I looked up and down the river and saw another dozen crocs, what the locals called "*pok poks.*" Rolly Maloney's movie idea was grounded in reality.

We got back in the boat and cruised upstream toward Francis's village. The last half mile of our trip upriver, the water became too shallow for the longboat. Steven shut off the engine and raised its propeller, and we got out of the boat and dragged it upstream.

The village was a short walk from the river, with fifty dwellings that housed about two hundred people. The houses were small and tidy, on wooden stilts, with roofs and walls thatched from sago palm leaves. Unlike Arawa, there was no trash anywhere. Colonial-era clapboard buildings, one a school and another a clinic, served as the village center.

A crowd of villagers waited for our arrival, an unusual occurrence for west side Bougainvilleans. More people trickled into the village center as we arrived from the river. West siders were primitive. Many didn't know English; some spoke only in local dialects and didn't even know pidgin. Most of the children had never seen a white man before. If people like us came to Karato, we weren't allowed to simply show up; we needed to be invited by a chief like Francis, and a ceremony and feast were required. We had given Francis money to stage something appropriate, the people knew all about it, and they had turned out in large numbers. Local dishes were laid out under a thatched awning. People pressed close, eyeing the food and the coolers of soft drinks we had carried up the river with us.

Before everyone could eat, we had to be welcomed. Village ladies in ceremonial dress sang and danced, and afterward washed our faces with leaves dipped in rainwater to spread good spirits. Then everyone ate. After lunch and some halting remarks from a local chief, we dropped off our bedding and supplies in the house where we would spend the night and set off for Mt. Bagana.

The boomtown was two miles away, at two thousand feet above sea level on a steep slope along the west side of the volcano. We arrived upon a frenzied scene. The bonanza strike had occurred when someone had first stumbled on a vein of gold running alongside a steep hill and pulled a nugget out of the ground. Word had gotten out, men had rushed in from all over Bougainville, and the camp had spread out from there. Hundreds of men, barefoot and shirtless, toiled in the jungle heat and humidity. It was a man camp, but there were women there too. Some were panning, but others were prostitutes.

Working a vein of gold was different than mining alluvial gold. A vein is a distinct, sheetlike deposit of ore, typically lodged within a rock formation. The vein in Karato probably held thousands of grams of gold. When a miner found the right place in a vein, he could be rewarded quickly with hundreds of grams of high-quality gold. By contrast, mining alluvial gold meant collecting tiny flakes and grains of alluvial gold and other precious metals, including substantial impurities, in the bottom of a pan. Three panners working together would be lucky to collect a gram of gold a day.

The claim-stake arrangements we saw were surprisingly orderly, better than camps would have been in the old days in Alaska or California under similar circumstances. When I said as much to Francis, he pointed across the way to where several men stood watching; they were larger guys not involved in panning or mining. "Ishmael's boys," he said.

The deposit area had been divided up. Rectangular work zones were staked out perpendicular to the mountain, each about ten yards wide, stretching twenty yards up the hill. Groups of panners worked within their space, scratching out cave-like excavations with crude picks and shovels. Up above them on the hillside, bucket brigades ran water along a primitive irrigation ditch from a stream a hundred yards away. The water was diverted through lengths of hose down individual sections of the hillside, washing material to the foot of what was an enormous slab of mud-covered rock. Workers below clawed the dirt and rock down to their feet where panners on the ground, totally covered in clay-red mud, sloshed around, panning and separating the material that held the gold.

Away from the digging, panners lined up to sell their gold to us. We ran out of cash almost immediately. Francis had told me about the bonanza, emphasizing how much gold was to be had, but I had not believed him. With our million kina, we bought seven kilos in five minutes. We could have bought another twenty kilos, but we would have needed a horse to carry the cash in and the gold out.

The amount of gold was staggering. I had been so consumed with establishing the Gold Dealer that I hadn't taken time to focus on the subject of the massive wealth contained in Bougainville's ground. It's one thing to buy twenty grams of gold from a panner for a couple thousand kina, but quite another to eyeball sheets and nuggets of gold worth millions. The connection between Bougainville and gold didn't hit home for me until Karato. The men I was watching were probably producing twenty kilos of raw gold a day. That was serious money, close to a million bucks. A day. As long as the vein held out—it might be gone in days, or perhaps could last a year—a bunch of barefoot guys with crude tools on an island in the middle of nowhere were generating twenty times what Davis Partners had produced in a year—a good year.

We purchased another seven kilos on credit, telling those panners who agreed to our terms that we would bring back their cash in a week. Others shook their heads and returned to their pits, not ready to trust us yet. When our business was done, we headed back to Francis's village before it got dark. Early the next morning, we walked the boat down the river and headed home, a million dollars of gold in our bags. A lot went wrong during my trips to the bush, but in Bougainville's defense—and with a big assist from Ishmael—I was never robbed.

"Tete," I said as soon as I returned home from Karato, "I need to speak to a first-class geologist." Someone, I explained to him, who knew a lot about the geology of Bougainville, but also a person who would inspire confidence with international financial institutions.

"That's Lawrence Queen," Tete said with no hesitation.

"Who's Lawrence Queen?"

Tete said, "W-W-When I started at MRA, he was the head of the PNG geological survey. He knows more about natural resources in PNG—i-i-including Bougainville—than anyone. He left and went to work for a mining company that made a lot of discoveries."

"Where is he now?" I asked.

"The PNG geologists are all in Brisbane."

"So he's Australian."

"No," Tete said. "He's American."

Lawrence Queen was easy to find on the internet. Tete was correct; Lawrence possessed impressive credentials and had an office on Eagle Street in downtown Brisbane. I called him up, introduced myself, and said I got his name from Tete, who he remembered well. I explained that I wasn't an experienced mining person, but was a gold dealer with some loyal landowner customers. I said I thought there was a good chance the Bougainville government was going to allow commercial mining to resume at some point, and that the landowners would want to team up with me.

"At least you're starting off in a good place," Lawrence said.

"I was up at a boomtown in Karato. I've never seen so much gold."

"Karato's got a lot of it," Lawrence said. "That's just the small stuff near the surface; wait until you see what's under the ground. Are you and your landowners going to file exploration licenses there?"

"I thought I would focus on alluvial mining licenses first. It seems simpler."

Lawrence said, "It's really all the same. Getting to know the chiefs is the hardest part. You're way out ahead of everyone else. I'd try to get as much land in central Bougainville under your control as possible. Filing for exploration licenses should be relatively simple there. Are they issuing them yet?"

"It's sounding like they may issue a few. Bougainville has had a mining moratorium since the Australians came in the 1960s. The chiefs need to request a lifting in their area first, and that hasn't happened yet. We heard that the president may have been influenced to lift it in Isina and Tinputz, but we've never bought any gold there, so we're not interested."

"I wouldn't worry about those places," Lawrence said. "I know the guys involved. Other than bribing people, their favorite pastime is telling geologists like me about geology."

"Okay, but when the time comes, what's it take to apply for an exploration license?"

"You've already got the most important thing: the landowners. Tete's involvement helps. Add some friends at the mining department, plus someone like me, and you're in business—as long as the government doesn't pull the rug out from under you."

"Where do you think would be the best places to file?"

Lawrence said, "Hard to say. Any place around the big enchilada would make sense."

"You mean the Panguna Mine?"

Lawrence didn't answer.

"This is going to sound just as stupid, but I'll ask you anyway," I said. "How come there aren't more mining companies sniffing around in Bougainville? With all these resources under the ground, why is it that only a couple of wannabe junior mining companies have showed up?"

"That's easy," Lawrence said. "One word: politics. Today, a mining company can't lodge a secure claim in Bougainville. Until that changes, the ground might as well be Swiss cheese. Mining guys want to mine; they don't want to mess with politics."

"What if they fixed that?"

Lawrence just laughed. "You don't know Melanesian politics."

"They're voting on independence soon, and have a presidential election right after that. Let's just say that for once, there was an honest leader in power. What then?"

"Time to go to Bougainville."

"So, subject to politics, Bougainville's worth going after?"

"You really have no idea, do you?"

"That's why I'm asking."

"You're in elephant country, Mr. Davis."

Elephant country…the mining industry's holy grail. I repeated the words to myself when I lay awake at night, wracked with worry. They had a galvanizing ring.

20

Chinese Squeeze Play

In 2017, President Liuman Mogol announced that commercial mining would return to Bougainville, after a thirty-year absence. By personal fiat, bypassing the House of Representatives so as to control the decision-making—and perhaps the governmental money-making—process himself, Mogol lifted the mining moratorium in a limited number of locations in central Bougainville. Mechanical alluvial gold mining would be allowed in the Panguna Tailings region, and exploration could commence in two villages, Isina and Tinputz. Foreigners could not apply alone for any type of mining license, but needed to partner with the landowners where the gold was located.

This was the starting gun I had expected when I first traveled to Bougainville two years earlier. Now, the landowner relationships I had forged through the Gold Dealer were about to pay off. By dint of hard work, we had become the landowners' obvious choice.

It wasn't a coincidence that at the same time I got Bougainville's mining news, an email showed up from my Chinese friend Miao. "Hey Jack," it read, "It's been a while. Didn't you say that you were down in the South Pacific on some island called Bougainville? I'm asking because I'm in the boardroom of one of my clients, Gao Gold, a big

Chinese company in the gold-mining business. Your former partner *Linzhong* is involved, and is here too. Lin is a major shareholder of Gao Gold, and calls the shots. You remember how crazy he is about gold. There's a black guy here pitching Lin and Mr. Jiang, the Chairman of Gao Gold. He says he's from Bougainville, is the commander of the army there, and will be elected president in the next election. The man's on the make. He's telling us that Bougainville has billions in gold, and commercial mining is about to start up again. He says if Gao Gold will back him, he'll deliver control of all the gold and copper on the island, including some huge mine called Panguna? Lin wants to do it, but Chairman Jiang needs to be convinced. If you're there and can help, maybe it's a way for you and Lin to start over. It could be worth a lot to you. I've attached a photo of the Bougainville guy. Do you know him?"

The person in Miao's photo was George Washburn. Even though it was April, Beijing could be cold in the spring, and someone must have warned George; sitting in Gao Gold's boardroom, he was all bundled up in a fluffy white ski sweater, looking like the Michelin Man.

Miao had always gone to great lengths to stay involved with me. He had been the same way with Lin, and I could imagine him adhering to Gao Gold's leader as well. But I had no interest in responding to his email. The last thing I wanted to do was help Lin and the Chinese. I deleted the message, but it was hard to push its disturbing subject matter out of my mind. Bougainville had no antidote for the Chinese Communist Party, whose leaders were obsessed with gold and copper and would do anything to get it. For Bougainville, their arrival would be like the second coming of the Black Death. George Washburn would learn the hard way what blatant racists his Chinese partners were, but Bougainville deserved better.

I tried to forget about China, and focused instead on getting an alluvial mining license. I knew the best mining sites because I knew where the panners found gold. Most of it was in the Panguna Tailings, so Tete and I went up there and scouted around. The best location in the Tailings was controlled by Chief Wendell Bittyman, one of the Gold Dealer's good customers. His land yielded lots of gold, and was the closest to Arawa in terms of driving time. There was one other thing I liked about Chief Bittyman's site. Above the chief's village in the hills was a water collection system and what looked like a penstock, the water conveyance conduit for a hydroelectric generating station. Maybe one day we could figure out how to convert the civil works into a crude hydroelectric project.

I negotiated a partnership agreement with Chief Bittyman. He was agreeable, on the condition that I had nothing to do with Lucien, with whom he had had several disputes concerning BROL. The deal's terms called for my company to pay all costs of licensing, constructing, and operating a so-called wash-plant mine on a bloc—five square hectares—of the chief's land. Chief Bittyman's clan would receive a 10 percent royalty on all gold sales and would be employed to operate the mine. The chief would also, when the deal was signed, receive a one-time, ritual fee of forty thousand kina, roughly fifteen thousand dollars, to pay for a ceremonial feast for the neighboring clans and families. Twenty pigs would be butchered and served, along with other local delicacies. As long as everyone in the area was invited to the ceremony, jealous neighbors wouldn't have a reason to complain about the mine.

Tete and I spent a month assembling our application. In May, at ten o'clock on the first day that the mining department would accept applications for alluvial mining licenses, I submitted the first one on behalf of us and Chief Bittyman. I had expected a line at the department door, but there was no one else around.

For four months I waited for a response, biding my time at the Gold Dealer buying gold from panners. In September, I still hadn't heard a word when rumors began to fly: A mysterious Chinese applicant had applied for not one, but ten alluvial mining licenses, on blocs up and down the Panguna Tailings. If granted, those licenses would monopolize the entire Tailings except for our site. The rumors arrived courtesy of what Bougainvilleans call the coconut news, a media unique to the islands where word of important outcomes floats over the land as if on a cloud of group consciousness, like a coconut on the sea, and typically makes landfall in a depressingly accurate manner.

"I don't know what to believe," I said to Tete when we heard the news. "Get up to Buka and check out the mining department bulletin board." Since Bougainville had no newspapers, important announcements like the granting of mining licenses were still posted physically on bulletin boards at the respective department's offices.

Tete called me when he got to Buka. "It's worse than we thought. The licenses have already been awarded. They must have already conducted the warden's hearings. We're surrounded. Whoever it is took all the available Tailings sites except for ours."

It felt like getting punched in the stomach. Although we had been the department's first license applicant back in May with a timestamped document to prove it, a Chinese interloper had grabbed ten alluvial mining licenses ahead of us, while our application hadn't even been reviewed. The whole process smelled.

"Whose name is on the Chinese licenses?"

"G-G-Gao Gold; w-w-want me to spell it?"

Punch number two. "That's all right. I know who they are." I felt sick, and stupid; when I got the email from Miao, I should have somehow done more. Gao Gold had probably started at the top and taken care of everyone, from Liuman Mogol down through Mining Minister Ferdy Mimosa to Gideon Donglu.

"Are they a big company?" Tete asked.

"Yeah. Does it say who the landowner is?"

"You're not going to like this," Tete said.

"Who is it?"

"George W-W-Washburn and BROL."

"They're not landowners in the Tailings!" I yelled. "They don't own a square inch up there."

"I-I-I'm j-j-just t-t-telling you."

I shouldn't have raised my voice; I knew it flustered Tete. "Sorry; I didn't mean to shoot the messenger. Come on home."

"There's more."

"Christ almighty. What?"

"The same Chinese company was awarded two exploration licenses too. In Isina. Some other guys—it looks like Australians—got two exploration licenses for Tinputz."

"That figures—a waste of time," I said. Isina was George's territory, but there was no gold in Isina; no alluvial gold, anyway. "Remember what Lawrence Queen told us about those guys: they spent a lot of money bribing people, but they don't know what they're doing."

A couple months later, our license application with Chief Bittyman was finally approved. We were the only guys to get one by following the rules, rather than via bribery. Once the news was posted on the mining department's bulletin board—Lesley called to tell me—we leapt into action. Tete hired Donald, a local chief, as a mechanic, and Max, a welder. They began fabricating our wash plant. Meanwhile, I flew over to Lae with a shopping list that threatened to drain our treasury. I bought two excavators, a new JCB model with a one-ton bucket, and a second-hand Shantui as a backup; two used dump trucks, a secondhand Toyota two-seater, an open-back crew truck with a winch; several tons of rebar; and a hundred meters of rubber sluicing material. That cost us a million kina, close to three hundred thousand dollars. I had always worried about money, but now I was petrified. The mine had to pay off quick, or else I'd be forced to go back to my investors for more capital. At that point, they'd probably tell me to swim home.

When I returned to Bougainville from Lae, Tete told me that as soon as our license was posted on the mining department bulletin board, Grumpy showed up across the river from Chief Bittyman's village in the Panguna Tailings. Driving a shiny new five-door, he sat chewing betel nut and taking photographs with a camera outfitted with a telescopic lens. Before he left, he stopped to yell at our workers constructing our mine, telling them they were trespassing and that their boss owed him money.

I was half expecting it when Lucien called me a day later; I hadn't heard from him in months. "I think it's time we had a drink," he said. "Can you drop by?"

An hour later, I walked up Lucien's front steps to where he was waiting for me on his porch. He shook my hand and said the civilized things one would expect from the Dr. Jekyll side of his split personality: he hadn't seen me in a while, and was sorry we'd lost track of each other. "Please sit down," he said as he led me into his office. "Can I fix you a drink?"

"I'll take a short one," I said. I fibbed, telling him I had a later commitment and couldn't stay long.

He went into the kitchen and rattled around for a while, coaxing ice cubes out of a tray. I heard a couple of them hit the floor, and figured they ended up in my drink. Lucien called to me from the kitchen, raising his voice over the racket he was making, "Greyson tells me he's seen your men building a wash plant up at Chief Bittyman's village. You should have asked my permission before you started doing anything like that with the chief. He's a member of BROL, you know." Lucien wouldn't have had the nerve to say those words if he had been sitting across from me.

"I can barely hear you," I said. "Do you want me to come out to the kitchen?"

He didn't answer. After a minute more, he appeared with two tall Bougainville Cocktails and a tin of salted peanuts.

"I think this is the first can of peanuts I've seen in Bougainville," I said, picking up the tin of peanuts and examining it. "You didn't have to go to the trouble."

"The airline gave them to me," Lucien said, shrugging, his schoolboy innocence in full flower.

I said, lifting my glass, "Here's to you." I took a pull of my drink and waited for him to do the same. "Chief Bittyman told me he wants nothing to do with you or BROL."

Lucien flashed one of those smiles people use when they're trying to demonstrate they're in control when they're not. "The chief's been known to be forgetful. For ten years, BROL's been the only organization representing the central Bougainville chiefs on gold matters. That's important for everyone up there in the Tailings to understand, including you."

"Sure," I said. "Is this the part when you tell me about Gao Gold?"

There's no doubt I surprised him. Looking like someone had smacked him in the face, Lucien took a few moments to recover. "I'm glad you brought that up. I didn't ask you here to argue. We need to find a way to cooperate."

"Honestly," I said, trying to be decent about it, "there's no chance of that happening."

In sales mode, Lucien ignored my words. "We've got a big opportunity. The Chinese have the money, and the Bougainvilleans have the resource, but you and I can remain in control of these deals if we show a united front."

"Thanks for the drink," I said as I stood up.

Lucien peered over at my glass. "You haven't finished."

"I've got an appointment."

Lucien took a document off his desk and handed it to me. "Please sit down and take a minute to read this."

I sat on the edge of my seat and examined the paperwork. Scanning the words, it occurred to me for the first time that Lucien might be truly off his rocker. The document proposed an absurd transaction between BROL and me, which, when consummated, would cause the Chinese to pay us a total of ten million dollars for control of the development rights to the Tailings.

Lucien grinned at me. "Looks pretty good, doesn't it? Gao Gold's ready to write a check."

I tossed the paperwork back onto Lucien's desk in front of him. "When's the last time you've done a deal with the Chinese?" I asked.

Lucien babbled until I put my hand up.

"It's all right to say you haven't. I'm trying to warn you for your own good. You're attempting to extract what the Chinese call 'the squeeze.' Their cardinal rule is that white guys aren't eligible."

Lucien just blinked at me, fumbling for a response.

I tried again. "George is the one who found Gao Gold, not you. They're Chinese, Lucien. Any Chinese guy is going to conclude what Gao Gold's saying right now: we know why we've got to give George Washburn a piece of this deal, but who's Lucien Sump and BROL?"

Lucien's face got red. "I've been paying George since before Jasper Kaboose died. He can't write me out of this transaction. There'd be hell to pay."

"My guess is he already has." I stood up once more. "Your deal has three problems: George isn't a landowner in Panguna and can't be trusted; the Chinese can't be trusted; and—sorry, nothing personal—neither can you. Thanks for the drink." I headed for the door.

He called after me, "We've got to speak with one voice here, Jack. Otherwise, the Chinese and the chiefs will collaborate, and that'll be the end of us. The Chinese say they know you. A whole group of them are coming soon. I can arrange for you to get reacquainted."

"No thanks."

Lucien followed me out to his front porch. "You don't understand, Jack. The Chinese are paying Greyson directly. I have no control over that."

Someone across the street was cooking something over a fire. The wood smoke reminded me of family camping trips. I tried to focus on that, and the pleasing sound of the crickets, as I walked down Lucien's front steps, out into the street, and home.

A few days went by uneventfully, and I was able to push the unpleasant subject of Lucien and his Chinese collaborators to the back of my mind. The weekend came, and Saturday morning dawned hot and humid. I lay in bed, the sweat on my chest cooling me under the twirling ceiling fan, listening to the geckos chirping as they crawled around inside the air conditioner housing. For some reason they liked hanging out in metal structures; every time I opened my electric meter box to pay the power company, I surprised a handful of them lounging inside. I glanced at my wristwatch; I'd never adjusted it from Eastern Time. It was Friday night back home; maybe one day I'd figure out how to get back there.

When I had taken the Bougainville leap, I had thought I had a reasonable idea about what I was getting into. I was wrong. There was no way to get the full effect other than to live through it. I wasn't looking for sympathy, but it wasn't easy. One day I was processing information for my tax returns—a ridiculously difficult task to accomplish from a remote island in the South Pacific—and needed to calculate the number of days I had been out of the country, hoping to avoid the onerous New York City income tax. Using the immigration stamps on my passport, I calibrated the days I had accumulated in Bougainville during the past year. I was stunned. I double-checked the number, and then for good measure duplicated the process for the previous year. In the last two years, I had averaged nine months out of each twelve-month period in Bougainville.

I ached for home. I missed the little things: waking up early and going for a walk in the neighborhood, the air clear and crisp, the streets clean, and the robins chirping; making myself a cappuccino in the kitchen and grabbing a handful of fresh blueberries from the refrigerator; and getting the news from a real newspaper, not an antiseptic, digital screen, and catching up with the world. Most of all, I missed America, the place all the songs are about: the vast beauty of the land; the people who liked you and wanted you to like them, differences be damned; the endless highways, always beckoning, offering a new life and new friends to anyone who travelled down the road. I became fixated on renting a car and driving across the country the minute I landed back on US soil. Bougainville would never be home.

It was getting late. I got out of bed, did my exercises, showered and dressed, made myself a cup of instant coffee, went out on the porch, and had a breakfast that consisted of a hard-boiled egg. I did my laundry in the sink in the utility room and hung everything out on the lines under the house to dry. The general store was next. I stocked up on cans of tuna and Spam, corned beef and coffee, and some fresh eggs. I returned, and cleaned the house. A month had passed, and it was time to scour the mold off the shower stall. I might as well have been in jail.

Monday was a busy day at the Gold Dealer. We bought almost two kilos of raw gold. By three in the afternoon, we had maxed our allocation of cash for the day. Out at the reception desk, I told Shirley to shut down the buying window. Joe and Clepson were working at the furnace out back, melting the last of the alluvial gold Doré bars. Leki and Moroa, a new cashier, were in the office totaling up the accounts so we could do a financial balance and everyone could go home. Steven and Ates had just returned from their day in the bush buying gold, and Tete and I were in the show room with them sorting out the transactions, when Shirley ran in from the reception area. "Someone just stole your car!" she yelled.

Everyone scrambled out the front door to the parking lot. Our Toyota five-door was gone. Leki said she was going to alert the police and ran down the street to the station house. Joe and Clepson got on their mobile phones and started via Facebook getting the word out to the neighborhood to be on the lookout for our white Toyota.

"What happened?" Charlie asked, looking dazed as he stood in the front door.

"Someone hot-wired it," Shirley said.

We all stood out front, not knowing what to do next. "I wasn't under the impression that a lot of cars got stolen here," I said to Charlie.

"They don't," Charlie said. "Someone's sending you a message."

The crowd in the parking lot grew rapidly. People spilled in from the main street, speaking loudly in pidgin as they heard what had happened. It was as if the rumor of the car theft was tangible, something in the air that people could reach out and grab, and it would pull them along toward the crowd. Many of them approached me, all with versions of the same message: whoever did this wasn't going to be able to get away with it; Bougainville needed the Gold Dealer and the Americans; we couldn't be treated in this manner; and not to worry, they'd get our car back and punish the criminals. For what it's worth, it made me feel pretty good.

A four-door, open-back pickup with bench seats in an elongated truck bed pulled into the parking lot and skidded to a halt, and the driver got out. He was familiar-looking, barefoot in a black T-shirt and jeans. "What happened?" he asked, giving orders to people at the same time, getting the men in the crowd organized.

"Someone hot-wired the boss's car," Shirley answered.

A young man came over to the black T-shirt guy and, in broken English for my benefit, said that he had been standing outside the Gold Dealer waiting for his gold to be melted when someone jacked open the hood of the Toyota. At that point a group of thugs jumped inside the car, fiddled with things for a minute, and then started it up and drove off.

A posse of men filled the back of the black T-shirt guy's truck, some brandishing bush knives, ready to ride. The black T-shirt guy got back in his truck, started it up, and then rolled down his window to pose one last question to the crowd. The chatter was immediate; everyone seemed to agree. I turned to Tete. "What are they saying?"

"One of the thieves was a r-r-redskin," Tete answered.

That's when it hit me: Grumpy had stolen my car. I turned to the man in the truck. "Do you know Greyson Trull?"

He looked at me. "I was thinking him too."

Just then, someone held his mobile phone in the air and started yelling. The black T-shirt guy slammed his door closed, backed up his truck, and yelled something out the window to Tete as he peeled out of the parking lot.

"Someone saw our vehicle," Tete said to me, explaining what the guy with the phone had said in pidgin. "A woman saw Joe's post on Facebook and texted him saying she saw our car speed past her fruit stand in Atamo, on the coast road going north. They're going to try to catch it." He started to walk back inside.

"Wait a minute. Who was that guy in the truck?"

"Which guy?"

"The guy in the black T-shirt; the one driving."

"That's Peacely, Ishmael's brother."

Peacely had our Toyota back under our house by ten that night. He and his posse brought it in, everyone speaking in pidgin, laughing and shouting, enormously pleased with themselves. I examined the truck; there were no dents or nicks. I shook everyone's hand, thanking them, and handed out bottles of water. They all were laughing about something. "What happened?" I asked Tete.

Tete laughed, "They caught Greyson up at Lucien's cattle farm. He and his gang of *raskols* had the car jacked up, and they were taking the battery out of it when Peacely and the boys drove up. Greyson ran off into the high grass and tried to hide behind the cows, so Peacely drove across the field, running him down." He kept laughing. "They said the cows were milling around in circles, forcing Greyson to jump through the mud and the cow dung while the guys chased him. Everyone herded the cows out of the way, until they ran Greyson down and tackled him. He was covered with cow shit. Peacely said they felt like a bunch of guys in a cowboy movie."

The next morning, Leki told me that Grumpy had turned himself in to the police, and I needed to go to the station house. I didn't understand why Grumpy would do that, but followed Leki down to the police station, a low, one-story building next to the bank. The morning was sunny and bright, but it was dark inside. A man Leki knew named Chris sat at the sergeant-at-arms desk. The front half of the room was the policemen's working area, while jail bars ran from one end of the room to the other, dividing it lengthwise. Grumpy sat behind the bars, alone on a bench.

When we came in, Grumpy hopped off the bench and pointed at me, yelling over to Chris, "This is the man, officer. Arrest him. He owes me one hundred thousand dollars, and he's trespassing on my property in Panguna."

With a bored look on his face, Chris looked at me. "Mr. Jack, what do you say to that?"

I had no experience with Bougainville police methodology, but wasn't inclined to go where this discussion seemed to be headed. "I don't owe him a penny. I'm assuming you asked me here to press charges?"

Now it was Chris's turn to appear confused. "We need to settle this. You got your car back, but this man's saying he's owed money and you're trespassing on his property."

I asked Leki to follow me back outside. It was a hot morning, and I was covered with sweat. "Listen, I don't want to show disrespect to your policeman friend, but I didn't come here to negotiate. Grumpy stole my car. I don't owe him a penny, and I'm not trespassing on his property. In the US, he'd be looking at six months of jail time. I don't think I should be here now, so you handle things. I'm going back to the office. I'll take care of this with Ishmael if I need to."

Leki said, "I'll deal with Chris. Do you care if Mr. Trull goes free?"

I said, "Of course I do, but I think you're going to tell me that he's going to walk out of here anyway."

"When there's a dispute like this over a business matter, they usually pay the police a small fine and leave," she said, wincing as she saw my reaction.

When I got back to the office, I tracked down Ishmael on his mobile phone and told him what had happened at the police station.

He waited until I had finished. "It's the worst part of the Bougainville Peace Agreement," he said. "The police force doesn't report to Bougainville."

I had never considered such a thing. "Well, who do they answer to?"

"PNG. The chief of police in Port Moresby."

"So the police here aren't really cops," I said.

"No," Ishmael responded. "Don't negotiate with them. That's just their way to take a cut."

"Sounds like the mafia."

"Yes."

"So when something truly goes wrong, who handles it?"

Ishmael laughed softly through the phone. "Not them."

I was starting to understand. "That's what you do."

Ishmael said nothing.

"Can you at least keep an eye on Grumpy?"

"He might play some games—sorry, I can't stop him—but he knows not to hurt you. He has enemies here."

I took Ishmael's word for things, even as I discovered that Grumpy was just getting started. In the middle of the night the following weekend, I was lying in bed when I heard something on the porch outside my bedroom. I looked out my screened-in, jalousie window and saw the dark shape of a man standing in the shadows. I yelled at him, and he ran down the stairs. I got up and put on my shorts, picked up my bush knife, and ran outside onto the porch. Downstairs, I heard someone climbing the chain-link fence; there was more than one of them. A moment later, they hit the ground outside the yard and ran down the street.

When Tete and I investigated in the morning, we discovered that intruders had used a stand of flimsy trees along the fence line of the yard as a ladder. The trees had snapped, and one of them had slipped and fallen on the barbed wire, cutting himself badly. There was blood all over the fence and the trees, the same person's blood as the stuff used for the crude graffiti painted on the walls outside my window. They also had stolen the spare wheel affixed to the rear of the Toyota. We recovered the wheel the same way as we had the Toyota a week earlier: Ishmael's brother Peacely put out an all-points bulletin for a stolen Toyota wheel. It was returned with apologies from an auto parts dealer. The man said Grumpy had sold him the wheel.

Grumpy's Chinese benefactors started showing up the following week. Their alluvial gold-mining project in the Tailings began as a typically staged, overseas Chinese Communist Party project: One day down at the Kieta wharf, forty Chinese workers showed up on a freighter. A few days after the men arrived, another ship followed with a fleet of excavators, backhoes, and trucks. They didn't hire a single Bougainvillean worker.

The Chinese built a self-contained man camp on the banks of the Jaba River, a mile downstream from our mining site. Their man camp's living area was formed from prefabricated metal and popped up in a couple of days. The buildings had doors, but no windows. If not for the air conditioners, the men would have suffocated. The compound had its own generator and was encircled with a ten-foot chain-link fence, its gates locked nightly. Out in the river, the Chinese workers began welding a massive gold-dredging machine with twenty buckets.

Upstream from the Chinese, Tete and his crew worked around the clock, seven days a week. They fabricated our wash plant along the banks of the Jaba River, built stone foundations to secure the plant up above the water line, and laid out the sluices and loading areas. The mine—christened Mine No.1—began operating months before the Chinese finished theirs. We planned to operate two eight-hour shifts, one during the day and one under the lights, with a dozen workers per shift. The crew was half-supplied by Chief Bittyman's family, with the rest of the personnel from the surrounding community. Crew who were not from the area slept in a house on the riverbank, and there was a full mess for all workers on shift.

Everyone knew that Sylvester, Chief Bittyman's youngest son, was an alcoholic, but it took Grumpy to take advantage of his situation. One day after Mine No.1 had been operating for a couple of months, Sylvester showed up drunk at the Gold Dealer and demanded to see me. When I met him in the reception area, his eyes so bloodshot he could barely see, he started waving around a piece of paper and saying that I owed him money. I relieved him of the paper and read it. It was gibberish—a fabricated agreement between Grumpy and the Chinese and me, wherein they purportedly bought me out for a big price, and I was obligated to pay Sylvester 10 percent of my purchase price for providing the landowner approval. I tried to explain that no such deal had happened, spent five minutes being polite as he told me he knew from Grumpy that it had, and then threw Sylvester out. In Sylvester's mind, this justified his next action, which was to go up to our mine, hot-wire our new JCB excavator, and steal it.

I called Ishmael. "I don't mean to trouble you, but I've got a problem with Sylvester, Chief Bittyman's son, up at the mine."

"Yes, yes." He didn't sound thrilled, and I didn't blame him. "I've known Wendell for a long time. I try to stay out of business disputes," Ishmael said, sounding like any other police-force captain who'd had a long day with little help.

I said, "I don't blame you, but that's not what this is about. Sylvester stole my new JCB excavator. Greyson Trull put him up to it."

"All right. What do you want to do?"

"Get it back before Sylvester damages it," I said, "and try to talk some sense into his father so this doesn't happen again."

"I'll pick you up in five minutes, and we'll drive up there," he said.

I got some cash from Leki and was ready to go when Ishmael pulled up outside the front door a few minutes later.

"Things good?" I said to Ishmael as I hopped into his truck.

"Today?" he said, and made a show of gazing out the windshield into the sky, as if questioning his maker, before he smiled, his eyes remaining on the road. "Always."

Once we were on the way to Panguna, I felt I needed to clear the air. "I'm pretty sure you know this, but Greyson Trull isn't staging these dirty tricks on his own. Lucien Sump is orchestrating things, but Chinese money is behind it all."

Ishmael said, "I wouldn't be that concerned about Sergeant Trull. People here have plans for him. It's only a matter of time."

"Who is it? Angry ex-combatants?"

"No, no. People from Toniva. I know them. There's a score to settle." Ishmael shrugged, his dark eyes holding no hint of kindness. "He's a marked man," he said, as if Trull was already dead.

I said, "I didn't know he was a sergeant. I like my nickname for him better."

Ishmael raised his eyebrows.

"Grumpy."

"Like the little guy in Snow White," Ishmael said, surprising me, and we both laughed.

Everyone knew Ishmael's truck. As he began driving across the Jaba River to Chief Bittyman's village, work at Mine No. 1 came to a halt. The crew stopped what they were doing, and some of the women ran toward the main house where Chief Bittyman and his family lived. A moment later the chief came out his front door and, walking toward the river, started yelling to the rest of his family and directing them to come inside.

When we pulled up on the other side of the river in front of the village, Chief Bittyman stood alone on the riverbank. He walked toward us and stopped when he was ten feet away. "I hope you're not angry," he said to Ishmael, ignoring me. "I don't want anyone to get hurt."

Ishmael didn't smile. "Chief, I'd like you to get Sylvester and the rest of your family and meet me in that shed over there," he said, pointing at the building that housed the mine crew's mess. When the chief didn't move, Ishmael said, "Go on now. This will be a family meeting. Mr. Davis won't be involved." He said some more words in pidgin to the chief and then turned to me, a serious expression on his face. "You can take a look around your facility and the equipment, make sure it's all okay, and just wait for me there. This will take about half an hour."

Ishmael left me, walked over to the mess hall, and arranged the seats in a hemisphere, with one seat in the middle. Chief Bittyman returned to his house. A minute later, his family members filed out of the front door and walked wordlessly into the mess hall. Ishmael directed them to take seats and stood and waited for everyone. More of the chief's family traipsed over, even the chief's wife. Finally, Chief Bittyman came alone. When he got to the mess hall, Ishmael stopped him and spoke to him in pidgin. From where I stood over at the mine, I heard him say the word "Sylvester" in English. The chief blustered for a minute, Ishmael remained firm, and the chief retreated back to the house. A minute later, a sheepish Sylvester appeared and, followed by his father, walked over to the mess, where they sat down in the circle of seats to face Ishmael.

I acted like I was inspecting the wash plant, but I wasn't. A quick scan of the site told me everything was there, except for the JCB excavator. Without staring, I listened to what was going on at the mess hall and occasionally stole glances that way. Sitting in the center of the group, Ishmael spoke to them as if he was a minister and they were his flock. His words were quiet but firm, with no lecturing tone, giving his audience dignity while discussing a serious transgression. No one from Chief Bittyman's family—including the chief himself—said a word.

It was over in thirty minutes. Sylvester slipped out of the mess hall and disappeared. The family members ambled back to their houses, done for the day. Chief Bittyman walked over to me.

"We'll go back to work tomorrow, Davis," the chief said to me, his haggard face blank.

"Sure, chief; these things happen."

"You've got to get rid of that redskin," the chief said. "It's his fault. My son," he said, shaking his head, "is not smart enough for that man." He looked at me with an expression only a father could understand. "He'll never be a chief."

I gave the chief a pat on the back. "He's still young. Just keep him away from the jungle juice."

"He gets it from the redskin," the chief said. Seeing Ishmael approaching, he uttered in pidgin what sounded like curses, saying "redskin" several times, and then spat on the ground.

Ishmael ignored the chief's outburst. "Ready?" he asked me. He leaned over close to the chief and said a few more words in pidgin. "Okay, see you," he said to him, and turned back to me. "Sylvester will say a few words to you," he said, gesturing toward the mine site.

I heard the excavator before I saw it. Sylvester was in the driver's seat as he drove the big yellow machine around from where he had hidden it in the bush behind the village. When he got to the mine, he made a big deal about laying the bucket down properly, flush to the earth. He turned off the excavator, jumped down, and walked over to me.

"Sorry, Davis," he said, looking at me momentarily with his blood-shot eyes before staring down at his bare feet. He stuck his hand out perpendicular like a slot machine handle, took my hand and shook it, and then ran off.

The chief watched us without saying a word.

"Okay, see you," Ishmael repeated to the chief. He said goodbye to a few of the chief's womenfolk and made some small talk, "*tok tok*" as the locals call it in pidgin, and we got back in his truck.

"Thank you for helping me," I said as Ishmael put the pickup in four-wheel drive and we began to ford the river back to the other side. "I'm sure you had better things to do today."

"It's okay," he said, bouncing the Ford over the boulders.

"What do I owe you for this?"

"Oh no, it's nothing," he said.

"I'm not going to let you do that," I said, both of us bouncing up and down as we hit the holes in the deepest part of the river.

He said nothing, and kept bouncing as he drove forward.

"I'm actually being selfish, you see, paying you," I said, hoping to loosen him up.

He glanced at me for a moment.

"I've got to be worth your while. Otherwise, when I have a serious problem, you're not going to answer my call," I said. "Then things could get much more expensive for me."

Ishmael laughed. "Yes; then you'll have to call the police," he said as we pulled out of the river on the other side. He stopped for a moment, shifted the four-wheel drive stick on the transmission, put the truck in regular gear, and headed up to the main road.

I handed him a wad of cash. "I'm giving you a thousand kina for today, plus a thousand each for the times Peacely and the boys helped me get my car and my wheel recovered. If I need to bother you in the future, you'll know I value your time. I'm not going to ask you to do something without paying you a thousand kina."

He put the money in his pocket. "Thank you very much," he said, making eye contact with me for a brief moment.

I said, "I listened to you speaking to the chief's family. I couldn't understand the words, but I didn't need to. You've been doing this a long time."

"Yes, yes." It was about four o'clock, and he seemed tired.

"How long?"

He was quiet for a while, and I was about to ask him another question when I realized he was thinking. "Since before the Bougainville Peace Agreement. Yes; before 2001."

"My God. That's twenty years."

He kept driving.

We finished the steep climb from the Jaba River and plateaued off west of the ruined mine. Wreckage began to loom up on both sides of the road. Ghoulish hulks of metal, mangled and burned—towers, tanks, and vehicles—lined the road as if carcasses in an infrastructure cemetery.

I said, "I could feel the tone of your words. You were very respectful, and they were very respectful of you, as if you were a teacher—or a priest." I watched the side of his head as he drove the Ford through the burned-out town. "My guess is there's no one else on this island that could do what you just did. I imagine being the head of the BRA has something to do with that."

He kept his eyes straight ahead. "I think so."

"What did you tell them?" I asked.

"I said that Greyson Trull and Lucien Sump work for the Chinese and can't be trusted. You're an American, and they're lucky to have you as a partner, but if Bougainvilleans treat American investors unfairly, you won't stay."

"The police are never going to be able to do what you do. You know that, right?"

"Yes."

"Neither is your current government."

"Yes."

The Ford cruised over the bridge into the center of Panguna Town, and Ishmael headed it up the mountain to the top of the ridge and home. We passed a flock of PMVs, dropping off people who had gone down to Arawa to sell gold, to deposit money in the bank, to shop, to be normal human beings for the day.

"Do you think this place can ever come back?" I asked.

"Maybe. After independence." He glanced over at me. "Do you?"

"Maybe, after independence," I grinned as I mimicked him and then added, "assuming Bougainville elects the right president."

He shifted into lower gear as we got to the steepest part of the hill out of Panguna Town, right before the crest of the ridge.

I considered my next question carefully. "Would you ever run for political office?"

He sighed. "I did before, but it was a disappointing experience. Now I'm too busy."

"I think you should reconsider." I was careful about what I said next; I didn't want to give him the wrong impression. "If you did—not that we would want to be the lead participant—my American investors and I would be the first in line to support you."

He kept his eyes on the road in front of him. "That would be a gift from God."

PART FOUR

ISHMAEL AND JACK

21

Two Minds Thinking Alike

When I went to Bougainville, I had no idea that my biggest nemesis would turn out to be the Chinese.

I should have. The news was full of their depredations in the South China Sea, which wasn't that far away. Bougainville was sitting on billions in gold, and the only thing the Chinese coveted more was jade. I wasn't surprised by their methods. What they had done in the Tailings—bribe people in the Bougainville government and grab all the mining licenses—was typical, and not a new maneuver. That made the outcome all the more embarrassing for me; I was supposed to be smarter than that. After all, in the hydroelectric business, I had run circles around them in their own country.

When I say the Chinese, I'm not speaking about people like Miao, my good friend and a wonderful person. I'm referring to the Chinese Communist Party—the CCP—a sinister, mafia-like organization led currently by its general secretary, Xi Jinping. The CCP and their agents like the People's Liberation Army, as I had discovered firsthand, are relentless, all-consuming predators. That doesn't make them all-knowing or all-powerful. In the end, their kind can—and will—be beaten. Their system violates human nature. To fight them, it helps to know when to bide one's time, and when one must attack, when their misanthropic nature has goaded them to try to reach down the throat of a people and rip out their ethos.

The CCP has been many things in its century-long history, but today it's a cult of mainland-based Chinese, one hundred million strong, who are focused on the re-elevation of China to the supreme position it occupied at the beginning of the nineteenth century (in their view), and the subjugation of all other peoples in the process. If you don't believe that, then you don't know Xi Jinping—whose position in China today is tantamount to emperor and, as such, above mere mortals.

It's not that Bougainville had presented me with no challenges other than the Chinese. I was experiencing pressure enough from our day-to-day business before they entered the picture in 2018. It was our third year in Bougainville, and if there was a sanctuary to which I could have escaped, I would have done so. Nothing I pursued had turned out as expected.

The Gold Dealer seemed like it should have been easy: we bought raw alluvial gold at one price, and sold it at a higher one, locking in a markup on valuable, non-depreciable inventory. When anyone knowledgeable in the gold-dealing business learned the spread we made on a Gold Dealer transaction, they salivated. They made the same, incorrect assumption that I did: Just because one could do a single gold trade successfully didn't mean they could hire staff, scale up, and turn repetition of that into a business. Not in Bougainville; financial projections were a useful tool in the rest of the world, but had no value—in fact, were dangerous—when employed here.

I had expected alluvial gold mining to be better. I'm not saying I thought bringing an alluvial mine into production would be easy. During our first weeks in operation at Mine No. 1, we encountered the same inconsistencies that occurred anywhere when breaking in a new manufacturing business: hesitant equipment, sketchy personnel, and weather. We also encountered challenges unique to Bougainville:

the failure of every mechanical device, more flat tires in one month than I had endured in a lifetime, whole crews leveled by jungle juice weekends, and really bad weather. I remained optimistic.

Tete and I tried to predict Mine No. 1's performance while rejecting heroic estimates. We massaged the numbers numerous times. When I was satisfied, I plugged the data into financial projections and sent them to Mt. Bagana Resources' investors as part of our periodic status reports. After a while, I learned not to do that. Projections require consistency. In the first two quarters of Mine No. 1's existence, we never operated successfully two days in a row. Not once. One day the excavator's radiator blew a gasket; the next, Chief Bittyman declared that we had to stop working until we served chicken with the mess rice bowl. The day after, the river reached flood stage. It was always something.

Stupidly, I had told my sons that as soon as we got our alluvial gold-mining license, we'd ton it. Initially, I had delayed telling them how mistaken I had been, hoping for an uptick that never came. After six months of miserable results, the jury was in. I took advantage of a good morning of internet functionality to email the boys my overdue confession.

> I know I haven't written in a while; sorry. We haven't had good internet service for the last few weeks, and I've been hard at work up at the mine where there's no network. Don't quit your day jobs; so far, I don't see any way this business will make the Davis family rich.
>
> My job at the mine, way up on a mountaintop west of town in a place called the Panguna Tailings, is adult supervision. I only play this role—watch the crew and referee disputes (which occur daily)—when my mine managers miss their shift, which thankfully doesn't happen that often. When no other person of authority can be there, I must be. It's not pleasant. It rains every day. I sleep on a wooden floor in a crowded crew house with no electricity. People smell. The bugs eat me alive. We have rice three meals a day. Everyone shits in the woods.

Most importantly, I must go up there because if someone responsible doesn't supervise the cleanout, there's no gold. A cleanout takes place at the end of the shift when the crew—a dozen men and women—remove from the sluices the plastic mats that capture the grains of gold—forget about nuggets—from the slurry coming out of the wash plant. A wash plant is a big metal machine that my machinists have fabricated that sits alongside the river. The wash plant extracts the gold by channeling the river's alluvial material through the machinery, first culling the rocks and stones, and then hosing the remaining gravel and sand-filled slurry down a cascade of sluices. At cleanout time, the women take the mats from the sluices and dump them into a big drum, scrub down the sediment, and then pan the remaining mixture with hands and pans, just like they pan in the streams in the old Western movies. When things go well, we produce around fifty grams of gold a day, worth something north of two thousand bucks. If I don't supervise the cleanout, the gold finds a way to disappear, and then we've worked all day for nothing.

If two thousand a day doesn't sound like a lot of money, it's because it's not. I'm not making much here, not nearly as much as I thought I would before I went to all the trouble to come to this miserable place and get licensed as a miner and buy all this equipment and employ all these people. On a good day, I cover my costs and produce enough additional cash to tide me over toward what I hope will be my next big enchilada, a bonanza somewhere in these hills that will make me millions. Two thousand's not great, but better than a bad day, when I lose my ass. There are plenty of bad days.

This depressing state of affairs is enough to make me want to leave, but I've taught all of you never to quit, so I'm not going to do that either—yet. I just hope I get out of here before I die.

It seemed impossible to turn a profit in Bougainville. One thing was clear: it was no place to establish a hamburger stand. Travel expenses alone put any normal business behind the eight ball. Only something with gargantuan potential—something big and insanely profitable like a world-class mine—made sense. Once a mine produced wealth for the surrounding community, opening up a hamburger stand next door might prove to be a decent business, but not before. Gold dealing and alluvial gold mining were hamburger stands.

There's a quicker way to say all this: doing business in a place where business hasn't been done, doesn't happen. Yes, of course, the solution—theoretically—is to find good people. This was not impossible in Bougainville. I had managed to come across a few. But I was starting to believe that locating enough good people in Bougainville to operate a legitimate business might require something far greater than simply improving my networking abilities.

Desperate, I had given a lot of thought to whether there was some other, less exotic way to make a buck in Bougainville—like something I had done in other foreign places before—or whether I should just wave a white flag and go home. In the past, whenever I had ventured into another country like China for the first time and needed something to fall back on, I had developed infrastructure projects—the first thing I did successfully after I left the investment banking business. I had been able to raise capital for the projects and pay myself in the process. The only infrastructure project I had seen in Bougainville that had any potential was the limestone project Lucien had shown me the first day I came to Bougainville, the one he said BROL owned with George Washburn. There were plenty of greenfield hydro sites around Bougainville, but they would all be impossibly expensive. I figured I probably needed another angle.

I had made a run over to Port Moresby to sell some gold and returned the next afternoon. Tete picked me up at the airport, and we arrived home in Arawa around six o'clock. Expecting to have dinner across the street at the Women's Centre, we encountered our first surprise of the evening: it was closed. The gates were locked, and some strange people could be seen inside the compound. Tete got the lowdown from the neighbors. Somehow, the staff had lost physical control of the property, and an army of squatters had forced their way into the place and taken over.

It didn't seem like the squatters planned to stay. They had moved the furniture out of the hotel rooms and stacked it up in a pile in the parking lot, as if they planned to haul it off. Having put a new lock on the chain-link gates and bolted the place shut, they were hunkered down inside. Outside, neighbors huddled along the fence, trying to see in the windows.

I grabbed a tin of tuna fish and a cold can of South Pacific beer and sat down in a wicker chair on the veranda to eat dinner. I had just popped open my SP when I heard a loud, booming report from across the street, followed by someone yelling at the top of his lungs. I stood up and looked over the porch railing.

It was Ishmael. He had used his truck to ram open the front gates of the Women's Centre and bust the new padlock into smithereens. He stood unarmed and barefoot in front of his truck in the driveway, yelling in pidgin at the squatters who were scurrying around like cockroaches. There were at least a dozen of them. I couldn't tell what Ishmael was saying, but they appeared to be very afraid.

Tete came out on the front porch.

"What's Ishmael saying to those guys?" I asked.

Tete said, "He's telling them they've got ten minutes to restore the rooms."

A couple of the squatters stood in front of Ishmael trying to jaw-bone him, but he shooed them away, pointing at the pile of furniture. The squatters gave up any hope of reasoning with him, and transported the furniture back to the rooms. Ishmael stood in the driveway and watched them until the job was done. Then the squatters assembled dutifully as a group around him and waited for their instructions. Ishmael pointed at the gate; they said a few words to Ishmael and left.

I looked over at Tete.

He shrugged. "He told them not to come back."

"What did they say to him?"

Tete chuckled. "They apologized."

Our next surprise came when Ishmael got in his truck, pulled it across the street in front of our house, and got out.

Tete ran down, and then came back upstairs. "Ishmael wants to speak with you."

I walked downstairs to where Ishmael stood outside the fence, opened the gate, and shook his hand. "Come on upstairs. I've got cold beer and water," I said.

"Water, please," Ishmael answered, and followed me back upstairs.

I went inside to the refrigerator, got three waters, and we all sat down on the porch. Ishmael seemed cheerful and unperturbed. I could have used the incident across the street to say that I wondered what Bougainville would do without him, but I had learned he was uncomfortable with anything that sounded like flattery.

This was the first time Ishmael had asked to speak with me; usually, it was the other way around.

"You said once that you thought I should consider running again for president," he said.

"Yes, I did."

"I told you that I lost because I didn't have resources or an organization. Those weren't the only reasons." Ishmael looked at me, his eyes as clear as an eagle's. "The voters asked me, 'What are you going to do for us?' and I hadn't thought as much as I needed to about what to tell them."

"Um-hum." I waited to see if he was going to ask me what I thought. Bougainvilleans didn't usually do that with foreigners, probably to spare themselves the pontification.

Ishmael said, "I have been thinking about it, and I've got some ideas, but I don't know if they're any good." He regarded me as he selected his words. "The ideas need money. I don't know if someone with money—like you—would think they're good or not."

"That makes sense. Do you want to tell me about it?" I asked.

He shook his head. "Not now. It would be best if I could show you tomorrow morning."

A few minutes later, we agreed to meet the following day at eight, and said good night. As usual, the next morning Ishmael was on time.

Once we were in his Ford pickup, I asked, "Where are we going?"

"First, we will see some chiefs up in Manetai," Ishmael said. "Do you know the place?"

"Yes, I know it. There's only a little gold there."

"No gold, but limestone," Ishmael said. "They have an old BCL factory, like the Panguna Mine."

I said, "You mean where those steel towers are standing along the coast road?"

"Yes," Ishmael said.

"When I first came to Bougainville, Lucien Sump and George Washburn told me they owned that place."

"No, no," Ishmael said, shaking his head and smiling. "After the Crisis, everybody says they own that place. The Manetai landowners own it. It's their land." His mobile phone rang. He excused himself, said a few words in pidgin, and hung up. "Sorry," he said. "My boys around the island need to stay in touch with me."

"Sure," I said. "Okay, let's say for now that the Manetai landowners own the limestone project. How can I help?"

"I told their chiefs it was a good project," Ishmael said. "If someone can get the money and put it back together, it would be good for the landowners and good for me if I decided to run for office."

As he looked over and saw me grinning, his expression turned quizzical.

I said, "I'm just smiling because ever since I first saw that project, I thought it was probably the best infrastructure project in Bougainville."

"Good." Pleased with himself, Ishmael pounded both of his hands on the steering wheel.

I added, "No guarantees. Normally I'd say developing a lime processing facility here would be very difficult, but I understand this project was up and operating for several years. That means the quality of the limestone must have been good, and they must have located willing customers, not only here in Bougainville but overseas. Other than the Panguna Mine, the limestone project was probably the biggest operation on the island. The most important issue is the one we've already discussed: ownership. It might be doable. I'd need to see some words and numbers."

"Yes, yes," Ishmael said. "The chiefs have their ownership papers to show you, along with some old BCL calculations. They'd like to show you the site today, and give you the papers to read."

I watched him drive a mile or so. "I'm just curious," I said. "Do you have a stake in this project?"

To my relief, Ishmael looked at me as if he didn't know what I was talking about. I didn't tell him that no one else in his position in the South Pacific would be helping out the Manetai landowners unless he had first cut himself in on a generous piece of the action.

As we drove up the coast road to Manetai, I prepared myself to experience the same sense of sadness the broken-down infrastructure at the Panguna Mine gave me. It didn't happen that way. The site of the limestone quarry, a sharply peaked mountain pebbled with white boulders sparkling in the green jungle, felt clean and hopeful. Maybe it was the color of the limestone, as white as coral—which, of course, is what it was, just in a more ancient form. There was an entire mountain of it, almost crystalline in consistency. I grabbed a few rock samples for testing. The rusting steel hulk of the crushing plant sat slumped over in the jungle just like the buildings at the Panguna Mine, but that could be made new. A quick review of the paperwork the Manetai chiefs gave me confirmed my hopes. They were indeed the true landowners. The numbers they produced were equally satisfying; extracts from BCL's original feasibility study, they described a profitable project, one whose size alone made it more than a hamburger stand. As we concluded our meeting with the chiefs, I told them and Ishmael that I would put together an updated feasibility study and send the samples to a laboratory in Port Moresby to test for calcium carbonate content.

The project was just the thing to rekindle my hope. If it was financeable, maybe I could make some money in Bougainville after all. When the chiefs said that they also owned Arovo Island, an island in the Arawa Harbor that had been a resort until the Crisis, and they wanted to give it to me to develop, it was easy to conclude that the morning's trip had been worthwhile.

At noon, we said goodbye to the chiefs.

"Where are we going now?" I asked when we were back on the road heading south.

"Up to Panguna."

We rolled slowly down the asphalt-covered coast road without saying anything. I took it as a good sign that the two of us felt comfortable enough with each other that there was no need to talk as we cruised along. The shore side of the road was cultivated and lined with banana trees; the west side was bordered by jungle-covered mountains. It was a pleasant day, sunny, with a few clouds overhead. A big hornbill glided over our truck, following us for a mile.

As we came around a bend, giving us a view of the sea several miles to the east, I said to Ishmael, "Lucien seemed so positive that he and George owned that project, but I guess I should know better by now."

"Yes," Ishmael said. He didn't say anything else, but it seemed like he wanted to. His eyes straight ahead on the road, he took his time as if choosing his next words carefully, and then said, "Ex-combatants shouldn't do that: take advantage of their position to grab things that don't belong to them."

"Does it happen a lot?"

Ishmael usually looked straight ahead when he drove, so when he looked over at me, I figured the pending words would be important.

Before he could say anything, his mobile phone buzzed, and he answered it. He spoke in pidgin to the caller, listened, and, after a minute, hung up. "Now, you will be able to see for yourself," he said to me. "Something's happening up at the Tailings, and it's too far for me to take you back into town first."

I sat silent in the shotgun seat and waited for events to unfold.

When we got to the intersection at Morgan's, Ishmael turned west toward Panguna. He gunned the gas, gave a short wave to the guard at the Me'ekamui gate, blew past the open toll bar, and accelerated up the long hill toward the mountaintop, his pickup hitting sixty. "Is your mine operating today?" he asked me.

I answered, "I think so."

"Tete and your crew are there?"

"They should be. What's wrong?"

"The landowners at the Chinese site have had enough."

I asked, "What are they doing?"

"Taking back what's theirs."

I knew nothing about the arrangements that Lucien Sump and George Washburn had structured for their Chinese handlers with the landowners downstream from us in the Tailings. I had assumed they were similar to what we had agreed to with Chief Bittyman, but now I wondered.

We drove over the crest of the mountain ridge and down to the main junction of Panguna Town, where Ishmael pulled over to the side of the road. Four of his boys climbed into the back of the truck and we continued through the town, past the derelict mine factories and down the road toward the Tailings. A mile along the road, we came around a bend that afforded a view of the Jaba River below. We stopped, and a few more men climbed onto the back of Ishmael's truck. Off to the right and down in the canyon below, I could see Mine No. 1 next to the river. Our crew had stopped working and was gathered along the riverbank by the wash plant, looking downstream where a plume of oily black smoke curled up from the Chinese site.

"What's burning?"

"The Chinese man camp," Ishmael said.

"What happened?"

"The Chinese always go through the back door. You Americans do it right. You go to the mining department, say hello, ask about the rules, and apply. No bribes. That's what Bougainvilleans call going through the front door."

"You're right about that. We're brought up that way."

"The Chinese never do that." Ishmael shook his head back and forth in frustration. "They go to the mining department, find out which person to bribe, and sneak around behind everyone to pay him. That's going through the back door."

"I agree," I said. "Unfortunately, with most corrupt governments, that's how it's done."

Ishmael put his forefinger up in the air. "Not in Bougainville, thanks to the Bougainville Peace Agreement and the constitution. They say the landowners control the resources under their land. If you don't make a deal with the landowners, you have big, big trouble. Lucien and George should have paid the landowners, but they didn't." He put the truck back in gear and accelerated down the hill. As we drove past Chief Bittyman's village, he glanced across the river at Mine No. 1. "Yours looks all right."

I looked across the riverbed and could see Tete and the others watching the happenings at the Chinese site. Downstream, crowds of people milled around in the gravel-strewn riverbed, but they weren't panning. Groups of men were walking toward the Chinese man camp armed with tools while others were returning, carrying furniture, mattresses, and lengths of tin siding. Smoke from the man camp billowed up into the sky. "Is that it for the Chinese?"

"Finish," Ishmael said.

I didn't have to ask about the specifics of what the Chinese did; everyone knew. Gao Gold had bribed people in the highest reaches of the government to lift the moratorium for mechanical alluvial mining in the Panguna Tailings, and to grant them their ten licenses. No surprise there. To the Chinese, that was standard operating procedure: bribe government officials, receive mining licenses. Everyone took Gao Gold's money, but no one—not Mogol, not the mining department guys, nor Lucien and George, who certainly must have lined their pockets too—bothered to tell the Chinese that the licenses were not theirs to sell. The only party legally entitled to receive and hold an alluvial mining license in Bougainville—the customary landowners—were ignored, and received no stake in the deal. Of course they were pissed.

"What did Lucien and George tell the landowners?" I asked.

Ishmael said, "They forced the Tailings landowners to agree to their plan and promised that BROL would be the local partner, get the landowners' money from the Chinese, and then pay them. The landowners didn't like it, but because of George, they waited for their money. Not anymore."

Ishmael turned the truck off the road and dropped down an accessway to the riverbed. In the middle of the river, men using tools were dismantling the big Chinese dredge, prying batteries and components out of the engine works. On the flat wash of stones and gravel alongside the river, some of Ishmael's boys had circled up the Chinese heavy machinery—excavators, backhoes, and bulldozers—like a wagon train in a cowboy western, and were guarding it in the face of a threatening mob of noisy locals. Ishmael's men in the back of the truck climbed down and joined the defense force.

The Chinese man camp was across the wash on the other side of the river. The chain-link fence still surrounded it, the gates open. Out front, a bonfire spewed black smoke. Inside the enclosure, Bougainvilleans were ripping the camp's buildings down to the foundations and carting off everything, while others were throwing loose clothing, housewares, and used tires into the fire. Behind the camp under some trees, a crowd of Chinese men cowered behind additional construction equipment, protected by more of Ishmael's men.

"Where are those Chinese guys going to go?" I asked.

"We're getting some PMV trucks to take them down to the dock at Kieta," Ishmael said. He looked over his shoulder, back toward the road. "The trucks should be coming now."

"They're leaving for good?"

"Yes. The big boss called me this morning to tell me."

"This is someone at Gao Gold?"

"Yes. Their number one guy; his name sounds like Jing?" Ishmael said, looking at me quizzically. "He has my number; he's spoken to me many times."

"Why are you here now?"

"So no one gets hurt," Ishmael said. "This Chinese boss says he gave BROL money to pay the landowners. But it's gone." He shrugged. "He asked me many times to fix that, but I said no. I never agreed for them to come here."

I asked, "Are you telling me that Lucien and George got paid, but the chiefs didn't?"

"Yes. That's it."

"Jesus. They're lucky to be alive." I looked around for Lucien's vehicle. "Are they here somewhere?"

Ishmael smiled as he spoke. "No, no. George always gets what he wants, and then someone else must clean up the mess."

I said, "That's what he did to you at the end of the Crisis when he stayed in New Zealand."

"Yes, yes," Ishmael said. "These Chinese men have been left here as meat for the crowd, but I can't let that happen. We'll sell their big machines and distribute the money to the landowners so they get paid for their gold, but they can't hurt the Chinese people. If Bougainvilleans do that to foreigners, we'll never get new friends."

"You're like a Texas Ranger up here," I said. "The sheriff."

Ishmael said, "We had something like that in the old days in Bougainville. Australian men called kiaps. They were the boss. They were white, but I didn't care; they did their job. Everyone needs law and order." Preoccupied, Ishmael said nothing more. He looked over his shoulder up the hill toward Panguna, trying to locate the PMV's. As if on cue, two large, open-back PMVs emerged from the jungle along the road, dropped down into the riverbed, and lumbered across the wash toward us. Ishmael put his pickup in gear, and we drove over to intercept them. He directed the drivers to follow him across the river to the camp, pointing to where the Chinese men huddled together near what remained of their village.

We bumped over the boulder field of the wash and forded the river. As soon as we got to the other side, Ishmael's guys herded the terrified Chinese men toward the big trucks, and they gratefully swarmed the PMVs, clambering up into the safety of their truck beds. Short and wiry and brown from the sun, most of the men had no possessions but the clothes they were wearing; only a few carried duffel bags or small suitcases. When all of the Chinese were aboard, Ishmael leaned out his window and gave instructions to the drivers. I watched the Chinese, herded like cattle into the truck beds of the PMVs. Some of them realized that the person driving the black pickup had saved them from an unspeakable end. "*Xie` xie, Xie` xie*," they called out toward us, a few of them holding their palms together in a prayer sign or giving us the thumbs-up signal.

"They're saying thank you," I told Ishmael.

Ishmael showed no reaction. When he was done speaking to the PMV drivers, he put his truck in gear and started driving back across the Tailings to the road. Neither of us said anything as the truck gained the road, and we started back up the mountain toward Panguna and home.

"Chinese are always the same," Ishmael sighed after a few minutes. "It's not their fault," he said, gesturing with his thumb toward the trucks of Chinese men behind us. "Their bosses make the mistakes. They always do the same thing. Mogol invites them here, and they give him money. Then the bosses think it doesn't matter how they treat the local people." He shook his head. "They come, do bad things, and then soon they must leave."

"This has happened before?"

"Yes, yes," he said. "Many times. Gold, timber, fishing; it's always the same. The Chinese pay Mogol, then they come and cheat the people, and the people run them off."

"What's going to change?"

"A new government."

"Plus ex-combatants who won't take advantage of people," I said.

Ishmael shook his head. "No, no. Ex-combatants are not the problem. Only a few greedy ones."

"What are the rest of them like?" I asked.

"Tomorrow is Remembrance Day. You can come and find out."

"Is Remembrance Day a national holiday?"

Ishmael grinned. "One day, when we are independent, Remembrance Day will be Bougainville's national holiday. For now, it's my holiday."

"I'll come," I said. "Where is it?"

"Right down the street from you, in the park next to the Bendaun Market."

"You were going to show me your other idea, remember?"

"Yes, yes," he said. "It's right next to you on the ground along this road."

I looked out the window. Running parallel to the road was the big steel pipe that ran down from the Panguna Mine past Chief Wendell's place. "You mean the big pipe?"

"Yes," he said, looking straight ahead.

I tried to pick my words carefully. "If you're thinking it could be used as part of a hydroelectric project, I agree with you."

"Good," he said.

I sighed. "The problem is that a hydro project needs a lot of other stuff before it could all be useful."

Ishmael didn't smile very often, but now he grinned. "It's already a hydro project. The other parts are lying hidden in the jungle. BCL was just about finished installing it before the Crisis started." He pointed up the mountain to the right. "From up there in Guava, I used to watch them working on it."

"You mean somewhere out in that bush, someone installed water conveyance systems, canals and drops, reservoirs and a forebay?"

"Yes, yes. I think it has all that."

"Well, I'd have to take a look; more importantly, my hydroelectric engineering friends would need to examine everything. But if all that's there, you may be right."

We were just cresting the top of the big hill leading out of Panguna Town when Ishmael turned and looked at me. "If those are good ideas, and you can help us by finding the money, maybe I should run for president next time—in 2020. That's the election right after the independence referendum, the most important one."

"I can help you do that if you want." From the ridge, I looked south down the Pacific at the blue gum-drop shapes of the Solomon Islands on the horizon. "To be honest," I told him, "if these projects are real, we'd be helping each other."

We started driving home.

I had put off the last topic until a good time came up, and it seemed as good a time as any. "I don't want you to think I'm trying to monopolize your day, but I'd like to request one more thing. Can I interview you for a book I'm writing on Bougainville?"

Panguna Jackals

A false dawn was lurking over the Pacific horizon on a November morning when my mobile phone with my American number rang. That never happened in Bougainville. I told everyone who needed to know that if they wanted to reach me via Bougainville's horrific communication system, the best method was to text me. Email was a distant second; and telephone calls? Don't even try. As the roosters under the house crowed, I rubbed my eyes, reached over, grabbed my phone off the nightstand, and checked out the caller ID display. The number had an 861 prefix—the call was coming from mainland China.

"Hello?"

"Hey, Jack; it's Miao," my friend from Beijing replied.

We spent a few minutes exchanging news about family members, mutual friends, and work, before Miao surprised me.

"I'm calling about APEC 2018," Miao said. "The big event in Port Moresby? That's near your island, right? Opening night's only two weeks away. I'm getting there the weekend before. When are you arriving, and where're you staying?"

I had made no plans to go to APEC 2018, and didn't feel like admitting to Miao that I couldn't afford it. I explained that while I was aware of the upcoming Asia-Pacific Economic Cooperation meetings in November, the nature of my current business meant that there was no longer any need for me to attend those kinds of soirees. I wished him the best of luck.

Miao just chuckled. "Come on, Jack. You've got to go. We've got a big meeting. You mean you haven't booked a hotel room? Man, have you heard what the government had to do? They've got cruise liners moored in the harbor as hotels. Gao Gold booked me a suite at some place called the Grand Papuan, up the hill from the conference center? If you can't line up something, you can use my couch."

I waited until it sounded like Miao needed to take a breath. "I just don't think I'll be able to make it. It's too bad we won't be able to see each other."

Miao's tone got serious. "You're joking, right?"

"Not really."

Miao said, "These meetings involve you. You've got to be there."

My good humor on hearing from my friend Miao started to dissipate; after all, it was five o'clock in the morning. "It would be nice if someone had told me."

Miao said, "I was going to tell you. What's your partner's name—Lucien? I spoke with him last night, and he said he told you all about it."

"He's not my partner, I haven't spoken to him in months, and I'm not interested in any meeting involving Lucien."

Now Miao's voice pleaded. "Jack, this is important. I'll be with Gao Gold and your old partner, *Linzhong*."

"To speak with me? About what?"

"About Bougainville, Jack. About you and your island. They've got a proposal for you."

Things weren't adding up. I needed a cup of coffee before I said anything else. "What time is it there, anyway?"

"A couple hours after midnight."

I scratched out a laugh. "Some things never change. You're always up late."

Miao laughed too. "So you're going, right?"

"I don't know why I would."

"Come on, Jack. *Linzhong*'s special friend asked him to tee up this deal. You know—the big guy. Lin introduced you, remember? He'll be there giving the keynote address. He wants Bougainville. I can't say any more over the phone."

"Great. So I get to hear another monologue about how before 1800 your country was the leader of the world with a third of its GDP, and the farmland in Iowa is nice, but Shandong's is better?"

Miao laughed. "He keeps harping on that nationalistic stuff, but I don't pay any attention." He took a deep breath. "You've got to come, Jack."

I had no idea what Miao was talking about, but it sounded important enough to consider going. Supposedly, the whole world would be attending. Maybe while I was at APEC 2018, I could pitch some investors and raise some new capital. While money was the main motivation, I confess I thought about how nice it would be to bump into the Filipina bartender at the Airways, but I was broke, and reluctant to allow testosterone to influence my plans. "Let me see what I can do about a room," I said halfheartedly.

"Like I said, in a pinch, my couch is yours. Meanwhile, do me a favor and send me something non-confidential on your company that I can hand out to these guys," Miao said. He hung up before I could tell him that's the last thing I would do.

Instead of going back to sleep, I got up, showered, and made myself a cup of coffee. Then I got on my computer to take advantage of the internet's availability during the early morning. It only took me thirty minutes to review everything available on Gao Gold; I learned nothing new.

I decided my trip would depend on my friend Sushil Gordon, the general manager of the Airways. I stayed at the Airways every time I flew to Port Moresby to sell gold, and Sushil and I had become friends; if he had a room, I would head over there. Sushil confirmed that the town was jam-packed, but no worries: he would find something for me. I thanked him, caught myself wondering if the bartender would be on duty at the Vue when I showed up, and rang off.

My PNG mobile phone rang a half hour later. It was Lucien Sump, his voice pleasant, as if we had no issues between us and had played a round of golf together the day before. Surely, I was planning to attend APEC 2018, he stated matter-of-factly, and then reminded me that he had told me that his Chinese friends wanted to get together. Thursday morning, November fifteenth at the Grand Papuan was convenient for them, he said, and hung up.

As long as I was going to go to APEC 2018, I needed to make the trip pay for itself by pitching some investors, so my next emails were to my investment bankers. Over the past couple of years, whenever I wanted to talk to investors about Mt. Bagana Resources, I had done so via Tom Curran, a friend from business school who was the chairman of Cordovan Capital, a Canada-based investment firm experienced in foreign infrastructure deals, and Bill Wright, a former geologist who was now with Larchmont Securities, a New York City investment banking firm focused on mining deals with strategic investors. I checked in with them. They both indicated they wouldn't miss APEC 2018, had already made arrangements, and knew potential investors who also planned to attend. They were both staying at the Crown Plaza across from the convention center, and we agreed to meet for breakfast at their hotel Wednesday morning.

After I booked my flight and hotel, I emailed Miao: I confirmed that I was going, and told him where I was staying and that I would arrive on Tuesday. Without getting into any more details, I suggested that I buy him a drink at the bar of the Vue on Tuesday evening, and he could tell me more about what was going on.

A week at the Airways would be like a vacation, but it didn't come cheap. To foot the bill, I would use the profit from selling a big slug of gold. Otherwise, I would be required to dip into our working capital, which I needed to maintain for funding ongoing gold purchases.

When we had first opened the Gold Dealer, we expected to ship our melted gold all the way to Australia in order to get paid. To our surprise, we learned that there was a very professional refinery—Italpreziosi South Pacific, or the "Italians" as everyone called them—in downtown Port Moresby.

Two weeks later on a Tuesday morning, I loaded up my backpack with four kilos of Doré bars—about two hundred thousand bucks' worth—winked at my friends the security guards at the Aropa airport, and took a seat on the plane going to Port Moresby. When I arrived in POM, as the locals called it by virtue of the airport's call letters, two Guard Dog guys with shotguns met me on the tarmac and drove me in their armor-plated vehicle to the Italians. Dario, Italpreziosi's manager, gave me ten thousand kina in a block of hundred-kina notes and wired the balance to the Gold Dealer's account at the bank.

In the afternoon when I was finished with my gold transaction, the Guard Dog guys drove me to the Airways and dropped me off. I checked in, was shown to my room, and showered and changed. It was the first time I had not worn my normal Bougainville garb, a T-shirt and shorts, in months, and even longer since I had put on pants and a jacket. As the sun was going down, I took the elevator up to the Vue to meet Miao.

It was a clear night, the air was drier than usual, and the moon and stars were just winking out as I entered the bar. I had never seen the room so crowded. I squeezed in next to Miao, where he was sitting on a barstool, and clapped him on the back.

"Jack!" Miao exclaimed, and stood up and embraced me. He and I had always been fond of each other, although I had learned the hard way during my years in China never to put complete trust in any man there. He looked up at me. "Your hair's getting gray."

"That's what happens to us *laowai*," I said as I examined him in turn. "It's not supposed to happen to you," I said playfully as I looked down alongside his temples where small thatches of gray had sprouted.

"Why aren't you doing what Xi Jinping and all your so-called leaders do, and use some black shoe polish up there?" I laughed.

"Shush," Miao hissed, raising his forefinger to his lips and looking around the crowd pressed together at the bar, his eyes concerned. "His men are everywhere," he whispered.

I glanced over toward the dining room, which was clearing out. "Let me order a drink, and then let's grab a table out on the balcony," I said, looking through the crowd for a bartender. There were several behind the bar, and the Filipina lady was among them. Serving a customer, I saw her glance my way.

"How are you?" she called to me over the noise from the crowd. "Your usual?"

"Yes, and another for my friend Miao here. I'll take his tab when we're finished. We're going over to the dining room where it's a little quieter, along the railing in the corner."

"Always a pleasure, sir."

I felt good about seeing her again, but duty called. I led Miao out along the balcony to a corner table where there was an unobstructed view of the Owen Stanley Range. The sun was just setting to the west over the harbor islands, and lights were coming on across the Jackson Parade airfield.

"None of your spies can overhear us here," I said to Miao.

He glanced around for anyone suspicious. Satisfied, he pulled out a chair and took a moment to take in the view before sitting down. "You didn't tell me how nice it is in Port Moresby."

"That's because it's not," I said. "This hotel is an oasis, and the rest of town is a dangerous mirage. Don't get too comfortable."

"The Grand Papuan seems nice enough," Miao said as the Filipina bartender appeared with our drinks. She had on the same attire she had worn the first night I saw her; I noticed that Miao was equally entranced.

"Here, you didn't have to do that," I said as I stood up and took the drinks from her. "I could have gotten them."

"No; I wanted to," she whispered in words meant for me, brushing her long black hair out of her eyes, looking into mine.

"Well, I can see that I don't need to ask how you are; you look terrific," I said. Her smile told me she didn't think I was being too forward.

She started to turn and walk away, but stopped. "It's Joy," she said.

I stared back at her, uncomprehending.

"My name," she said, laughing.

"Oh; stupid me. I'm Jack."

"Maybe I'll see you later, Jack. The crowd clears out by nine."

I felt Miao staring at me as I stood watching Joy walk back to the bar.

"How come that doesn't happen to me?" Miao joked. "She's fantastic."

I retook my seat, a big smile on my face, thinking he was right. Joy sure looked good; what's more, she seemed interested. That hadn't happened to me in a long time, although I had to admit that I had not been very encouraging over the last few years. I still had no idea what I would ever tell my sons if something developed. After a moment's blissful reflection, I turned back to face Miao, and the reality at hand. "You were telling me about the Grand Papuan."

"It's right up the road from the convention center," Miao said.

"I was about to ask how you're getting there from the hotel."

"Gao Gold's got a bus."

"Fine. Don't walk," I said in a firm tone. "Cheers," I said, holding up my glass of white Burgundy. "Now tell me about Gao Gold; other than the typical propaganda, there's nothing material about the company on the internet."

Miao explained that Gao Gold was one of the largest gold-mining companies in China. They owned several gold mines across the PRC—mainly in Tibet and Inner Mongolia—and now wanted to extend their interests outside mainland China. They had their eye on sites in the Asia-Pacific region. Lin Boxu, my former partner, was a large shareholder of Gao Gold, and, more importantly, was their princeling—their trusted conduit to the highest reaches of the CCP.

"I remember the feeling. It was intoxicating."

"*Linzhong* has changed," Miao said in a low tone, still nervously scanning the room. "You remember how focused he was on his collection of Chinese antiquities?"

"Sometimes it was the *only* thing he focused on."

Nodding his head up and down, Miao said, "That's the way he is now about gold—and copper too—ever since the prices bottomed out and started to move higher. He told us early on that he had a feeling about both metals, and as they've run up, it's become like a religion to him. He thinks he's Warren Buffet. The funny thing is, so far he's right. The prices keep going higher."

"Which leads to Bougainville."

Miao said, "You're missing a step. When Lin first started to believe he was right about gold's future, he told his special friend, and the big guy loaded up on gold. Now he thinks Lin's a genius."

"That's the connection?"

"All I can tell you is that when it comes to precious metals, the only person the big guy listens to is Lin. Gao Gold doesn't care as long as the government keeps funding their budget; they'll do whatever Xi and Lin tell them. The big guy told Lin he loves gold, but he needs copper more. He's obsessed with the stuff. To be number one in electric vehicles, China needs mountains of copper. He's telling all his military guys that when electric cars rule the world, the shipping lanes in the Strait of Malacca are no longer important," Miao said, looking across the table at me, "and the US navy won't control the world." He scanned the room again. "Sorry."

"So Lin's going to deliver a twofer: the Panguna Mine has both."

"It's a twofer, all right." Miao cleared his throat. "He's recommended Gao Gold buy the Panguna Mine—and you."

Hearing Miao's words, I was dumbfounded. "Me? What do I have to do with this?"

Miao had noticed two Chinese men sitting about twenty feet away. They were seated off to one side in the regular dining room, and I didn't think they could hear us, but Miao raised his forefinger to his lips, lowered his head, and whispered, "Those are Gao Gold guys over there. I guess you know something about what happened to them in Bougainville? Some place called the Tailings?"

I nodded. A waitress floated by, and I ordered another round.

Miao said, "Gao Gold was just testing the water in Bougainville with that deal, but they were disappointed with the results, and don't want to make the same mistake again."

"I don't blame them," I said, keeping my voice down, "but they teamed up with the wrong guys."

"That's the point," Miao said.

"I don't get it."

Miao kept his head down and whispered some more. "Gao Gold did their homework. They found out you haven't had the same problems with your landowner at your mine. They asked Lin about you, and he told them you could be trusted. So Gao Gold told Lucien that the only way they'd proceed in Bougainville is with a trustworthy partner on the ground—you. That's when Lucien told them he was already partners with you." As Miao finished his last words, he looked at me with a quizzical smile on his face, like he was wondering why I hadn't jumped out of my chair with joy.

There was no percentage at that point in telling Miao I would never do business with either Lin or Lucien. "You say, 'the only way they'd proceed in Bougainville.' Tell me exactly what that means."

"Sure," Miao said. "Liuman Mogol? Bougainville's president? He's agreed with the big guy to sell Gao Gold the Panguna Mine for one billion US dollars."

That was so absurd it was funny, and I couldn't help grinning. Mogol never stopped. "That's one percent of what it's worth, but that's not the point. Mogol can't sell something he doesn't own. That's what went wrong for Gao Gold the first time; the only deals that work in Bougainville are the ones with the landowners."

Miao shrugged. "All I know is that Mogol agreed to the price, and is flying in here on Friday to collect his money. Gao Gold is prepared to write a check, subject to the landowners agreement."

"How's that going to happen?"

"That's your team's job."

I couldn't help it—the hilarity of the scenario Miao was suggesting overcame me like a drug, and I started to laugh. Envisioning myself running around Panguna trying to coax landowners to agree to a deal with a bunch of thieves was, well, so suicidal it was funny.

Miao was watching me, a confused look on his face. "You think all this is amusing?"

"No, not really," I said, trying to straighten up, deciding I wasn't going to play any cards at that point. "I'm just trying to imagine what someone would have to do to convince a bunch of chiefs who were ready to cut some Chinese guys to pieces that they all should join hands and smoke a peace pipe."

"Hey, Jack," Miao said, "As you used to say to me, I'm not stupid. I realize the last few years haven't been kind to you financially. Gao Gold has authorized me to tell you they're prepared to pay a ten percent fee to you guys for delivering the landowners and keeping the peace."

The waitress approached our table with menus. "Do you have time to stay for dinner?" I asked Miao.

He looked at his watch. "Sorry; I was supposed to meet Gao Gold ten minutes ago."

I asked the waitress for the tab. After paying the bill, I walked Miao down the open-air walkway to the parking lot entrance, where his car and driver waited.

"So?" he said to me.

"You know me, Miao. The meeting's a couple days away. Let's see what happens."

"I'm happy for you, Jack. It's a lot of money."

"Yeah; sure." I shook Miao's hand, watched him get into his car, turned around in the darkness, and almost bumped into Joy, who had walked up behind me.

"I'm off duty now. Can I buy you a drink?"

"Not in there," I said, looking over her shoulder at the noisy bar. "We won't be able to talk."

"I could take you to the VIP salon on the third floor."

"I'm not a VIP."

"You are to me."

"Okay, lead the way, but I'm buying."

She laughed "No; my treat." She looked me in the eye. "That's my polite way of keeping you at arm's length," she said. "For now."

I followed her to the VIP lounge on the third floor. When we said goodnight a couple hours later, she rose up on her tiptoes and kissed me. It took a lot for me to let her go. Next time might be different, I said to myself, wondering if she had thought about me, an older man, the same way I had thought about her. I wondered about a lot of things that night, but doing a deal with Lin and Lucien wasn't one of them. As my father once said, life's too short.

When I met Tom Curran and Bill Wright the next morning, I was doing my best to forget both the conversation with Miao and my evening interlude with Joy, and focus on raising money for Mt. Bagana Resources. After breakfast, we walked down the street and got our first look at the new convention center built for APEC 2018. Unfortunately, there were a lot of people around who wouldn't let the subject of the Panguna Mine go away, including three junior mining companies inside the mining section of the convention center—BCL, PBJ, and Cruks Mining—with fancy display booths all trumpeting the same message: *We've got the keys to Bougainville.*

In light of my conversation with Miao the night before, the statements seemed ludicrous.

BCL's booth was festooned with photos and slogans proclaiming Bougainville as the company's private backyard. Standing across the aisle, Tom Curren whispered, "Jesus, Jack. You didn't tell us another outfit was so entrenched in Bougainville."

"That's because they're not."

Bill said, "BCL's got to be. They've played the lead role on the island since the '60s."

"Yesterday's news," I said. "They've had no presence to speak of in Bougainville since the Crisis. They work out of a small office in Port Moresby." Dodging passersby touring booths along the aisle, I looked across the hallway at the BCL booth. "See the man with the pointer?" I said, referring to a balding, fifty-ish fellow speaking to a single visitor in front of a map of Bougainville Island. "I think he's the president. I'll think of his name in a minute."

"It's Bailey," Bill said.

"Right," I said. "A year ago, I sat next to him on a plane flying from Port Moresby to Buka. He introduced himself as the president of BCL, and then you know what he told me? It was the first time he had been back in Bougainville since they pulled out at the beginning of the Crisis in 1989."

Tom asked, "What was he doing there?"

"Trying to save their exploration license at the Panguna Mine," I said. "We had a nice conversation. When I told him I was from Wall Street, he said that Rio Tinto had cut them loose, and they needed money, asked me for a business card and said he would be in touch."

"What happened?" Bill asked.

"Lucien Sump was on the plane," I said. "When we landed, he came over and started talking to me. Bailey and his people saw us together and must have assumed the worst. I never heard from him."

"Do the BCL guys have a problem with Lucien Sump?" Tom asked.

"I'm sure they despise him," I answered, watching as the BCL people in the booth surrounded their sole guest, who was probably beginning to regret his visit.

"Why?"

"They must blame him for their misfortune. After the Crisis, BCL still had many Bougainvilleans bamboozled, and their lawyers took advantage of that by trying to preserve their historical rights in everything from the Bougainville constitution to the mining act. Even when Mogol got elected president in 2010, he said that when the Panguna Mine reopened, BCL was the odds-on favorite to renew their role as the operator."

"Is the Panguna Mine going to reopen?" Bill asked.

"It's got to, if Bougainville wants to become independent," I answered.

Tom said, "I want to hear what Lucien did to BCL."

I said, "After Lucien's deal with the first president collapsed, everyone thought he would leave. Instead, he stuck around and tried to carve out a leadership role for himself on the island. That made a rejuvenated BCL his biggest enemy, so he teamed up with all the die-hards who hated BCL. Over time, BCL's contractual rights on the island, which were already eroding, evaporated. The Bougainville Peace Agreement negated their original deal, and when the constitution and the mining act came into play, they lost their leases on the lands around Panguna. Bailey was flying over there to try to preserve their last asset, their right to renew their exploration license at the Panguna Mine, but they didn't get it."

Over at the BCL booth, the visitor extracted himself and started walking away. "I can't imagine what they could offer an investor at this point," I said.

"I'm going over there to find out," Bill said, and walked across the aisle to the BCL booth.

Tom said to me, "After the Crisis, I'm surprised Bougainvilleans are even willing to talk to BCL."

"Some don't," I said. "But as far as most Bougainvilleans are concerned, BCL and mining and the Panguna Mine are all one and the same. I don't think it's entered their minds that if they wanted to reopen the Panguna Mine, they have choices."

Tom asked, "Do they understand that Rio Tinto, the mother ship with all the money, has left the nest, and BCL is a financial orphan?"

"Nope."

Tom gazed down the aisle of the convention hall. "It looks like there's a TV camera in front of the PBJ booth. Head on down there, and I'll fetch Bill."

I walked down the aisle to the PBJ booth. Out front, wires and people created a jumble of commotion as a film crew wielding lights and a journalist brandishing a microphone positioned themselves to shoot an interview. A crowd of onlookers edged toward the set. Inside the booth, I watched the management team huddle as they readied themselves. A bookish woman was doing most of the talking.

"Ready, Jesse?" asked the journalist.

"Ready," the woman called out in a voice with an Australian accent, tossing a jacket onto her thin frame and straightening her hair.

"Okay, rolling," the journalist said into his microphone. He moved toward the screen, lights arrayed behind him, speaking into the mic, "One…two…three…And now I have the pleasure of introducing PBJ's own Ms. Jesse McGrue, the president of the company and…the queen of Bougainville!"

Tom and Bill walked up behind me. "The queen of Bougainville?" Tom said, while Bill, his geologist's face disdainful, watched over the heads and shoulders of the crowd.

"Her Highness in the flesh," I said.

Ms. McGrue must have seen a show featuring the wannabe journalists at the Me'ekamui gate, because she used the same script. She breathlessly described the all-powerful Me'ekamui as the overlords of Panguna and PBJ's partners in the redevelopment of the Panguna Mine. Feigning regret, she cautioned that she was prohibited from saying anything more specific about Bougainville because the company was in the midst of a financing, but, she winked, they had high hopes to reopen the big Panguna Mine soon. She went on to say that a large chunk of the proceeds of the recent financing would pay for them to expand their footprint in central Bougainville, a place that to her felt "just like home."

"Have you ever seen her before?" Tom asked.

"Never."

"They're partners with the Me'ekamui, though," Bill cautioned. "That counts for something. I've read about those guys."

"Well, the Me'ekamui were a factor in Panguna during the Crisis, but if you ask me, they were overrated even back then," I said. "I can't understand why PBJ would make the mistake of selecting them as partners."

"Why is that a mistake?" Bill said.

"They're bitter enemies with the current Bougainville government, and if that wasn't enough, many of them are not bona fide, customary landowners."

"What does that have to do with anything?" Tom asked.

"No mine can get licensed in Bougainville unless they've got a local partner, and that party must be a bona fide, customary landowner."

After Jesse's presentation ended, we drifted down the hallway. "What did BCL say?" I asked Bill.

"Panguna Mine's in the bag," he said, his face a blank before he broke into a grin.

We kept walking, past scores of booths extolling the value of the exhibiting companies' shiny stuff under the ground in crazy places. Bill checked his map of exhibitors. "What about Cruks Mining? I heard their booth airs a helicopter tour of Bougainville Island."

"I saw it yesterday," Tom said. "If you've never seen the jungle from a thousand feet up, it's worth stopping by; otherwise there's no point. It didn't sound to me like they have any angle for the Panguna Mine," he added.

"Do you guys care about the Panguna Mine?" Bill asked me. "I don't think I've heard you speak about it once."

"Sure," I said, "in due course. If you're a newly arrived white guy in Bougainville and you want to command respect, you learn not to mention it. It's the interlopers who bring up the Panguna Mine—the suits who fly in, look around, and leave. The Bougainvilleans have been through dozens of those guys. They want to see that you're going to live and work with them before they're going to talk to you about the jewel in their crown."

"On that note, it's time to meet Mongolian Royalties," Bill said, referring to a mining company he had convinced to consider making a strategic investment in Mt. Bagana Resources. At breakfast, Bill had told us they were one of the hottest junior mining companies at the conference, and it had taken a lot to line up the appointment.

Bill headed for the front door of the convention hall, and we followed him back up the hill to the Crown Plaza. The cityscape around us had been totally transformed by the Chinese. For them, it was a big deal that at APEC 2018, Xi Jinping—not a Western leader—would be the keynote speaker. They spared no expense in surrounding Miao's so-called "big guy" with a suitable setting. Not only had China spent fifty million dollars on the convention center, but they had spent millions more transforming much of Port Moresby's old downtown waterfront known as Ela Beach. New roads, sidewalks, lighting, and landscaping sparkled—incongruous when compared to the balance of Port Moresby's urban squalor.

Bill was thorough, and as we waited for the Crown Plaza concierge to show us to our meeting room, he took me through last-minute pointers. "Remember, they're not going to be interested in the Gold Dealer or the alluvial mine."

Tom asked, "What are they interested in?"

"Exploration," Bill said. "It could be a fishing expedition," he cautioned. "But maybe they're smart. If so, they'll realize teaming up with guys who have already paid the price of getting in on the ground floor will be, in the long run, much cheaper than trying to do it themselves."

When the concierge showed us to our designated conference room, we found a large, bearded man already inside. He was dressed in what looked like my grandfather's three-piece suit and ignored us, engrossed in a conversation on his mobile phone. I started to sweat just looking at the guy, and went over to the wall and lowered the temperature of the air conditioner by ten degrees.

When our guest ended his phone call, Bill took over. "Jack, this is Jansen Erik, the president of Mongolian Royalties."

I shook Jansen's hand, took a seat, and opened a copy of my presentation. Whenever I was in Jansen's situation, I always assumed that the company leader across the table from me, who lived with his business every day, had a presentation honed to perfection. If not, there was either something wrong with the company, him, or both. The best bet was to sit back and evaluate not only the presentation, but the way the presenter delivered it.

Jansen didn't operate that way. Apparently, he didn't need to hear anything I had to say. "I know you're involved in gold dealing and alluvial mining," he said before I could open my mouth. "We're not interested in that."

"Bill explained that to me," I said, setting aside my presentation.

"The only reason I took the meeting is to find out about Bougainville's exploration opportunities, and whether or not you can deliver the Panguna Mine," Jansen said with a straight face.

"All right. The Panguna Mine's off-limits for the moment, and I wouldn't advise you to spend any time on the subject until you've been in Bougainville for a while. As far as exploration licenses, what's your level of interest?" I didn't think it was a difficult question, but Jansen seemed confused. "Look, we don't have any exploration licenses now," I explained. "We'd need to prepare applications, then go through the process to get the licenses. We can do that—we've just done it for our alluvial mining license—but at a cost. If we were willing to move ahead with you guys on the exploration front, what's in it for us?" I smiled, trying to put someone who seemed unusually stiff at ease.

Jansen said, "When you put it that way, my level of interest is zero. I can just go over there and get the exploration licenses myself. Actually, that's the first thing I thought when Bill told me about your company."

While Bill was starting to look uncomfortable, I replied to Jansen, "That's not really an option for you; you'd be better off working with us. You didn't ask me, but I would have told you that you need a customary landowner partner to apply for a license. Typically, that's a chief," I said, trying to be helpful, although Jansen didn't deserve it.

"I don't need you. I could send someone to Bougainville to tick the chief box tomorrow," he said, sounding more moronic after every word, although that didn't prevent him from appearing self-satisfied with his statements.

I couldn't help myself. "Tell me how you're going to do that."

"What's to tell?"

"Go ahead, just for yucks. You get a ticket to fly to the end of the world, and you arrive in Buka. Now what?"

"I'm not sure I know what you mean."

"I know you don't; I'm trying to help you. You've got to find a chief, right? That's the reason you went there, remember? How're you going to do that?"

He just looked at me. I couldn't tell whether Jansen was getting pissed at me, or if he had started to comprehend how stupid he sounded.

I said, "Bougainvillean chiefs don't wear badges. It takes a year on the ground just to figure out who they are." I grinned at the oaf, trying to leaven the situation.

"Forget the chiefs," Jansen said, definitely irritated with me. "I can just go to the government and cut a deal, like we did in Mongolia." He looked over at Bill like he expected points for his repartee.

Bill had told me that Jansen was an American from Colorado, but he might as well have been a Chinese guy from Gao Gold; I was tempted to say it, but bit my tongue. "The government can't help you in Bougainville. They're not the landowner."

I glanced at Bill. He was embarrassed by Jansen's behavior, and looked like he was trying to disappear into his seat. On the other hand, sitting there in a sweltering room in the midst of a horrid conversation, I was having an epiphany. Listening to myself educating the man across the table, the value of Numa Numa's position crystalized in my mind; how could I have missed it until now?

Jansen wanted the upside associated with exploration licenses, and no part of gold dealing or alluvial mining, the pedestrian business in which we were currently involved. But because of the relationships Numa Numa's approach enabled us to forge with the landowners, our way was the only route to the big stuff. Mongolian Royalties or Gao Gold, it didn't matter who was talking—their approach reflected every carpetbagger's misguided scheme for Bougainville. No wonder Bougainvilleans were suspicious of foreigners. Fly over to the island, find someone to bribe quick to land a big fish, and then fly out. That made success impossible. But to do things the right way—what my company had done—to live and work there to win the trust and confidence of Bougainvillean landowners, was hard, expensive, and took forever. Only a crazy person would do it. Even though we had wasted a lot of time and money, I started to realize we were on the holy side of the issue, and things might work out in the end. Just not with this bozo.

I looked at my watch, and then winked at Tom and Bill. "Jansen, it's been real. Best of luck to you."

As Bill led a confused Jansen to the door, Tom's expression remained morose. "I didn't want to pop your balloon, but everyone I've talked to says the same thing," he said. "They don't care about alluvial gold mining. They want to see exploration licenses before they'll invest."

"Then we'll get them. We've done everything else," I answered, my mind made up. It had taken a mining conference to educate me, but now I saw our path clearly: we would get the exploration licenses, not because everything else we had done was wrong, but because they were the icing on the cake.

But this icing would be expensive. I wouldn't be able to talk any of my investors into ponying up the dough; I knew they'd never do it. I would have to do it myself. When I got to my room, I emailed my bank and told them to empty my account and wire the money to the company. I had never done that before. If the whole deal went south, I would be wiped out financially. I refused to dwell on it. Bougainville was going to happen; in the meantime, I would neither accept defeat, nor surrender. I would get the exploration licenses, no matter how difficult. Then surely Mt. Bagana Resources would be worth a fortune, and so would I.

My mobile phone rang in the late afternoon. It was Lucien. I had been expecting his call.

"I told you if we stuck together, the Chinese would have to treat us well," he said when I answered, his voice oozing cordiality.

"You're going to have to tell me what you mean."

"Didn't Miao explain things?" he asked, a little startled.

"I'd rather hear it from you."

"I'm staying at the Grand Papuan; come on over, and I'll buy you a drink."

"Tell me over the phone."

Lucien didn't like that answer, but I wanted a straightforward conversation, with no booze involved. "They want to be partners with us," he finally said, somewhat exasperated.

"Who's 'they,' and who's 'us'?"

"Come on, Jack, what's with this cat and mouse stuff?"

"Hey, this is your deal. You called me," I said. "If you don't want to explain things, we can talk some other time."

"No, no, wait a minute," Lucien said. "Just hold on." He put his phone down, and I heard him open a pop top. "Gao Gold—the big

Chinese company we're working with in the Tailings—wants to be partners with us in Bougainville."

I said, "What else is new? You guys are already partners in your mine in the Tailings—what's left of it."

"They're just getting started, Jack. You know the Chinese."

"I don't see what this has to do with me."

"Your friend Mr. Lin controls Gao Gold, and they've told me you've got to be involved."

I'd listened enough. "Let me make this easy for both of us. On behalf of Xi Jinping, Gao Gold thinks they're going to pay Mogol a billion and buy the Panguna Mine. They already got their pocket picked in the Tailings, so Lin told them to ditch you guys and use me."

"Now, wait a minute," Lucien protested.

"It doesn't matter what you say," I said, cutting him off. "This isn't a real deal. It's never going to happen. Mogol can't sell the Panguna Mine; it doesn't belong to him. Gao Gold would run into the same problem in Panguna they had before in the Tailings."

"The checks are already cut. Don't sell George short; he's had a lot of conversations with the chiefs up in Panguna about getting their approval. We get ten percent of Mogol's purchase price, Jack. That's a lot of loot to spread around."

I said, "I already told you the Chinese don't pay foreigners the squeeze, but it doesn't matter. George isn't going to be able to lie to the landowners again; this time, they'll cut him into little pieces."

"Are you coming tomorrow morning or not?" Lucien asked.

"I haven't made up my mind yet. Who's going to be there?"

"Xi Jinping himself," Lucien said.

"Get real. The so-called leaders send someone for this type of thing."

"You're talking about your friend Lin Boxu, your princeling, as Miao explained to me."

"No. For this deal—with a head of state—he's a lightweight."

"Who then?"

All I could think about was his wizened face, those lizard-colored eyes, and his rust-yellow teeth. "Your worst nightmare."

In the early evening, I asked Eki to take me over to the Grand Papuan so I could case out the place. The hotel was rated five stars. I wouldn't quarrel with that, but it wasn't on the same level as the Airways. The meeting rooms occupied the entire twentieth floor, and there was a separate lounge area for business and VIP guests. I made conversation with the concierge and verified that Gao Gold had a room reserved the next morning at ten o'clock. When Eki drove me back to the Airways, I gave him two hundred kina and asked him to meet me there again the next morning at eight thirty.

That night, Tete texted me the news that was just announced on the floor of the convention center: Mogol and James Serape, the new prime minister of PNG, had agreed that Bougainville would conduct its independence referendum in 2019; the only thing left to do was to pick a date. Bougainville was getting more interesting by the day.

The next morning, reluctantly, I put on a suit and tie. After breakfast at the Vue, Eki picked me up in front of the Airways, and I was at the reception desk of the Grand Papuan's twentieth floor business center by nine. It was crowded. I introduced myself to the concierge and explained that I was expected for a meeting at ten. When she asked under whose name the room was reserved, I feigned ignorance and shifted around next to her to view her schedule. I put on my biggest smile, explained I had forgotten my glasses, and bent over to study the names on her morning calendar. Gao Gold's name was listed next to the Pearl Room at ten, together with a dozen names including mine. Right next to Lin's name was the one I expected to see from the first time Miao had told me there would be a meeting with Lin about an investment involving foreigners.

I pointed out my name to the concierge. She explained that the meeting required extra security, and asked to see my ID. I showed her my passport, and then she pointed toward the Pearl Room, a glass-walled boardroom with mahogany double doors that monopolized the end of the hallway. I thanked her, picked up some day-old newspapers, and poured myself a cup of coffee from the urn at the buffet. Then I found a stuffed wingchair off in a corner where I could observe people getting off the elevator, but they'd have a hard time seeing me. I found myself thinking that it was Sunday, and wondered if Joy had the day off.

The Chinese security team showed up at nine thirty. They whispered to the concierge for a few minutes, and then she pointed my way. As one of the men walked toward me with a list in his hand, I pulled out my passport and flashed him my photo. They didn't bother me after that.

Lucien and George were next, accompanied by four Chinese guys, including a well-dressed man who had to be Chairman Jiang of Gao Gold, and Miao, looking dapper in a suit as well. They huddled around the reception desk, conferred with the concierge, and then walked down the hallway to the Pearl Room. From where I was sitting, I could see through the glass walls on either side of the mahogany double doors, and I watched Lucien and George whispering together off in one corner of the room.

A minute later my American mobile phone vibrated, and I looked at the caller ID. It was Miao. "Are you coming?"

"I'll be there if I need to be," I said.

"What does that mean?"

"I'm being inscrutable," I said, and hung up.

Lin and Mr. Zeng were next, accompanied by two uniformed PLA army officers. Wearing his customary double-breasted blue blazer and gray slacks, Lin looked nervous and much older. As his eyes darted around, he looked right at me. I froze, not knowing how to handle what might come next, but then Lin looked off in another direction, his eyes jumpy. Mr. Zeng, whose appearance hadn't changed since the last time I had seen him seven years earlier, took Lin's elbow and drew him off to a seating area. They sat down in a huddle, and Mr. Zeng placed a call on his mobile phone.

Mr. Zeng was speaking in an animated state, unusual for him, when Liuman Mogol and a couple of his thugs walked in. Mr. Zeng looked up and saw them, shut off his phone, and nudged Lin, and the two of them went over and started hob-knobbing with the Bougain-villean leader. A moment later, they all walked down the hallway into the Pearl Room and closed the doors.

I looked at my watch. It was already after ten. I was trying to decide what to do when there was a big commotion at the elevator. Xi Jinping, surrounded by an entourage including a television camera-man and someone carrying lighting equipment, walked off the lift toward the reception desk.

I guess he really wanted the Panguna Mine.

The concierge scurried out from behind her desk with a big bou-quet of flowers. A Chinese aide practically tackled the concierge and grabbed the flowers before they got to Xi, demanded to know where the Gao Gold room was, and then recovered and guided the leader and his retinue down the hallway to the Pearl Room.

Less than ten minutes later, I saw the television lights go on, and then there was a long, pregnant pause. Too long, I was thinking, just as the double doors of the Pearl Room blew open and Xi, his face darkened, came down the hallway like a locomotive, his minions trail-ing behind.

In the aftermath, as the disappointed deal mavens waited at the elevator, I believe that most of them saw me. I know Miao did, his eyes squinting at me through his gold, wire-rimmed glasses.

I called Eki, and got back to the Airways around noon. I had just called Joy, learned she didn't have to work until six, and agreed to meet her at the National Museum and Art Gallery at three. Then Miao called.

"You knew all along, didn't you?" Miao laughed.

I was glad he wasn't angry. "I don't know anything. What happened?"

Animated, Miao set the stage. Everyone was there in the room, happy and shaking hands. The big guy's finance officer had placed a check on a signing pad on the table, and Liuman Mogol wore a greedy grin on his face. Lucien and George were already congratulating each other when Mr. Zeng's cell phone rang.

"Zeng went off into a corner on his phone while everyone was talking," Miao continued, "and then he came over and grabbed Mr. Jiang and the big guy, pulled them together and whispered to them—and then Xi grabbed the check off the table and everyone stormed out."

"And?"

"Chairman Jiang told me that Mr. Zeng was on the phone with a special guy in Bougainville, a leader that Jiang knew. The guy told them the deal was no good."

"Who the hell was it?" I asked.

"He rescued Gao Gold's men from the Tailings," Miao said. "Some guy named Ishmael?"

23

Trojan Horse

I hung around APEC 2018—romancing Joy more than I should have, and pitching investors, the latter unsuccessfully—until the conference ended, and then caught a flight back to Bougainville. Since it was Saturday, there was no plane to Aropa, and I was forced to fly to Buka. Walking up the airstair to enter the plane, I encountered a curious scene. All eight of the business-class seats were occupied by Catholic clergy: six nuns, one priest—and one four-foot-tall plastic statue, snugly strapped into its seat belt for the flight. An hour later as the pilot leveled off on his approach into the Buka airport, the senior nun—the one with the beads around her neck—stood up to address the passengers. She explained that the statue was the so-called Pilgrim Statue of Our Lady of Fátima, on an international pilgrimage to Bougainville. Her arrival would be marked by celebration of Mass on the grounds at the airport, presided over by Bernard Unabali, the bishop of the Diocese of Bougainville. Everyone was invited. As we circled the airfield to land into the wind, I looked down out of the window and saw a crowd of over twenty thousand people surrounding the terminal. It looked like a rock concert about to get underway. Close to 10 percent of Bougainville's population had come to say Mass. Off to one side of the landing strip, a red carpet led from the tarmac across the grass to where a temporary altar had been erected. The nun finished her remarks by telling us that after Mass, Our Lady would be driven the length of Bougainville Island's coast road, stopping at all the Catholic churches and schools along the way.

We landed, the priest and the nuns carried the statue down the airstair and across the red carpet to the altar, and I went on my way. There was no way to get a ride from the airport to the Passage—the road was lined bumper-to-bumper with churchgoers, cars, and trucks—so I walked the two miles to town. After my longboat conveyed me across the Passage to Kokopau, the village on the south side, I noticed a change: The trash was gone. There was no garbage anywhere. Even the betel nut stains had been washed off the streets. I wondered what was going on; I had zero sense that under normal circumstances, the local denizens could ever be motivated to behave that way. I negotiated the shotgun seat in a PMV for the four-hour trip to Arawa. As we left town, I noticed that the roadway was also spotless. Then I saw the bamboo stakes. Every five yards along both sides of the road, six-foot high bamboo stakes adorned with orchids and other flowers had been placed in the ground, like decorative ornaments at a Hawaiian garden party. As we kept driving south, the bamboo stakes and flowers continued. I asked the PMV driver who was responsible.

"Oh, that's the bishop. Bishop Bernard Unabali," the driver said in a respectful tone.

"We've driven several miles already," I said. "How far do these decorations go?"

The driver grinned, and waved his hand forward. "All the way to Buin, man. A hundred miles."

Bishop Unabali was one powerful guy; I made a mental note to meet him. Soon, I had an opportunity. It was announced that he would be coming to Arawa to celebrate Mass at the Catholic church down the block from me, and I attended. I had heard the bishop was interested in solar power. After the service, I introduced myself and dropped a few comments about solar. That was enough to get an invitation to dinner later that night at the Diocese's house in Arawa.

"Are you a religious man, Mr. Davis?" the bishop asked me over a boiled chicken dinner.

"Well yes, I suppose. In a foxhole, anyway."

"You must be praying nightly here in Bougainville," the bishop said with a straight face.

"How'd you guess?"

The bishop laughed. Yes, the man was powerful, but any bishop who could laugh at religion was a man I wanted to befriend.

After APEC 2018, my mission was clear: Mt. Bagana Resources would become the dominant owner of exploration licenses in Bougainville. The licenses would allow my company to throw a net around the majority of the prospective mineral resources in central Bougainville. Then, investors would line up at our door.

The gating issue was Bougainville's mining moratorium, which had been in place since BCL perfected its mining rights in 1971. Unless the local chiefs filed a written request with the government to lift the moratorium—accompanied by documentation indicating strong community support—no mechanized mining or exploration was allowed. On the other hand, if the chiefs requested it, the government was required to grant their wish. No one had yet applied for any exploration licenses except in Isina and Tinputz, where Mogol had exercised his presidential fiat to lift the moratorium. In the past, those few parties who had wanted to explore for mineral resources had concluded that the route through the front door—getting the chiefs to cooperate and going through the mining department's Byzantine process—was too difficult, expensive, and, most importantly, time consuming; they had taken the back door. No one had even tried the front door. Mt. Bagana Resources would be the first.

I wasn't concerned. I lived there. The chiefs weren't adversaries; they were my friends. Tete and I contacted Lawrence Queen, and over the next few days we hammered out a plan to prepare applications for exploration rights to the most prospective areas in Bougainville. The government wasn't issuing exploration licenses for the Panguna Mine itself, but all other lands were eligible. Lawrence evaluated the areas with encouraging geological and geophysical information; I compared them to the data from thousands of alluvial gold-buying transactions we had completed at the Gold Dealer; and Tete went out into the bush and solicited willing chiefs. We applied for exploration licenses in every area in which the positive information overlapped. When we were finished with our paperwork, we would hand-deliver our applications and get them timestamped, so as to remain first in line.

Our business day lengthened as we dealt with an increasing agenda. In cooperation with Ishmael, we were also developing the Manetai limestone project and the hydroelectric project in Panguna. The hydro project needed a different set of permits, but the limestone project needed all the same paperwork we required for our exploration licenses; it was a mine too.

Tasked with filing the topological maps for our applications, Tete spoke frequently with the mining department staff regarding verification of geographical coordinates. One day he called me up, excited. Sheldon Yomama, the secretary of the mining department, wanted me to send him a letter explaining what the mining department could do in order to encourage the redevelopment of the Panguna Mine. I fashioned what I considered a brief but helpful answer and sent it along. Yomama never replied, or even had the courtesy to thank me for the letter.

A little while later, Tete approached me with another mining department request, this one more troubling. Gideon Donglu, the unctuous executive director of the mining department and Tete's colleague from the MRA, had jumped on one of Tete's phone calls with a department staff member. Gideon told Tete he had an urgent matter to discuss and demanded that he visit him soon in Buka. Tete told me he thought it would be a bad idea to meet Gideon alone.

Convinced Gideon's intentions were nefarious, Tete and I decided to stave him off until we were ready to submit our applications. We hadn't seen Gideon since he had taken our alluvial mining license application first, and then ignored us while awarding ten alluvial licenses to the Chinese, but that had been enough to learn his methods. Besides taking payoffs from carpetbaggers, it was hard to figure out what Gideon did all day. In the four years I had lived in Bougainville, the mining department had issued two alluvial mining licenses, to us and the Chinese, and four exploration licenses to the carpetbaggers in Isina and Tinputz. That was it.

My company's applications were completed by late January 2019. Tete called Gideon on a Friday and arranged to meet him in Buka on the following Monday; he didn't mention that I would accompany him. At four thirty Monday morning, a Buka-bound PMV pulled up outside our front gate. Lugging two sets of license applications, we let ourselves out under a clear sky, the Southern Cross and the moon and the stars in the heavens lighting our street as if it was the middle of the day. It was quiet—the roosters weren't even crowing yet—as we rolled north out of town in a Toyota ten-seater. Tete nodded off immediately, but I always stayed awake on the ride up to Buka, enjoying the scenery along the highway. By six, as the sun peeped over the clouds lining the eastern horizon, our vehicle's inhabitants were awakened by the crash of waves breaking along the road in Wakunai, halfway to Buka Town.

Tete scheduled his meeting with Gideon at Reasons for nine o'clock. Gideon wasn't there when we arrived, but we hadn't expected him to be. Reasons served the only decent breakfast in Buka Town, and after being on the gravel washboard from Arawa for four hours, we were hungry. I ordered one of their omelets, and Tete devoured a stack of pancakes. A few longboats, loaded to the gunwales with people and freight, motored by. Young boys frolicked below us on the coral rocks, leaping into the riverine blue water of the Passage.

Gideon made his entrance a little after ten. He wore a Stetson-style leather hat, the kind favored by Australian mining types. Dressed the part of an Australian miner, too, in a long-sleeve gabardine shirt, khaki pants, and work boots, he was paying the price—his clothes were drenched in sweat. As he came through Reasons's restaurant and out onto the balcony where breakfast was served, a frown developed on his face when he saw me sitting next to Tete.

Gideon sat down without saying hello. He was from Sepik, the PNG province that bordered the western half of New Guinea Island. When he removed his hat from his sweat-beaded, bald head, he wiped a brow that appeared more Indonesian than Melanesian. The waitress came over, handed Gideon a menu, and turned to go.

"Where do you think you're going?" he said to her. "I'm hungry." His lower lip fluttered petulantly when he learned they were no longer serving breakfast, but he recovered by ordering a steak. He put the menu down and focused his attention on me. "I didn't expect to see you this morning."

I reached under the table and handed Gideon one of the canvas satchels containing our applications. "We wanted to give you a separate copy of these."

"What are they?" he asked, taking the bag from me.

"Applications for exploration licenses," I said. "You'll find copies of each application. They're color-coded by subject."

"This bag's heavy. How many applications are in here?" he asked in an unhappy tone as he set the bag on the empty chair next to him, pulled out the bound pamphlet on the top of the pile, and flipped through it.

"Five," I said, and recited the respective villages they covered.

Gideon's steak came a few minutes later, but it seemed as if he'd lost his appetite. He kept returning to the subject of our applications. My antenna started to rise. Something was up any time Gideon paid attention. He dropped the first application on the table and pulled out the second. He examined its initial pages, and then did the same with the third. He stopped shuffling through the bag and looked across the table at me and Tete, his expression dark under his chrome dome. "You're applying for the rights to most of central Bougainville."

"That's what you want somebody to do, right?" I said, forcing myself to grin. "How else is your department supposed to make any money?"

He snickered, his amber eyes snakelike. "It's a little late for that. I haven't been paid in three months, and there's been no toilet paper in any government bathroom since last June."

Tete and I said nothing.

He stuffed another piece of steak into his mouth. "I heard you guys were getting ready to give me something, but I didn't expect all this," Gideon said, his mouth full of food. Then he tossed his silverware on his plate, pushed his chair away from the table, and leaned back, his potbelly resting in his lap. He pulled a folded piece of paper out of his back pocket and handed it across the table to me. "Here's your admission ticket. I was going to discuss this with Tete alone, but I guess you're the one paying the bill."

The document was an invoice from PNG's largest auto dealership, Ela Motors, which had a branch in Buka. It described a new Toyota five-door, including a lengthy list of optional features, with a total cost of 189,000 kina. The quotation was made out to the Gold Dealer. I read it and handed it over to Tete. "Thanks, but we already have a five-door."

Gideon snorted. "Since you chose to treat this as a joking matter, I'll add something else to your tab while I'm here." He pulled a pen out of his shirt pocket, scribbled some information on his napkin, and tossed it at me. "Those are instructions for wiring my daughter's school fees to my bank account. I'll need the vehicle to be ordered by the end of the week. You've got a little longer for the school fees; her classes don't begin until February. Send me a confirmation when your wire hits the Ela Motors account, and after that I'll see what I can do about getting you at least one of the exploration licenses you're seeking." He stood up and walked away from the table.

As soon as Gideon passed through the exit door, Tete started punching numbers on his cell phone. "Something's going on," he said. "He seems desperate. I'm going to get his wife on the phone."

I asked the waitress for the check. "Who's his wife?" I said to Tete. "She's from my hometown."

Tete had an extensive gossip ring, so I let him do his thing. He was still dialing when we went downstairs to Reasons's hotel lobby. I flagged a taxi and asked him to take us to the mining department. On the way, Tete located Gideon's wife and started having a telephonic conversation in pidgin.

We arrived at the department's office five minutes later, and while Tete remained on his phone in the car, I took the second sack of applications inside. I asked for my friend Lesley at the reception area. When she came out, I drew her outside. "How are you? Tete thinks something's going on here. Can you talk about it?"

"Not now." She looked around, and when she looked back at me, I could see she was afraid.

I explained the contents of the satchel and that we wanted a time-stamp for each application.

She looked around. "Do you have a car?"

"Yes; we're right over there," I said, pointing to our taxi.

"Wait there, and let me see what I can do," Lesley said.

"We just had breakfast with Gideon. He wants me to give him something for his help."

"Don't do it."

She came out ten minutes later and handed me five receipts. "I don't know whether these will help you or not. Read the papers tomorrow," she hissed. She pushed my door shut, saying "I can't lose my job," and ran back inside.

Tete didn't hang up with Gideon's wife until the taxi driver had delivered us to the longboat dock at the Passage. "I was right," he said. "She said a bunch of Australians have been camped out in the mining department all week, and they're meeting with members of the House of Representatives right now."

I said, "Forget going home today. I think we'd better hang around town a little longer. Let's get the driver to take us back to Reasons, and we'll book rooms for the night."

We went to bed as soon as the sun went down. The next morning, the headlines were all over the internet: *Mysterious Australian Group Seeks to Steal Bougainville Minerals for $US150 Million*, as one Fiji rag put it. In my room, I made myself a cup of instant coffee and scanned the airwaves. The preliminary reports sounded god-awful. If the described events came to pass, my company would be wiped out with the stroke of a pen. Everything we were doing or planned to do in Bougainville—the Gold Dealer, alluvial mines, exploration licenses, and the limestone and hydroelectric projects—would belong to some Australian guy who might as well have just flown in from Mars.

I stayed on the internet. By ten o'clock in the morning, a journalistic consensus had congealed. According to reports filed across Asia-Pacific, Liuman Mogol had somehow stumbled upon an Australian miscreant named Jeffrey McGuffin, head of an organization called the Cabal Group. McGuffin's career exhibited an arc similar to Lucien Sump's: an Australian whose first venture showed promise, his later pursuits devolved into recriminations among all concerned. McGuffin's Cabal Group had delivered a proposal to the Bougainville government which had a familiar, Lucien-like ring to it: in order to "jump-start its economy," the Bougainville government would sign binding legislation tossing out Bougainville's constitution and its mining act, which were "too complicated and inhibited progress." The new constitution and new law would require that Bougainville's landowners forfeit all ownership of the mineral resources under their respective ground to the Bougainville government, who would assign the rights to everything to "Newco," a new entity organized by the Cabal Group. Newco would become the exclusive licensing agent and owner of any mineral right, development, or mine in Bougainville, with the Bougainville government—read Mogol, not the landowners themselves—retaining a 60 percent interest, and McGuffin's Cabal Group owning the other 40 percent. Any capital required to finance mines would dilute the government's interest further. Since henceforth all mining would be done by Newco, there would be no need for Bougainville's mining department, which would be abolished.

Like Lucien, McGuffin required that the laws be changed before any money was exchanged. Once Bougainville's leaders had executed the binding legislation and Bougainville handed over its resources to Newco, McGuffin would then become Newco's chief executive and use his best efforts—no guarantees—to raise the 150 million US dollars—with the proceeds going to Newco, not the Bougainville government—to pay for various costs of Newco's pursuing the mining business in Bougainville. It was even possible that a few kina would dribble back to the government, so that it could buy toilet paper.

The plan was so absurd that I wasn't that concerned with its chances—I had never seen a worse example of government malfeasance, or a sillier financial scheme—until another, much more ominous headline floated out onto the internet around noon. It hit me like a locomotive: *Bougainville Legislation in the Backstretch.* While I was having my morning coffee, right up the road from me, the Bougainville Executive Council, a group comprised of President Mogol and his cabinet cronies, had met and approved the required legislation. It was headed to the floor of Bougainville's House of Representatives for ratification, and could become law in a couple of days.

Shocked, I started dressing while double-checking the article I read to make sure I wasn't mistaken, and then scanned the internet until I found more newscasts trumpeting the same horrific message. Pulling on my shoes and grabbing my room key, I went next door to Tete's room and knocked on his door. "Tete? Come on, we've got to go."

We scrambled along the sun-drenched outdoor balcony of Reasons's hotel rooms that overlooked the Passage and around the corner to the lobby of the hotel.

"Where are we going?" Tete asked, following behind me as I ran down the hallway.

Rather than answer him, I pushed open the door of Reasons's reception area and greeted the receptionist. "Can we please get a taxi to take us to the office of the Diocese of Bougainville?"

Tete asked, "Why are we going there?" as we waited in the coolness of the air-conditioned room while the lady at the desk dialed a taxi.

"It's a long shot," I confessed. "I can't think of anyone else who's in a position to tell Mogol to stop."

"He was a priest, after all," Tete said, shrugging his shoulders as if he'd need to see it to believe it.

The taxi arrived, and we asked him to head for the Diocese, a place I had never visited. As we traveled down Buka Town's main drag paralleling the Passage, I watched throngs of Bougainvilleans walking up and down the quay, talking and laughing and spitting prodigious amounts of betel nut. Most were undoubtedly just trying to get by. For some, perhaps, this might have been the day they had chosen to move ahead, when for whatever reason they had finally decided to do something meaningful in their lives. Meanwhile, people no different than the ones I observed out on the sidewalk, forty men and women who had been slightly more fortunate and lucky enough to win membership to the House of Representatives, were getting ready to sell them and all other Bougainvilleans down the river. For what? Twenty pieces of silver? Forget it—more like twenty pieces of lead.

The taxi snaked through the crowd for a half-dozen blocks, and then traffic thinned out and the driver picked up speed. Heading due east, in a mile we passed the airport on the left and threaded the flats between the end of the runway and the sea, and then snaked up a hill toward a promontory. I wasn't surprised: in the colonial days, the Catholic Church always snagged the choice properties. As we gained the summit of the hill, a sign surprised me: "Autonomous Region of Bougainville: House of Representatives."

"I had no idea that the House of Representatives was up here," I said to Tete.

The taxi driver heard me, and said, "President's house here too." He pointed to a corporate-looking dwelling under a grove of trees less than a hundred yards off from the building housing the legislature. Both structures were modern, unwieldy, and seemed totally out of place.

I thought we would continue on up the road, but we didn't. Momentarily, we reached another sign welcoming us to the Diocese of Bougainville. We turned off the road onto a long roadway that paralleled the driveway to President Mogol's house. Off to the left was a multi-acre, grass-covered campus with playing fields surrounded by tidy bungalows. It reminded me of the Boy Scout camp that my twin brother and I had attended when we were teenagers.

I said to the taxi driver, "We're here to try to see Bishop Unabali."

"You want the main building," he said.

We pulled up to a wooden, one-story building raised above the ground on stilts. The structure was painted green, with a high, wide stairway leading up to a set of double screen doors. It was a busy place; people were walking in and out as we paid the taxi fare.

I led the way through the screen doors and inside. A U-shaped reception area separated visitors from staff, who were numerous and sitting at desks or doing filing. "We're barging in, unfortunately," I said to a kindly-looking nun dressed in a gray habit and sitting at the desk closest to the front. "We don't have an appointment, but the bishop knows me," I said to her, and reached over and handed her my card.

She asked us to wait, and we took a seat outside along with several others. Ten minutes later, someone fetched us and took us around the corner to a two-story house overlooking the sea and surrounded by tropical plants and palm trees. As we walked across the grass,

Bishop Unabali stood waiting for us up on the second-floor balcony. Smiling down, he said, "You see, the Lord rewards me every day with this wonderful view," pointing east out over the sun-dappled Pacific headlands toward the wave-tossed eastern entrance to the Passage. "I'm not the only one who felt this way about our location. Take a look down below in the high grass; the hillside is still lined with Japanese fortifications."

I looked down off the ridge where we stood and saw the remains of a network of concrete bunkers and ramparts. "Sorry to barge in," I called up to him. "Our topic will only take a few minutes, but it's important for all Bougainvilleans if you want to avoid another war."

"The stairs are around the corner. Come on up," he said, and disappeared inside.

Tete and I said hello to the group of retainers, who congregated under the porch on the first floor, and climbed the stairs to the bishop's simple apartment. We entered a room that functioned as a kitchen, dining room, and living area where a lady named Elsie welcomed us, showed us to seats around a dining table, and told us lunch would be served shortly.

It appeared that the bishop had been working on his computer. It sat engaged on a card table at one end of the room, with his Microsoft Outlook page projected onto a blank wall that acted as a screen.

"Now you know my secret," the bishop said, a smile on his lean Bougainvillean face as he emerged from what looked like his bedroom in a white T-shirt and khaki pants and flip-flops. "I'm nearsighted." He shook my hand, and I introduced him to Tete.

I asked, "Since you're on your computer, is it possible for you to reach the internet on this machine?"

"Why yes, of course," the bishop said, and looked over at the kitchen where Elsie had busied herself a few minutes earlier. Without a word from the bishop and not breaking stride, she glided into the room where we sat, placed a sandwich on a plate at the bishop's setting at the head of the dining table, put another sandwich in front of me, and went over to the bishop's computer and looked up at me for instructions.

"I believe the site's www.rnznews.com," I said, and thanked Elsie when the page came up.

She whisked back to the kitchen for Tete's sandwich, grabbed it, came out and put it in front of him, and then adjusted the bishop's computer for the Cabal news story, as if she had already read it herself.

The bishop leaned over the computer, and then looked up and squinted at the screen.

"That's the subject of our visit," I said. "Please take your time and read the whole story."

The bishop made the letters a little larger, and then glanced at us. "I'll be two minutes. Eat; it's lunchtime," he said as he took my hand and Tete's and said grace. Then he looked up at the screen again and kept reading. When he was finished, he leaned back in his chair. "My goodness; what will the man do next?" the bishop said, and took a bite of his peanut butter and banana sandwich.

The three of us ate in silence while the bishop continued to squint up at the words on the wall. When we were finished and Elsie cleared the plates, the bishop asked me if the Cabal proposal would be bad for the economy. I told him that I didn't want to exaggerate, but yes, absolutely. The impact wouldn't simply be financial, I told him. I feared the net result could be much worse; I didn't see how armed conflict could be avoided. Not when Bougainvillean landowners would be told that everything they had fought for, and twenty thousand people died for, would be taken away and given to an Australian who had appeared out of nowhere. "The news has been out for a day now. Why aren't all Bougainvilleans more upset?" I asked him.

"Oh, ho! Don't get me started," the bishop said. "That's what I ask them all the time. Right, Elsie?"

Elsie bustled around her kitchen, a faint smile crossing her face.

The bishop asked if the Cabal proposal would harm my company. I understood why he asked the question. He was smart; he was trying to determine if I was using the power of the Diocese to advance Mt. Bagana Resources' fortunes. I admitted to him that we would lose money, but I added that such a setback wouldn't radically change our way of life. On the other hand, if Cabal's proposal was ratified, the average Bougainvillean landowner's future would be dashed, potentially forever.

He looked at me as if his mind was made up. "What can I do about this?"

"How well do you know Mr. Mogol?"

"Liuman and I were in the seminary together," the bishop said. He looked over his shoulder at Elsie working in the kitchen. "Mind you, he was a lousy priest," he said in a low tone, smiling. "Too political." He pointed out the window. "He's my neighbor. He lives right over there. I speak with him all the time."

"Could you write him a letter asking to stop this fiasco?"

"I was thinking the same thing," the bishop said. "I email him advice all the time." As if on cue, Elsie came out of the kitchen, helped the bishop adjust his seat, and switched the computer to a clean page of Microsoft Word. "You can read my words as they spit out right up there on the wall. When I get far enough along, tell me how I'm doing."

It took us a couple of hours to write the bishop's letter. I asked Tete to call over to Reasons and book us for another night. A little before seven when the last of the language was typed and edited, Elsie transferred the bishop's letter into an email. The bishop clicked on the "send" button, and the letter was gone. He asked us to stay for dinner, but we thanked both of them, saying we had taken enough of their time. We called a taxi and went back down to Reasons.

The next morning, my iPhone rang. I looked at the caller ID. It was a now-familiar foreign number.

"Hi, Miao. I wondered if I was going to hear from you."

"What do you think this time?"

I said, "I figured your friends were behind this crazy scheme. That Australian highbinder doesn't have access to a hundred and fifty million, and Mogol wouldn't do something like this without a big slug of cash in the bank in advance."

Miao laughed. "Jack, I love your American idioms. I must learn all of them. Which Australian highbinder—McGuffin or Lucien Sump?"

"They're both reprobates."

"To give credit where it's due, it was Lucien's plan," Miao said. "McGuffin used to go out with his sister."

"Why all the intrigue?"

"Look at what happened at the Grand Papuan, Jack. The Chinese want to avoid negative headlines—and loss of face is worse. This scheme is like that trick those guys played on the Greeks in that fable—the one with the wooden horse. What's the name of it again?"

"Yeah, but your partners are made of straw."

Miao laughed some more. "Speaking of reprobates, you should see what the PLA's cryptology guys have planted out there. It's all over PNG's Facebook that some Somali Muslim is the Cabal Group's source of money. No one's mentioned the Chinese once. It might work in the end, Jack. Cheaper than a billion—so far."

"Your guys are persistent. I'll give them that."

Miao said, "I told you. The big guy really wants the Panguna Mine. There's still room for you if you're interested."

"No thanks. By the time this is all over, a lot of feelings are going to be hurt."

"Jack, you know the Chinese," Miao said. "They'll come over there with a boatload of gifts and make nice with everyone."

"Yeah, well, my advice would be to bring a gun."

When I hung up with Miao, I was quite sure it would be the last time I spoke to him on the subject.

Over coffee that morning, Tete related the latest gossip. It was Wednesday, and Friday was the last day of the current Bougainville legislative session. The Cabal proposal was slated for a vote that day.

There was only one other thing I could do: call Ishmael. I dialed him up, and, by chance, he was in Buka. I told him about the problem and asked if I could take a half hour of his time. We agreed to meet at noon in a house he maintained for his security guys on the backside of town.

When Tete and I sat down with Ishmael, I was concerned at first. He hadn't followed the issue closely. It was clear that he viewed some of the members of the House of Representatives and their kind as worthless windbags. The other thing that was obvious was that I wasn't the first foreigner who had asked Ishmael for help on business issues similar to this. From his eyes, I could also see the cynicism he had developed. At a point in the past, some foreigners probably had had a business spat, and had wasted Ishmael's time in a selfish attempt to gain advantage, when his attention was needed on matters more important for the overall community.

This was different, and he needed to see that. "Let me ask you a question," I said. "You signed the Bougainville Peace Agreement. What's the most important thing in it?"

He said nothing. I had interviewed him many times for my book by then, and he knew me well enough to know that if I asked him a question like that to make a point, the best thing was to wait for me to answer it.

"It says that Bougainville's customary landowners control the resources above and below their ground, words which became the primary point in the Bougainville constitution."

"Yes, yes." That was a given, his expression said.

"McGuffin and Mogol want to take that away. The resources will belong to them."

He laughed, his eyes disdainful. "They can't do that."

"I realize that when you say that, you know that no landowner would allow it. They would take up arms," I said. "But that's a long-term solution to a problem that can be stopped today. Mogol must have paid a lot of members in the House to sign the legislation—big money, enough so most of those guys can't afford to say no—and apparently, they've taken it. They're going to sign the legislation into law on Friday. Then, it's going to take another twenty years of your time, Mr. Sheriff, to sort out another Crisis. That won't happen if those guys don't sign."

"I will tell them my way," Ishmael said, standing up. The meeting was over.

The next morning the internet contained some minor good news. A host of articles indicated that Mogol had decided that he personally shouldn't cast a vote regarding the McGuffin matter. The issue would be addressed, and decided upon, by the other members. He was confident that they could determine what was best for Bougainville.

The bishop's letter had struck a blow, but only a glancing one.

The other internet item of note on the Cabal topic was a notice from New Dawn Radio, an FM station in Buka and Bougainville's only radio channel. Ishmael, the BRA chief of defence, would address listeners on the subject of the Cabal proposal Thursday afternoon at one p.m. Bougainville time.

Tete and I weren't about to leave Buka. When we extended our room reservation for another night, we asked the people at Reasons if they had a radio. We wanted to listen to Ishmael's speech. To our surprise, they indicated that they did, and would be setting it up on the second floor in the restaurant, as many of their customers wanted to tune in as well.

A few minutes after one in the afternoon, a woman's voice introduced Ishmael, and he was live. He spoke in pidgin, and all I could do was observe people's reactions. Ishmael's address lasted only three minutes. It was less a speech, and more a set of instructions. His language sounded clear and precise. As soon as he uttered his last words, some people in the crowd gasped, while others, the whites of their eyes widening, shrieked as if in anticipation of havoc. Whatever he had said, everyone seemed to be backing Ishmael as they tossed down their drinks and ordered more.

I looked at Tete, who was laughing with the rest of the crowd. "What did he say?"

"Okay," Tete said, struggling to straighten up. He cleared his throat. "Ishmael said he respected the members of the House of Representatives. He said he understood that an Australian and the president had collaborated on a plan—the Cabal proposal—and that legislation approving the proposal had been submitted to the House for a vote on Friday. Then he said that he understood that the Cabal proposal would change what the Bougainville Peace Agreement stands for, the document he signed that embodies what he and his fighters fought for, and Bougainvilleans died for, in the Crisis." Tete looked me in the eye. "Then he said, 'I want each member of the House of Representatives to know: whoever approves that legislation will answer to me personally.'"

On Friday, the Bougainville House of Representatives did not open due to lack of a quorum. The legislation underlying the Cabal proposal did not leave committee, and expired.

24

Coming to America

Bishop Unabali and I dreamed up the idea of taking Bougainville-ans to America. I don't know who learned more from the trip: the Bougainvilleans or me.

It was a good time to get out of Bougainville, as the collapse of the Cabal proposal left an incapacitated government in its wake. Neither Mogol nor the legislature retained an ounce of credibility. After McGuffin and the Chinese had handed out cash like candy, Gideon Donglu abandoned any semblance of propriety and slumped into a primordial state, like a Komodo dragon waiting to be fed. Mt. Bagana Resources might as well have filed applications for licenses to explore the moon. During another interview for my book, Ishmael told me the Cabal event convinced him that fighting street crime wasn't enough. White collar crime in Bougainville—government corruption—was worse. In the future, he could no longer leave the government to the politicians.

Relief was in sight: a new government might be in the offing. The one legitimate thing Mogol had done at APEC 2018 was to announce, together with PNG's prime minister, James Serape, that Bougainville and PNG had agreed to conduct the independence referendum stipulated by the Bougainville Peace Agreement. In the past, PNG had made similar promises, but always reneged. This time, the two men validated their joint statement by setting an actual target date: autumn of 2019. To Bougainvilleans, this was the sign they had been waiting for. The kingdom was coming. After decades of futility, the Bougainville people would choose whether they wished to be part of someone else's destiny, or forge their own.

The potential for drama in Bougainville's political future didn't end with the independence referendum. In its aftermath, Bougainvilleans would elect a new president. Mogol was a lame duck. Subject to the outcome of the referendum, the new president would not be merely the head of an autonomous unit of PNG, but instead the leader of what could become the newest nation on earth. For Bougainvilleans to get their kingdom, they would need a messiah. The combination of the two pending events monopolized Bougainville's attention.

Squabbles continued to fester over what had been the underlying, yet central issue in the Cabal proposal: the fate of the Panguna Mine. On one side were the children who wanted the keys to the mine, although they couldn't drive the vehicle—BCL, PBJ, and, to a lesser extent, Cruks Mining—while on the other was the nasty stepfather—Mogol—who continued to plot how to use the mine's rich inheritance for his own ends. A solution was nowhere in sight.

The Chinese weren't giving up either. "What do you know about PBJ?" Miao asked when he called me one evening.

I was surprised. I hadn't spoken to him since the Cabal fiasco, after which I had assumed his masters had taken Bougainville's message loud and clear and ended their mission. "Why doesn't Xi Jinping forget about Bougainville and go hang out closer to home in Southeast Asia?" I said. "Those countries are more his style."

Miao chuckled. "They don't have a Panguna Mine. Seriously, do you think my client could work with those PBJ people?"

"I don't know. I'm not sure who's less trustworthy," I laughed.

Even the bishop wanted to discuss the subject of the Panguna Mine, encouraging me to drop by the next time I was in Buka. When I showed up at the Diocese on the weekend a few days later, the nice nun in the front office asked me to wait while she called over to the bishop's house. A moment later she got off the phone and smiled, saying he was getting ready for a service, but wanted me to hurry over anyway. As I got halfway across the grass, the bishop came out on his balcony and called to me. "I was just up at my family's home in Panguna; the people up there keep fighting. Ishmael's going to have to open an office there to keep the peace."

I walked up the stairs and into his rooms and sat down. In his T-shirt and khakis, the bishop sat across from me while Elsie circled him, flitting in and out of the room like a bird building a nest, getting him outfitted for his upcoming service. Already a thin man, it had only been a couple of weeks since I had last seen the bishop, but it looked like he had dropped ten pounds.

"Can any of these companies really do anything with the Panguna Mine?" the bishop continued as Elsie made him stand up to don his linen robe.

I wanted to avoid tainting the holy surroundings by exaggerating the incompetence of the parties in question. "No chance."

"Then what are they trying to do?"

I said, "In the US, we have an expression, 'Throw mud up against the wall and see what sticks.' Do you use an idiom like that here?"

The bishop smiled. "Yes; that one."

"That's all."

"Can they add anything of value?" he asked, peering at me.

Again, I tried to sound Christian. "BCL could, perhaps. I'm sure they own a lot of data describing what's in the ground around Panguna, but that's their limit. PBJ brings nothing to the table."

The bishop frowned. "That's not what I hear when I go home. Up in Panguna, some people say PBJ's the chosen developer of the mine."

"Yeah, but they were chosen by the Me'ekamui, which is a non-starter," I said. "Why do you ask?"

"That mine is the root of our problems," the bishop said. "It causes corruption, but it doesn't even operate. At least if it were working and paying Bougainvilleans, they could learn to live with it. I know it's valuable, but only in the right hands. Why can't we talk to somebody who has the capacity to truly fix it?"

I said, "You're asking the same question that Sheldon Yomama, the secretary of the mining department, put to me a few months ago. You need two things. First, a smart mining organization that understands how to live and work in a place like Bougainville. A lot of these mining executives should have taken more liberal arts courses; they don't see the big picture," I said, thinking of Jansen Erik, the buffoon at Mongolian Royalties. "Second, solve the issue defined by two words, to quote our geologist Lawrence Queen: 'political risk.' Until Bougainville's word means something, the mining world's going to avoid it."

Sitting down and leaning over the coffee table, chin in hand, the bishop lapsed into thought. "Ishmael and I could convince anyone we're a God-fearing people."

"Bingo," I said. "I agree. We've just got to figure out how to get Bougainville and the rest of the world into the same room."

The bishop still looked unconvinced. "Even if we were lucky enough to elect Ishmael as our new leader, we need to educate others to grow up like him. We must be able to teach our young people the perils of corruption; it's the bane of the South Pacific."

As I listened to Bishop Unabali sitting there in his vestments, Elsie walking into the room with his mitre, holding his headdress with two hands, I got an idea. I imagined the bishop, regal in his robe and mitre and a staff in his hand, walking into a boardroom at Barrick Gold, and then doing the same at Morgan Stanley. Showing up with a Bougainvillean like the bishop would certainly get people's attention. Once they were listening, the good organizations—those with people of intellect and scope—would grow more interested. The Panguna Mine was the carrot to attract that audience. The hydroelectric and limestone projects also required lots of capital, but not Morgan Stanley's flavor. The kind of capital those projects needed was best found at international aid organizations.

If we could get stateside, we could kill two birds with one stone: make progress on a fix for the Panguna Mine by introducing some impressive Bougainvilleans to a few big mining companies and investors in New York City; and then do the same thing for the limestone and hydroelectric projects by heading south and pitching aid organizations in Washington, DC. As long as we were in DC, addressing the bishop's concern about education was easy.

"Did I tell you I went to Georgetown?"

"No." He was quiet for a moment. "I've dreamed about that place. It must be magnificent."

"How'd you like to see it?"

The bishop struggled to keep his face placid as he looked back at me in silence, as if, if he spoke, his vision might shatter. His eyelashes opened and shut slowly, as he seemed to hold his breath.

"If you don't mind wearing your full bishop regalia to some meetings with mining companies, investors, and government officials, think about coming to America with me," I said. "The goal would be to get a few members of the audience to reciprocate and pay a visit to Bougainville. As far as the teaching part, I could take you to Georgetown. I've got good friends there. Since the independence referendum is coming up, maybe we could ask the university to send some people here to conduct a lecture series on how to be a good citizen in an independent country. It would have to start small, of course, but who knows what might transpire over the long run."

"Who would go?"

"That's a good question. For now, you've got to understand, we're just talking," I said. "I'd have to discuss this with my shareholders. I think it makes sense, but they might disagree, and if they do, forget it.

Even if I get the green light, money will be a primary issue, so it could only be a small group. I'm thinking you, one chief from Manetai for the limestone project, one from Dapera for the hydroelectric project, and we've got to have one from the Panguna Mine area as well. Given the matrilineal nature of most of Bougainville, at least two of the guests must be women."

"I agree. I think you're going to tell me I can't take my vicar as an assistant."

I chuckled. "Do you have any idea how much this is going to cost my company?"

"I'll be fine alone," the bishop said.

"I would bring Tete to make sure you'll be comfortable, if that's any help."

The bishop was already planning. "The trip would be apolitical."

"That's the idea."

"I hope you don't change your mind," he said before he left for his service.

Our shareholders probably flinched when I ran the idea by them, but in the end they agreed it would be good for all concerned, as long as the costs were controlled. It was April, and if we booked flights six weeks or more in advance, the trip would be cheaper. The bishop and I figured out a schedule that threaded the needle calendar-wise. A mid-June trip would be optimal. In Bougainville, we had time on our hands: nothing was going to happen until the independence referendum in the fall. In the US, dates were more complicated. We would need to get to New York before July when the corporate chieftains left for summer vacations. At that point, Congress would still be in session, and while Georgetown would be done with graduation, the administration would still be on campus. We nailed down a mid-June date to leave Port Moresby. The trip would take two weeks, with ten days on the ground in America.

After not seeing the bishop for a couple weeks, I went up to his place in Buka to put together our presentations for the US. When I climbed the stairs and met him at his front door, his appearance was shocking. He had lost another ten pounds. Elsie had gotten him a cane, and he was hobbling around.

"What's the matter with you?" I said, first looking at the bishop and then over his shoulder toward Elsie in the kitchen. "Elsie, has he been to a doctor?"

"It's nothing, it's nothing," the bishop said, as if muttering to himself. "I haven't been hungry."

I looked at Elsie, her face lined with concern. "What's going on?"

"He won't eat," she said. "I've tried everything."

"You've got to go to a doctor," I said to the bishop.

"I'm doing that next week," he said. "Now come on, while you're here let's get to work."

We focused briefly on the upcoming trip. One of the last agenda items was selecting proposed topics for the lecture series that we would discuss with interested Georgetown faculty.

"My guess is that both the Bougainvillean audience and the Georgetown contingent would appreciate provocative subjects," I said.

"How provocative?" the bishop asked, the Catholic priest in him coming out.

I said, "Well, one subject might be guns: you know, the pros and cons of the police being armed, or instituting armed forces if Bougainville becomes independent. With future economic development, you're going to get a more diverse population—like back before the Crisis—and then Bougainvilleans might feel safer if the authorities had weapons."

"What else?"

"I would think racism might be a good topic, but you tell me. It's a huge subject in the US these days."

The bishop nodded his head. "Yes, it's bad here too."

I was surprised. "You think so? To be honest, I haven't noticed anything close to what I would call racism. Of course, it would be difficult for people like me to exhibit racist tendencies here in Bougainville—we're a little outnumbered. I'm practically the only white guy in town."

The bishop said, "No, no; I'm not talking about racism between whites and blacks, especially Americans. Bougainvilleans loved the Americans in World War II. I know how they feel about you, and I can see you feel the same way about them. We don't have any black-white racism here now." He looked at me, his face showing traces of affection—or was it sympathy? "White people don't have a monopoly on racism, you know; black people can be just as bad."

"What are you talking about?"

"Why, the situation with the Chinese, of course."

"For sure," I agreed. "I experienced that firsthand when I lived in China for ten years. They can be terrible racists with respect to black people. My partner Lin was horrible; he refused to go with me to Los Angeles on a fundraising trip because he read that the black people there had torn the town apart in a riot. I tried to explain that it took place twenty years earlier, but he wouldn't budge."

The bishop laughed. "No, no. I'm not talking about the Chinese—I'm talking about the Bougainvilleans. My people. They can be brutal—especially when they feel that another race is taking their jobs—like the redskins—or competing with their businesses—like the Chinese."

I was surprised. "I know about the tension with people from PNG, but there's no way for me to observe what you say about the Chinese. I don't think there's a single Chinese person in Arawa."

"That's why," the bishop said. "They've all been run off."

We also needed to plan which mining and banking people we would see, and which governmental officials would confirm meetings. Back in the US, Elizabeth recruited Tom Curren and Bill Wright to help line up investors and mining companies in New York City. Tom's fund did a lot of investments with international aid organizations, and he was able to arrange meetings for us with a host of agencies in

Washington, DC. He also pulled some of his Irish-Catholic strings and lined up Cardinal Dolan to give everyone a tour of St. Patrick's Cathedral, and arranged for Bishop Unabali to be able to celebrate Mass on the Sunday he was in New York City. I arranged for us to have an audience with Jack DeGioia, the president of Georgetown University, and a more business-agenda-type meeting with Kelly Otter, the dean of the School of Continuing Education, the part of the university we all agreed was the best fit for what the bishop envisioned for Bougainville.

Taking the chiefs to America cost my company approximately one hundred thousand dollars, but that was nothing compared to the years it wore off my life. Negotiating travel documents and tickets for the group took two weeks: not two weeks of periodic problem-solving, but two solid weeks of days filled with encountering, and then surmounting, one problem after another. Two of the chiefs—Judith and Wendy—had never left Bougainville. Visas and passports? They didn't even have photographs, let alone driver's licenses. After all, who had a car?

I got the call from Elsie the day before we were scheduled to leave Buka for Port Moresby. "You better come quick."

When I got to the bishop's house, Elsie explained that he was exhausted, and sleeping. I told her it was okay; I'd wait for him and, when he was rested, we'd go to POM together.

She shook her head. "He's not going to be able to make it."

"He's got to," I said.

"Look," she said, and nudged open the door to his bedroom.

I looked into the room at the bishop, asleep on his bed, strung up with tubes. He couldn't have weighed more than a hundred pounds, and seemed barely alive. After a few minutes, I knelt down, said a prayer, kissed him on the top of his head, and left. The bishop died two weeks later. My guess is the trip had been the only thing keeping him alive.

We took a vote, and decided to go anyway; the Bougainvilleans were sure he would have wanted that. The vicar went in place of the bishop. Getting the amended paperwork finished on time was hair-raising, but we made the deadline with some welcome help from the US Embassy staff and finally caught our flights out of POM via Manila to New York City's JFK airport.

On a gorgeous, clear night over the rural reaches of New York State, our plane dropped into its approach as the pilot guided it down the Hudson River. "Welcome to the Big Apple," I said to the group as we cruised over the twinkling towers of Manhattan.

"I can't believe that's real," Tete said.

JFK was my first direct experience with profiling. Getting off the plane, I shepherded my flock down a long hallway until the immigration gates separated US citizens from the other passengers. At that point, it was eleven thirty in the evening. I didn't see them again for three hours. Later, Tete explained to me that when they reached the head of the line and went to the immigration window, each of them was interviewed for fifteen minutes, while most other people breezed through. Customs was worse. I had told everyone to pack light, taking only a carry-on bag; we didn't want to be delayed with lost luggage, and we'd be buying them plenty of tourist garb as souvenirs. That didn't sit well with the Customs police, Tete said. They couldn't make sense of why these black islanders would fly all the way to New York City without all of their family belongings, like all the other immigrants.

"Sir, these folks say they're with you," one of New York's finest said to me when he popped out of a side door near where I had been waiting, my group of weary travelers trailing dutifully behind him.

"That's right, sir. Did they tell you that three of them are chiefs, and one's a priest?"

The white-haired sergeant looked at me with surprise, his rosacea turning bright pink, as I did my best to regale him with stories of a special South Pacific region and its noble people, five of whom he had been unfairly interrogating. He released them and said goodnight a minute later, albeit without offering any apology.

"They said they thought we were drug dealers," Tete said.

On Saturday morning, their first day in the city, I let everyone sleep. No one stirred until the afternoon. After lunch and lessons about how to dial up television shows and movies, the group returned to their rooms. We met later Saturday evening in the hotel restaurant, ate dinner, and turned in early. Sunday was scheduled to be our tourist day in New York City. Everyone straggled into the breakfast café by eleven o'clock. I laid out the schedule: Our first visit would be the United Nations. After that, we would take our rental van and make a few stops in Central Park, and then visit the Museum of Modern Art. That seemed all right with everyone.

"Tonight, I thought you might want to do something different and go to Harlem," I said. "Does anyone know what Harlem is?"

"Isn't that the black neighborhood?" Tete said. I was learning on this trip that Tete was unusually informed about American culture. There was no American movie he hadn't watched, and he could sing along with most of the American pop hits we heard playing on the radio.

"That's one way of putting it," I answered. "It's a famous area. There are some good restaurants serving special food from the American South that you might like. If we have time afterward, maybe we can visit a club."

As I was speaking, Wendy, Judith, Simon, and the vicar stopped listening, and huddled together on the other side of the table, whispering in pidgin.

When they were finished, Wendy announced, "We don't want to go to Harlem."

"It's dangerous," Simon said. "Everyone there is a drug addict, and they have guns and shoot people."

"That's not true," I said, tempted to laugh, their comments were so unexpected. "You've been watching too much American TV."

Judith leaned forward. "I don't want to go there."

That was that. We made do with an Italian dinner in Little Italy.

Tom Curren had helped us line up people at the United States Agency for International Development, and we had sent them a preliminary proposal about receiving financial assistance for the hydroelectric and limestone projects. As two female chiefs from the Panguna region who were old enough to have experienced the Crisis and spent their lives in the dark, Judith and Wendy were excited about the prospect of getting electricity for their homes and families. Elizabeth worked with them to prepare a presentation they would make about the hydroelectric project to the USAID audience. It hit the high points: hydroelectric power was much cleaner than diesel power, and the electricity would enable the women to manage better households and businesses, while the children could study at night.

Tom had done a good job teeing up senior officials for the meeting. We were ushered into a large boardroom where a half-dozen people, including the head of the agency and a group of women officers, greeted us. Wendy and Judith began by handing out Bougainvillean handicrafts, and then made an excellent presentation.

"I'm not sure this project ticks enough boxes on gender equity," opined one of the women officials, smiling as she said it.

Even though their English was excellent, Wendy and Judith didn't understand the inane comment and were confused. Elizabeth huddled with them, explained it, and they fashioned a response. Then Judith sat up straight in her chair, clasped her hands together on the table, and looked across at the assembled professionals. Other than fending off Defence Force soldiers during the Crisis, I was quite sure she had never done anything as intimidating in her life. "I'm a poor mother. I raised eleven children in the Crisis. I need electricity." Things improved markedly after that, and we spent the next two hours fielding questions.

When we met with the Development Finance Corporation, USAID's sister agency for international aid investment, Simon made a presentation about the limestone project. No one remarked about any deficiencies in his presentation, but he didn't get a single question about financial viability. All of us, including me, were getting an education that day about raising money from international aid organizations: the secret was neither the technical nor financial viability of the projects, but whether or not they 'ticked the boxes' and fit into the government's aid menu du jour.

That night at dinner, all the Bougainvillean chiefs asked me the same question in multiple ways: when would they get the money? There was no concept in their mind that it might not be forthcoming, or of the substantial preliminary work and expense that would be required to lay the groundwork. If you had asked them if money in the US grew on trees, they would have laughed and said no, but if you had said, "No seriously—where does it come from?" they simply had no idea.

Their favorite city was Washington. They were afraid of New York, they said. The buildings were too high, it was too dark, and the people talked too fast. Their favorite place in America? It was unanimous: Washington's National Zoo.

On our last day, we drove north from Washington toward New York City. I planned to put the visitors on a plane at JFK, then stay in town to begin a round of capital-raising for Mt. Bagana Resources. We stopped at an old-fashioned diner. Over cheeseburgers and fried chicken—their two favorite US meals—I asked what they would remember most about the trip.

We went around the table. When it was Tete's turn, he said, "I learned what's different about your country, Jack. It's time. I can see now why you get angry when things are delayed in Bougainville. Time has a totally different meaning to an American. It's something that can't be replaced. In our country, we don't worry about time. I don't know if we can ever learn how to be like people are here."

Tete wasn't the only one who learned something surprising. After the group flew home and I recuperated, I met friends and explained what I had been doing. My friends' response was universal. "Those people must have been so grateful…for them, it had to be the experience of a lifetime…they'll probably never get over the opportunity." Things like that. I nodded my head in agreement. It had been unforgettable, and I know Tete and the chiefs felt the same way. Our company and I had been happy to do it, and we were pleased that we could impact some deserving lives in a positive manner.

A few weeks after the Bougainvilleans had left, I received an email from the vicar. He was the most sophisticated of the travelers, and had a computer. He explained that on the way back, he and the chiefs had a conversation in which they expressed their mutual surprise that I, an American, was pushing for the projects as much as the Bougainvilleans were. My company Mt. Bagana Resources was going to benefit, they realized. Therefore, the vicar concluded, they had been working for me. Speaking for himself, he needed to be paid; an invoice was attached. He never expressed a word of thanks.

Ultimately, the trip paid off. The original intentions that the bishop and I had for it—that it could serve as a way for American institutions to get more comfortable with Bougainville—were realized. The potential investors we met were enthusiastic, the mining companies interested, and the politicians and diplomats were happy to know they had friends in that corner of the world.

The dividends the trip paid back home in Bougainville were more pronounced. Tete put all of the photos he took on the trip on Facebook, and within hours they were all over Bougainville: the chiefs in front of the White House, at the Lincoln Memorial, the Washington Monument, and the Martin Luther King Memorial. The chiefs had been taken by Americans to America, and the marriage had been consummated. The Bougainville rumor mill picked up the story and blew it over the island like a cornstalk in a Nebraska dust bowl. People waved to me and nodded their head my way inside the general store.

After a successful fundraising jaunt, it was time for me to return to Bougainville. Tete and the chiefs had been home for a couple of weeks. I was on my way, changing planes in Hong Kong, when I saw Tete's email. He said Ishmael had contacted him and asked when I was coming back. Ishmael needed to see me, Tete said, indicating it sounded important. The plane was just about to take off when I called him. "What do you think it's about?"

"The Chinese," Tete said.

25

Independence

My flight from Hong Kong via Port Moresby landed at Aropa Airport around three in the afternoon. I had checked no luggage and was the first person through security. Tete was waiting at the bottom of the stairs. As we walked across the parking lot and climbed in our five-door, I started to ask him about our aborted conversation the day before regarding Ishmael and the Chinese, when I noticed someone sitting in the back seat.

"Welcome back," said a voice from the darkness. A hand attached to the voice thrust forward to shake mine. "Bougainville thanks you for caring."

I peered back at a man wearing a baseball hat pulled down over his eyes, and realized it was Jeremiah. He was a pastor in Arawa. I had run into him a couple of times involving community support meetings for our development projects. I had no idea why he was there, but guessed it had something to do with Tete's correspondence about Ishmael; Jeremiah and Ishmael were friends.

I wasn't going to put Jeremiah on the spot by asking why he was there, but his presence meant I'd have to wait to ask Tete questions. The entire time I had spent in the air from Hong Kong, I had puzzled over his last words before I got on the plane. Why would Ishmael want to speak to me about the Chinese? Whatever the issue, I hoped it meant that Ishmael needed my help. I liked him, but I was uncomfortable in relationships as one-sided as ours had been. Ishmael had done many things for me in Bougainville and could do many more, but I was careful not to endanger our friendship by asking. When we spoke about the book I was writing on Bougainville, it was clear he liked reminiscing about history and battles, and I believe he would have been glad to talk more, but I was parsimonious with his time. I was pleased I had been able to help Ishmael with the limestone and hydroelectric power projects. The best thing would be if there was something else I could do with him like that.

Mt. Bagana Resources' future was at a crossroads. Our gold-dealing and alluvial gold-mining businesses were operational, but their financial performance was marginal. It was clear that if we were going to make real money in Bougainville, it would be by pursuing exploration licenses, as well as redeveloping the limestone and hydroelectric projects. To do all that, I needed permits and approvals. As long as the lazy, corrupt Mogol government sat on their hands, my company could not move forward. Bougainville couldn't either. It had all the potential in the world, complete with fools like me trying to help extract it, but a few low-life barnacles in the government's engine room had succeeded in gumming up everything.

If Jeremiah held any clues about Ishmael's state of mind, he wasn't divulging them. He remained silent. When we pulled up to the gate in front of my house, he finally revealed his mission. "Ishmael is over in the Women's Centre," he said. "He asked me to arrange for you to join him in an hour."

We agreed, Jeremiah walked across the street, and Tete and I went upstairs, unlocked the house, and turned on the porch lights.

"Do you want a beer?" I said to Tete from the kitchen.

"There should be two cold ones in the back of the fridge," he said, and joined me out on the veranda a minute later. The Arawa night was balmy, the gentle air enveloping me like a down blanket. It was Bougainville's best time of day.

I took a long pull from my can of SP. "What's Ishmael want to talk about?" I asked Tete.

He said, "I asked around. I think he's going to tell you that he's running for president."

Tete didn't say things like that unless he was sure it was going to happen. "That's good, but what's it got to do with China?" I asked.

"You'll find out."

Even though he wasn't volunteering anything, I assumed Tete had already spoken to Ishmael. "As long as you seem to know, what's it got to do with me?"

He looked at me like I had asked if night follows day. "He needs your help."

I knew two things about political campaigns: they were expensive, and there were a million ways to lose. Over the years in the US, friends tried to lure me into getting involved with political candidates, all of them guaranteed to change the world. I had resisted strenuously. I didn't get worked up over politics to begin with, plus the odds of backing a candidate always seemed lousy. I never spent a dollar on a race, but that didn't prevent me from following the results. Everyone who had asked me for money ended up a loser. In Bougainville, I couldn't see myself behaving differently. It was one thing to encourage Ishmael to run, but footing too much of the bill was another. I chugged the rest of my beer. "I definitely think he should run, but we're in no position to be heroes here," I said to Tete as we walked across the street.

Around the corner from the hotel's open-air entrance, a board-room lined the left side of the main walkway. The door to the room was open, and Ishmael was inside with Jeremiah. The two of them were fussing with a computer and an old-fashioned video projector that sat on a table. Plastic chairs were pulled up to the table on either side of the equipment. The projector was on, casting a white, circular spot on the blackboard on the wall. Both Ishmael and Jeremiah stopped and said hello, and then went back to hooking the computer together with the projector. A minute later, things were ready, and the four of us sat down.

"Have you seen *60 Minutes* yet?" Ishmael asked.

"No," I answered, having no idea what he was talking about.

Tete said he'd heard their crew had been in Bougainville.

Ishmael explained, "We provided security to them when they were here, and they gave this film clip to us. They said it will be broadcast next month."

Jeremiah hit a button, and I learned that there was a *60 Minutes* other than the one in the United States. A logo and trademark for the Australian Broadcasting Corporation rolled across the screen, followed by credits for their version of *60 Minutes*. A newscaster from Sydney explained that the viewer was about to watch a special, hour-long television newscast on China-creep in the South Pacific. The man said that there would be three segments: the first was on the Solomon Islands, the second on Kiribati, and the third was about Bougainville. I settled back in my seat, half expecting to see Lin or Chairman Jiang pop up on the screen.

The first two segments were damning, albeit rendered in the same smug, self-congratulatory style as employed by *60 Minutes* in the US. When those guys got someone in their crosshairs, even Jesus Christ didn't stand a Chinaman's chance, as my father used to say. As the film wound through the first forty minutes, it portrayed teams of journalists visiting the Solomon Islands and then Kiribati, each nation led by a corrupt despot in recent receipt of excessive largesse from the Chinese. In both locations, as soon as the leaders realized that the reporters were on muckraking missions, the police showed up and forced the interlopers to flee.

Then it was Bougainville's turn. The format changed. The newscaster back in Sydney explained Bougainville's circumstances, and then the camera panned to a conference room where George and Francine Washburn sat across a table, eyeing a reporter next to a camera. George appeared comfortable, but for some reason, Francine wore a fierce expression, as if she was going to slug the reporter the minute the show was over. They were portrayed as Mr. and Mrs. Bougainville, and didn't do anything to dispute the description. The reporter asked them how they felt about China. With a broad smile across his handsome face, George stood up and expounded on all the benefits to be bestowed by his good friends from China on his Bougainville homeland. He pulled out storyboards covered with artist's renderings of major new infrastructure—highways, bridges, airports, and ports—and, last but not least, a redevelopment of the Panguna Mine. After a few more minutes of questions and answers, Mr. and Mrs. Bougainville faded out, and the show ended.

Being filmed together with two crooks confirmed the Washburns as corrupt, something which probably flew over George and Francine's heads. That's what they got for talking to *60 Minutes*.

"There's something else you should know," Ishmael said.

Tete and I studied Ishmael where he sat on the other side of the projector, clad in his jeans and T-shirt atop bare feet.

Ishmael said, "Something like this happened to me last month with George in Vanuatu. I went to a meeting there with some Chinese guys who tried to convince me to sign a document agreeing to work with them." He laughed. "I had to escape." Then he turned serious. "If it was up to George, Bougainville would turn into a Chinese colony."

Miao was right, I thought. The Chinese would stop at nothing until Bougainville was theirs. "What's this have to do with us here tonight?"

In situations like this, Ishmael sometimes got downright shy. With a diffident smile, he said, "One time you said you thought I should consider running for president."

"You know that's the way I feel."

Ishmael said, "I said before that I didn't think it was a good idea." He looked up at the screen. "Now I don't think I have a choice. I can't let George become president of Bougainville, especially when we have a good chance to become an independent country."

"I can see why you feel that way," I said, counting to three. I had to be very careful. "I also don't think these things are easy. You'd be up against some serious obstacles. I'm sure the Chinese are prepared to throw a lot of money around."

"George is already bragging on Facebook that they gave him seven million kina," Tete said.

Jeremiah said, "He's not the only one the Chinese are backing. They're funding Ferdy Mimosa too."

Ferdy Mimosa, the corrupt minister of the mining department, was the biggest slimeball in Bougainville. If the Chinese were backing a reprobate like Ferdy, they would truly stop at nothing. The election might as well be over. If I had had a choice at that point, I would have hightailed it before spending another dime on the island.

"They say he's getting seven million too," Tete said. "It's all over Facebook."

Ishmael grinned. "Don't worry. Bougainvilleans are smart. They'll take the Chinese money, but they won't take the Chinese."

"That's right," Jeremiah said.

Ishmael looked my way. "I need someone to back me. I know I can win, but I need help."

"I'm sure you can, too, but there are issues," I said, staring back at him. "Big ones. Do you have a staff selected?"

Before Ishmael could respond, Jeremiah pulled a bound presentation out of his bag and handed it to me.

The presentation was labelled Bougainville Peoples' Alliance Party. I skimmed it. It didn't answer my question; it was a legal document to register a political party in Port Moresby. I said to Jeremiah, "This is a start, but it's a plan for a political party, not a candidate. Are political parties important here?"

Both men chimed in, explaining that they were. If Ishmael was to be elected as a new president, he would need party loyalists in the legislature to get things done. *Terrific*, I thought. As if jumping into a presidential race wouldn't be enough, an entire political party had to be created—and paid for.

"My first question still stands," I said to Ishmael. "You're going to need good people, and," I said, grinning at him, "I for one would really like to hear what you're going to tell the voters."

"Yes, yes," Ishmael said, the way he answered questions when he wanted you to know that he had thought about it. "We're working on that. Maybe we can meet again in a week?"

After Tete and I said goodnight and walked back across the street, the first thing I did was call Miao. "I'm trying to check out a few rumors," I said when Miao picked up. "Are you guys horning your way into the upcoming election here?"

"As Deng Xiaoping said, there's more than one way to skin a cat."

"That's not what he said," I scoffed. "He said it didn't matter whether a cat was black or white, as long as it caught mice. Are you?"

"I don't think I can say."

I didn't blame him for being cagey. "Okay, fine. I'll do the talking. If you didn't already know, it seems your friends may be taking a new approach here. A political one."

"If it's true, I don't blame them. The other way was getting them nowhere. Maybe politics is better. Would you agree?"

"For you guys? I'm not sure. It's not like the Chinese have a lot of experience with voting." I laughed, and so did Miao. "What happened to Lucien?"

"Things never panned out. We won't be working with his crew anymore."

"I suppose I should be thankful. Maybe his henchman Grumpy Trull will stop harassing me. You're not working with George either?"

"I didn't say that," Miao said, a little too quickly.

"All right; just asking. Listen, one last thing: I'm going to do the big guy and your boss an enormous favor. As far as George, good luck to you both; you deserve each other. I can't say the same about Ferdy Mimosa. If there was any way to document people's transgressions here—unfortunately, there isn't—the guy would have a rap sheet as tall as you. Embezzlement, sexual assault, you name it. Tell your guys they don't want anything to do with him."

"I'll pass that on," Miao said, his laugh cynical.

"So seriously, your guys are behind what's going on here?"

"I told you. The big guy will do anything to get Bougainville. If he can't buy the Panguna Mine outright, maybe he can buy the election. In China, that's legal."

We hung up a minute later. Things couldn't have been clearer. The Chinese were going to do anything it took to grab Bougainville, and anyone standing in the way had better jump to the side. It harked back to the stories I had read about Bougainville during WWII. When the Japanese took control of a village from the colonists, they chopped off the heads of the chiefs who had resisted them and posted them in their village on bamboo poles. I shouldn't kid myself; I was in the same situation as Ishmael. If a Chinese-backed candidate won, Bougainville wouldn't be a place either one of us would want to call home.

A week later, my PNG mobile phone woke me at five in the morning. "Hello?"

"Mr. Jack Davis?"

"Who's this?"

"I'm sorry to disturb you. This is Dr. Gupta from the Pacific International Hospital in Port Moresby. We have a patient here who will die unless we operate. He gave us your name."

"Who is it?"

"He was difficult to understand," the doctor said. "I believe his name is Greyson Trull."

"What? Greyson Trull? What's this got to do with me?"

"I'm truly sorry about this. Mr. Trull was left on the front steps of our hospital a few minutes ago. He has multiple stab wounds and is bleeding to death. As I said, he gave us your name." Doctor Gupta cleared his throat. "I searched our records, saw you were a patient of ours, and took the liberty of calling. My apologies."

"Don't worry about it." The phone crackled in the silence. "I guess I still don't understand why you're calling me," I finally said.

"He's going to bleed to death, Mr. Davis."

"So fix him up, for God's sake."

Doctor Gupta sucked in his breath. "He's penniless, Mr. Davis. We are not authorized to operate unless someone pays."

Now it was my time to remain silent. "That's why you called me?"

"He used your name. He said you would agree to pay," the doctor said. "I thought he was a friend."

"Hardly."

"I'm afraid we're out of time," Doctor Gupta said. "I'm sorry to have disturbed you."

"Hold on," I said. "I'm not going to just let him die."

"Whatever you want me to do, you must tell me now," Doctor Gupta said.

"Go ahead and operate on him."

"Thank you, Mr. Davis. I'm sure Mr. Trull will thank you too. I have your credit card on file; may I use that?"

"I guess so. Let me know what happens."

"We will, of course. Hopefully, Mr. Trull survives surgery. In that case, his recovery will take some time. When you're next in Port Moresby, you could stop by to see him—and to complete our paperwork, of course," the doctor said.

That evening we had our second meeting with Ishmael. I had pondered the subject of his election campaign since we were last together. The reasons behind Ishmael's candidacy were compelling, but I had an overriding issue: money. Mt. Bagana Resources was barely scraping by, and we weren't in a position to be magnanimous. If Ishmael expected my company to match the Chinese financially, he was dreaming. We had limits.

Tete and I walked across the street to the Women's Centre. Six people were waiting for us in the boardroom, seated around the tables that had been rearranged in a square. It was the first group meeting I had attended in Bougainville where I didn't have to wait for someone to show up. Ishmael invited us in, and then he introduced us to his campaign staff.

It appeared that no one was experienced at what we had gathered to do, and people were a little nervous. I got the sense that Ishmael had told them that I was the reason he had invited them to the meeting, and everyone including him acted as if I should pick the tune. I suggested we sit down, go around the room, and say some words about ourselves. Lenore, the woman on my left, went first: she was a media expert, specifically Facebook. That sounded good to me. The next person, Geoffrey, actually wore a jacket and tie, and said he was the campaign's lawyer. Jeremiah went next, indicating his role as strategy. The large man to his left, Easton, turned out to be Jeremiah's brother; the campaign platform and planning was his thing, he said. Isaac, a clean-cut, handsome guy with a sandy complexion—not a Bougainvillean—was in charge of finance.

Ishmael looked at me as if proud for assembling his team. He should have been—these things didn't get done in Bougainville often. I asked him if he had anything to hand out. As he hesitated, Jeremiah pulled out another bound pamphlet. He had only one copy, and gave it to me. Ishmael didn't have one in front of him, and I got the feeling he hadn't seen it in advance.

I didn't look at the pamphlet at first because Ishmael started speaking. He said that the election process wouldn't start until the first quarter of the following calendar year, but he felt strongly that his campaign had to begin immediately, due to the pending independence referendum. The referendum and the election were tied together, he said, and around the room people nodded their heads.

Jeremiah said, "People on the street ask Ishmael two important questions: Are you for independence? And if you are, where's the money come from?"

Easton crossed and dotted his brother's remark. "Ishmael must be seen to be Bougainville's number one advocate for independence, because that will be the number one issue in the presidential election."

Even if he looked half-asleep, Easton made sense. Preliminarily, I assumed he might be useful, and I had already seen the pastor in action and knew he was an eloquent speaker. Other people grew confident and started talking. Lenore sounded like she was skilled as far as using Facebook in the campaign, and seemed like a keeper. Isaac answered any financial query I posed, which in Bougainville qualified him to be minister of finance, as far as I was concerned. As I listened, I flipped through the pamphlet Jeremiah had given me.

As my eyes focused on the bottom line of the summary page at the back of the document, it felt like something knocked the wind out of me. According to this document, the purported cost of Ishmael's campaign was five million kina. As others kept talking, my insides still fuzzy, I looked up to see who was watching me read the pamphlet. Ishmael was paying no attention, but Jeremiah and Easton were both studying me carefully. I kept reading. The largest line item was labelled salaries: Jeremiah and Easton were listed up top, receiving amounts they couldn't earn in their wildest dreams anywhere else in Bougainville. So much for getting involved in a political campaign; at least those guys had made it easy for me to say no.

To be polite, I waited for an interlude before taking my leave. Several minutes later, I told everyone it was getting late and thanked them for their time. Ishmael looked concerned, not an expression I was used to seeing on his face. As I got up to leave, he leaned over and whispered to Tete in pidgin. Shaking everyone's hand and thanking them, I waited for Tete while he finished with Ishmael. As the two of them stayed in their seats and kept whispering, Tete explained to me that he needed more time, and I should go ahead.

Back across the street, I grabbed a beer and sat out on the veranda. The stars were out, and so were the Bougainvilleans, strolling down the sidewalk, the lilt of their voices floating up on the air. Off in the distance, the sea rustled like a white noise machine, a wave finding its way across the reef and crashing on the shore every few minutes.

I should have known what would happen. Jeremiah and Easton had been tasked with preparing a plan and a budget, had heard the number the Chinese were willing to pay, and figured I was a ripe target for an amount in the same neighborhood. I didn't hold it against them—it was a classic Bougainvillean move when dealing with a wealthy foreigner. I doubted Ishmael even knew what they had prepared. I opened the pamphlet and read more. Some of it was laughable. The campaign was supposed to expend huge amounts supporting party members from remote villages who were running for seats in the House of Representatives. What could someone there possibly spend all that money on? As far as I was concerned, all a Bougainvillean election campaign needed were the same things my company expended when we sought community support for our projects or exploration licenses: fuel for the transport vehicles and food for the people. That, and a few bucks to manage a Facebook page and some text blasts, ought to be ample.

A few minutes later, I looked down from my veranda and watched Ishmael's group strolling out of the gates of the Women's Centre, saying good night to each other. Tete came out alone and walked across the street. He got to the locked gate and called up to me. "Can you come back over? Ishmael wants to talk to you."

I went downstairs, and Tete and I walked across the street. "He knows you didn't like what you saw in the budget," Tete said as we crossed the gravel parking lot of the hotel.

Ishmael sat at the table. The look on his face was so baleful, I felt like I should ease his pain. "I hope I didn't mislead you. I'll support your candidacy; I told you I would. I just don't have five million kina—or anything near that. Even if I did, my shareholders would never approve me spending that kind of money on something like a political campaign. No offense, but it's a crapshoot."

When he heard me state the number, Ishmael laughed. "Five million? That's their number, not mine," he said. "I saw your face. I asked those guys to come up with a budget, but they didn't ask me before they gave it to you. I don't even have a copy."

"Look—you've got to understand: even half that number is way too much for us."

"I don't need much money," he said, shaking his head as he kept his eyes on mine. "Tell me what you're comfortable with, and that's fine with me."

"Campaigns in other places have guys raising money," I said. "Do you have anyone like that here?"

His smile was wistful. "No."

"So I'd be the only one."

Ishmael nodded his head as he kept me in his sights. "You're an American. That's all the support I need."

I owed it to Ishmael to set him straight. "I'm American, but I don't represent the government. I'm just a private citizen—and not a rich one either. As you know, I just finished a trip to America with some of your fellow Bougainvilleans, and all the government officials back there were tripping over themselves to tell us how impartial they must be—while they know full well China's eating their lunch across the Pacific. They said the rules won't let them support Bougainville in its referendum, let alone an individual in a presidential election. It makes me wonder how we're going to maintain our place in the world."

"It doesn't matter," Ishmael said, his feelings unfettered. "You're American. Everybody knows you've lived here a long time and you're helping. You're the right man for me."

I stood there mulling things over. "I'd better write down some numbers," I said after a minute, and walked to the back of the room where I saw a desktop strewn with paper and pencils. I grabbed what I needed, returned, and sat down, scribbling down a campaign budget. "Fuel and food are the basics, right?"

Ishmael signaled thumbs up.

"Tete, do me a favor. You and Ishmael estimate how much fuel it takes one truck to go the length of Bougainville and back, figure out how many times people need to do that, double it, and give me the number for fuel. After that, do the same thing for food: drinks, cookies, things that he needs to pass out at the village meetings."

While I tried to think of everything else, Tete pulled out his phone and pressed the calculator key, and the two of them put their heads together for a few minutes and produced some numbers. I recorded them, annotated the other line items in a column down my page, and started a tally. After a moment I looked over at Ishmael and said, "You did good to line up that staff. They seem qualified, but if you ask me, the only ones you need right now are Lenore and Isaac. I'm not saying the others won't be useful later, but they won't have anything to do at this point."

"Yes."

I kept making notes. "The budget they gave me had fat salaries. That won't work. Back in the US, campaigns do pay some level of salary, but typically starvation wages. People don't work on campaigns for big salaries; they work out of loyalty to the candidate and the party and the issues, and the hope that they will be offered a job in the government if they win. It shouldn't be any different here."

"It's the same."

When I was done writing everything down, I double-checked my figures, at the same time asking myself if I really wanted to do this. I didn't, but I didn't see what choice I had—not if I wanted to prevent the Chinese from stealing Bougainville and forcing me off the island. "All right," I said, turning my seat toward Ishmael. "My company and I could probably go ahead and support your campaign, starting now, including the independence referendum and running all the way through the election…with a budget that would pay for the essentials of the campaign that we have discussed here tonight; no salaries, and no extras," I said. "I know that's maybe not what you expected…"

Ishmael stood up, extended his hand, and started to shake mine while I was still in my chair. "That's good; very good. Thank you very much."

I stood up, so did Tete, and I looked Ishmael in the eye. "All right then," I said, still dubious, and knowing the feeling wasn't likely to go away for a while. "Here are the rules. We are not going to do anything that violates Bougainville campaign financing guidelines. We're not handing any money to you personally; we're doing what's legal, paying the expenses involved in supporting your campaign. The only person on your team I trust with money is you. Each week you tell me how much you need for the campaign's support expenses, and I'll give it to you, and you alone. Everything's cash; please don't incur any campaign liabilities that will bite us in the ass later. Also, you must take care of the campaign's vendors; please don't make me have to deal with a bunch of different mouths to feed. I'll keep a running tab on the total cost, and you should too. When I'm out of money, we're done."

Ishmael gave me his trademark high sign, putting both thumbs up in the air. "We'll make it happen."

"One last point on which I know we both agree," I said. "You don't owe me or my company anything for this. We're supporting you because we believe in you, know you're honest, and assume your agenda for Bougainville is the same as ours."

"Yes, yes."

I walked home in a daze. I had been conservative and left a margin for when we went over budget—which I was sure we would do—but otherwise the grubstake I had just promised Ishmael was all the money we had left in the company; Mt. Bagana Resources was making an all-or-nothing bet. I'd try to explain it to the shareholders, but it was clear to me that we had no choice. The shareholders wouldn't like hearing it, but when they understood the facts, they'd agree with me. If Ishmael won, we were heroes and our business would evolve as expected; if he lost, the Chinese would take over Bougainville, and I might as well swim home.

I waited until the next day to call Miao about Grumpy. "Tell me why your guys did that to Sergeant Trull."

"How could you suggest we had anything to do with something horrible like that?"

"Come on, Miao. I haven't even told you what happened yet." Sometimes Miao could be like the CCP guys—rarely, thank goodness.

"All right, all right. The truth is, it was some Chinese guys who beat him up," Miao admitted, "but no one from Gao Gold was involved. The guy was an addict; he had a death wish. He owed a fortune to a pachinko parlor in Port Moresby."

"How did you find out what happened to him?"

"He called Lin first from the hospital—before you," Miao said, sounding tentative.

"What's that about?" I asked.

"I'd rather not say."

"Come on."

"Lin told Trull he wouldn't pay, but you would."

"What? Why?"

It took Miao a while to speak up. "Do we have to talk about this?"

"Yes."

"Because you're an American. That's what Americans do."

In a way, Miao was right about Americans, just like Ishmael had been. In the South China Sea, the Chinese had determined that they could push the Americans around. In Bougainville, the people believed the Americans would help them. Whether either party was right in the end remained to be seen.

As our independence campaign revved up, Ishmael transformed himself into a human whirlwind, and I hung on by my fingernails. Ishmael, his American in tow, carried the message of independence all over Bougainville. We visited remote villages in the clouds and took longboats through heavy seas to the atolls. Most of our meetings were at night when the villagers had returned from working in the fields and the seas. I couldn't see what we were given to eat, but it didn't matter: I was starving, and it was usually delicious.

The first part of our plan couldn't have been more successful. In December 2019, the independence referendum's results were announced: thanks in large part to Ishmael's efforts, 98 percent of Bougainville's registered voters choose independence, rejecting any further affiliation with PNG. My guess was that most of the 2 percent minority were voters whose ballots had been filled out improperly. By the referendum's terms, independence was not guaranteed, but its outcome pointed the way to freedom for Bougainville—and success for Mt. Bagana Resources—depending on the people's choice of the president to steer the ship. Ishmael declared his candidacy the same weekend.

26

The Silent Majority

Two geologists trespassing on customary land met violent deaths in Bougainville in the immediate aftermath of the independence referendum. I didn't view the events as completely coincidental.

The referendum's overwhelming majority vote in favor of independence did something new for Bougainvilleans: for the first time, it gave them a strong dose of mutual identity. Other than the unifying pride Bougainvilleans have always taken from their striking, ebony-colored skin, the concept that they were to become members of an independent nation brought them together like nothing had ever done before. Independence was something virtually every Bougainvillean had voted for, and could believe in. The degree of the unanimity of the vote was unprecedented worldwide. So was the peoples' satisfaction that a nationwide referendum had been conducted with decorum. Universally praised by international observers, the independence referendum demonstrated to the world that Bougainvilleans knew what they wanted, and were accustomed to democratic conduct.

In a Bougainville enamored with this new image of itself, miscreants trespassing pursuant to backdoor mining deals picked the wrong time to assume that people would continue to react passively, however tragic the potential outcome.

Up in Tinputz, it wasn't like the landowners hadn't warned Cruks Mining's geologist before. He had been run off many times. His abrasive manner and PNG provenance hadn't helped matters. When confronted they had told him, the locals later testified to the authorities, that his foreign sponsor had made a backdoor deal with the wrong people, pushy types who had intimidated the true landowners, promising to share the spoils when received from Cruks Mining. The scoundrels had never done so, but the man kept trespassing. He had been discovered there the day before, but had eluded their capture. This time, when the landowners found him trespassing once again, they cornered him on a rocky outcrop. Rather than face an angry, machete-bearing mob, the geologist had attempted to escape by scaling down a cliff. He slid and fell, hit his head on a rock, and died at the scene.

Down in Isina, Andy—Lucien's Thai geologist, now working with George and the Chinese—met a more premeditated fate. As local landowners testified later, Andy encountered in Isina the same problem I had experienced with him when we visited Isina together years earlier. Over the period separating the two events, George had continued to fib, saying the land in question belonged to him—that is, to Francine—when it didn't. Back in 2016, when I was probably the first unauthorized visitor to the Isina hills, the landowner was polite, and I was lucky. My group and I were asked to leave, did so, and weren't stupid enough to return. Over the years, I heard many reports describing how Isina's landowners, angry with George's lies, continued to reject foreigners from their land. I would have thought Andy would have learned from all that and stayed away. Instead, he hiked in from Kongara, someone up in the Isina hills encountered him, and Andy ended up shot and killed.

In a way, Liuman Mogol's latest stunt—conspiring to remain in office as president indefinitely—was probably seen as similar to trespassing. In the past when Bougainvilleans were sheep, it might have been accepted. No longer. Now, Mogol's arrogance violated Bougainville's new persona and underscored how estranged he had become from the people. It would have been fascinating to be a fly on the wall inside Mogol's mind, observing the perverse machinations he must have fabricated to convince himself that there was not just one, but a second good reason to stiff his people and revoke Bougainville's constitution. All right, so the first reason—he needed the rights to the people's mineral resources to get bribed by the Chinese in the Cabal proposal—had come a cropper. The second reason had a nobler logic: In Liuman Mogol's concept of himself, he was no lame duck. No, like Richard Nixon, he believed he was loved and admired by a "silent majority," a vast number of Bougainvilleans who wanted him to remain in office for life. This devout group of lambs cared not for their constitutional rights, but only to be led by the good shepherd, President Mogol. If it restricted his efforts, the constitution could certainly be amended, or even discarded.

None of this was known to us when, after the results of the independence referendum were in the books and a short break was taken for the Christmas holidays, Ishmael and I and the team went back to work on his presidential election campaign at the beginning of January 2020. I pushed ahead with a profound sense of relief. No longer was Mt. Bagana Resources to be plagued by the perfidy and sleaze of the Mogol government, nor did we need to spend time and energy watching our backside. We simply needed to focus on what was right in front of us: Ishmael's campaign, including his platform and speeches; housekeeping items like purchasing media and such swag as T-shirts and stickers; selection of the party's constituency candidates for seats in the House of Representatives; raising money; and, most importantly, meeting with and soliciting voters. What a concept.

We registered the Bougainville Peoples' Alliance Party in January, which coincided with my introduction to Rachel Eto. Ishmael selected her to manage the day-to-day business of both his campaign and his party apparatus. From Ishmael's village of Roreinang, she had been raised by Ishmael's family, and he had paid for her to graduate with a business degree from a university in PNG. She was bright and indefatigable, brooked no nonsense, and was totally dedicated to Ishmael. We converted the single-floor, thatched-roof auxiliary building next to the Women's Centre into BPAP's headquarters. Rachel moved into a room in the hotel and could be found in one of the two locations at any time of the day or night.

Bougainville's 2020 election was to be administered by the Office of Bougainville Electoral Commission and George Manners, its commissioner. OBEC had published rules about the upcoming process. Candidates could announce themselves as Ishmael had in December, but they were not allowed to begin campaigning until the end of March, when OBEC would file the writs ordering the election of the president and the legislature. The winners would be announced in mid-June.

That was the election schedule everyone was using as a road map when we first learned of Mogol's skullduggery. As usual, I heard about it first from Tete, who got it via the coconut news. It seemed that Liuman Mogol's silent majority had turned vocal. Of course, he was only acting on their behalf. The people wanted—no, demanded—that he remain as president of Bougainville. How else would the important matter of independence from PNG be addressed? Certainly, no one else could manage it.

Once the news of this situation was made public in February, Mogol agreed to an interview in Port Moresby. "The matter of independence is too important to be left to a new, inexperienced candidate for president," he had proclaimed, and then invoked the famous phrase favored by despots around the globe: "I need to finish the job." How long would that take? A reporter asked Mogol, who wasn't sure. "Five years, perhaps?" In order to do so, there was only the minor matter of amending the constitution. Mogol was pleased to inform the reporter that the revised documentation had already been delivered to the House of Representatives, where it was being considered expeditiously.

Until it wasn't. Ferdy Mimosa had always been a loyal soldier in Mogol's camp. The relationship had paid off: Ferdy had lined his pockets with Mogol's crumbs, and had been happy to do so. Like most other venal politicians, once Ferdy was financially comfortable, he grew dissatisfied. Higher office awaited; Ferdy wanted to be president too. The unexpected news that His Excellency planned to remain in office indefinitely could postpone Ferdy's ambitions…indefinitely. That wouldn't do.

To amend the Bougainville constitution so that Mogol could remain president, a minimum of two-thirds, or twenty-seven members of the forty-person House of Representatives, needed to agree with his proposed legislation. Within the House, thirty-three members represented geographic constituencies, three at-large seats were reserved for women, and three more were reserved for ex-combatants—but only until independence was achieved—and one seat was reserved for the president.

Put another way, a bloc of fourteen votes in Bougainville's House of Representatives wielded considerable power. No material legislation—the important kind requiring two-thirds majority, like amending the constitution—could pass if such a bloc declined to support it. Ferdy recruited other members, lured them with God-knows-what, and formed a group he called "The Bloc," specifically to thwart Mogol's ambitions. In mid-February when Mogol's proposed legislation cleared committee and came up for a vote of the members, Ferdy's plan worked. Mogol's presidency would not be indefinite.

Our campaign team had originally believed that George Washburn and Ferdy Mimosa would be Ishmael's competition. In retrospect, they were child's play. Ishmael had always maintained that until he was truly down for the count, Mogol was his most formidable foe, and now I understood why. Which was why when we read that

Mogol's bid for permanent office had been defeated, I was elated and relieved. Back to work.

I thought. We were about to learn what Ishmael told us he had learned since the end of the Crisis: it was never wise to underestimate Mogol. Whatever the psychology books define as the disease caused by an overwhelming greed for money and power, Mogol had it—and was terminally infected. When a week later Tete informed me that the coconut news threatened more trouble, I felt like a stupid foreigner. Ishmael had said Mogol would be back, and I hadn't paid attention.

It was the beginning of March, a couple of weeks after his legislative defeat, and time enough for Mogol to turn magnanimous. Perhaps it wasn't democratic to remain in office indefinitely. The honorable members had been right. Leave it up to the people; the silent majority could choose. Simply amend the constitution to allow him to run for a third term as president. What could be the harm be in that?

The real news articles validating the coconut news—as the sequence always transpired—appeared the next day in both Port Moresby newspapers. Mogol had accepted defeat on his proposal to remain in office indefinitely, but wasn't going away. As a compromise, he now proposed that the members be sporting and pass legislation giving him the right to run for a third term. The Bougainville constitution was clear: a person could only serve two terms as president. Mogol's new proposed legislation would also require amending the constitution, and the attendant two-thirds approval vote by the House's members.

Also in both Port Moresby papers, small articles in their obscure international pages commented on the growing world anxiety regarding a new, SARS-like virus. A coronavirus discovered originally in Wuhan in the People's Republic of China in December 2019, the threat was termed COVID-19 for short. The newspapers both pointed to the Johns Hopkins statistics on COVID-19, which had quickly become the world's ranking system for COVID-19 infection cases. While the United States had zoomed to the top in terms of total cases, both papers took pride in the fact that PNG sat at the bottom of the table. There had been one case detected in PNG—perhaps—and that person had later tested negative and had already left the country. Bougainville had zero cases.

Ferdy Mimosa, together with at least a half-dozen other members in his group with designs on the Bougainville presidency, must have thought his next move would be a simple one: roll out The Bloc and fire the same salvo as before. This time, when Sheldon Greenstreet, the jumbo-sized speaker of the House, counted the votes and announced that Mogol's second proposal had suffered the same fate as the first, Mogol stood up, waddled to the front of the chamber, and objected. According to journalists with press credentials who were present, Mogol indicated that the votes of the ex-combatants were not valid constitutionally. The Bougainville constitution stated that ex-combatants were only allowed at-large eligibility prior to independence. Obviously, Mogol argued, the independence referendum results recorded in December 2019 were valid proof that Bougainville was indeed independent. As of that date in the prior calendar year, the ex-combatants should no longer be considered valid members of the House, and their votes should be disqualified. Since the vote had been twenty-six for Mogol's proposed legislation versus fourteen against—the fourteen including all three ex-combatant votes—when those votes were nullified, the revised vote was twenty-six for, and eleven against. His legislation passed, Mogol indicated, and sat down, appearing pleased with himself.

Chaos ensued on the floor of the House. That is where a speaker earns his keep, and Mr. Greenstreet did his job. He stood and announced that Mogol's logic was faulty. In his view, Bougainville would not be independent until it had negotiated and executed an independence treaty with PNG, which could take years. The proposed legislation was therefore defeated. When the newspapers printed the story the next day, none of us working with Ishmael on his campaign assumed that the matter was finished. It wasn't.

By the end of the week, Mogol had said nothing more about his proposed legislation to monopolize the presidency. He did announce, however, that he was forming a COVID-19 task force within his government to take all necessary and appropriate steps, as he put it, to advise the people how Bougainville should address COVID-19. At that point, PNG still had zero bona fide cases of infection, and Bougainville remained at zero as well. The announcement was picked up and printed by news media around the South Pacific. Little attention was paid to the last paragraph of the language, which indicated that international aid organizations had sent two million kina to Bougainville to be distributed to qualified recipients for COVID-19 educational purposes.

The following Monday, Mogol announced that he was suing the government and the speaker of the House of Representatives for improperly advising the members regarding his proposed legislation to be able to run for a third term. His objections were too numerous to print. He filed his suit in the Supreme Court of Papua New Guinea.

When Ishmael, Tete, and I heard the news, we didn't know what to think. We had no idea what Mogol's suit claimed. The PNG Supreme Court had a reputation for taking its time. A fair assumption was that the Bougainville government could be in limbo for months, or even years.

"That's what he's doing," Tete said. "I know how the PNG Supreme Court works. They've tried cases over there that have taken a decade. He's going to tell the members that things must be the same until the court makes their decision. He plans to stay in office until he dies."

I said, "Yeah, but if I was Ferdy Mimosa, I'd say 'We're not waiting. To hell with the court.'"

Neither of us was right, but we weren't wrong either. What Mogol pulled the next day came totally out of the blue, but was up to his devious standards. He made two announcements, both by press release.

"My fellow Bougainvilleans, it is with a heavy heart that I announce I am asking your House of Representatives to join with me in invoking a State-of-Emergency for Bougainville to help our government and our people combat COVID-19. If the members see fit to do so, the SOE will have the effect of postponing the 2020 elections until further notice. In the meantime, rest assured that your government is in good hands." Of course, he didn't embellish the fact that his release pertained to a viral infection that most Bougainvilleans still didn't even know existed, let alone made them sick.

Mogol's second announcement seemed innocuous by comparison. "I am also announcing that I may see fit to distribute the proceeds of a two million kina grant received from international aid organizations for COVID-19 awareness to the individual members of the House for their use in serving you, their constituents."

In the US, this type of political maneuver had received a lot of attention recently. Otherwise known as a *quid pro quo*, Mogol's message to the House was clear: support my declaration to enact an SOE postponing the election, and you'll get a proportionate piece of a two-million-kina pie. The greedy members trotted up to the trough and voted to approve the SOE that afternoon. Later, it was reported that each member received fifty thousand kina of COVID-19 awareness funds. They were supposed to use the money to assist their constituents in combatting COVID-19, but how they did so was up to them. I'm sure most simply deposited the cash into their personal bank accounts.

While the members were celebrating, Ishmael and I and our campaign staff were despondent. Not only was the election delayed, but the news describing the rapid advance of what was now being described as a worldwide pandemic provided no clarity as to when the SOE would be lifted.

Our problems were nothing compared to those of normal Bougainvilleans. Mogol's SOE brought life in Bougainville to a complete halt. The planes stopped flying, and the ships stopped sailing. Vehicles were not allowed to travel up and down the coast road beyond certain limited checkpoints, and PMVs were banned. The police loved the SOE; it enabled them to boss people around at the slightest provocation. Social distancing was enforced indiscriminately to settle old scores; people were arrested for being less than six feet apart on their front steps.

Stores and businesses shut down. BSP limited banking customer activity to deposits only. Since we couldn't fly, we couldn't tie up our cash in gold that would sit in our vault, so I was forced to shut down the Gold Dealer. In a single stroke, the two spigots of cash for all of central Bougainville turned dry. Most critically, Bougainville's markets were all closed. Separating the market from a Bougainvillean is like removing milk from a bowl of cereal. Bougainvilleans go to the market every day to do two things: sell their garden produce, fish, etc., and use the proceeds to buy their family's dinner. The market closures were enforced by the police. The scenes I watched at Arawa's markets would have been comical if the circumstances weren't so dire. Women materialized out of nowhere, illegally located themselves in a remote corner of the market, and arrayed their produce for sale. As the cops detected their transgression and moved in, the ladies' next move was to scramble to grab their stuff and flee to another corner. Then finally, out of hiding places, they stood in a group and refused to vacate, shaking their collective fists and yelling at the top of their lungs at the cowering police. As the SOE wore on, the markets were where I figured things would first erupt.

Liuman Mogol knew that the entire land's means to eat and make a living were being compromised, and was also aware there were no cases of COVID-19 infection in Bougainville—and implemented the SOE anyway. His plan was obvious. The SOE would delay the election schedule until the Supreme Court upheld his appeal of the speaker's decision. At that point, he would give himself an election boost by cancelling the SOE—whoops, sorry folks, I've fixed things now—and then enter the fray, run for a third term, and prevail. Meanwhile,

Mogol would remain president and govern Bougainville as long as it took the court to decide. He had been expected to step down by mid-June. By the end of March, it was clear Mogol wasn't going anywhere for what could be a very long time—unless someone did something.

We refused to bring Ishmael's campaign to a stop. Although the SOE put the election process on hold, we pushed forward. Ishmael travelled to dozens of villages, sometimes with members of our team, sometimes alone. When we went with him, we saw that, in a way, the SOE wasn't all bad news. Ishmael was using the interim period to refine and polish his pitch and his ideas. He sounded better every day.

Rachel was constantly trying to recruit and upgrade our BPAP members from Bougainville's constituencies who would run for membership in the House. One day, she waved at me from across the street at the Women's Centre. "Someone told me you know Matty Savant," she said when we met on her side of the road.

"I do," I said. "Why?"

"Central Bougainville is Ishmael's weakest region. There's a lot of competition here," she said. "Matty's running for the North Nasioi member seat, and he's probably going to win. I'd love to get him to join our party; he could give us a boost here."

"How is it that Ishmael isn't going to dominate the vote in central Bougainville?" I exclaimed. "This is where Ishmael helps people the most."

"Show me one grateful Bougainvillean, especially among the elites who live here in town," Rachel answered.

I thought about Matty; he seemed different, but I really didn't know him that well. "I'm not sure. Matty used to be on George and Lucien's BROL team. I did hear that his wife, Anita, is unhappy about that. I'll see what I can do."

Matty had always struck me as a loyal guy, and I was concerned about any remaining affiliation with BROL. I doubted he would return my call. Instead, I dialed up Anita. Landlords usually try to keep their large tenants happy, and Anita sounded accommodating.

When I brought up Lucien and George and BROL, she was dismissive, saying Lucien owed both her and Matty money, and that neither of them wanted anything to do with BROL. We agreed that she would stop by the Gold Dealer with her husband the next day.

"You sure picked a tough time for your introduction to Bougainville politics," Matty said when he and Anita and I sat down in my office.

"Why do you say that?" I asked.

Matty smiled, his face offset by whitish hair creeping up his temples. "You don't know?" he said, and then when I shook my head, he continued. "This is going to be the most corrupt election in Bougainville's short history." Matty had been around, and knew what he was talking about. He verified that both George and Ferdy had received millions from the Chinese. "But that's nothing compared to Mogol."

I must have looked clueless sitting there saying nothing, so Matty kept talking.

"Mogol's been funded by the Chinese since he was the ambassador from PNG to Beijing. Don't forget, I was Kaboose's minister of finance. After he died, I served out my five-year term, and I was there when Mogol entered the picture in 2010. I could show you exactly how the Chinese bought his election—and how millions disappeared from Bougainville's treasury once he was president. He's fixing to do it again."

"You mean take Chinese money?" I asked.

Matty laughed. "My guess is both countries will be bribing him."

"What do you mean, both countries?"

Anita couldn't contain herself any longer. "He's talking about PNG," she said. "Mogol's half Chinese, and the other half's PNG. He's not Bougainvillean at all—look at the color of his skin. PNG doesn't want Ishmael negotiating the independence agreement; they're afraid of him. That's why PNG owes Bougainville so much money; Mogol never pushed them to pay us."

"Well, in a way, what you're saying is a positive thing," I said. "I'm sure a lot of Bougainvilleans will come to the same conclusion about Ishmael out-negotiating PNG. Hopefully, that will push a lot of voters his way."

Matty sat across the desk from me, pursing his lips and shaking his head.

"What?"

He said, "You can't win with the popular vote here." His eyes regarded me with what looked like pity. "That's less than half the battle. You've got to beat the fraud. Otherwise, you can take all Ishmael's votes in the ballot boxes and dump them in the sea—because that's where they'll be when Ferdy and Mogol's boys are done with them."

Miao called me that night. "What's Ishmael going to do if the SOE stays in place?" he asked.

"I'm not sure what you're asking me."

"Come on, Jack. Ishmael's a warlord. Is he going to tell the people to riot?"

The thought had crossed my mind, but only in idle moments— not that I was going to share that with my Chinese friend. "I'm just a stupid foreigner here, Miao. I can't answer that, any more than I could have told you what Lin was going to do when the PLA forced his hand with Middle Kingdom."

My conversation with Miao was short, but it wasn't totally useless. It gave me an idea. I had thought the wild card in the delayed election process would be the PNG Supreme Court. Now, I started to change my mind. Ishmael was stopping by that night, and I decided to try it out on him. "I've been online, studying decisions made by the PNG Supreme Court," I said to him when we sat in our wicker chairs on my veranda.

Parsimonious with his words the way he always was, he waited for me to fill him in.

"They're not above being influenced politically. The verdicts in some of their cases look downright questionable."

"They take money," he said, but it was a question.

"I'm not saying that. It's impossible to tell. I'm just saying that it seems that they bend to the government's will from time to time."

"Yes."

"Do you think Prime Minister James Serape would feel responsible if the Supreme Court found in favor of Mogol, and then the people of Bougainville rioted?"

Ishmael laughed, his eyes twinkling pools, but did not answer.

I said, "My guess is, that's the last thing he wants. Think about what it would do to the negotiations on independence. You know, with the international NGOs and do-gooders looking over things and all. I'm just curious: if you came out and told Bougainvilleans *not* to riot, how do you think Serape would interpret that message?"

Ishmael didn't utter another word, but I knew him well enough by that point to conclude that he understood exactly what I was saying.

As Bougainville slogged through the month of May with the SOE in place but a complete absence of infections, tempers boiled. The SOE wasn't the only issue. Bougainvilleans were demanding to know what COVID-19 services were being provided, and where had all that money gone? With no infections, why couldn't Bougainville hold its elections? Anxiety levels reached the point where the government began to panic. Mogol and the members of the legislature started to point fingers at each other. The conspirators decided to stage town meetings across Bougainville to calm things down, social distancing be damned; no one was doing it anyway.

Arawa's town meeting was held at its largest venue, the Town Market. Mogol was too afraid to attend, but several members of the House of Representatives braved the crowd, albeit with an entire company of Bougainville Police Service escorts. A printed agenda was distributed. The program was supposed to start at ten, so I decided not to show up until eleven. When I did, I was surprised—there were already thousands of people there, jammed underneath the tin-roofed market and spilling out into the sunbaked streets. No one wore masks. The government bloviators were speaking first, after which an open microphone would be made available to the public. Everything was in pidgin. Ishmael, barefoot and clad in his jeans and a T-shirt, showed up late after several government speakers had spoken, as if letting the people know that the session wasn't important to him. I sat with Tete, and whenever something was said that caused a stir in the crowd, I asked him to explain.

As I listened to the government windbags and watched the crowd absorb the nonsense, I wrestled with the same puzzle I had debated a dozen times. Were these Bougainvilleans simply polite and well-mannered, or were they just sheep? When were they going to wake up and demand change? They were smart people. Why in God's name did they tolerate these idiots?

The government finally yielded the floor to the public, and a few Bougainvilleans started taking some shots. Each person who came to the microphone sounded more strident than the last. For over an hour in the hot sun, the crowd remained under control, but the cordon formed by the police around the government stooges tightened noticeably. Finally, the moderator announced that the open microphone portion was over, and the program would be ending shortly. The crowd didn't like that. A wave of agitated complaints rattled the roof over the market like a thunderstorm. I couldn't tell what was bothering everyone, and asked Tete what was going on.

He nodded toward the microphone. "They want to know what Ishmael thinks."

People started to clap in advance of Ishmael stepping to the microphone. Speaking in pidgin, his remarks lasted only a few minutes. As polite applause rippled over the crowd, Ishmael handed the microphone back to the moderator and disappeared into the throng.

"What'd he say?" I asked Tete.

"He told everyone to remain calm," Tete said, "and said that none of us could control COVID-19. He finished by saying that he was sure that the government would reschedule the election by June." Tete laughed. "That's next week."

That night, Ishmael stopped by my house and told me he wanted to put some words together that would be used on his Facebook page and in a speech that he would make on the radio shortly. He wanted to speak in more detail about the issues he had addressed that day in the Town Market—the ideas about exercising patience with the government and waiting until June, when things were sure to get better. He gave me some concepts that he wanted included, and we agreed to compare notes the next day. Ishmael had many ideas, but sometimes he wanted new ones. That was when he might ask me to write down some thoughts. When I was done, he would thank me, take the paperwork, and use the words in his own way. I found him very sophisticated that way; I'm sure leaders in the US did much the same thing.

I assembled some words for the Facebook page, and wrote a speech too. The next day, Ishmael took the paragraphs of text for the Facebook page and indicated what he wanted changed. I made the edits, and then sent the language to Jason Osborne and his partner Ryan O'Dwyer, the political consultants from Washington DC we had hired to help us with media for Ishmael's election. They were expensive, but the shareholders and I knew that I was a political novitiate, and we couldn't afford to make ignorant mistakes. Ishmael handed me the speech I had written for him, thanked me, and told me it was fine the way it was. He had booked time with New Dawn, the FM radio station in Buka that he had used before. We would go up to Buka the next day.

Ishmael gave his speech at one p.m. on the last day of May. New Dawn's studio was comprised of a couple of bullpen offices and a small, soundproofed recording studio on the second floor of a building in Buka Town. The staff gave Ishmael a folding chair and some earphones, and swung a microphone in front of him. The studio was carpeted, and Tete and I sat on the floor in front of Ishmael. He held a copy of my speech, but he spoke in pidgin, and the words that he spoke were his. The session was over in thirty minutes. The station staff promised to email us a digital file containing the speech. We said goodbye and walked down the stairs to the street below.

A crowd had already gathered at the bottom of the stairs. More people were coming, cheering and yelling as they emptied out of the stores and ran across the road. As we made our way through the throng, Ishmael didn't pay much attention to the escalating group of admirers. When he saw someone he knew, we stopped for a minute.

"What's going on?" I asked Tete. "I know what the words said; I wrote them. I didn't write anything that would make people react like this."

"It was your words," Tete said, "but at the end this time, he wasn't speaking to the people, but the government. He said something like, if you don't announce the election schedule, I can't be responsible for what's going to happen. Then he ended by saying to the people, 'Don't riot; be patient.'"

The silent majority was the wild card. Not Mogol's bogus silent majority, but the real one: the Bougainvilleans who were mad as hell, and weren't going to take it anymore. Even if numbskulls like Mogol didn't absorb that message, more astute observers like the Supreme Court and Prime Minister Serape did. The Bougainvillean people were out there, knew what they wanted, and, via Ishmael, had spoken.

On the second day of June, the Supreme Court of PNG announced their decision: Bougainville's constitution was clear on its face, and Mogol's appeal of his legislative rejection was denied, with prejudice. The court also made it clear that PNG harbored no desire to involve itself in what it viewed as Bougainville's internal political affairs.

OBEC wasted no time. George Manners, the OBEC commissioner, made it official: The 2020 election was finally underway. Campaigning could begin immediately. OBEC, an entity independent of the Bougainville government and therefore, supposedly, beyond conflicts of interest, would supervise the process. Writs issued by the government for the candidates would be filed in two weeks, on June seventeenth, at which point campaigning would commence. Campaigning would end August twelfth, and polling would begin the next day. Voting would end on the first day of September, and counting would begin. Winners would be announced by mid-month. The election was on, and would not be further delayed.

27

The Prophecy

Bloviation was my favorite term to describe the speaking style of Ishmael's competitors in the presidential campaign. The longer their speeches, the more the oration edged toward bloviation. It helped if the bloviator had flaccid cheeks that expanded and contracted like a large sea bass. No women were guilty; all of Bougainville's bloviators were men. It was as if they were trying to mimic Martin Luther King's wonderful speaking style but hadn't been able to get past the cosmetics. Successful at plagiarizing the sonorous rhythms and lilting tones, they couldn't create legitimate material to fashion into sentences. The result was empty chains of pompous words signifying nothing.

Ishmael was no bloviator. When he spoke, which was only when he needed to, his words were concise and direct. Before campaigning was allowed to officially commence, Ishmael used the time to learn from his people. He crisscrossed Bougainville, meeting leaders, chiefs, tribes, clans, and families. He didn't dominate conversation; he listened. When we drove to a village together, he voiced his thoughts and I made notes. As the starting gate to the campaign loomed, we hammered out his position on issues.

Ishmael's platform was straightforward: he stood for independence from PNG, improved law and order and elimination of corruption, and electrification and economic development. The voters would want specifics, so I wrote a dozen one-pagers—we called them narratives—containing key concepts and ideas that Ishmael could use when speaking on the road.

Prior to June, rumors had swirled about who would be presidential candidates. Most Bougainvilleans did not get any form of media, so rumors ruled. Supposedly at least one hundred candidates were running. When OBEC finally published the official list, things became only slightly more manageable. Twenty-three men, and two women, had registered. Six were sponsored by political parties; everyone else was independent.

It was difficult to even envision a presidential race contested by so many entrants. George Washburn and Ferdy Mimosa were on the list, but that was no surprise. Everyone knew they were running; the rumors about them both being awash in Chinese election money had been floating in the coconut news for months. I learned that another dozen people on the list—like Joe Wobely—ran every five years, no matter what. Their motivation had to be hubris or self-absorption, since it wasn't cheap to run—there was a ten-thousand-kina registration fee—and I couldn't imagine anyone voting for them. If Liuman Mogol's name had appeared on the list, I wouldn't have been surprised, but it wasn't there. Instead, we learned that Mogol and his Chinese buddies were backing a puppet: Tipsy Racket, an officer in the Defence Force who wasn't even retired from active duty. My gut instinct was to dismiss his candidacy as ridiculous, but by then I knew better. Another surprise was Joe Louie, who was an elected member of PNG's parliament. In order to run for president, he was required to resign his membership, a comfortable position. Hope sprang eternal.

I was also surprised at who had decided not to run. I breathed easier when I didn't see Sam Acoatie's name on the list. Also an elected member from Bougainville in PNG's parliament, Sam was a formidable politician with credentials and a power base. I had met Sam and his brother Paul when they asked me to look at a hydroelectric site up in the mountains west of Wakunai. If Sam had entered the race, I would have thought he'd give Ishmael a run for his money, but what did I know—I was still learning about Bougainville politics.

When I had first met Ishmael and the subject of politics had come up years earlier, I had gone to the office the following morning to test political ideas on Leki. "Do you think Liuman Mogol is doing a good job as your president?" I asked her when she arrived at the office.

If I asked Leki a question and she looked straight ahead at the wall for a prolonged period of time as if I weren't there, it meant the topic was too sensitive to discuss with a foreigner. I dropped it and went out to make myself a cup of coffee until Moroa arrived. "Do you think Liuman Mogol is a good president?" I asked her as soon as she came in. Moroa's reaction was the same as Leki's.

"All right, then; forget I asked. Here's a different question for the two of you. If the presidential election was tomorrow, who do you think would win?"

They both doled out more of Bougainville's silent treatment.

"Come on," I said. "It's a harmless question, and it's just the three of us in here. Nothing goes outside these walls."

Moroa cracked first. Turning to look at me the way she would if I had just asked whether a dollar was worth the same as a kina, she said, "Everyone thinks Father Simeon will win."

"Who?"

"He's a priest," Leki chimed in, as if that's all she needed to say about the guy.

"I gathered that, but why would people vote for him?"

"That's how Mogol won," Moroa sniffed, and the discussion was over.

I tried to learn everything I could about this priest named Simeon, but couldn't uncover anything notable. When I did my research on Bougainville's recent history with democracy, it confirmed the theorem: if a Catholic priest aspired to be a governmental leader of Bougainville, with its large Catholic population, he would automatically be a factor in any race—perhaps even the frontrunner. Looking down the list of the twenty-five, there he was, right above Ishmael.

Father Simeon worried me, but Ishmael's candidacy for president was so compelling, I assumed he would still be considered one of the favorites. Even if they preferred someone else, certainly Bougainvilleans would agree on the merits of his candidacy. I was mistaken. I hadn't anticipated the snobbish conceit of Bougainville's so-called elites, what passed for its intellectual class. Those fortunate enough to have gone to any kind of institution of higher learning overseas—a university, college, seminary, business or technical school—were considered members of what Bougainvilleans termed the elites. The elites wielded substantial influence in Bougainville regarding any exchange of ideas, especially concerning politics. Ishmael wasn't one of them.

My first experience with the phenomenon occurred one day in late June with my bank manager. I was sitting in his office withdrawing some cash for the Gold Dealer and figured I would pick his brain on the campaign.

"Barney, forgive me if this question is too personal for these parts, but who are you supporting for president?"

Being a Bougainvillean and a professional bank officer, there was no way Barney was going to answer that question from a foreigner, even though I was a good customer of the bank. Unlike Leki's silent treatment, he did give me the courtesy of a response.

"I didn't realize you got involved in local politics, Mr. Davis."

"I don't think I have a choice. If you guys don't make the right decision, it's going to affect me too."

"Yes, I suppose you're right." He returned to the paperwork on his desk, tallied up some numbers, and then looked up at me. "Pardon me for asking, Mr. Davis. Do you have a preference for a candidate?"

"You guys would be crazy not to elect Ishmael."

Barney peered at me through his spectacles in unadulterated surprise. "Ishmael?" He stared down at his desk for a moment, and then looked at me as if I was a child who had just uttered something foolish. "He's a good man, but…he doesn't have a college degree."

As the word got around that my company was supporting Ishmael, many of the elites approached me on the street or in church or at the market. They were curious as to why I would support an uneducated man. They pointed out that he had also been a guerrilla. After the Crisis, the behavior of some ex-combatants had been less than stellar. I was glad they asked, and tried to provide them with what I hoped was logical reasoning. I had heard the warlord objection from the days when I first arrived in Bougainville, and found it easy to rebut: "I guess you're telling me you'd be happier with the riot squads back in town?"

Whatever the elites' concerns, Ishmael and I needed to convert them into supporters. Like every other place in the world, Bougainville's opinions were shaped by its intellectuals; perhaps even more so than elsewhere. The obstacles were surmountable. When Ishmael provided specific ideas underlying his platform, some of the smart folks might realize that just because he had been out in the bush defending their freedom and had sacrificed his chance to attend a university, didn't mean he wasn't intelligent. Hopefully, the smarter ones would change their minds, and tell their friends.

Out on the campaign trail, we were more convinced that the broader population welcomed Ishmael's candidacy. Across Bougainville's heartland, the people knew Ishmael and the hope that he alone represented. Leading the BRA in the Crisis, he had risked his life for them, and was primarily responsible for not only winning the war, but also the Bougainville Peace Agreement, an advantageous settlement witnessed by the United Nations that promised current stability and future freedom. From the Crisis up to the present, Ishmael had volunteered to play the role of Bougainville's unofficial protector of the peace. As of December, thanks to the positive vote in the independence referendum that he'd personally spearheaded, liberty was at hand. To the people, Ishmael was the signal that it was their time. He was the one who could lead them out of past misery to a better place.

On the first day of campaign season, Ishmael's brother Peacely drove us to a series of appearances on the northeastern coast of Bougainville Island. Ishmael wore his normal jeans and a T-shirt over bare feet. Having stupidly imagined I should get more spruced up, I had donned a collared shirt, and dripped sweat like a wet sponge all day. I asked Ishmael how he'd arranged the gatherings, and he explained that he sent messengers ahead who prepared the way.

Our first stop around noontime was mid-island at a country store and filling station south of Wakunai. As we arrived, vehicles sat in line waiting for fuel, the station providing both diesel and petrol through clear plastic tubes that dangled through a lattice of chicken wire. Along the front of the store's tin roof, a ubiquitous red Digicel sign advertised mobile phone top-ups. Like any similar establishment anywhere in the world, a couple of half-assembled jalopies languished in the weeds alongside the sheds that comprised the store and the dark maw of the repair shop. Unlike those other places, Wakunai's weeds were full of flowers topped with orange and yellow blossoms, and the warm air smelled of the sea.

The meeting began Bougainville-style: when we showed up, no one was around. A barefoot teenager in shorts and no shirt manned the store in front of an array of greasy shelves offering only canned drinks and junk food: Chinese knockoffs of Cokes and Fritos. Over in the garage, three boys peered under the hood of a beat-up Toyota. As Ishmael got out of Peacely's truck, a couple of guys emerged from the wild sugarcane along the road as if they had been hiding there. I climbed down out of the truck and looked around. Off to the left was the sea, deep blue and glassy on the sunny, windless day, with the green-cloaked Mt. Balbi rising out of the background. Fishermen in dug-out canoes crisscrossed the lagoon inside the reef. A four-foot wave crested and broke over a coral ledge on the outside edge of the harbor. I watched the wave through several sets of swells; it looked like a decent surf break to the right. Behind the store through a line of frangipani bushes, men had been working on the framework of a new house. When they caught sight of Ishmael, they hammered a few more nails, then dropped their tools, climbed down, and shuffled along a path through the trees to join us.

While he waited, Ishmael spoke to each of the men who showed up as if he knew them. In the beginning, there were no women present. A guy wearing a ski hat over an Afro arrived in another vehicle and greeted Ishmael with an embrace. He appeared to be our host. After he had said hello to everyone else, the man looked around and then held his hands to his face megaphone-like and called out loudly in several directions through the sugarcane and undergrowth. More people trickled in. Behind where I stood, I gazed up and down the curve of the coast road. Twenty men and women ambled toward us, taking their time. As guests arrived, some went up to Ishmael and exchanged words, some approached friends in the crowd, and others were content to take seats in the grass.

A circle of people formed around Ishmael. When enough of a crowd had materialized, he began speaking. All in pidgin, I caught snippets of his words, especially the English terms that had no pidgin equivalent: independence, law and order, and electrification. Ishmael possessed the moves of an excellent public speaker. He used no notes, but spoke extemporaneously. He connected with his audience, look-ing people in the eye as he spoke to them and gazing back and forth across the crowd, including everyone. His voice had a good baritone quality, not strident or emotional, and he spoke loud enough to be heard over the occasional crashing wave, even by people standing in the back rows.

Ishmael kept talking as stragglers filed in. After the crowd maxed out, he wrapped up his stump speech, thanked people, and asked for questions. Typical of Bougainvilleans, no one in the crowd had any at first. Finally, an old man stood up. His hair and beard were white, and he couldn't have weighed more than a hundred pounds. The man surprised me, both with his question and his use of English. "Why is this foreigner here? George Washburn wants to give Bougainville to the Chinese. Are you offering it to the white people?"

Ishmael's expression was tolerant. He said, "Someone asked me why we must allow foreigners to come here from other parts of the world. I told him we don't need to, if we want to keep doing the same things we've been doing: cooking dinner over a fire and shitting in the woods. I don't think you people in Wakunai want that. Most of us want to improve life for ourselves and our families. Foreign investors can help us."

The subject turned to economic development. People said they were afraid that seeking independence would antagonize PNG, and they would turn off the cash spigot. Ishmael responded that despite the potential economic hardship, Bougainville needed to become independent, and gave a deadline: five years. He conceded that Bougainville's financial picture had to improve rapidly to allow that, requiring enhanced foreign investment and increased foreign aid. He ticked off the projects that would generate foreign investment, jobs, and taxes, including the Manetai limestone project and the hydro-electric utility in Panguna. "Roads," he added with emphasis. "We're going to build better roads." He went on to say that no society could succeed without roads. Until Bougainville had good ones, it wouldn't have the strength to compete in the world. He said he was a cocoa farmer, and he knew how hard it was to transport his beans to market.

"We've been living along this road all our lives, and the government's never improved it," a young guy said from where he stood in the back of the crowd. He was dressed in slacks and shoes, probably just back from overseas. "What can you do that's any different?"

Ishmael countered with something that he and I had dreamed up together. "To make sure we have funds for road improvement, I'm going to tax the foreign gold dealers five kina per gram," Ishmael said, staring back at the guy for emphasis. "We project a million kina in the first year. It's a start."

The young elite looked surprised, and so did others in the crowd, pleasantly so. Specific financial remedies were probably unheard-of in Bougainville politics. The meeting progressed, and Ishmael got stronger after every exchange. When the crowd's questions lapsed and the session seemed finished, I was ready to head to our next destination. Ishmael explained that they were about to serve food. We needed to stay for a little while to be polite, and then we would move on.

The man who owned the store and his wife and children wheeled out a cart covered with platters of local food. In the center was a plastic container full of chunks of raw honeycomb smothered in honey. Next to it was a plate of something that looked like deep-fried grasshoppers. Most of the attendees lined up to eat, but some people brought over their children, and others offered Ishmael their babies. He patted the children on the head, took the babies in his hands, and raised them to the heavens.

We left Wakunai and drove up the coast road. Our next destination was Siara, a farming and fishing village north of Wakunai. Thirty minutes later, Peacely slowed down and turned east off the road toward the ocean. We drove down a grassy lane through rows of tall palm trees and came into a village that looked like it could have been Gaugin's retreat in Tahiti. Raised on wooden stilts above the sand, twenty bungalows formed an arc around a packed-earth village center. Their roofs and walls thatched with tawny palm fronds, the structures' front doors faced the village's common area. At the rear, each house opened to a garden plot and beyond that to the sea, twenty yards through the trees. Dugout canoes dozed in the high grass, while chickens scampered everywhere.

Under a mammoth shade tree, people were already gathered at a crude amphitheater formed by hemispherical rows of wooden benches and fronted by a smoldering fire pit. A few women lifted the last strips of what smelled like a delicious early dinner off the grill and laid them on wooden boards.

Ishmael had warned me in advance that Siara was an unusual place. He knew it well, since his father had been attached to the United Church missionary team there as a young man. The mission's ministers placed a high emphasis on education. A majority of the villagers had attended the mission school and then had gone overseas to study at institutions of higher learning. Most had remained away during their careers, and returned to Bougainville for retirement. The people of Siara prided themselves on their academic capabilities. Ishmael's speech and any ensuing discussion would be in English. The chief, a lady and a strong political leader, had been a teacher at the Siara primary school during and after the Crisis. As a student, she had graduated from Hutjena Secondary School, the highly regarded high school on Buka Island that both Ishmael and George Washburn had attended. Ishmael told me that the chief had married her headmaster at Hutjena, and then pointed him out in the crowd. A slight, older white man wearing an Aussie-style cowboy hat, he sat up front on a bench by the fire pit.

In Siara, the people had gathered before we arrived, so the food came first. Helping themselves, villagers sat in small groups. The former Hutjena headmaster approached me and introduced himself. We spoke about Bougainville history; the man was an encyclopedia of local lore. As Ishmael was preparing to address the crowd, I said, "You must be proud of Ishmael."

The headmaster replied, "I was disappointed that he left early. George Washburn was a better student."

Ishmael started speaking. I excused myself and started handing out pamphlets containing copies of the narratives. Ishmael had only spoken for five minutes when the chief interrupted him. "Bougainville is an agricultural society. As you know, here in Siara, we grow coconuts and cacao. We would like to remain simple farmers, but I'm afraid you will tell us we must change."

Ishmael said, "We're going to keep expanding our agricultural base, but it won't be enough. Agriculture alone doesn't have enough of a gross margin to pay Bougainville's bills," he answered, and then kept talking.

Someone raised their hand and interrupted. "Did you say gross margin?"

"Yes," Ishmael replied. "Revenues less variable costs? It's the fundamental yardstick of profitability for an industry," he said, looking over at me and winking.

As Ishmael continued speaking, people looked at each other; some smiled, in an admiring way.

"We will continue to emphasize coconuts and cacao, but we won't just grow them," Ishmael continued. "We must form industries around them, like one of my dream companies: Bougainville Chocolate. Bougainville cacao beans are the finest in the world, but growers here don't make much money because middlemen take all the profits. We must organize a cooperative with a website, and make and sell our own brands of chocolate bars and other products over the internet to the world. That's how agriculture can lift Bougainville."

When people starting clapping, I was surprised. Several members of the audience asked more questions, but as Ishmael kept speaking, it was clear some of our ideas resonated, even with this sophisticated group. Ishmael continued the agricultural improvement theme, telling the audience about virgin coconut oil being used for cosmetics, and people remained enthused.

He finished ten minutes later. "We are lucky," Ishmael said. "Unlike most other South Pacific nations, Bougainville is blessed with resources. Yes, we are sitting on billions in copper and gold, but we have lime, timber, and fish as well. This is a true privilege the Lord has given us—but we must use it. Thank you for listening."

People applauded as Ishmael waved and spoke to a few friends, and then he, Peacely, and I headed for our vehicle. As we walked toward the car, I passed the headmaster. He didn't say anything, but tipped the brim of his hat. "Ishmael was a better soldier," I said as I walked by, making sure to smile. We piled into the car, and Peacely pulled away.

As Peacely drove north on the Buka Road, no one spoke. Up in the shotgun seat, Ishmael got a call on his mobile, answered it in pidgin, said a few words, and shut his phone off. He leaned back and yawned, and I thought he was going to take a nap. I was thinking about doing the same thing when he twisted partially around and stared over the top of his seat at me. "What do you think?"

I grinned. "You remind me of the former mayor of New York City, this guy named Ed Koch. Especially when he was in the midst of an election campaign, he used to walk up to strangers on the sidewalk and ask, 'How'm I doing?'"

Ishmael asked, "What was his name again?"

"Ed Koch."

Ishmael looked out the window as he mouthed words to himself. Then, he whispered the name. "Ed Koch." He sighed. "The mayor of New York City," he said to himself. Then he turned back to look at me once more, and spoke slowly. "How'm I doing?"

"You keep doing what you're doing today, and we're going to win."

At the wheel, I saw Peacely grin.

Our last stop was Teop Island. Only ten miles north of Siara, Peacely turned toward the water again. The sun was starting to go down, and a sunset painted fire across the ceiling of the western sky. Once more, we drove east down a quiet lane lined with flowers and greenery. This time, we were surrounded by groups of people moving along with us, including pet dogs running alongside them. Walking from the agricultural fields that lined both sides of the coast road, carrying rakes and hoes, the men and women were laughing and joking after a day's work as they headed toward the shore. As Peacely slowed down, I looked up ahead. On the ground under the trees along the beach were dozens of outrigger canoes, scattered everywhere like bicycles on a workday in an Amsterdam square. Through the trees, I saw Teop Island.

The island sat flat on the sea like a green confection, its palm trees feathering over the land, about a half mile offshore in the middle of a wide lagoon. On either side of it, breakers crashed where the surrounding reef met the ocean. Beyond, the eastern heavens across the Pacific had turned a deep blue. Towering cumulus, burnished orange and raspberry by the sunset, rose up out of the sea like a line of coppery buildings in a distant city.

As we arrived at the shore, Peacely parked the car while the locals fanned out to their canoes. The dugout portion of each canoe was short and could only hold two people. Whole families used one canoe each, the mother placing her youngest facing her in the dugout and taking the paddle, her husband and older children lashing their farming tools across the outrigger. The group of them, mother paddling with her baby and husband and sons and daughters and dogs swimming alongside like a bob of seals, headed across the lagoon to their home.

Teop Island's paramount chief—the head chief of the island—skippered his motorized longboat inland across the lagoon to the shore of the mainland, picked us up, and ferried us back over. On the way, Ishmael told me that the paramount chief admitted that George Washburn had learned earlier that Ishmael was scheduled to speak that evening, and had preempted him by showing up two nights ago. The chief also confided that George had handed out packets of kina to anyone who asked, even small kids.

By the time we landed at Teop Island, it was almost dark. The paramount chief nosed the longboat halfway up a beach. We all got out and pulled the boat up into the soft sand, and the chief tied it to a tree. The island stretched a mile from north to south and a little less across. A broad path led from the beach through a thicket of palm trees toward the center. Three villages of thatched bungalows occupied the northern, western, and southern shores of the island, with their outlying neighborhoods meeting in the middle. Around a cleared area of packed earth, an array of crude stores and low community buildings formed a public square. Next to a church-like meeting hall, a generator hummed, and lights shone over rows of benches. Even though it was dinner time, dozens of people were already seated or wandering in.

Ishmael knew many of the people and spent close to an hour meeting and greeting. Standing next to him, I must have looked tired. The paramount chief came over, tapped my shoulder, and led me toward a plastic chair. The sky overhead had turned black, and the stars had come out by the time the meeting got started.

This time, the island's political leaders spoke prior to Ishmael. The audience paid close attention. At first, everyone spoke in pidgin, but when the paramount chief stood up and spoke, he used English. So did Ishmael, although sometimes to make a point, he'd repeat the words in pidgin too.

Ishmael's last performance that day was his best. After an hour, he took questions. The people didn't want him to stop, and neither did he.

A woman in the front row stood up. "Is our government corrupt? With all our resources, why don't we have any money?"

The crowd laughed, and so did Ishmael. "Of course our current government is corrupt," he said. "How else could our president, according to an international magazine survey, be the seventh richest man in Papua New Guinea? According to this same magazine, PNG's ten richest people are all government officials."

The crowd's humor evaporated, and turned to grumbling.

"Don't worry," Ishmael said. "If I am elected, I'm going to Buka with a broom."

As people cheered Ishmael's remark, a man stood in the back. "George Washburn gave us money. How much are you giving us tonight?"

"I already gave you my life," Ishmael said. "I'm not handing out money. If you want to join my party, it costs five kina," he laughed, and the crowd laughed with him. Then his face became serious. "Many lost their lives so that you could have a vote. Don't shame them by selling it."

Finally, the paramount chief stood. "Thank you, Ishmael. Thank you for winning for us the chance to be independent." Then he grew serious as he looked at Ishmael. "I'm concerned. Look at us here," he said, making a show of waving his arm across the breadth of the island. "On Teop Island, we're already independent. I'm not sure Bougainville's independence will be worth it for us."

"Who's your daddy?" Ishmael said, smiling back at the chief and the crowd. "Who's your daddy?" he repeated. "It's one of my favorite expressions, because it describes Bougainville—until now. We're always described as belonging to someone else, as if we were a child. Colonialism relied on us to accept that. Our colonial powers—France, Germany, Australia, and Japan—took turns looking on us this way, as if the natural order of things was that they were the father, and we were the son. We accepted that then, but Papua New Guinea? We are not Papua New Guineans; we are Bougainvilleans. Our government should be Bougainvillean. If I am elected president, we will belong to no one. We will be free. Thank you very much."

After Ishmael had said goodnight to everyone, the paramount chief guided us back to the beach and his longboat. A group of young boys with flashlights served as advance scouts, fanning out ahead through the trees. When we arrived at the beach, pulled the longboat into the water, and pointed it toward the mainland, the scouts took dugout canoes and set off ahead of us, their flashlights blinking in the night like a flock of lightning bugs. The paramount chief called ahead to them in the night, "Prepare the way for the leader. Make a straight path for him to the shore."

28

The Walls of Jericho

August twelfth marked the last day of campaigning. The next day, polling began, and counting commenced after that. It was time to gear up and deal with the back door. Everyone, from experienced Bougainvillean politicians like Matty Savant to American political experts like Jason Osborne, had warned us that this phase—after campaigning was over, but before the results were counted—was when Ishmael's election would be won or lost. When they told me these things, their expressions invariably sober, I nodded my head in agreement as if I understood. The truth was, I didn't have the slightest idea how election fraud worked. I was about to learn firsthand.

We had conducted Ishmael's presidential campaign through the front door. No one was paid a kina for improper favors. We had been as proficient as political amateurs knew how to be, and had done anything and everything we thought was necessary. Ishmael had led the way tirelessly. He had traveled thousands of miles and had spoken eloquently and fervently in hundreds of locations across the islands, to anyone who wanted to speak with him. The campaign staff had backed him, doing their best to make sure Ishmael was viewed in an optimal light. Media had been employed with expertise and frequency:

Facebook pages, text blasts, and radio shows had been conceived, printed, and performed. Swag—hats, T-shirts, stickers, and posters—had been ordered, procured, shipped, and distributed, with people all over Bougainville fighting for the stuff. Speeches and narratives had been written, distributed, and discussed with the voters. We were satisfied with our effort; given the time allowed and our resources, the campaign could have done no better.

Bougainville's voters were required to register at their local village. I was informed that the registration process in all South Pacific island elections was difficult, and highly localized; many places didn't use numeric addresses, and most individuals did not own authentic identification, making verification impossible unless the polling official was a knowledgeable neighbor. Thankfully, the 2020 election got underway only a few months after the independence referendum, when similar infrastructure and procedures had been paid for and deployed by international agencies.

Bougainville's population was approximately three hundred thousand. Slightly more than two hundred thousand Bougainvilleans had registered for the independence referendum, and about one hundred ninety thousand had actually voted. The experts told us that if Bougainvilleans were like other Pacific Island populations, more would vote in a special, one-time event like an independence referendum than a regular election. They expected one hundred forty thousand people to vote in the 2020 election.

Bougainvilleans could only vote if they were over eighteen years old and had previously registered. Polling was scheduled to take place for two weeks. At the end of the voting period, counting would begin, and was expected to take several days. When I first heard that, I was immediately dubious. That's where the fraud would rear its head—how could counting take more than a day? That was before I learned the complexities of the process. Nothing was mechanical, let alone electronic. All voting and counting was done by hand—and each ballot required a number of tasks. Voters were provided with four eight-by-eleven-inch, color-coded ballots to fill in: the blue paper ballot was to vote for the presidential candidates, the pink for the three women at-large candidates for membership to the House of Representatives, the yellow for the three ex-combatant candidates, and the green for constituency candidates. That was only for the national elections; there were local elections going on at the same time. According to OBEC, a total of four hundred forty-six candidates were contesting in the 2020 election.

As if that wasn't enough, the Bougainville electoral system was a so-called preferential one. Bougainville couldn't afford run-off elections; events needed to be finalized in one shot. To do so, voters were required to vote for three candidates, by descending order of preference, regarding each office being contested. When voting for president, the voter used the blue paper ballot on which were arrayed the names of all twenty-five candidates; next to each name was a blank space. The voter placed the number one next to their preferred choice, the number two next to their second choice, and so on. If, after the initial counting, no candidate won a plurality, OBEC would count the number two votes, and perhaps even the number three votes, until someone edged over the 50 percent, majority line.

OBEC established one hundred twenty-one polling stations across Bougainville's islands, including six different locations in PNG since many Bougainvilleans lived overseas. The polling stations were arranged in a fashion similar to polling stations everywhere. Inspectors and other officials milled around out front. Party supporters were also allowed to kibitz nearby, subject to certain spatial limits. A table marked the front of the station where voters lined up to submit their names to be checked against their registrations. The station fronted multiple voting booths, each a tent-like affair to ensure privacy. When voters were finished filling in their ballots, they handed them to an election official for inspection. The inspector examined the ballot to make sure it was filled out with three preferred candidates and no other markings were present on the paperwork, and then folded it twice into a quarter-size ballot for confidentiality. The blue presidential ballots were deposited into a special presidential ballot box, while the three other ballots were placed in a separate box.

Once voters were finished with the process, they were free to go, which was, in my experience, what happened after any election in which I voted in the US. Not in Bougainville. Voting was a big deal for Bougainvilleans, and many wanted to share their experience. That's what our so-called scrutineers were for, among other things. At each station, Rachel organized two BPAP scrutineers. We paid the scrutineers a subsistence stipend, but also provided them with two items they coveted: Ishmael campaign T-shirts and hats. Rachel also provided the scrutineers with paper pads, pencils, and water to distribute to thirsty voters. Their job was two-fold: scrutinize the proceedings, reporting any false moves by the election officials to Rachel, and obtain post-voting feedback from the voters. If they saw inspectors urging voters to change their ballot, they'd report it to Rachel and lodge a complaint. OBEC could remove inspectors for obvious and repeated offenses. Did you vote for Ishmael? The scrutineers might ask a voter when they emerged from their booth. Terrific; who'd you pick for number two? Who are your neighbors and friends voting for? With the two-week polling period, if we learned things were trending poorly in an area, we could send in reinforcements.

The ballot boxes were nothing special. They looked like the plastic storage boxes for sale at Home Depot or Walmart, except they had a wire-based, combination lock on the handle. Each ballot box was numbered, and their lock combinations scrambled. Someone could probably figure out how to compromise the ballot box system, but I doubted that it could be done on the fly while in the polling stations.

As polling commenced and the calendar wound through the second half of August, we felt cautiously optimistic. Our scrutineers across Bougainville verified what we had learned on the road over the summer: Ishmael had given his all for Bougainville, and the people appreciated him, thank goodness. Where salt-of-the-earth

Bougainvilleans lived—in the south, on the west coast, in the atolls and the northern parts of Buka Island—it sounded like Ishmael did well. In the more urbanized places where money and human weakness had turned parts of the elite population snobby and cynical, things might be different. The popular vote seemed to be going the way we expected, but of course we wouldn't know until the end.

Polling ended. The ballot boxes were to be collected and shipped via police-escorted trucks from the polling stations to OBEC's offices in Buka. After an overnight hiatus, counting would start the next day, leading to the announcement of the winners during the following week. All the people whose opinions I respected on the subject said that when the counting commenced, our fraud problems were over: Counting took place in a secure, public space with official observers; even credentialed press could attend. Assuming fraud was a factor in the election, it had to happen before the counting. Armed with this advice and determined that our year-long effort not be in vain, we still had no idea how, and from what direction, the enemy would attack. That was where things stood when the three Chinese-backed candidates—George, Ferdy, and Mogol—panicked, and conspired to wend their evil ways.

The first inkling I got that something was amiss was on the last Friday of August, the day after voting had finished, right before counting was supposed to begin. Rachel had dispatched a group of our scrutineers to wait outside OBEC's offices in Buka, with instructions to watch the off-loading of the boxes from the trucks for any suspicious activity. The scrutineers called Rachel around midnight. The trucks never showed up.

We didn't learn until Saturday morning from a nervous OBEC commissioner that the ballot boxes had been deposited inside the Buka station house of the Bougainville Police Service. Not to worry, the commissioner told a disgruntled audience. OBEC's offices were not large enough or secure enough to house the ballot boxes. They would be safer in the police station. The crowd mumbled; some yelled.

If that was the case, why was it printed on the official instruction forms that the ballots would be stored at OBEC's offices? In any event, surely observers would be allowed inside the station house to verify the integrity of the ballot boxes? No, he said, visibly sweating; the ballot boxes were being stored inside a secure area in the station house. No one except uniformed police officers was allowed inside. He offered no reason for either the change in storage location, or the fact that the boxes would be in an unobserved, potentially prejudicial site. When would counting begin? Commissioner Manners wouldn't answer the question, and ended his remarks a short time later.

At least now we knew. This was how and where the fraud would take place—inside the police station, of all places. When Rachel told me, I was crushed, and torn. The ballots were in the possession of a bunch of unsupervised, corruption-prone police? Hopeless; we might as well pack our bags. On the other hand, I tried to envision how some bonehead cops could possibly replace a meaningful number of Ishmael ballots with bogus ones over the weekend. I couldn't. These guys couldn't get arrested. What were they going to do to doctor the ballots? That was before I spoke to the experts, who told me I shouldn't derive any comfort from my inability to figure out how to commit ballot fraud. I was just a stupid foreigner. There were plenty of people out there who did this for a living; and who knew the fraudsters, or how to employ them, better than the police?

The developments didn't seem to bother Ishmael. When I met him, he was calm. "Albert and my boys are on it," he said, speaking about Albert Mague, one of his trusted ex-combatant leaders. "They know what to do."

I told him I hoped he was right, even as I harbored a sick feeling that the naysayers knew more than we did and were laughing at our ineptitude. What fools we were to think we could win an island election on the merits. Now we'd learn the way of the world.

The Buka station house sat back from the street on the avenue that ran parallel to the Passage. The desk sergeant-at-arms sat right inside the front door. The structure was surrounded by other build-ings and a few trees and bushes. In both the front and the rear of the building, parking lots provided space for police vehicles.

Saturday night was moonless, and a thick cloud cover hung over Buka as the sun went down. The night shift was over at eleven, and most of the duty officers vacated the building soon afterward. The town was noisy until midnight, and then turned silent. Other than a light shining over the front door, the station house appeared deserted. Albert and the rest of Ishmael's boys positioned themselves every-where, just not where they could be seen: across the street and in the bushes and the trees, even up on the roofs of the station house and the buildings next door.

Albert told me later that the two Toyotas with tinted glass pulled into the rear of the station house around one in the morning. Men in dark clothing with hats pulled down over their faces scurried out of the vehicles, carrying new ballot boxes and ballots and following their leader, who approached the door with a keychain. When he unlocked the door, they filed inside like a pack of wharf rats making for the hold of a ship.

Albert dispatched one of his guys to break open the back door. The thieves were so confident and nonchalant that they had left it unlocked. Albert whispered patience to his boys. He wanted to give the villains inside enough time to perpetrate some visible damage, and then catch them in the act. At three in the morning, Albert gave the high sign. He and his men pressed on their phone lights, got their cameras ready, and rushed though the building's back door until they found what they were looking for.

Ferdy Mimosa and Greyson Trull, the ringleaders of the fraud-sters, were caught red-handed, sitting with their feet up on a police desk next to a pile of damaged, discarded ballot boxes. Next to them, two guys dropped their hacksaws, and the other two stopped switch-ing ballots and raised their hands.

Albert and Ferdy knew each other well. Albert told me it was all he could do not to laugh, while Ferdy was pissed and complained about his rights being violated. Albert snapped a selfie of himself between Ferdy and Trull with the altered ballot boxes in the background; it made the newspapers Monday morning. The most amusing part of the episode occurred when Albert and the boys dragged Ferdy and Trull and their accomplices out the back door and around the front door to present them to the desk sergeant on duty.

As Albert recounted the events to me over the weekend, I tried to estimate the extent of the damage. From the way he described things, it seemed like it could have been a lot worse. I learned that committing election fraud was much easier than I had imagined. Apparently, Bougainville's polling stations were littered with tens of thousands of unutilized ballots corresponding to registered people who had not showed up to vote. In the wrong hands, it was a snap to fill those out with Ferdy named as the preferred choice, and substitute them for Ishmael's ballots. Not having any idea how many ballots the crooks had been able to process, I did some calculations. Even if Ferdy and Grumpy had been accompanied by the Harry Houdini of ballot box fraud, it didn't sound like those bozos could have done much damage in a couple hours. Perhaps some fraudulent ballots were able to squeak through undetected. Ishmael might get scammed by a thousand votes—two thousand at the most. Now that the crooks had been apprehended, hopefully, the ballots could be restored, and we could breeze to a victory. Feeling better, I thought that was the end of it. I should have known. Every time I came to that conclusion in Bougainville, something bad happened.

Ishmael continued to maintain that things were under control. I wanted it to be true. The first hint that I would be disappointed occurred when I read the Monday morning newspapers. The stories were borderline ridiculous. It seems that there had been a misunderstanding. Ferdy Mimosa's company had a maintenance contract to clean the police station, and he had been there in the middle of the night checking up on things. No one was arrested. Ferdy remained a candidate.

Monday came and went without a peep from the election authorities; so did Tuesday. By Wednesday, when Commissioner Manners announced that he and the police chief would conduct a press conference in front of the station house at eleven o'clock, everyone suspected something was up. A crowd gathered. George Manners and the police chief appeared, bloviated for a few minutes, and explained nothing. None of us in the audience paid attention to their hot air until an Australian journalist in the crowd said, "I assume counting will begin henceforth?"

"Ah, no." Manners said that he would let us know and bolted off the stage with the police chief behind him.

I was thinking about getting drunk when Miao called in the afternoon. "Hey, Jack, look, I'm really sorry. I know you worked your ass off down there."

Miao would just keep talking unless you stopped him. I didn't.

Miao said, "It's over, right? The election?" Papers rustled in the background, and then he continued, "Yeah, I've got the schedule right here. Sorry. You know it wasn't my fault, don't you?"

"Sure."

"You have no idea what you were up against, Jack. The three guys we were backing flipped a coin, and Ferdy won. My chairman told the three of them to pool their money and grab Bougainville for China, no matter how much they had to spend to win. 'Anything it takes,' he said, and he kept telling them that his words came straight from the big guy." Miao started laughing. "I've got to tell you, I'm not sure what you guys see in that island. Their women sure sound a lot different than ours."

"What do you mean?"

"Oh man, let me tell you. I was sitting here with the chairman when Ferdy called. We were on the speakerphone, it was turned way up, and in the background some woman was shrieking, 'Ishmael will win over my dead body.'" Miao laughed. "I'm telling you, she sounded mean. The chairman asked Ferdy, 'Who's that?' and Ferdy said, 'I'm inside the station house. She's a cop.'"

"I guess I'm not surprised about anything."

"It's not fair, Jack, but these things happen. What are you going to do now? Want to come back to China?"

I hung up a minute later. Most Americans think they know the CCP's limits, but it's not even close.

By Wednesday night, it was clear why Miao was so confident. The police and the perpetrators stopped attempting to disguise their efforts. Bad guys were seen coming and going from the station house with fresh ballot boxes and ballots at all hours of the day. Everyone in Bougainville was aware that fraud was going on and would continue, while the counting had yet to start, but no one was doing anything about it. Bougainville had been bought. The Chinese would keep throwing money at Ferdy and the police, and whoever else was necessary to be bribed, and the fraudulent counting would continue inside the station house until the desired result was achieved. Then in a week or so, the authorities would act like nothing had happened, announce the tainted vote, and declare Ferdy the winner.

I couldn't help but wonder if Ishmael had considered a coup. On Wednesday afternoon, when I asked, he told me. In the absence of a threat of violence to the people, he would never do that, he said. It wasn't the Melanesian way. He would be greatly disappointed to lose his bid for the presidency—much more so for Bougainville than for himself—but he would demonstrate to all that the law must be obeyed. The election would take place, come what may, and then everyone would go home peaceably.

Ishmael's remarks put Bishop Unabali's frustration about Bougainvillean apathy in a different light. Yes, the fact that everyone knew a fraud was being perpetrated but did nothing about it was a damning indictment of Bougainvillean indifference; but at least the people were peaceful. After all, the one time that Bougainvilleans had not sat on their hands—the Crisis—had been, for most, a disaster. Violence was never the best choice. If Bougainvilleans choose to wait for a better day, so be it.

Except for Rachel and the scrutineers. Rachel employed two hundred forty-two scrutineers for the campaign, two for each polling station. I admired their enthusiasm. Pound for pound, they were our most exemplary campaign team members. Most of them were young. Paid a pittance, they didn't care. They worked for the best candidate, and weren't shy about reminding their counterparts.

Rachel asked me if she could work with them to devise a plan to rectify things. I encouraged it, because at that point I was convinced we were going to lose but thought it might make everyone feel better. When conceived, their plan was simple: raise a noisy—but peaceful—ruckus on a twenty-four-seven basis. They would encircle the station house and chant and make a racket as they tromped around it, all two hundred forty-two of them. While the crooks were inside the police station committing fraud, the noise would reverberate around the town, drummed into the airwaves until hopefully it became too much of an embarrassing din for all concerned. The scrutineers would deliver to the criminals and the public a message no one could ignore: We know you're in there. We know what you're doing. We're not going away. We want you to stop. We're free and independent Bougainvilleans.

I gave Rachel money to truck all the scrutineers to Buka. She rigged up a loudspeaker to play Bougainvillean war chants, and mounted on pushcarts some Bougainvillean wooden drums used in the old days to send signals from village to village. At ten o'clock Thursday night, they were ready. The scrutineers encircled the station house, each carrying a mobile phone or a flashlight. Rachel turned on the loudspeaker full blast, the drums began beating, the scrutineers began walking and chanting, and the entertainment commenced.

"We know you're in there. We know what you're doing. We're not going away. We want you to stop. We're free and independent Bougainvilleans." Boom, boom, boom.

"Again!" Rachel yelled.

"We know you're in there. We know what you're doing. We're not going away. We want you to stop. We're free and independent Bougainvilleans." Boom, boom, boom.

For several days, morning and night, the scrutineers circled the station house. They got smart and started working in shifts. People began to gather, and after a while a permanent crowd of onlookers formed. Soon, the crowd began to chant along, too, and then dozens of them began joining the conga line.

"We know you're in there. We know what you're doing. We're not going away. We want you to stop. We're free and independent Bougainvilleans." Boom, boom, boom.

As the chanting got louder, the crowd grew every day and spilled out into the streets. A couple of policemen tried to pick on individual scrutineers, but the crowd swarmed in, fending them off. The police chief came out and tried to intimidate everyone by threatening mass arrests, but got pelted with fruit and vegetables for his trouble.

On Friday, a reporter in town to cover the election from one of the Port Moresby newspapers interviewed Rachel. "What's your objective in all this?" he asked, leaning close to hear her response over the din.

"Who knows?" Rachel said. "Maybe if we keep it up, the walls will fall down." She looked over toward her charges. "Again!"

"We know you're in there. We know what you're doing. We're not going away. We want you to stop. We're free and independent Bougainvilleans." Boom, boom, boom.

Ishmael and I drove to Buka to observe the spectacle firsthand. We took a longboat across the Passage, and disembarked on the street in front of the police station. The people saw Ishmael, and a roar went up from the crowd. Out in front of us, accompanied by a thunderous drumbeat, the massive parade of people swirled around the police station.

We both watched in silence for a minute.

"None of this makes any difference," I said to Ishmael. "Right?"

Looking in another direction, Ishmael chuckled at my words before turning and seeing the tortured look on my face. His expression turned to one of concern. It was the first time I had seen him evidence sympathy toward me. I was just a foreigner, after all; I didn't understand.

"You must think like a guerilla," he said. "Use bows and arrows at first if you have nothing else. Remain confident that as your strength grows, the enemy's cannons and tanks will never be enough to defeat you."

"Do you really think we have any chance of winning?"

"I'm not sure how long it will take. What I do know is that we'll never surrender."

The scrutineers' performance was heartening, but it couldn't last forever. Rumors swirled regarding next moves. Finally, Tete said he heard via the coconut news that either the fix was in, or the police had had enough; in any event, the election results would be announced on Monday. I had no idea what to believe. It was a fitting way for things to end in a remote South Pacific island called Bougainville.

PART FIVE

ISLAND OF HOPE

29

Election Day

The winner of Bougainville's presidential election would be announced Monday morning in Buka. Ishmael remained in Buka over the weekend. I decided to return to Arawa and wait out the weekend at home. I liked praying in my bedroom there. It had a musty smell, the air hot and drier than outside, like the atmosphere in the bunk rooms of the old clapboard buildings in the church camps we attended when we were kids. I planned on praying a lot that weekend.

If things ended badly on Monday, the last thing I was going to do was tell myself I had no regrets. I wouldn't accept the words from anyone else either. At this point, platitudes were inexcusable. Bougainville was my last artwork. I was either going out a winner or a loser, and that was the way I would be remembered. I leaned back in my bamboo chair, where I sat on the veranda and looked out over the street. Encouraged by the afternoon wind, palm trees cast undulating shadows across the wild sugarcane lining the road.

Thinking about the time I had spent on the island, not just the year of the campaign but the whole five years, it was easy to conclude it had been wasted. That was what people I was close to at home told me when they felt angry; the same ones who said they loved me, anyway. As much as anything, that made it easier to feel regretful. I couldn't do that now, though; not when I was marooned at the end of the world in what could be my end of days. The ramifications could be permanent.

I looked around for a distraction. Off to the west over the Panguna foothills, the last rays of the sun peeked through castle-like thunderheads, their minarets burnished with pink and orange. It was the only time all day I had seen anything other than gray sky. The rain had poured down for hours, plump raindrops thrumming on my tin roof. At least the island's showers were pleasant. Never cold or harsh, a Bougainville downpour might be a soaker, but afterward one felt cleansed. Now the air was dry, and people were starting to come out. That was another thing about the place: people weren't afraid to walk in the dark. It was like they waited for the sun to go down. Probably because—even for them—it was too hot. Or perhaps they'd rather not be seen, their ebony-colored Bougainvillean skin blending into the night. They weren't malicious people, not most of them anyway.

As darkness fell, women and children and crippled old men from the war emerged from the shadows and floated along the sidewalk on the other side of the street where I lived. Some strolled silently in the grass next to my house. Passing under my porch, they resisted looking my way, through the fence surrounding my yard, up where the only white man in town sat watching them. A car rumbled by every five minutes or so. In the meantime, a few intrepid souls walked down the middle of the street, its ancient asphalt poured fifty years earlier when the big Panguna Mine had been going full blast.

Night arrived. I couldn't see the people anymore, but they could see me. I went inside and got ready for bed.

I locked the front door and the porch doors to my study and the kitchen, and mixed my one drink of the day. When I had first come to the island, as the ninety-degree heat and humidity conspired to bake my brain and bathe me in sweat by the time I finished break-fast, when for relief I had started drinking cold beer by noon and the hard stuff over ice by four, I had learned enough to impose a rule: one beer with dinner, and one drink when I turned in. That was it. I had stayed sober, and each time I returned from civilization, I lost twenty pounds.

I took my pills for atrial fibrillation. God help me if I had a second incident and needed another tPA injection. It took at least four hours to get from where I was to the Aropa landing strip and over the Solomon Sea to Port Moresby, even if I managed to contact Global Rescue, stay coherent, and get the chartered plane that their emergency response services guaranteed. I'd never make it.

Opening a fresh package of mosquito wipes, I extracted one and swathed my face and the bugs' favorite dining spot, my ears and temples. Ishmael had suffered through periodic bouts of malaria all through the campaign, but so far, I'd been lucky. I took another towelette and applied it over the pebbly bumps formed by the rash of creeping crud spreading across my chest, telling myself it was time to take my boat out on the reef and burn the jungle rot off my body before things got serious.

I slept eight hours that Saturday night—but like most others, woke up constantly. Since it was the weekend, the power would go off at some point before daybreak. The guys down at the power plant would get drunk on jungle juice and neglect to fill the fuel tank, and the single diesel gen-set would wheeze to a stop. Usually, it happened around three in the morning. Weekly. My ceiling fan—whose job it was not only to keep things cool but blow the mosquitoes under the bed—would cut off, and I would find myself in a sweat, under insect siege. Sure enough, later I rolled over, my sheets sticking to me. I examined the quiet. The night was still. Beyond the silence, I heard the waves crashing on the reef a half mile out in the Arawa harbor. I never heard the waves if the fan was on. The first mosquito buzzed up ten seconds later.

In the blackness, I got out of bed and found my way to the shelf along the wall that functioned as my dresser. I pulled on my shorts and shoes, picked up my mobile phone for light, and opened my bedroom door. The heat in the hallway smacked me like I had walked into a furnace. I stumbled to the utility closet, reached inside for the hook along the wall, and grabbed the set of big black keys to the emergency generator. I unlocked the front door, walked down the stairs to ground level, and crossed the grass to the generator shack. The noise of the waves pounding on the reef was louder, the strangely soothing, thudding sound rolling up the street from the beach. I stopped where I stood in the yard and looked up at the moonless sky. It was clear, the stars beguiling. Suspended above my house, the Southern Cross shone down as if to bless the foreign sinner. The night was kind, the heavy air whispering South Pacific verse as it caressed me—but Bougainville's morning would bring rain once again.

Shining my mobile phone light on the control panel of the generator, I inserted the key in the ignition and cranked it up. The security lights in the car port under the house blinked back on. I looked at my watch: three a.m. on the nose. I went back inside and fell asleep.

On Sunday morning, after taking a shower, I heated water for instant coffee. I selected from the refrigerator one of the ripe papayas I had picked off the tree in my garden, sliced it in half, and scraped out the dark seeds. I made myself a cup of coffee, put both halves of the papaya on a plate, and went out on the porch to have breakfast. Earlier it had been sunny, but the clouds were already drawing a curtain across the roof of the sky. I went into my study, turned on my computer, and started writing, trying to put a dent in the pile of emails I owed people on the other side of the world.

The light rain that had been falling for two hours ended. I stopped forcing myself to write and walked out onto the porch. The sun had broken through the clouds—a hot noontime sun that broiled the land. Steamy mists rose from the wet spots on the road. Geckoes romped in the garden, their tongues flickering as they scampered after bugs hiding in the dewy grass, wet wings too heavy to fly.

I called downstairs to the room where Tete kept his office and asked him to organize the gear so we could take an hour and go fishing out on the reef. I changed into my bathing suit and covered my face with sunscreen. I rubbed a thin layer of sunscreen on the rash across my chest and midsection, then grabbed my keys, locked the doors, and walked downstairs.

Two men were waiting outside the fenced driveway gate. I knew to ignore them.

Tete also ignored the men. He stood waiting for me at the bottom of the stairs, with the tackle box and the big rods. I took the tackle box, told Tete to leave the rods, and grabbed the trolling line. Tete got excited when we went outside the reef into the Slot after the big yellowfin tuna and dorado, but I didn't want to do that. Ishmael might call. We just needed to catch some fish for lunch, and then I would return and take another stab at my emails. While Tete pumped some gasoline from our fuel drum into a four-liter container, I rigged a single trolling line with a small bucktail suitable for skipjack.

Tete unlocked the gate. On our way out, he spoke briefly in pidgin to the two men who had been waiting outside the fence. After Tete finished speaking to them, they walked away. Tete relocked the gate, climbed back up into the driver's seat, and put the Toyota in gear, and we headed down the street.

I asked what the men wanted. The usual, Tete said, in the clipped, lilting English he had inherited from the nuns at his Catholic school growing up in Finschhafen: money.

We turned right at the end of the street and headed south on the coast road. After ten minutes, Tete pulled the car off the road and parked next to the water. Beyond a rough coral beach, a collection of longboats floated on an emerald-green lagoon. A mile offshore sat Pok Pok Island, and, past it, the wave-lined reef that ran around most of Bougainville. The swell was up. I could hear waves crashing on the reef. After Tete reeled our longboat in from its mooring to the shore and scooped out the rainwater, I climbed aboard and organized the trolling rig on the foredeck.

The wind was coming onshore from the north. Tete headed the longboat to the leeward side of Pok Pok, where the surface of the lagoon was still glassy. When the boat was clear of the shore and doing five knots, I tossed the shimmering bucktail off the starboard stern and paid out fifty yards of line. As the line sank, Tete picked up speed. We scanned the sky for seabirds. I saw them first—a big, rambunctious flock diving in clusters out by the reef. I pointed toward them, and Tete headed their way. As the longboat came into the birds, they scattered and flew off, but the water's surface still roiled. I hooked a skipjack, pulled it in, threw the fish into the cooler, and tossed the bucktail back in the water. I peered down into the sea. Sure enough, the birds had been diving for fish, the water thick with tuna feeding on minnows, one school chasing the other, churning up the lagoon.

As the longboat eased alongside the coral reef, the surf roared as large waves pounded outside. On the inside of the reef where the sea remained calm, I peered again into the depths. The water was gin-clear down to thirty feet. I saw flashes of silver as a big school of tuna chased its prey. Frantic minnows broke the surface of the lagoon, the ravenous tuna right behind them. Some of the fish appeared larger than those I typically caught inside the lagoon; they must have come in on the big waves. On a different day, I would have followed the school and used a rod to go after them, but today I trolled for forgettable skipjack, not wanting to miss a call from Ishmael. I caught two more tuna in five minutes. When we'd caught enough, I told Tete to head for shore.

After we drove home, Tete cleaned and fileted the fish. I fetched some of the dough we kept upstairs in the refrigerator to make bread and gave it to Tete to flatten and place on metal sheets in the oven. Ishmael had asked us to commission some ovens that his campaign could give out to villages, and we had bought one to use ourselves. The children in the neighborhood liked the bread. We had bought some soccer balls for the campaign to hand out, too, and we rolled out a couple of those so that the kids could play in the yard. They loved playing with real soccer balls, and we would let them play with them out in the street on the weekend in good weather. Tete gathered a pile of dry wood from the stack underneath the house while I hauled over a bushel of dried palm leaves. The oven didn't need wood, just leaves. Tete assembled the sticks and some newspaper in the pit he used as a grilling fireplace and lit a fire. He lit the leaves in the stove too. As the sticks burned and reduced to coals, Tete added more wood. After he had built a pile of hot coals, Tete laid two cooking stones over them. The stones were clean and thin. As the coals warmed the stones, Tete licked his forefinger and touched the surface of the stones a couple of times. When they were hot, he placed the fish filets on the stones.

While we were at work, the kids began to gather at our front gate, staring through the chain-link fence.

I got some platters from the kitchen, a cold beer from the refrigerator for me, and a bottle of cold water for Tete. I was violating my one-beer-a-day rule, but it was the weekend, and I was hot. When I was hot, nothing but an ice-cold beer would do. When Tete was done, he spread out pieces of fish on one platter, took the loaves of bread out of the oven, cut them into slices, and put them on the other platter. I watched him, and when he was done, I unlocked the gate and the neighborhood kids poured in. I handed out the soccer balls, but most of them went for the food first. They were always hungry, and it seemed like there were more of them all the time, but we always seemed to have enough to eat.

After the day ended, I sat back down at my computer and tried to write some more emails. The words flowed this time, and I finished a bunch. After a while, I got up from my computer and went into the kitchen to mix a drink. When I took the drink and a cigar out onto the porch, it was almost dark. I lit my cigar and gazed out over the street. The drink tasted much better with a cigar.

I could feel people watching me but couldn't see them in the night. Maybe if we won the election and hit it big, I'd move out of the house in town and build a place for my sons and their families out on Arovo Island, the place the chiefs proposed to give me to redevelop as a resort. We'd catch fish off the rocks and lobster under the reef, grill on the beach, and tell stories around a campfire, listening to the surf pound and waiting for the evening clouds to lift so we could watch the shooting stars, the way we had done the same back in the old days in Watch Hill. Maybe someone like Joy would like to spend a vacation there with me. They would love it here. Bougainville could surprise a person that way. It wasn't such a bad place after a while. I felt good thinking about it until I caught myself. False optimism—my nemesis—never let me alone; it was what had shanghaied me there to begin with. Who was I kidding? No one would ever come to visit me in Bougainville. There was no chance Ishmael was going to win the election. Things like that didn't happen anymore. I went inside, locked the doors, and got ready for bed.

Aftermath

On September 22, 2020, Ishmael was elected president of the Autonomous Region of Bougainville, and was inaugurated on September 29. Due to Bougainville's overwhelmingly affirmative vote in its 2019 independence referendum, it is expected to separate from Papua New Guinea. In that event, Ishmael will become the leader of the newest nation on earth. Since he was elected to office, I have spent much time with the president. He has never ended a meeting without taking my hand in both of his and expressing his gratitude for our support.

About the Author

John D. Kuhns is the author of three previously published novels, including *China Fortunes, Ballad of a Tin Man,* and *South of the Clouds.* He writes stories derived from his personal experiences. He is also an investment banker, investor, and businessman who has established five companies and grown them from original concept through their initial public offering to maturity. He first went to Bougainville in 2015 and has lived and worked there during a majority of each year since then. Mr. Kuhns is chairman and chief executive officer of Numa Numa Resources Limited, a company developing and investing in infrastructure and other business ventures in Bougainville. He graduated from Georgetown University, where he was a captain of the football team and elected to the university's Athletic Hall of Fame; earned a Master of Fine Arts from the University of Chicago, where he was an art and culture critic for *The Chicago Maroon,* the university's independent student newspaper; and received a Master of Business Administration from the Harvard Business School.